LOST ROSES

Lost Roses

A NOVEL

Martha Hall Kelly

BALLANTINE BOOKS · NEW YORK

Copyright © 2019 by Martha Hall Kelly

All rights reserved.

Published in the United States by Ballantine Books,
an imprint of Random House, a division of
Penguin Random House LLC, New York.

BALLANTINE and the HOUSE colophon are registered
trademarks of Penguin Random House LLC.

Hardback ISBN 978-1-524-79637-2
Ebook ISBN 978-1-524-79638-9

Printed in the United States of America
on acid-free paper

randomhousebooks.com

246897531

FIRST EDITION

Book design by Barbara M. Bachman

For Katherine and Mary,
bound by a silver thread

LOST ROSES

LOST ACRES

Luba

1912

I ONLY PUT THE CENTIPEDE IN ELIZA'S SLIPPER SINCE I thought she was stealing my sister Sofya from me. I was eight years old and had just lost my mother. I couldn't lose Sofya, too.

Eliza Ferriday, an American friend of the family, had taken us in for a week at her Paris apartment, two Russian cousins to the tsar forced from our St. Petersburg home before Christmas. Our father had remarried and gone to Sardinia on honeymoon with his new wife, Agnessa, who loathed me since, when she visited us in November, I first practiced my centipede skills on her. She especially hated my favorite interest, astronomy, and convinced Father to take away my maps of the constellations, saying they distracted me from French lessons. Though she tried to lure me out with the gift of a doll-sized Limoges tea set I spent most of November barricaded in my bedroom.

Once Sofya was on break from Brillantmont School in the Swiss Alps we'd met in Geneva to take the train to Paris. Pale and thin, still shattered by Mother's sudden death the previous spring, Sofya said little on our train ride and immersed herself in the stack of books with which she'd filled her suitcase. As we pulled into the Gare de Lyon, she sat and pondered our fellow travelers on the platform. Thinking about Mother, who'd often met her there on school breaks?

Alone in Paris, awaiting the arrival of her husband and daughter from New York, Eliza dedicated every waking hour to our happiness, not leaving us alone for one second. The first day she brought us to a soup kitchen in Le Marais, and I watched as Eliza and Sofya's bond grew by the moment. How easily she got my sister to laugh. They worked as one, side by side, ladling soup from a giant silver pot, while I retrieved the used bowls from the tables.

The next day I watched, envy coiling in my chest, as the two walked the Christmas market, arm in arm, discussing the merits of goose versus duck for dinner and which chocolates to buy at À la Mère de Famille candy store. As the week wore on, at night by the fire, we played cards and they let me win so they could move on to conversation about novels and men and other boring topics, and then stay up half the night talking more. How I yearned to go home to St. Petersburg and have Sofya to myself.

The night before we left for home, shortly after I'd gone to bed, the two came to my bedroom and woke me, embers still glowing in the fireplace.

"Wake up, my darling," Sofya whispered in my ear. She brushed the hair back from my forehead as Mother so often had done. "Slip your coat over your pajamas and come with us."

"We have a surprise for you," Eliza said.

Half asleep, I followed the two out into the cold night air. We walked through a still Paris toward the Tour Eiffel and once there, stopped under a massive, dark globe that loomed above us.

"What is this place?" I asked.

Eliza and Sofya hurried me up three flights of metal stairs and through a pair of heavy, velvet curtains to a dark room. In the inky blackness I could make out a few inclined chairs close to us, like those on the deck of a ship but upholstered. Eliza and Sofya chose their seats and I lay between them. To our left and right others did the same.

"You woke me for this?" I whispered to Sofya.

"Just wait," she said.

She held my hand as the domed ceiling above us came alive with constelled stars, reproducing the heavens as I'd seen them one hundred times from earth. The light of the stars revealed a whole auditorium full of people inclined as we were, gazing up at the massive ceiling.

"It's called the Celestial Globe," Eliza said. "A planetarium."

I lay there stunned as the constellations appeared against the indigo sky. Libra's scales. Bright Scorpio. Even usually dim Draco the dragon snaking past Ursa Minor.

Sofya leaned close and whispered, "That is where Mother lives."

I barely breathed as we watched the moon drift by, fading from full to milky crescent, and a sense of joy I'd not felt since before my mother died filled me.

Eliza took my other hand, warm in hers. "We hoped you'd like it."

As we lay there, the celestial world playing above us, it struck me that I had never lost my sister. Just acquired a spectacular new one.

Part One

CHAPTER

I

Eliza

1914

I T WAS A SPRING PARTY LIKE ANY OTHER HELD IN SOUTH-
ampton, with the usual games. Croquet. Badminton. Mild social cru-
elty. It took place at Mother's house on Gin Lane, a sprawling white
clapboard place surrounded by a swoop of tawny lawn, which eased
down to meet the ocean. The Queen Anne cottage, known to most as
Mitchell Cottage after Father's people, stood with her sisters lined up
along the treeless South Fork of Long Island, New York, like passengers on a ship deck facing out to sea.

If I paid more attention that day, maybe I could have predicted
which of the boys who laughed over croquet wickets would soon die in
the forests of Argonne or which women would exchange their ivory
silk dresses for black crape. I wouldn't have pointed to myself.

It was late May and too unseasonably cool near the ocean for a fete
of any kind, but Mother insisted on sending our Russian friends, the
Streshnayvas, off in style. I stood in the cool, wide living room at the
back of the house. Like a steamship wheelhouse it provided the perfect
view of the backyard through the picture window, the glass hazed with
salt from the sea. It gave the scene a blurry look as guests drifted down
the lawn to the dunes.

I felt two arms wrap around my waist and turned to find my eleven-year-old daughter, Caroline, already almost to my shoulder in height, her hair the color of summer hay and pulled back in a white ribbon. Her friend Betty Stockwell stood at her side, a complete opposite of Caroline, five inches shorter and already blossoming into a dark-haired beauty. Though dressed in matching white dresses, they were as different as chalk and cheese.

Caroline held her arms fast around my waist. "We're going to walk the beach. And Father says he's sorry he dressed without your help this morning, but don't deprive him of his Dubonnet."

I smoothed one hand down her back. "Tell your father color-blind men who insist on sneaking yellow socks into their wardrobes cannot be forgiven."

Caroline smiled up at me. "You're my favorite mother."

She ran off across the lawn and down to the beach, past men who held on to their straw hats, their white flannel trousers flapping in the breeze. Ladies in canvas shoes and suits of cream linen over dainty lingerie shirtwaists turned their faces to the sun, back from places like Palm Beach, happy to feel northern breezes again. Mother's suffragette friends, most outfitted in black taffeta and silk, lent dark contrast to the otherwise pale lawn, like strutting crows in golden flax.

Mother came and linked arms with me. "A bit chilly for a beach walk." My seventy-year-old mother, Caroline Carson Woolsey Mitchell, referred to as "Carry" by her sisters, stood as tall as I did, six feet, a staunch New Englander sprung from ancient Yankee stock that had weathered as many heartaches as hurricanes.

"They'll be fine, Mother."

I squinted to see my Henry, Caroline, and Betty already walking down the beach, the skirt of Caroline's white dress wind-puffed, as if ready to fly her skyward.

"They have their shoes off?" Mother asked. "I do hope they come in soon."

The wind stirred whitecaps on the ocean as the three walked, heads bowed.

Mother wrapped her arms warm about me. "What do they even talk about, Caroline and Henry?"

"Everything. Lost in their own world."

The breeze grabbed Henry's straw boater, leaving his auburn hair shining in the sun, and Caroline darted to pluck it from the surf.

"How lucky she is to have a father who dotes on her," Mother said.

She was entirely right, as always. But would Caroline be up coughing again half the night from the sea air?

Henry waved from the beach, like a castaway stranded on a desert island.

I waved back. "Henry will burn with his fair skin."

Mother waved to Henry. "The Irish are so delicate."

"Half Irish, Mother."

Mother patted my hand. "They'll miss you."

"I won't be gone long." Sofya and her family had been visiting from St. Petersburg for a month and I was due to travel back with them to St. Petersburg the next day.

"I do worry. Russia is so far. Saratoga is nice this time of year."

"This may be my only chance to see Russia. The churches. The ballet—"

"The starving peasants."

"Keep your voice down, Mother."

"They eliminated serfdom but the tsar's poor are still enslaved."

"I'll go mad if I stay cooped up here. Caroline will be fine with Henry."

"At least there's no war on. For now."

For those who read the papers thoroughly, reporters predicted conflict with Germany, but the world had been on the brink of war so many times, many New Yorkers treated the subject with only passing interest.

"Don't worry, Mother."

She hurried off and I stepped out onto the terrace, the salt wind in my hair, into a polite stew of conversation punctuated by great thuds of surf and the occasional knock of a croquet mallet. I pushed through the crowd, squeezing past smooth silks and cashmeres, in search of my friend Sofya.

Mother's and Father's friends split into two distinct camps. Though Father had been dead and gone for a few years, Mother still included his friends in any gathering. He was once head of the Republican Party for New York and his friends reflected that: fellow lawyers and their wives, financiers, and the occasional self-made tycoon.

Mother's friends were decidedly more lively: actors and painters, suffragettes of all shapes and sizes, and several members of the international set from far-off places that Father's friends only gossiped about: Nairobi. Bangkok. Massachusetts.

To find the Russian contingent, I simply listened for raised voices, since they were a refreshingly raucous bunch, prone to heated discussion in a mix of French, English, and their native tongue at any time of day. I passed the Streshnayvas' physician, Dr. Vladimir Leonidovich Abushkin, a squat, balding man wearing a lynx coat over his morning suit, chest to chest with Mother's physician, Dr. Forbes.

"I don't care what they do in St. Petersburg," Dr. Forbes said, his face drawn and heavily joweled from years of late-night deathbed visits and baby deliveries. "If you want a healthy child born, Sofya should not be traveling. She needs bed rest and calcium."

Dr. Abushkin threw back his head. "*Ha*. Calcium. We have two months before the birth. She's sound as a roach."

"But she is at high risk. Two miscarriages. Extended travel is risky."

I found the Russians gathered on the far end of the back terrace, around my actor friends: silver-haired E. H. Sothern, kneeling on bended knee, and his wife Julia Marlowe. Julia addressed them all from my bedroom window above as she and E.H. performed the balcony scene from *Romeo and Juliet,* one of their most famous.

"'Tis almost morning; I would have thee gone—" Julia called out, one arm stretched over the crowd, my bedspread around her shoulders.

The Russians watched the little play, wearing serious expressions, while the rest of the party milled about, immune to the greatest American Shakespearean actor and actress of their day, having seen them perform often. One might ask how Julia and E.H. at forty-eight and fifty-four years old played the famously pubescent couple, but one only had to experience them onstage to be convinced of their talent.

Julia finished the scene to enthusiastic applause and Russian *hurrah*s from the Streshnayvas. They were a jolly group out there on the terrace. Ivan, the patriarch, cousin to tsar Nicholas II, stood and surveyed the pounding surf, his shirtsleeves fluttering. A kind, trim man with a certain European flair, Ivan had met Henry years ago when my husband was a young fur buyer for Poor Brothers Dry Goods and Ivan represented the Russian trade board.

Ivan's second wife, the countess, stood with a decidedly pregnant Sofya and her soldier husband, Afon, and described at length how she sent her personal linen from Russia to Paris to be laundered.

Most guests were well-mannered enough not to gaze openmouthed, but the aging Russian beauty was a sight to behold, dressed in last year's French couture and festooned with sable stole, ropes of pearls, and diamonds the size of which had never been seen before the dinner hour in Southampton.

Sofya caught my eye, smiled, and raised an eyebrow. Pregnancy suited her; it left her with a respectable expectant figure, unlike my own before I delivered Caroline and looked as if I carried a Shetland pony.

The countess ignored the brewing fight between the doctors and pulled a housemaid aside. "Fetch me a soda water, would you, and do remember the ice?"

The maid rushed off and the countess lit one hand on Sofya's shoulder. "You really must sit. Think of your miracle child and how long you've waited, dear. And *do* stop eating or Afon won't touch you after the baby is born."

Sofya shook off the countess's arm. "Please, Agnessa, you've asked for two soda waters already and left them untouched."

"Americans have ice cubes to spare, dear."

I was thrilled to be leaving for Russia the next day, the trip of a lifetime. Not only would I get to see Sofya's baby born, I would finally tour St. Petersburg—the bejeweled Church of the Savior on Spilled Blood, its interior covered entirely with jeweled mosaic, and the Rembrandts at the tsar's Winter Palace. Best of all I could visit with my dearest friend every day.

I pulled Sofya by the arm to the dining room, a room big enough to fit an enormous mahogany table loaded with platters of hors d'oeuvres and desserts and a rose damask sofa.

"Thank you for getting me away from them. Agnessa is terrified the baby will emerge any moment."

"This is the heir, after all. You know how mothers are."

"Stepmothers. And Afon is a wreck—becoming a child himself as birth nears."

"I'm thrilled we're leaving tomorrow, darling. They'll worry less at home."

She reached across the table and held up one of Mother's cookies. "What's the name of this?"

I loved the sound of Sofya's soothing voice. Her Russian-accented English had few hard edges and often caused people to stop what they were doing, lean in, and listen.

"A butterscotch crisp, a Civil War recipe." I'd asked the kitchen to prepare Grandmother Woolsey's family recipes. Fried apples. Teacake cookies and blackberry cordial.

Sofya finished the crisp in three bites. "Wish I could stay here forever and live on butterscotch crisps. The trip home will be terribly long—"

"Sail to France and train to St. Petersburg? Sounds heavenly. I love having a reason to leave New York in the summer."

Sofya reached for another butterscotch crisp. "How can you say that? Back home, half of Russia is on strike. You don't appreciate what you have here. The beach and Manhattan . . ."

"Either stuck out here in a wet bathing costume or holed up in a hot apartment in the city? Trips abroad are the only cure."

"There's always service work."

"And join the society do-gooders, braying about their milk funds and church sociables? Not Mother, of course, but most of them incite little real change and certainly don't expand their horizons."

"You sail . . ."

"Only at gunpoint. The boats I'm interested in are steamers due east. And besides, I miss Luba."

"I do as well. If only Agnessa hadn't convinced Father she needed to study for her—"

Sofya placed one hand on her belly and winced.

"The baby?" I asked, a bit dizzy at the thought. It was too soon.

"It's nothing."

Guests congregated about the table, inspecting the offerings. Unfazed by the battling doctors, Mother sailed past us, her strong Woolsey chin high. She left an oddly pleasant mélange of salt air, Jicky perfume, and mothballs in her wake. As usual, her way of dealing with trouble was to smile and ignore it, ride it out like a sudden squall.

I felt the cold, velvety softness unique to sheared beaver brush my arm and turned to find our neighbor Electra Whitney leaning across the table for a canapé, her face like the weathered side of a barn. Electra lived in a grim sarcophagus of a mansion several houses down from us on Gin Lane, every door attended by liveried footmen. She was alone that day, not flanked as usual by her fellow members of the Pink and Green Garden Society.

Electra helped herself to smoked salmon and lingered. Eavesdropping?

Our gardener, aptly named Mr. Gardener, stepped into the room, two hands supporting a silver Revere bowl filled with his signature antique roses, from creamy white to a deep fuchsia.

Sofya gasped, one hand to her swollen bodice.

"We thought you'd like them," I said. Sofya had once been on the path to becoming an accomplished botanist and still pursued the study of plants for pleasure. When not walking the dunes in search of beach roses she spent hours in Mother's greenhouse grafting orchids.

Mr. Gardener placed the bowl on the polished dining room table, the felted bottom quiet on the mahogany, smoothed his hands down the front of his white coveralls and turned to leave. Mr. Gardener's people had known Mother's for two generations. He was infinitely kind and a fine-looking young gentleman: tall, with a plowman's physique, and dark as the loamy earth he worked.

Sofya caught him by the elbow. "You are just a genius with roses, Mr. Gardener."

Electra edged closer to the table and looked Mr. Gardener up and down. Her gaze slid to the roses.

Each blossom was lovelier than the next: a William Lobb moss rose in ballet pink, with spiky, mosslike growth on her sepals, a deliciously scented, flesh-colored Madame Bosanquet.

Sofya breathed in their essence. "I've never seen anything like these. The fragrance is remarkable. Just in from China?"

"No, ma'am. These are antiques. Some of the finest old roses just grow wild nowadays."

"He finds them in the most unlikely places," I said. "The cemetery, the lumberyard."

"I imagine they're disease resistant, too," Sofya said. "You're a magician, Mr. Gardener. The creamy white one with a tangle of golden threads at her heart—"

"Mrs. Mitchell's favorite, and mine, too," he said with a smile. "Katharina Zeimet—such a hardy repeat bloomer. All she needs is water and a little fertilizer."

"He'd be happy to crate some for you, wouldn't you, Mr. Gardener?" I asked. "To take home to your hothouse."

Electra stepped closer. "It's illegal to propagate a plant still under patent without paying a royalty. Some might call it stealing."

Mr. Gardener stood taller and directed his gaze at the floor.

I turned to her. "Taking a cutting from a wild plant is not stealing and is no worse than eavesdropping, Electra Whitney."

"You never used to see such a thing in Southampton," she said.

"You never used to see people speaking unkindly, either."

Electra drifted off as Mother led a crush of guests from the terrace, waving them into the dining room, and Mr. Gardener took his leave with a bow.

When would Electra Whitney learn to mind her own business?

"Come now," Mother called.

Guests milled around us as maids bearing silver trays topped with flutes of bubbling amber fanned out into the crowd.

Afon came to stand near Sofya. In civilian clothes Afon was simply a standard, good-looking young man, but in his navy blue uniform he became unquestionably Russian, with his thick-lashed brown eyes and shock of blue-black hair.

"Your mother's been looking for you, Sofya," Afon said. "And Eliza, Dr. Abushkin just pushed your doctor into the tea cart."

"Oh no," Sofya said, her brow creased.

Mother mounted a footstool, her posture still ramrod straight, from years of standing with a broom handle threaded across her back between her bent elbows. She hooked the wires of her spectacles behind her ears as her suffragette friends gathered around us, their silk dresses rustling.

"Thank you all for coming!" Mother shouted, arms spread wide.

"Hear, hear!" some in the crowd called out.

I tapped a spoon to my glass and the room quieted.

Mother cleared her throat. "It isn't every day that we host such—"

The French doors from the living room banged open and the doctors emerged, the countess not far behind.

"Would someone call the authorities about this man?" Dr. Forbes called to Mother. "He's intoxicated and may have broken my wrist."

Mother turned. "*Gentlemen*. Doctors. We are celebrating here—"

"Oh no," Sofya called out from the sofa and cradled her belly. "Eliza—"

I rushed to her as Afon knelt at her feet.

The countess paced the room, fanning herself with her hands. "*Dieu, sauve-nous!* She's in labor."

Mother rushed toward us, folding back her sleeves.

"Get my bag," Mother called out, and our housemaid, Peg, ran for the black medical bag.

Sofya reached for my hand. "Don't leave me, Eliza."

I held her hand and prayed the baby would be fine, with a sinking feeling I would never see St. Petersburg.

Sofya

1914

ONCE MY OVERLY PROMPT BABY BOY MAXWELL STRESH-
nayva Afonovich arrived in the middle of Eliza's party, we spent a fort-
night at the hospital. Soon, due to Father's pressing Ministry business
we set off for St. Petersburg, Eliza by my side. She said tearful good-
byes to Henry and Caroline and promised to be home by August.

The journey home lasted more than two weeks but flew by, for Eliza
and I talked about everything—Paris, art, politics—well into every
night, stopping only to eat, sleep, and tend to baby dear.

Once back in St. Petersburg at our townhouse on Rue Tchaikovsky,
my sister Luba and I showed Eliza every literary café and museum,
stepping on and off our excellent system of electric trams, which criss-
crossed the city like patient beetles, fed by a web of wires above the
streets. Luba hosted a star night on our roof to show off her new tele-
scope, a gift from Father, and Eliza bought us lovely old copies of
Walden: Or, Life in the Woods for the three of us to read together, stopping every few chapters to discuss.

Though our home was not far from the tsar's Winter Palace and the
fashionable shopping street Nevsky Prospekt, much to Agnessa's cha-
grin, we lived in the second-best part of town, near the embassies. At
night, we heard increasing unrest in the streets but thought little of it.

One afternoon we gathered in Agnessa's personal rooms, dressing for a Persian costume ball at Anichkov Palace, home of the tsar's mother. Rain fell outside the open window as I sat on the satin-covered love seat, infant Max sleeping warm in my arms, his breathing labored from a head cold.

How I longed to stay at home with him, but Eliza looked forward to the ball. Plus, it was one of the last events of the season, before the St. Petersburg society that was left would decamp to vacation spots like Crimea and Finland and the city left to janitors and scullery maids.

Russian society seemed more eager than ever to escape the city and tense talk of war. Archduke Ferdinand of Austria had been assassinated by a Serbian, which caused Austria to sever diplomatic ties with Serbia, Russia's ally, and Austria mobilized for war. This led to endless, nervous speculation about Russia being drawn in as well.

The royal ball invitation requested guests wear Persian dress and my stepmother, Agnessa, called in Nadezhda Lamanova, a former theater costumer and dressmaker to the tsarina. Madame Lamanova, a buxom, dark-haired woman with a permanently bored expression on her doughy face, produced two trunks of exquisite Persian costumes.

Eliza stepped about the dressing room admiring Agnessa's furnishings. Once Mother's, it was the largest room in Agnessa's bedroom suite, with high ceilings, floral wallpaper, and, on the mantel, a Limoges vase sprouting pink gladioli. The blossoms fluttered in the soft breeze and a shudder went through me.

Gladioli. That dreadful flower.

It was yellow gladioli the woman was delivering when the terrible thing happened. Soon after Agnessa married Father she ordered flower deliveries from Paris even in the dead of winter. I opened the front door of the townhouse one January morning after a violent snowstorm, to find a young peasant girl half dead on the doorstep, bamboo basket of gladioli in her arms, snow drifted around her. She lay there, eyes half closed, the flowers in the basket encased in glittering ice.

I helped the pantry boys pull her into the vestibule and pumped her chest until the ambulance came, but it was too late. I arranged her funeral and then kept to my room, unable to shake the thought of her frozen face. How unfair it was, to die so young, just so a spoiled woman from Moscow could have her flowers.

Soon after, Father and I opened Fena's House for impoverished women and named it after my mother, Agrafena. Her name meant "born feet first," a perfect name for her, always on the run doing things nonstop.

Madame Lamanova unlatched one trunk, the sound wrenching me out of my thoughts. She pulled with two hands on one side while Eliza took the other, and they pried it open like an oyster shell. The two huddled around the trunk, sorting through the racks of gold brocades and fur-trimmed cloaks.

Madame Lamanova drew out an ivory-colored, sable-trimmed, brocade coat. "For Mrs. Ferriday?"

Eliza slid off her robe, slipped her arms into the coat. "What will you wear, Sofya?"

"I'm going like this." I had simply augmented my white evening dress with a cashmere shawl from my closet.

Agnessa walked to me. "You must at least *try*, my dear. People judge you first by how you look and second by what you say."

How I hated that, her favorite expression. "Please, Agnessa—"

Madame Lamanova offered me a feathered turban and I waved it away.

Agnessa stepped to her jewelry cabinet and returned with a necklace draped across her palm. As she drew closer the emeralds glowed under the electric lights.

"You must wear this tonight."

Growing up, I'd seen my mother wear that emerald necklace on the most formal occasions. Luba and I would sneak to her jewel box and run our fingers over the humps of cabochon emeralds and two rows of round diamonds. The tsar's mother had given it to Father for performing some financial wizardry and he'd given it to Mother on their honeymoon in Biarritz. Now Agnessa wore it on occasion.

"Father's wedding gift to Mother?"

Agnessa's mouth tightened, as it always did upon mention of Mother.

"What if it falls off?" I asked. At a similar costume ball the tsar's younger brother had once famously lost one of the crown jewels, a diamond the size of a duck's egg, never found.

Agnessa fastened it about my neck. "If you won't wear a Persian costume, this is all you need. The sultans loved their emeralds."

I touched the heavy platinum and cool stones at my neck. I was no great fan of jewelry, but there was something empowering about that necklace.

Agnessa turned her attention back to the trunks, and then Eliza insisted on making up my face in her version of the Persian way, with kohl-rimmed eyes and scarlet lips.

The rain continued that night and Agnessa allowed Father, down with the cold as well, to stay home with Luba and Max. Father seemed relieved he would miss his least favorite activity, dancing, for guests were all to perform a Persian-style ballet, an audience-participation event. I shared Father's feelings about dancing but looked forward to presenting Eliza to the tsar's wife, Tsarina Alexandra, who would be in attendance.

Eliza and I set off from our townhouse, side by side in Father's carriage, driven by our coachman Peter, who, in his city uniform of high fur hat and scarlet jacket, made quite a show of it, whipping the horses.

How good it was to have Eliza all to myself. Agnessa and Afon took a separate carriage so she could come home early to check on Father. I wanted to arrive at the palace relatively dry, introduce Eliza to Tsarina Alexandra, and return home to curl up with infant Max in my arms.

We made good time down Nevsky Prospekt, the fine shops shuttered for the night. Halfway to the palace we passed a group of ruffians near a liquor shop confronting a well-dressed young gentleman, clearly pressing him for money.

"Criminals?" Eliza asked. "On the best street in the city?"

"They call them 'hooligans.' Nothing new." Hooliganism was an established practice heralded by the newspapers, where unemployed, drunken men used petty violence to intimidate the wealthy—often women. Rogue gangs bumped and badgered, robbed and mugged, let loose wasps' nests on the trams, and, from tea shop doorways, threw hot tea on passersby for sport.

Eliza craned her neck as we rode by. "Should we alert the police?"

"They rarely come."

"It seems to be getting worse just in the time I've been here. How is the tsar helping?"

I shrugged. "He believes if he supports the rich, prosperity will trickle down to the people. Private individuals pick up the slack. Like the women's home Father and I opened. Father funds it himself."

"The tsar hasn't helped the others still living in the slums."

"New York has no slums? Here, it's the Bolsheviks' fault—stirring up discontent. They called for another factory strike."

"I'm afraid for you, Sofya. The people are getting desperate. The tsar's solution seems to be to kill all protestors."

"What of your Mr. Rockefeller's guards just machine-gunning striking coal miners to death? Eleven children died there."

Eliza looked out the window at the dark streets, silent, the reflection in the window showing her pained expression. Had I been too harsh? She was right, of course. Perhaps it was better if we had a successful revolution, installed a more modern form of government. Half of St. Petersburg seemed ready to sweep out the tsar.

The carriage approached Anichkov Palace, the four-story white facade aglow, even more beautiful than usual, washed with rain.

"We're almost there, Eliza. I'll make sure you meet the tsarina."

"Will she expect an expert curtsey? Mine's a bit rusty."

"Yes. And she speaks English and French. Prefers English but you'll impress her with your French. Ask her about her son, Alexei, the heir. You'll get extra time."

We joined the crowds of Persian-dressed guests streaming into the high-ceilinged entry space and followed the crowd up the red carpet, past the usual magnificent guards at attention in their gold-braided, black jackets. We'd visited Anichkov Palace many times with our parents to call on the tsar's mother and it was always one of my favorites, more intimate than the tsar's official residence that was just minutes away, the immense Winter Palace.

Though I was in no rush to speak with them, I knew most of the *belaya kost* there, the "white-boned," the blue-blooded Russian families full of princes, dukes, counts, and barons that held most of Russia's wealth.

We entered the ballroom through gilded doors thrown open to reveal a wide ballroom, the walls shining in turquoise silk. Tall mirrors reflected the guests' brocades, silks, and beadwork lit entirely by flickering wax candles burning in the chandelier above. Great clusters of towering palms, flowering orange trees, and great blooming azalea gently swayed in the breeze of the open windows.

Eliza drew a quick breath. "Oh, *Sofya*. I've never seen such a place. The plants alone."

"The gardeners use massive hoists to lift these in through the windows—all from the tsarina's imperial greenhouse. You should see it, Eliza: three stories high, full of lilacs, her favorite. Before I went off to school, I practically lived there."

At the far end of the room, the dowager empress, the tsar's mother, and the tsarina sat on golden thrones, with a throng of guests already jockeying for position before them, lining up to pay respects.

In the corner sat bearded men in evening dress, a string quartet segueing with ease from our Russian hymn to Persian melodies. They would accompany the Persian ballet we would all dance later.

"Can you imagine growing up here?" I asked. "It's the tsar's childhood home."

We walked toward the golden thrones, which were placed just far enough apart that the two women didn't have to speak to each other. After years of competition between daughter-in-law and mother-in-law for the heart of the tsar, their rivalry was well-known but only whispered about. Their public personas were very different. The tsar's mother, beloved by the people, was more open and gracious, fond of dancing, while the tsarina Alexandra remained terribly aloof and barely tolerated public events, preferring quiet pursuits and family time.

"I shall introduce you to the tsarina, but we must wait our turn," I said, steering Eliza to the end of the line.

"I can't imagine what we'll talk about."

I pulled Eliza close to whisper in her ear and the heron feathers of her turban brushed my cheek. How many poor birds died to outfit this one party?

"She'll ask you questions, mostly about whether you have children. She has a buzzer under her foot that she presses when it's time to move on and her ladies-in-waiting will lead you away."

The line moved slowly and as the room filled with guests we grew warm and the fur costumes smelled of wet animal. As we inched closer in line toward the tsarina I caught a glimpse of her, wearing her usual bored expression, a blaze of diamonds at her chest. Did she realize her face betrayed every thought?

I recognized many of her ladies-in-waiting, for I'd once been one of them, well before Max was born. They hovered near the tsarina, dressed in their white muslin dresses, the empress's diamond monogram *chiffre*, a glittering letter "A" for Alexandra on a blue ribbon, pinned at each woman's left shoulder. Madame Wiroboff stood at the tsarina's side, a round, self-effacing woman with sleepy eyes, the empress's best friend.

Eliza leaned toward me. "The tsarina is beautiful. Though not at all happy."

"She hates big parties. Much rather be reading."

"Where is the tsar?"

"Down in Kracnoe-Celo. He has a full plate right now."

How tense things had become for the royal family with all the strikes and unrest on top of a looming war. Rumors abounded that Tsar Nicholas, afraid for his life, had food tasters check his dinners and would not allow even his longtime valet to shave him for fear of assassination. Though a dedicated ruler, the tsar was not at all suited to the monarch's life of high-pressure decisions. He was happiest in the country at his beloved Alexander Palace, with the tsarina and their five children, playing tennis or dominoes.

I felt a hand at my back and turned to find Grand Duchess Olga, the royal couple's eldest daughter, flanked by two colossi in palace dress.

"Whose idea was it to dress in fur in July?" Olga asked in English, with a smile. Dressed in a white chiffon gown of the Grecian style and necklace of seed pearls, she was a natural beauty without even a trace of powder.

I curtseyed. "Cousin."

Olga kissed me three times, alternating cheeks.

"Grand Duchess Olga Nikolaevna Romanova, may I present Mrs. Eliza Woolsey Mitchell Ferriday of New York?" I asked, using the full complement of Eliza's names, in the Russian tradition.

Eliza curtseyed low and Olga nodded back. "So nice to meet you all the way from America."

With her wide smile and candid, blue-eyed gaze, it was impossible not to be enchanted by Olga. For a woman of her regal position she remained remarkably down to earth.

"Did you come by rail?" Olga asked. "Such a long trip."

"Yes, steamer and train. It flew by—Sofya and I talked the whole way."

"I am terribly jealous of you having a bosom friend. What did you talk about, if you don't mind me asking?"

"Oh, our favorite paintings. Sofya's dream garden and what she would plant. Which philosophers truly understand the female mind—which is none, we decided."

"We graded the world's best cities," I said. "And, of course, we chose Paris as our favorite, for the best museums and the profiteroles."

"May I say you and Sofya look remarkably alike?" Eliza asked.

I glanced at Olga, with her tipped-up nose and waved hair pulled up in a chignon. "That is what they say. Maybe a *much* older sister."

Though I was several years older than Olga who was eighteen at the time, for distant cousins we shared many other similarities: the same height, round face, and almond-shaped eyes.

Olga smiled. "Of course, I didn't get your glorious hair."

She linked arms with me, drew me closer, releasing a sweet scent of orange blossom soap and cinnamon. "I've met a new officer," she whispered. "He wants to call on me soon. Can you advocate for me with Mother?"

"Of course, my darling, but remember, men know you are sheltered for a reason. They like a challenge, so remain refined. And keep to your reading. Men may leave, but books will always remain true."

The guards shifted in their boots and Olga released my arm. "Here it is I've found you and now have to go. Mother is nervous as a cat—there's trouble at the factories."

The guards rushed Olga off through the crowd and she called back to us. "Tatiana is getting a little dog, a French bulldog. You must visit when she comes."

Olga exited through a side door and we continued in line, inching closer.

Eliza stood on her toes to better see the tsarina. "She surrounds herself with noblewomen. Does she greet the common people as well?"

"No. Only when they summer in the Crimea. Too dangerous to be out among the people here, with every vagrant about."

A tall, red-haired woman hurried toward us through the crowd.

I leaned closer to Eliza. "Here comes Karina, cousin on my mother's side."

"Heavenly day, is everyone here related?"

"Karina was in prison for two years, been out for one year. I helped her return to society—she spends her days at my women's home, completing her sentence with service to the country."

As Karina grew closer, the bell sleeves of her white caftan fluttering behind her, she seemed less like a criminal and more like a great, kind moth.

"Whatever for?"

"Her boyfriend, from a fine family himself, belonged to a secret society whose object it was to bring violence to subvert the state, to bring down the tsar."

"Why would a nobleman want to hurt the tsar?"

"Not every person of wealth is a monarchist, Eliza. Many here oppose the tsar. Being young and silly, Karina had allowed her boyfriend to keep his printing press in her apartment. A gifted pianist, she played her piano loud enough every day to conceal the sound of the press in the back room."

"How were they arrested?"

"An informant loyal to the tsar turned them in but only Karina was caught. Received a fifteen-year sentence."

"The boyfriend escaped?"

"He has a talent for evading the authorities while others take the blame. She's not seen him since, but holds out hope. They would've sent an ordinary girl to the mines but the tsar has always doted on Karina and he considered two years' confinement enough. She's not allowed to play the piano again. And is never to see Ilya again, either. Not sure which is worse for her."

Karina made it to us and embraced me. "How good to see you, cousin. Welcome back to Russia. You look better for childbirth."

She turned to Eliza. "I'm sure Sofya told you about my sordid past."

"A bit."

Karina smiled. Her skin glowed pink, almost translucent in the candlelight. Such an oddly beautiful girl and altogether different from me, taller and thin, with a glorious head of deep red hair. Hard to believe we were from the same family.

"My life so far is stranger than any novel, but I confess it's good to be out." Karina pulled me closer. "Ilya has sent word he will contact me."

"You believe him?" I asked. "There are so many good men here tonight."

"Of course I believe him. He may be reckless, but not a liar."

"He always gets off free as a bird, Karina, while others—"

All at once there came a great commotion echoed in the front vestibule, of shouting and ladies' screams. At the golden doors, a man in velvet palace dress appeared, held high a gun, and shouted, "Long live freedom!"

Eliza put her arms about me as the man shot his gun into the ceiling and plaster rained down on us both. The musicians stopped playing and stood.

I barely breathed as guards rushed the tsar's mother and the tsarina out of their seats, their ladies-in-waiting following. Other guards wrestled the man to the ground, then hustled him away.

The crowd stood stunned, holding gentle conversation. A member of the palace guard turned on the monarchy?

The scent of gunpowder wafted through the air as waiters wandered the crowd with their silver trays, craning their necks to catch a glimpse of the gunman. In seconds the string quartet resumed their song and the crowd huddled in groups to discuss the gunman's assault, looking strangely out of place in their Persian clothes.

We lost Karina in the crowd and Afon rushed to us, his face pale against his deep blue uniform.

"I am taking Agnessa home," he said. "She had to be revived with smelling salts. I only have room for the two of us."

He hurried off, pushing through the crowd, with only a glance back at me.

"Will Peter know to come early to get us?" I called after him.

"I'll be back as fast as I can," he shouted back over his shoulder.

Soon, with the festive mood broken, guests started for the gilded doors and the musicians packed their instruments. Eliza and I joined the great crush of the crowd moving down the red-carpeted stairs, now muddy as the streets, wet with muck from Persian boots and shoes.

At the bottom of the stairs an American woman I recognized

brushed by us through the crowd and I touched her arm. "Princess Cantacuzène."

She turned, a tall, handsome woman with kind, expressive, dark eyes, beautifully turned-out in a deep emerald and gold coat trimmed in sable. An American by birth, her husband, Prince Mikhail Cantacuzène, was a decorated general in the tsar's army and a regular at court.

"Sofya." She took my hand in hers. "Just dreadful, that shooter. With all the tsarina has been through."

We joined the crowd, spilling out into the rainy night. As one motorcar came and went, I searched the night for our coachman.

Princess Cantacuzène leaned closer and I caught the scent of jasmine and ylang-ylang. "I would drop you at home but our coach has not arrived, either. The roads are flooded."

"We could take the tram," Eliza said.

"Princess Cantacuzène, Countess Speransky Grant, may I introduce Eliza Woolsey Mitchell Ferriday of New York?"

"Lovely to meet you," Eliza said. "Grant?"

"President Grant was my grandfather. Under better circumstances we will compare notes. But for now, I doubt any of us are getting home anytime soon."

A friend of Agnessa's, Count von Orloff, wedged his turbaned head into our little circle. A small, thin-faced man, he'd taken the Persian costume directive seriously. In his ostrich-feathered turban, embroidered, thick, velvet coat, and with kohl makeup lining his eyes, he could have been mistaken by an actual Persian as one of their own.

"The tram is the reliable way home," the count said. "I hear the rain has closed two streets."

"I never ride trams at night," I said. "And besides, they cannot pass on flooded roads, either."

The musicians rushed by us toward the tram stop, instruments in hand.

"Look, half the party is catching the tram," the count said. "The rain will keep the hooligans away. Only a cat hates rain more than they do. And besides, I will protect you all."

Princess Cantacuzène pulled me close. "The Cossacks are guarding these trams on the Nevsky."

A bad feeling grew in my belly as we followed the crowd to the tram stop, but it was a short walk and the rain-slicked, red tram soon came along.

The conductor stepped down from the rear platform, a bearded man in a black, belted uniform tunic and pants and knee-high boots, with a leather bag slung over his shoulder. From his chest hung paper tickets of all colors for the different routes. He helped each of us up the single step into the tram and then pulled a rope, which rang a bell up front near the driver.

"Yellow tickets, next stop!" he called out as the car set off.

What a relief to make it onto the brightly lit car. The princess, Eliza, and I found room near the driver, who stood at a big red wheel. We sat on the long, slatted, wooden seats that ran lengthwise along the walls of the interior, and shook the rain from our clothes.

The princess handed the conductor sterling for our fares.

"You're lucky," the tram driver said to us over his shoulder. "This number four is still running all the way to the Neva. It's my last run though. Things are bad outside the city."

Halfway down the tram sat the cellist, an older man with a pronounced widow's peak and sad eyes, his instrument clamped between his legs. He pulled from his pocket a bottle of the *Arak* from the party and passed it around the tram. The violinist, a younger man with graying hair, squeezed his violin chinpiece between neck and shoulder and played a rousing chorus of *Katyusha,* which had been my mother's favorite.

Eliza clapped to the music and called out to me across the aisle, high color in her cheeks. "I have no idea what it means, but I feel so Russian."

The *Arak* soothed my sore throat and we all sang. How it raised my spirits to hear everyone sing as one.

All at once the tram slowed.

In the glow of the headlights we could see a group of ten or so roughly dressed men blocking the way.

"Bandits," I said, trying to keep the tremor from my voice.

The driver rang his jangly little bell, operated by a pedal at his foot, to warn the men, but they stood fast.

"God help us," the driver said under his breath as he braked.

Eliza sat up straighter. "Button your coat, Sofya."

Of course. Mother's necklace. With trembling fingers, I pulled my coat up.

The music ended abruptly as we ground to a stop and the men surrounded the tram, peering in the wide windows.

A stout fellow wearing a wool fisherman's cap pounded on the driver's glass door. "Open up!" he called in Russian.

The driver brandished his radio. "I've called the police."

The stout fellow laughed. All at once the glass door fell to pieces and he scrambled onto the tram, hammer in one hand, a jagged-edged knife in the other. He slipped the hammer into his jacket pocket and removed his cap to reveal a smooth, bald pate that shone in the electric lights overhead, a ring of tangled, mouse-brown hair around it like a furry halo.

He walked down the tram shoving his hat at the riders. "Contributions to my university fund. Don't be shy." Passengers eyed his knife as they removed earrings and bracelets and pocket watches and placed them with a muffled clink into the hat.

The bandit kicked Count von Orloff's pointy-toed boot and the count retracted into his thick coat like a snail in its shell. People of good breeding, we awaited our fate in silence.

He moved on to the conductor and with the tip of his knife raised the flap of the leather bag. "Open that up, good fellow."

"I have nothing yet. This is the first run."

"I know you have change. It's not *your* money. Just give it up and we'll part friends."

The conductor handed the bandit a stack of bills.

"And the sterling."

The conductor reached into his bag and handed him the coins. "There was a time when people acted properly."

The bandit added the money to his hat. "I'll act as I want."

He walked back to the front of the tram, stopped and considered me, his stance wide, head tipped to one side. Up close, it was hard not to notice one side of his face had been burned somehow, as if a pointed iron seared the flesh there and it healed ham-pink and shiny. I tried not to look at the dirty fish knife in his hand.

"Well, well," he said. He opened the collar of my coat with the tip of the knife, so close to my face I could smell the metal of it.

My whole body shook. Could he see?

"I do like emeralds," he said with a smile.

One look at his teeth, black with decay, caused me to avert my gaze.

He ran the tip of his knife under the heavy platinum, the blade cool against my skin.

"I dug them when I was in prison. So, I guess these belong to me, don't you agree?"

He dumped his stolen goods into his jacket pocket, replaced his cap, and took my hand in his, surprisingly warm and smooth. "Let's go, madame. This is your stop."

I tried to pull free, but he yanked me from my seat.

Behind him, Eliza stood and grabbed his arm. "Let her go."

The bandit turned, lashed out with his knife and the whole car cried out with terror at what he did to my dear friend.

Varinka

1914

"BOIL, DAMN YOU!" I SHOUTED AT THE SAMOVAR, stuffing more pinecones down its tin chimney. Right away I was sorry for yelling at the poor water boiler, the last thing we had of Papa's. It stood on the table next to the giant white oven Papa had forged and I ran one hand down the warm, copper side of the cauldron, our one precious thing. Yelling at it was like ranting at poor, dead Papa. Would I wake Mamka?

Mamka. She slept upon the bench, which ran the length of our one room *izba,* on her back, mouth agape, still and gray-faced as a cadaver. I stepped to her in the darkness, smoothed her dark hair back off her forehead. How warm she felt, delirious with fever. We'd had a bad night, her up coughing as I held her, willing her to breathe. I brushed oven soot off her coverlet and pressed two fingers to the bones of her wrist.

My gaze flicked to the icons in the holy corner opposite, the golden faces of the tsar and the Black Madonna shining above the rose-scented candles burning there. Would the saints take her from me? How could I live without Mamka? We would bury her next to Papa in the pine grove.

The thought sent me rushing back to the samovar. I touched one finger to the metal side. The water was finally heating and soon it would hiss with steam.

I opened the *izba* door, shielding my eyes from the blast of sunshine, and with my apron waved out the soot from the oven.

I looked up and my heart banged inside of my chest when I saw two men coming down our front path, one skeleton-skinny with a springy step, leaning on a black cane, the other round and big, both in city clothes. Taxmen. Their carriage rested at the head of the path in the sun, loaded with household items: a brass birdcage, a baby carriage, and a tall clock.

I hurried to the samovar. How to hide it behind the oven? It was too heavy with water for me to carry by the silver handles. I wrapped my arms around the cylinder and lifted it, the heat searing through the linen of my apron and sleeves. The hot water inside sloshed against the metal as I stepped behind the oven and set down the samovar there, my chest and arms on fire.

I rushed back to the open door just as the men arrived.

"Fathers," I said, using the most reverent form of greeting we all did. I bowed low to the skinny one and stared at his boots. My arms and chest pounded with the burns.

"Don't kowtow to me," the skinny one said. "I'm no father of yours. I need to speak with Rafa Rafovich Kozlov immediately on imperial business."

"My papa's dead," I said into the leather. I brushed the water from my eyes. I had to keep my wits about me and, above all, keep my temper down.

The old man pushed by me. "Get up, I said. Why do you live so far from the others in town?"

"It's just a short walk from Malinov."

I stood and watched him take in the room, his weasel eyes magnified in his wire-rimmed spectacles. He was a census man from the zemstvo, his face lined and cracked like a dry riverbed, his mustache waxed sharp at both ends: a bureaucrat taxman, the most hated kind in the village.

The other man I recognized as Mr. A., a large man and good-natured, owner of the Malinov general store in town. He brushed the bottoms of his felt boots against the doorjamb and entered. He held a little paper book close to his face and wrote in it with a pencil stub.

The old man walked about the room as he spoke. "One room country dwelling known in the local parlance as *izba*." Suddenly the man turned. "Does a person named Taras Walidovich Perminov live here?"

"He once was my Papa's apprentice." This was true, after all. Taras's alcoholic parents had sold him to Papa. I pointed to the far wall. "Sleeps in the toolshed through that door."

"Back from prison?" Mr. A. asked, writing something in his little book.

The tiny pencil in his big hand made me want to laugh.

"Yes. Back two months now. But he's not here."

The old one stepped toward the beautiful corner and eyed the icons. "Where is he? On what business?"

St. Petersburg, of course, but what to say? Since Taras had been back from prison he'd been going to secret meetings there and I'd found pamphlets in his boots.

"Only God knows."

The two exchanged a look.

The prickles on the back of my neck rose. "He served his time."

Mr. A. stepped toward me. "I heard he met a bad element there...."

I took a deep breath. "Prison changes a person."

"Turn around," the old man said to me.

I stared at him for a long moment, and then quickly turned.

He considered my figure. "Are you and this Taras to be married?"

"No," I said.

"Unmarried women pay additional tax." With one hand, he grabbed my jaw and forced open my mouth. "Good teeth. You may be the only unmarried one in Malinov. Most have a passel of brats by your age."

That was certainly true. Thanks to Taras and the arrangement, I would never marry. Never have children.

The old man bent and peered out our only window. "How much tillable land?"

"We've had no harvest since Taras sold the ox."

"You could pull the plow." He turned to me and squeezed the top of my arm through my linen sleeve. "You're strong enough." My skin burned as I yanked back my arm.

His hand slid across my chest and grazed my breast.

"Old pig," I said under my breath.

Mr. A. directed his gaze out the door, looking like he'd tasted something sour.

"The tsar has sent people to Siberia for saying less," the old man said.

"We tried tilling the land. Taras hitched me and Mamka to the plow and we worked the soil until she grew sick." I waved toward Mamka on the bench. "She lies there ill with the cough, probably from pulling the plow like an animal."

Both men took a step back.

"Soil quality?" the old man asked.

"Bad. Even with both of us hitched we could grow only beets."

The old man shook his head. "Decreased harvest? Not good. Household budget?"

"We have no *budget*. I make peppermint oil I sell in town and use it to buy bread. Groats." My scalded chest and arms pulsed with heat.

Mr. A. bent to speak to me. "We ask, for we must know to tax you fairly, Varinka."

Such a kind man. How many times had he given Mamka thread on credit? She always tried to pay him back but he often told her to keep her money.

"Own any household items?" the old one asked.

I nodded toward the wide, tin basin leaning against the bench. "That washbasin there."

"Things of *value*. Jewelry? You cannot expect to pay no tax while your neighbors sacrifice. The tsar needs this money to provide famine relief."

"We are in famine," I said.

The old man waved in the direction of town. "You could work at the linen factory."

"They won't have me." I glanced at Mr. A. and he looked at his boots. He knew how those in town shunned us, three odd ducks living out there in the woods. They threw handfuls of dirt at me as I passed on the street. Accused me of being the witch's daughter and living unmarried with Taras, and they called me bad names. "And if you don't mind, I need to tend to my mamka."

The old man bent at the waist, opened the iron oven door and peered inside. "Your father was an artisan? No wonder you've been left in this state."

"Yes. But all we have left of him is this *izba* he made."

"Seems fairly well-crafted," the old man said.

How dare he doubt Papa's skills? "Papa made every bit himself, sturdy in the old style. Cut his own logs, daubed it with river clay he carried on his back, carved the flowers above the door himself. Even buried a coin in each corner for good—"

I regretted those words even as they came out of my mouth.

"Coins?" The old man hurried to one corner and poked the dirt with his cane.

I hurried to him and pulled him by one bony arm. "It's bad luck—"

He shook off my grasp, dug deeper, and soon the cane's silver tip hit metal and he bent to retrieve Papa's coin. The old man continued to the other corners and murmured happy little grunts as he dug up each of the coins Papa had planted so many years before.

How could I be so stupid? I took deep breaths to control my rage.

The old man stepped to me, leaving deep holes surrounded by horrid little piles of tilled earth. "You now owe the tsar four kopecks less."

"And you now have years of bad luck for yourself," I said.

He slid the four coins into his vest pocket and patted them. "Any other items of value?"

"Not a thing."

All at once from behind the oven came a great hissing sound. At last the samovar water boiled.

The old taxman glanced at me with eyebrows raised and followed the sound behind the oven.

I trailed him. "Please—"

The old man waved Mr. A. over. "Really? You have not a *thing*?" He pointed with his cane behind the oven. "This seems to be a household item."

Mr. A. lifted the boiling samovar from my hiding place, holding it by the silver swan-head handles, and placed it back on the table. "Jesus, it's hot."

"Well, that's a start," the old one said. He ran one finger along the samovar's sterling silver band, fastened like a belt around a man's waist, stamped with the seals of winning at every samovar competition Papa entered it in. "Look at all those awards."

"He was a great artist," I said.

The old man waved Mr. A. away. "Take it to the wagon."

I fell to my knees. "Please, no. We need it for my mamka—"

The old man wagged a finger in my face. "It's better off in a fine home, not here where the roof probably leaks on it."

Mr. A. wore a weary look as he dumped the steaming water out of the samovar just outside the door and carried it toward the carriage. I covered my face with my hands.

"Get up." The old one yanked me up by the elbow.

"Please, my mamka sews beautiful things. She can make you a fine sash with silver beads. Or tell your future. She is a seer."

He pulled me close and I smelled on his breath beets and stale beer. "How old are you?"

"Fourteen. Please don't take our samovar."

He smiled and ran one hand down the front of my *sarafan*, hurting my burned skin. "Why do you girls wear so many layers?"

I tried to move toward Mamka but he pushed me against the hard clay of the tall oven.

He kissed my neck, his greasy hair cold against my throat. "I can bring that samovar back if you cooperate."

I froze. I'd never kissed anyone, even Taras. I glanced at Mamka, lying there on her bench along the wall, deep in a fever-sleep. Who would know?

"Bring it back, first," I said.

He laughed. "You're a smart one. No. But I promise if you give me what I want, then the samovar comes back."

"On God's honor?"

He raised his hand to cover his heart. "On God's honor." He then dug that hand between my legs, through the folds of my long skirt.

Taras had never done that before, either.

"I can show you a few things," the old man said in my ear, the point of his waxed mustache pricking my cheek.

He moved his hands to my breasts and squeezed them like a person kneads bread dough. "Do you like that?" he said, sending his sour breath around me like a cloud.

I nodded, though it felt terrible being squeezed that way, my burned skin raw under his hands. Up close, his spectacles were covered with white flecks from his hair. The thought of kissing him made my stomach queasy. "Bring back the samovar and I will do what you want."

All at once the light coming from the doorway dimmed as a figure stood there. Taller and broader through the shoulders than Mr. A. I recognized the shape of his hunting jacket, his *brodni* boots that left no sound as he stalked his prey. The leather bag he wore was slung across his chest. The outline of one of his many knives, sheathed at his side. He made those knives himself, sharp enough to slice leather like butter. Taras.

The old taxman took his hands from my chest and turned. He blinked in the light and swallowed hard. Out the door I saw Mr. A. whip his horse as the carriage left with a clatter. Mr. A. knew better than to stay around an angry Taras.

"I think we are certainly done here," the old man brushed off his pants as he stepped toward Taras. "Your tax bill has been satisfied for now."

Taras stepped aside and watched the old man scurry by, down the path, and off through the woods toward town without a look back.

I rushed to Mamka and found her still asleep, felt her forehead, cooler, and relief washed over me.

I turned to Taras. "I'm sorry. I know I violated the arrangement." No contact with other men was one of the first rules.

Taras stepped toward me.

"You are disgusting, letting him paw you that way." He dropped his leather bag on the floor with a thud. "I can't trust you."

"But he took the samovar." I bit the inside of my cheek to keep the tears away.

"Who cares? It's just a stupid boiler. We have no tea anyway."

Taras snatched the washbasin from the bench and pushed it toward me.

I held it to my chest.

"I won't be long," he said. "Don't finish until I'm back."

I knew what to do with it, of course, as much as I hated it. And I knew where Taras was going. He'd given the old man a head start, for the thrill of the chase. Taras made his way out the door and I poured water in the basin. I unbuttoned my skirt, removed my clothes and prepared to follow the rules of the arrangement, knowing Taras would indeed be quick. The old taxman would not make it even halfway to town.

CHAPTER

4

Eliza

1914

HOW QUICKLY IT ALL HAPPENED, THERE ON THE TRAM. The bandit turned and slashed his blade, remarkably sharp for such a crude-looking knife, down the length of my thumb. I didn't feel it at first, but the blood came fast and thick and flooded Madame Lamanova's white brocade coat. What would Grandmother Woolsey do? Apply pressure?

I sat stunned and light-headed as my fellow passengers rose up against the bandit. The driver himself received a wound to the leg as he forced the man's knife to the floor, where Princess Cantacuzène pounced upon it and held the bandit at bay. The conductor and violinist helped hold the terrible man but he wrestled free.

"Grab him!" the driver shouted as the man melted into the foggy night just as the Cossacks arrived on their small horses. Though dressed in their dark blue everyday uniform coats lined with red, not their famous scarlet dress coats, they were a rare sight to see, circling the tram, skirts flying. The whole thing was quite exhilarating, almost worth the stitches, and I might have enjoyed it despite my gaping wound had dear Sofya not been traumatized. She hovered over me, face drained of color. How close she'd come to not only losing the emerald necklace, but her life.

The tram driver telephoned Sofya's house and a gaggle of my fellow passengers accompanied us to the Streshnayva's townhouse, on the front steps of which every servant and family member stood waiting, lights ablaze. Even Mr. Streshnayva rose from his sickbed.

They lingered while my old friend Dr. Abushkin, his hair fresh from the pillow, still spiked about his head in the German style like hedgehog quills, made a great fuss of cleaning the wound, announcing to all that if not for him I would surely lose the use of my hand.

The next morning the incident was in the newspaper, *The Petersburg Sheet*, which Sofya translated for me. The headline read AMERICAN HEIRESS STABBED ON TRAM DURING STRIKE, which was surprisingly accurate for the sensationalist newspaper, except for the heiress part, arguably an exaggeration.

THE VIOLENT STRIKES ENDED by July eighteenth, returning St. Petersburg to normal, and I continued to enjoy the city by day with my hand bandaged with a length of gauze that could have reached to the moon and back. Sofya and Luba were excellent tour guides and we spent many lovely nights on their roof deck admiring the stars, but by July's end I was ready to leave.

I'd spent nearly six weeks with the Streshnayvas and been offered every comfort: the house, with its large, well-appointed rooms and the quantities of flowers and handsome silver, a view of the wide Neva River running by my bedroom window, and my own little Russian maid. But I missed my family and also could not help feeling terribly uneasy. The talk of war escalated and though the tsar had suppressed the strikes, every day the discontent of the people grew, while the Streshnayvas chose not to see it.

On my last day Sofya and Luba accompanied me to the Niko-layevsky railway station. I was planning to leave the way I came via France and beat the war if it started. I wore my newest acquisition, a famous Orenburg shawl of goat hair and silk, so thin and finely woven it would pass through a wedding ring, yet large and warm when shaken out to full size.

We rode down fashionable Nevsky Prospekt, a second carriage following with valet and two house servants. The street looked abandoned, as the September streets often did in Paris, with society away.

But as we neared the station the real St. Petersburg emerged, the streets teeming with beggars, panhandlers, chimney sweeps, and women in vivid peasant dress. Men huddled in groups, holding up hand-lettered placards and red flags that said *Surrender your guns, bourgeois!* and *All land for the peasants.* It sent my heart pounding while Sofya and Luba barely noted it.

According to the newspapers, the people's rebellion was gaining momentum but the Streshnayvas and friends adopted a curious denial of the flames rising around them. The tsar seemed oddly disconnected from his people and the tsarina showed no love of them at all. Surely the royal couple would save themselves in case of a successful revolution, but what would happen to Sofya? I suggested they repair to Paris and ride this all out, but my suggestions fell on deaf ears.

Luba and I sat facing Sofya, little Max dozing on my lap. I would miss my godson, almost as much as his mother. The carriage bounced, he shifted closer to me and I felt his cheek. Such a handsome baby, indulged at every cry by all adults and dressed in pleated Irish linen, Belgian lace, and cashmere. His diapers came by post from a convent in Lyon, made of French cotton flannel with the edges basted in silver thread, and were affixed around his royal loins with golden safety pins. His name and the year were even embroidered into each one, *Maxwell 1914.*

How Max had grown in the short time I'd been there. At two months old, he was already less a newborn and more a robust child, and on his sweet head had sprouted wispy, white-blond curls.

The coachman navigated the missing cobblestones, which made our passage slow.

"Have your traveling papers?" Luba asked. "Passport?"

"Leave Eliza alone," Sofya said. "She can manage herself."

I was happy to spend more time with Sofya's ten-year-old sister Luba. How much she had matured since our time in Paris two years earlier. A handsome child with quick, bright eyes and a ready smile, she'd inherited the refined look of her father, but none of his careful restraint. Blessed with remarkable charm for a girl her age, her intellect far exceeded my own, but she was not off-putting as some child savants can be. The name Luba means "love" and the child personified the word.

I rested my injured hand on the seat beside me. Still wrapped in white bandages, big as a catcher's mitt, it throbbed as we arrived at the station. Sofya smoothed her skirt. "I wish you were not leaving so soon." She looked out the carriage window, eyes pooled with tears. Sofya was good at everything but farewells.

I passed the baby to Luba and moved across the carriage next to Sofya. "Please don't be sad, dear. Would you ever consider another trip to the States? We can meet in California this time. I have a travel specialist who can arrange it."

"I would love that. Can you send us the name?"

"Of course."

She held me close, her chest heaving with silent sobs, and then handed me a slip of paper. "I'll write every day—letters sent by Father's Ministry mailbag should still get to you fairly quickly in New York. And if you ever need me immediately, call our number here in the city or in the country, there's a telephone at the general store in Malinov. The proprietress Mrs. A. makes sure we get messages."

"If the mood hits her," Luba said.

Sofya removed the glove from her right hand and we made the sign of the cross over each other, as Russian friends did.

"I'll miss you, my dear," I said, my own eyes tearing.

Sofya handed me a tiny, bright blue charm. "I want you to have this to remember me by."

I took the charm, a tiny enamel telegram in French blue.

"It opens," Luba said.

I lifted the tiny flap of the charm, which revealed the French phrase *Ne m'oublies pas!*

Don't forget about me.

Luba leaned in and looked closer at the little telegram. "Father's first ever gift to Mother."

"I can't take this, Sofya."

"Promise you'll think of writing to me every time you look at it."

The coachman tapped the ceiling above us with his stick. "Hurry, madame. You will miss the train."

I slipped the charm into my pocket and stepped out of the coach, into a raucous ocean of Russian mothers and children, men and boys, most unkempt and dressed in little more than tatters, some taunting the well-to-do travelers that tried to navigate around them. Even in the short time I'd been there those gathering on the streets had grown more confident, cocky almost, as a group somehow. I held my bandaged hand to my chest as the valet led the way and two other fellows followed with my trunk.

A sudden darkness fell upon me. Would the Streshnayvas be swept up in this dreadful tidal wave one day? I'd arrange a trip for them to the States as soon as I returned. That would solve the problem.

At the station door I turned one last time and watched the carriage rumble off, swallowed by that angry sea.

I MADE IT SAFELY home to New York in August, just as Germany declared war on France and poured into neutral Belgium and Russia mobilized. How I kicked myself for not bringing Sofya and her family out of Russia with me. With the war on it would be harder for them to leave.

Henry and Caroline met me at the ship with a great spray of pink roses and spirited me home to the apartment. How lovely it was to feel terra firma and hear the sounds of New York: our big American horses clopping about the city and so much English spoken, all cocooned from the troubles of war-torn Europe.

I kept Sofya's little blue charm with me at all times for it calmed me to feel it smooth and cool in my hand as we read the war news pouring in from Europe. We followed every new development, but soon Henry and I became preoccupied with our daughter Caroline's terrible cough, for which Dr. Forbes suggested a respite from the Southampton salt air. Henry pounced on this opportunity to hire an energetic, young real estate agent named Noel Bishop, and we prowled the hinterlands of Connecticut for a country home. Mother's people, the Van Winkles, had been up in Litchfield County for years, but it seemed a pointless pursuit, motoring about, peering into ramshackle estates, Mother in tow.

We drove up through the Nutmeg State to Bethlehem, winding down country roads on an unseasonably chilly, early September afternoon in our convertible Packard Phaeton, top up. Mother's fresh-scrubbed driver Thomas Whitmarsh manned the wheel, splendid in his navy blue uniform, posture erect.

Mother sat in the back with me, and Caroline sat between us on the persimmon leather seat, arms linked in ours. Having come straight from school, Caroline wore her Chapin uniform, black stockings, a white cotton blouse with a sailor-style collar and dark green tie, topped with a light green tunic.

Henry sat up with Thomas, Noel between them on the wide seat. Alert as a ship's captain on the lookout for icebergs, Henry scanned the countryside, his arm and cigar out the window.

"Bethlehem was first inhabited in 1734 by pioneers," Noel Bishop said. "Soon after, young Joseph Bellamy ended up conducting the first theological school in America at the house we're about to see."

As we glided over gently rolling hills passing farm after farm, Henry said, "One feels a certain freedom up here."

Mother smoothed Caroline's hair. "Some are more suited to the farmer's life than others, I suppose."

Henry flicked his ash and a shower of orange sparks flew past my window. "I confess I'd like to till the earth a bit."

"Must be in the blood," Mother said. "Of course, all those Louisiana plantation people once owned their fellow human beings."

"Henry's *uncle* owned the slaves, Mother. In 1860. Are you forgetting your own grandparents owned fellow humans? In South Carolina I—"

"I'll never forget Charleston," Mother said, tugging on one glove.

How many times had she told us the story of her mother taking her eldest sisters to witness the terrible slave market there? They spoke with a young mother who'd just watched her husband and children sold and led away in chains, which seared a staunch abolitionist streak in Mother and her seven siblings.

Henry turned to us in the backseat with a smile. "You're not still holding that against me, are you, Mother?"

Mother tucked a stray lock of hair behind Caroline's ear.

As if sensing familial discord was about to hurt his sale, young Noel sat up straighter. "We're coming into Bethlehem now."

We slowed to a crawl and slid under great arches of ancient oaks and elms, past the village green with its army of spring grass already thick as the bristles on a boar's head brush. It was a pretty little village, with a town center so small one could send a rock across it with little trouble.

"Up on that rise is Bird Tavern," Noel said, holding out an arm in the direction of the commanding colonial home on the gentle rise just off the green. "It was once a stop on the underground railroad."

Mother perked up at that.

"Just to your left, that Federal house you'll see as we pass the green is our destination."

Caroline squeezed my hand tighter. "I see it. I can already tell I'll like everything about it."

Though dusk was falling, there was enough light to see up the gentle slope to the wood facade looming above us. It was painted an unbecoming shade of yellow, its shape marred by various verandas and outcroppings.

Thomas had barely stopped at the curb before Caroline, Henry, and the agent unfolded themselves from the car and sprinted up the hill. They ran under the porte cochere and disappeared through the front door.

Mother and I remained in the car.

"It's a wreck, Henry!" I called out the window after them.

Mother craned her neck. "That porte cochere isn't original to the house. I'm sure the outhouse is."

I touched Mother's sleeve. "Must you bait Henry, Mother? Hasn't he proven himself by now? He lives to please us."

Mother turned to face me. "This place is quite a project."

"I was immensely lucky to meet Henry. He's spontaneous and colorful and dedicated to seeing the world with me."

Mother kept her attention on the house so I played my trump card, her words. "And after all, Mother, aren't the principles of good breeding found in generosity?"

Mother patted my hand. "He's a fine man, dear, and seeing the world is an admirable pursuit."

"If I could sprout wings, I'd be gone again today."

"But 'though we travel the world over to find the beautiful, we must carry it with us or we find it not.'"

"Can you just say what you mean, Mother?"

"Just remember to appreciate your own backyard."

THOMAS PARKED AT THE side door of the house and after a suitable interval to show her displeasure, Mother agreed to let Thomas help us out of the car. We stepped onto a side porch, under a Chippendale trellis, heavy with an ancient wisteria vine thick as an elephant's trunk, and entered the house into a small dining room. The empty house had a musty smell, which came from being closed up too long, layered with that New England–house scent of beeswax and honesty.

We walked about the dining room, a plain space with so many doors it recalled the theater set of a French comedy, and then wandered into the living room with its small fireplace and steep staircase rising from the front door.

Mother opened a window and the scent of fresh-mown hay wafted in. "This old place has potential, actually."

"So does the tomb of Queen Tiyi, but would you want to live there? Besides, there is nothing to do up here."

"It's the country, dear. That's the point." Mother stepped to the front entry. "What a lovely staircase for Caroline to walk down on her wedding day."

Energetic young Noel came in pursuit of us. "Theological students lived here while Reverend Bellamy grounded them with preaching instruction."

I shook the banister and it wobbled. "Too bad he didn't preach indoor plumbing. It's like the Dark Ages."

We stepped back through the dining room to the kitchen, trying to shake Noel, but he stuck with bird-dog zeal. "The young seminarians lived dormitory-style on the third floor. It's been used to store apples but it could be put to better use."

The kitchen floor sagged as we stepped onto it. "Careful, Mother, these floorboards are worn through. I can see the cellar, here." A deep, white porcelain sink stood on one wall, and long glass-fronted cabinets down another.

Noel followed. "It just needs a woman's touch. The Hulls have enjoyed it here, left a few bottles of wine in the root cellar. This place can be your Alamo. Papers say if the war ever makes it to our shores they'll have us all talking German."

"Perhaps then we'll have the stomach to join the fight," I said.

Mother stepped through the doorway and swatted a cobweb away. "If those Huns make it to Bethlehem, Connecticut, we'll have worse problems."

Mother bent and peered up the dining room chimney. "You'll need to bring staff up, dear."

"No maid will set foot up here. And who would dress Caroline?"

We stepped out the back door to the yard. Mother ran one hand down the trunk of a massive maple tree and waved toward a stand of lilac bushes. "Lilacs grow like weeds here. Nothing lovelier. And you can plant a garden."

I laughed. "Wouldn't that be a sight? Me in overalls and a straw hat."

Caroline ran to us, one hand to her ribs. "Thomas and I found grapes growing on the arbor, so warm and sweet. And you should see the barns, Mother. Father says they could hold any number of animals. Horses, cows."

"Animals require hours of care."

Caroline stood her ground. "I'll do it."

"You say that now, but when your friends call, Peg will be stuck with it."

Caroline sulked and Mother wrapped her arms around her. "Animals can be of tremendous comfort, dear."

"Don't wish a little dog on us, Mother. Another clubwoman with her flat-faced Pekingese? That would be the death of me."

Henry called out from the west barn and Caroline hurried out. I followed across the side lawn in the direction of three large, white barns, which faced one another around a grass courtyard. I looked across the meadow, which was peppered with rows of the gnarled, flowering apple trees of an aging orchard. It stretched out to the road beyond, Munger Lane, bounded by the sort of lichened, blue stone wall one sees crisscrossing all of Litchfield County like a Chinese jump rope.

I stopped and watched Caroline run toward the far barn, hair long

and blond, caught up in a scarlet ribbon. At eleven years old she was all
arms and legs.

"Father, there's an old schoolhouse back here," Caroline called out
from behind the barn. "With its own stove."

Henry shouted to her from the barn door. "We can move that out to
the meadow for a playhouse. Would you like that? We'll fill it with
Shakespeare for you."

Caroline ran off through the orchard. "Most definitely," she called
back over her shoulder. "'Joy's soul lies in the doing.'"

I stepped into the low-ceilinged barn and inhaled the scent of hay
and cedar chips. Sparrows chirped in a nest in the loft and two rows of
abandoned horse stalls lined the walls. I stopped at the sight of Henry
in the barn, standing on the hayloft ladder brushing a beam with his
finger.

"Look. In the old days, they counted bales of hay here with chalk."

"It's getting dark, Henry."

He climbed down off the ladder and walked to me in the clothes I'd
laid out for him that morning, his tweed jacket and flannel trousers, in
the colors of the Scottish Hebrides, russet, teal, and tawny sage, as if
made for him with his strawberry-blond hair and grand mustache.

"They were horse lovers," I said.

Henry took me in his arms and pulled me close, the sweet scent of
him puffing up from the warmth of his chest. It was his favorite,
Sumare, a woody fragrance with just the right amount of pine, and it
mixed beautifully with the musky scents of the barn.

"Oh, you're right, Eliza, this place is a wreck."

I slid my arms about his waist. A ray of light from the hayloft fell
across his flushed cheek. "Gentleman farmer suits you."

"We should scrap the whole idea." Henry kissed me, long and deep,
transporting me to our honeymoon on the French Riviera, color-blind
Henry emerging at breakfast, so proud of his wide, blue Cote d'Azur
trousers, red beret, striped pink Riviera shirt, and lavender Basque es-
padrilles.

I held one cheek to his shirtfront and felt his lungs expand.

"It would take so much work," he said.

"This place is not so bad, I guess."

"Oh, it isn't practical."

"There's an orchard," I said. "You do like preserves."

"But you'd prefer a Tuscan villa. Though this is a lot easier to get to."

There was a reason Henry had become such a rising star at Poor Brothers. He had all the qualities that made a man successful back then: ambition, boldness, and a flair for sales.

"I wouldn't mind a visit here now and then as long as it didn't prevent my travels. Caroline could have a pony and I could keep horses. With ninety-six acres there are plenty of trails to explore."

"But, with Southampton, we'd have two summer places."

"With Caroline's lungs—we need this, Henry."

"I don't know," he said, toeing the wood chips.

Henry was selling me, of course. But it was lovely being sold by him.

"You must have imagination, Henry. Given time and money, I suppose we could make that kitchen workable."

"We can just stay in the city. Who needs the fresh air?"

"If you don't buy it Henry, I will."

He smiled at me, his blue eyes bright in the growing darkness. "If you insist. All right then, consider this place ours. We'll call it 'The Hay' after Grandfather's place in England and I'll have a pony delivered for my girl, a little gelding with pinto markings. How does that sound?"

He held me out from him. "And don't worry, you won't be stuck here. I wasn't going to tell you until the *day of*, but I'm arranging a trip—"

"Oh, Henry."

"I can't tell you where we're going, but I know you'll like it." He smoothed one hand down my cheek. "I want to go everywhere with you."

I clasped his forearm. "Please tell, Henry. Via the Orient? We can't go anywhere near the fighting in Europe, of course. It feels wicked to plan a glorious trip when Sofya is stuck at home in such dire straits."

"This war will be over soon and she'll come visit you. If the conflict winds down soon she could even meet us."

"Is it India, Henry? Sofya would love the Pink City."

It was all I could do not to shoot through the roof with happiness. How could one person be so lucky? What a picture that trip conjured— Mother, Caroline, all of us, trunks loaded, traveling the world together, Sofya and family, too.

We all piled back into the car that afternoon as darkness descended on The Hay, a new lightness to us all, the feeling one gets when embarking on a momentous purchase, no matter how impractical—the feeling your life is about to be enlarged, profoundly changed, with no going back.

"Well it looks like we've found another house," I said.

"Let's put the top down," Henry said. "Celebrate."

"But—"

He turned and smiled at me in the backseat and lit his cigar, the blue flame turning the tip of his cigar the color of molten lava. "Let's live a little."

"Yes, let's," Mother said. "It isn't every day you find a house that needs you this badly."

Thomas stepped out of the driver's seat and wrestled the canvas top down, and as we turned out of the gravel driveway the top of the windscreen knocked the branch of a chestnut tree and smooth white blossoms rained into the car.

Mother tilted her face up to meet them. "What a wonderful omen that is," she said as we headed off toward Manhattan.

Part Two

Sofya

1916

MORE THAN TWO YEARS AFTER ELIZA LEFT US AND made her way home to New York, we shuttered our townhouse and fled the city. Once Germany had declared war on Russia, France, and Belgium, things had gradually worsened. At first Russia greeted the news of war with joy, sending soldiers off to cheers and marching bands on Nevsky Prospekt. But after our huge defeat and retreat from Galicia things spiraled downward.

There were no lavish dances those winters. The young men who enjoyed the balls two seasons before never returned and lay fallen in far-off forests. The war ruined our economy and gobbled up precious food. Soldiers deserted and joined sailors and other hungry Russians in the streets shouting for an end to the fighting.

By the autumn of 1916, a rash of terrorist robberies of the treasurer's carriages had the Finance Ministry worried and Father's colleagues tapped him to take important documents to the country for safekeeping. Father judged it safer there for the family as well, so we returned to our country house an hour south, near the village of Malinov, two carriages of luggage and attendants in tow. How I yearned for the shelter of that sweet house.

We left at daybreak to attract less attention, but the rabble quickly recognized our escape since we traveled by showy carriage, the Ministry's motorcars having been requisitioned for the war effort. Agnessa, Father, Luba, two-year-old Max, and I sat in the first carriage, the gaudiest, its gilded doors painted with naked cherubs and dancing nobility, the tsar's imperial crest painted on every panel. A line of people waiting for cigarettes outside a tobacco shop wound into the street and slowed us, causing unfortunates to swarm the carriage.

There was a chill in the air as the sun rose.

A coatless mother held a wasted infant up to our window. "She's starving."

Our eyes met and I looked away, feeling the shame of my own well-fed child on my lap.

Men in ragged military uniforms converged upon our convoy and brought us to a crawl. They craned their necks to see into the carriage and hoisted a red banner: *Land and Freedom!* How many German spies were there in that crowd spreading propaganda of unrest? A cold wave ran through me. It seemed a vast, hideous dam was about to break.

On leave from military school, where he trained cadets, my husband Afon rode next to us as best he could, his horse skittish as he held his crop above the reach of grasping hands.

A pebble struck Agnessa's window, causing us all to jump, and a starburst crack spidered through the glass. My son cried out and buried his face in my skirt.

"Ivan," Agnessa said. "Tell the coachman to turn back. We'll try another day."

To Agnessa's window, someone lifted a brightly kerchiefed old woman no bigger than a child, and the crone waved and smiled to reveal toothless gums. Expecting a kind gesture, Agnessa waved back, whereupon the old woman spat upon the window.

Agnessa turned to me, tight-lipped. "I can't do this."

Father adjusted his spectacles, held Luba close with one arm and hugged his green, metal box with the other, gaze fixed on the crowd. "There's no turning back now, my darling. But they could take this carriage apart in minutes if they chose to."

All at once the coach lurched to one side and then the other.

Agnessa brought one hand to her throat. "Ivan—"

I leaned toward the window to see soldiers in dirty uniforms, their epaulets ripped off, press their shoulders to the carriage and rock it to and fro. Most brandished sabers and flags, the bayonets of their rifles poking out of the crowd at all angles. A group sang "La Marseillaise," which had started to replace our Russian anthem.

The carriage tipped and Agnessa slid toward me on the seat, pinning Max between us.

Afon slapped one of the soldiers with his crop. "There are children here."

The soldier swung around, holding his shoulder as if stung. "Bourgeois pig."

A voice came from the crowd. "Hold on. That's Captain Stepanov. From the academy."

"I'll be," said another. "Make way, citizens!" The men pushed their way through the masses shouting, "My good teacher coming through!"

"Why should we?" someone in the crowd called out. "Take them all."

"Be courteous, comrades. He's an old friend."

Soon the crowd gave way and we picked up speed.

"This was a one-time pass," one of the men called out as we rolled by.

"Don't expect such special treatment again," another shouted and we left the rabble behind.

Afon doubled back to free the other carriages and I wiped my palms dry on my skirt. How often Afon's good reputation had helped us through such situations lately.

Agnessa touched the cracked window. "How can they deface the tsar's property?" She reached under her seat and released her little dog Tum-Tum from his canvas carrier. "I worry about the tsarina, alone with the children."

I smoothed one hand down my son's back. "Please. This is her fault."

Father sent me a warning glance, for he seldom allowed criticism of the imperial couple. But how frustrating it was to see the tsarina run beautiful Russia into the ground.

Little Max pulled himself up and stood on the seat next to me, his eyes extra blue with unshed tears, angelic with his mass of baby curls.

As the carriage swayed I held him around his waist and searched for signs of injury, running my fingers along his arms and legs.

He cupped my cheeks in his two hands and turned my face toward him. "Mama?"

"Yes, my love?"

"Un biscuit?"

I pulled a biscuit from the wicker hamper at Agnessa's feet and he took it in his fist.

Max settled on my lap, burrowing himself into the soft folds of my silk coat and I breathed in the luscious scent of him, of French baby soap and sour milk. What a lucky child he was. If not for an accident of birth he might have been in that crowd.

Luba rode next to Father, their backs to the coachman above. She was a perfect, scaled-down, female echo of Father, with his wide brow, oval face, and keen eyes that missed nothing. Almost twelve years old, Mother's "late in life" child, Luba sat coatless, the yellow scarf the tsarina herself had given her for her name day looped about her neck, a black smudge of ink staining the left cuff of her dress sleeve. She tucked a tangled lock of hair behind one ear, aimed Father's old sextant out the window, and squinted through the eyepiece.

"Do put that thing away," Agnessa said in Russian, which she only spoke when she was cross with us or to the servants since her own mother had only allowed French spoken in their Moscow home. She unearthed a cotton wool–wrapped orange from among the tinned delicacies in the lunch basket. "No man will marry a girl so fixed on the stars, Luba."

"Well that's good, Agnessa, since she's twelve," I said. "Trying to marry her off like a peasant girl?"

Agnessa lifted the orange to her nose and inhaled its sweet perfume. With its vivid color and pebbled skin, it looked like a thing dropped from another planet.

"Marriage stifles creativity," Luba said, adjusting the sextant mirror. "I'm more interested in determining latitude."

"Dear God," Agnessa said. "Mind the paneling."

The tsar himself had loaned us the carriages and we five rode in the first. I brushed two fingers along the red velvet–upholstered seat and shuddered. The whole coach interior was covered in it, tufted, like the inside of a nobleman's casket. I was happy Agnessa kept the windows closed, still jumpy from the mob scene in the city.

"This coach belonged to Catherine the Great," Agnessa said.

Luba squinted at the ledger in which she wrote her celestial calculations. "It would be greater if it had a lamp—" We hit a pothole and all bounced up off our seats. "And better springs."

The second coach, plainer but completely serviceable, held five household maids and Max's Swiss nanny Justine who sobbed most of the day from homesickness and jumped at the smallest sound, expecting the Germans to be at our doorstep any minute. The third, an ordinary transport coach, held the luggage: Agnessa's six seal fur–covered trunks, one packed tight with tissue-wrapped family silver and six wood-painted icon panels of her favorite saints, and a box containing her dog Tum-Tum's canopy bed. Our three small valises and a crate of Mr. Gardener's Katharina Zeimet roses, which had been flourishing in the Ministry's hothouse, fit in between it all, tight as a Chinese puzzle.

I relaxed a bit as Afon rode up next to us on his favorite brown gelding. Would he be able to protect us there in the woods, until his service orders came? From a distinguished military family, Afon Afonovich Stepanov was tired of teaching at the academy and eager for battle.

How had he come to love me, this handsome man? It would have been lovely to ride in that second carriage, alone with Afon and our baby—to talk about his impending departure and have little Maxwell all to ourselves.

But soon I'd be free to walk about the grounds with our son. To ride with Afon in the woods and maybe find a mossy bower where we could—

Agnessa slung the curtain back from the oval window behind our seat. "The last carriage is lagging. . . ."

Father slid his metal box under the seat and then opened his newspaper. "Perhaps the horses suffered strokes from hauling the contents of your sitting room."

"You'd prefer to sit on sacks stuffed with hay?" Agnessa asked.

What did Father see in Agnessa, so unlike my carefree mother in every way? Had he wanted a model replacement mother for his daughters, to teach them the ways of court? If so, his plan backfired, for my one goal was to live a simple country life as my mother had.

Father turned his attention to the newspaper, as his felt bowler hat, gray and soft as a mole's underbelly, sat on the seat next to him, hopping about as if alive with each bump of the carriage.

I pulled a stack of letters from my hamper. Just seeing Eliza's fine handwriting on the envelopes calmed me. I opened one and read aloud as Max batted the rest about.

Henry has plunged into agriculture, bought a decrepit country house, and is planning to inhabit it, as if there is no war on at all. How I hate the word "neutral." If I could spur this country to the aid of Europe and Russia, too, I would. The kaiser is a common thug and the thought of France falling to him is almost as terrible as him barreling into Petrograd harming you and darling Max! I have a terrible feeling Germany will stop at nothing. . . .

"I can't get used to hearing St. Petersburg called Petrograd," Luba said. "Seems ridiculous to change a city's name just to make it less German-sounding."

Agnessa looked out the window. "I'm tired of the war."

"Eliza is entirely correct about the kaiser," Father said. "Says right here Germany is using poison gas at Verdun."

Agnessa batted the thought away. "That paper reports the most hideous things."

"Should they only report news you are happy with?" Luba asked.

"Yes, actually. They say now the ladies-in-waiting give the tsarina only good news."

"The ostrich puts its head in the sand at its peril," Father said.

The fighting had grown worse every day for Russia, as Germany and Hungary stomped over the tsar's troops and our allies Belgium and France. Would Afon be sent to France? How good it would be to have Eliza there next to me, to help make sense of it all and keep our spirits high.

Luba pulled Father's handkerchief from his pocket and dabbed at his brow.

"This is a war without end," he said. "We need to start living more modestly."

Agnessa sulked. She looked beautiful even when cross, which was much of the time. "In London, their sitting rooms are never under-equipped; Paris, too. If only we could be in Tsarskoe Selo with the tsar and the rest of good society. It will be a long winter out here."

I slid Eliza's letters back in the hamper. "We'll make do. And you can be there in half an hour by carriage from Malinov."

How often we'd visited the royal family at Tsarskoe Selo, "Tsar's Village," a lavish compound of palaces and parks, fifteen miles south of St. Petersburg. It was home to Alexander Palace, the royal family's favorite summer retreat, and the lavish Catherine Palace, the walls inlaid with lapis lazuli or amber.

"Alexei has a real motorcar there at Alexander Palace," Luba said. "Rides it through the halls."

"When you are heir to the throne, you can have a motorcar," Agnessa said.

"Perhaps the tsarina will call on you here," Father said.

Agnessa smiled at that and settled back into the red velvet. "The tsarina? In Malinov? No. They all prefer the seaside. Perhaps I'll lure them with a visit to the fortune seer—"

"That poor woman in the woods?" I asked.

"You'll have callers," Father said.

"From the *village*? No one suitable."

Agnessa's little dog roused and squinted as if seeing us for the first time. The phenomenon of dog and owner resembling each other was never stronger than with my stepmother and her Russian Toy, Tum-Tum; the slight frame, the amethyst collars tight around their necks, the auburn sable coats, the wet brown eyes, and alert expression. Having birthed no human children of her own, it was as if the dog were a product of her own womb. The size of a plump quail, Tum-Tum would provide no protection.

"There's town!" Luba called out as we passed the turnoff to the village.

Malinov resembled every other good-sized village in northern Russia, with one main dirt street down the middle bisecting two high rows of simple log homes known as *izbas* and small shops, the imposing white, onion-domed church in the center of it all.

Just past the village turnoff we passed the old imperial rope factory, a square, brick building, which Father had bought and converted into a linen factory. He'd convinced the tsar to electrify the old place so villagers could work two shifts weaving flax imported from other villages into linen, and he split the proceeds with the tsar. Father smiled as we passed. That factory saved so many peasants from backbreaking days working the fields.

Father craned his neck as we passed. "There are crates stacked up in the yard. I'll stop by tomorrow and see they're taken away."

"Those peasants," Agnessa said. "They practically live at church but it's you they should worship."

Father went back to his paper. "They deserve every kindness."

Max burrowed into the crook of my arm and slept as I dozed, half alert for bandits. I woke as we drew closer to home, the trees closing in on the road splashed with autumn colors. Luba opened the carriage window and slapped the leaves with her hand.

She sighed. "I do love the life of the *dachniki*."

Agnessa slid Tum-Tum's silk bootie onto his front paw. "This is not a weekend house, Luba. This is an *estate*—"

"An estate in need of *plumbing*," Luba shouted to the trees.

Agnessa looked out her window. "And ice cubes."

Luba pulled an orange from her own basket, tossed it out the window, and turned to face Agnessa with a smile.

Agnessa slumped in her seat. "*Luba*. You spoiled girl."

Luba shrugged. "What a nice surprise it will be for someone. I do it all the time. The local people suffer from a lack of vitamins, which causes scurvy." She clasped the windowsill with both hands and hung her upper body out of the window. "The gate! I see the gate!"

Home was an estate named *Malen Koye Nebo*, "Little Heaven," which the tsar had years ago given to Father as a reward for devoting himself to the imperial family's finances day and night. Surrounded by uninterrupted expanses of the tsar's imperial fir forests and flat, boggy steppes—vast, open marshes covered in tall grasses—it was a hunter's paradise, strictly controlled by our dear gamekeeper Bogdan.

In the mid-1800s, the estate had served as laundry and stable for the tsar's rope factory and had been converted to a home. The fence, a masterwork of black iron spears, just tall enough for a deer to leap over, extended around the house and outbuildings and had once kept intruders from stealing the tsar's horses. Each spear stood firm, tipped with a sharp diamond. The gates were almost twice as tall, topped with an archway of iron leaves entwined about brass letters that spelled Father's favorite phrase, *Welcome to Heaven*.

"Slow your gallop!" called the coachman as we neared the gates, Afon riding at our side. Two guards stood at attention, members of the tsar's palace grenadiers, men who served the tsar well enough to earn honorary roles. They stood dressed in the autumn uniform of their ranks, a dark blue suit covered with gold bars down the chest, and holding a musket over one shoulder. The tsar loaned us the same two, Aleks and Ulad, for years.

The carriage slowed and Afon returned the men's salutes. Luba held her hand out to Aleks, the older, more amiable one.

He reached up and took her hand in his. "Welcome home, my lady."

The horses stamped the ground, impatient as the rest of us to get home.

"You may open the palace gates, my good man," Luba said with a smile.

Each guard pushed his full weight against half of the gate. Once each reached its full arc, the men stood at attention and the horses pulled onward.

We again picked up speed and were less than a verst from the house when there came a great moaning sound echoing through the trees and the coachman slowed the horses.

Luba sat down next to Father and slapped her hands to her cheeks. "Look!"

I turned my gaze to the woods and found a pack of men—four or five—surrounding a large brown bear, in the usual way hunters capture a bear alive to be displayed in the circus or the fair.

One poacher sat astride the poor beast and struggled to affix a leather muzzle to its snout while the others held him by whips with balls at their tips, which they'd looped around his neck. The animal continued his pitiful moan, clacked his teeth in that terrible way bears do, and thrashed about as the men jumped to avoid his claws.

At the sound of our carriage drawing nearer the men dropped their whips and scattered.

I could barely breathe as Max tried to lunge past me to see the bear. I snatched him back and tucked him between Agnessa and me.

Afon drew his pistol and fired at the retreating men. Luba held Father's hand as the horses snorted and heaved against their harnesses. The fog of gunpowder clouded my view of the woods and when it cleared the men were gone.

"Dear God," Father said, his face drained of color. "Recognize them?"

Agnessa placed a cold hand on mine. "How did they get past the gates, Ivan?"

Freed from his captors the bear lunged across the road in front of us, dragging the leather muzzle, one whip still looped about his neck.

"He's free!" Luba cried.

Afon bent down and peered into the carriage. "All well?" he asked with a forced smile.

My heart thudded so hard against my chest I could only nod.

"Don't worry," Father said. "Bogdan will get on this."

Agnessa sat, stunned. "There's only so much one decrepit gamekeeper can do, Ivan."

Father rested one hand on Agnessa's knee. "Nothing will happen to us with Afon by our side. But I'm afraid we all must be more careful now—"

Agnessa smoothed Max's curls as the carriage lurched forward, the horses still skittish. "*Careful?* These are imperial woods. Those men should be hanged."

"We just need to be more vigilant," Father said.

Luba stood and leaned out the window. "I can see the roof!"

"And we can see your underthings," Agnessa said, her voice brittle. "Sit down at once."

Father pulled his metal box from beneath the seat and clutched it to his chest.

Luba leaned farther out the window. "Everyone's out front—Bogdan, Raisa . . ."

I gathered my gloves and tried to calm myself before greeting the servants.

After all, there was little one could do to change what God had in store for us.

Varinka

1916

T HE NIGHT THE COUNTESS VISITED OUR *IZBA* ON THE outskirts of town to have her fortune told, the wolves were quiet. Smart animals, wolves. They know when they've met their match.

Darkness fell and I dressed Mamka in a clean nightdress for the countess's reading. She sat in the bed Taras crafted for her out of birch logs, which stood next to the whitewashed oven Papa had forged, tall and wide as an elephant, which took up the whole back wall of the room. I slept atop it, the best bed in any *izba*, warm from the fire below.

Since Taras had hunted down the old taxman two years before and gotten our coins back we still had a little good fortune. Like a dying flower that tries to bloom one more time, Mamka recovered some strength and started sewing and telling fortunes again. The taxman had no good luck though. He lay somewhere in the forest, fallen to Taras's knife.

Luck could not help our roof, though, the thatch black with age; and the cold rain at night caused it to leak in places. Autumn had come to our woods just outside Malinov and our breath came in white vapor. The oven was making quick work of the last of our birch logs and the room was cold, but the tallow candle on her bedside table showed Mamka's forehead shone with fever. She pulled at the neck of her nightdress and gulped air. Maybe consumption, an old midwife had said the week before, charging extra for a night visit. Maybe not.

I combed Mamka's hair, long and waved about her shoulders, and helped her slip into a bed jacket of her own making, the silver embroidery down the placket some of her best work. I placed a pearled headdress on her head, her own mother's *kokoshnik*. How the sickness had aged her. Though not yet forty years old she looked at least ten years older there in the shadows, but the hollows under her cheekbones gave her a regal look. That made sense since her father had come from a good family, had been a respected teacher, and had even seen the royal yacht.

Mamka held up one hand. "Don't get too close, *lyubov.*"

"Hush. Save your strength for the reading. And don't forget to ask the countess if I can work for her."

"You're better off staying safe here with me."

I stepped away from the bed. "I can't stay cooped up forever."

"Don't be cross, Inka."

I knelt by the bed and took her hand in mine. "I imagine she pays a good wage."

What was it like in the estate? Images of stylish ladies like the tsar's daughters, the grand duchesses, floated before me. Their white dresses. Leather shoes.

"Please may I go?"

"Perhaps." She stared at the flickering candle. "Maybe they need kitchen help?"

"*Ask.* She will say yes if the reading is good."

Mamka folded her arms across her belly. "I'm afraid, Inka."

"This will be the last reading, I promise, no matter what Taras says."

"Stay close?"

"Of course."

The rain grew louder on the roof. Would it leak on our special guest?

I set a cup of boiled milk on the bedside table for the countess and placed our one chair close to the bed, but just far enough away for our visitor to think she might escape contagion. Predicting the future for clients had become harder on Mamka, for as she grew older the visions became more vivid, too real, but people came all week looking to have fortunes told and the money helped us buy food.

"My cards . . ." Mamka said, patting the bed around her.

I took her grand oracle cards, tied with a red cord, from my pocket. They felt good, smooth and worn, French cards: *Cartomancie Française*, but written in Russian. Each card was a little colored masterpiece and, best of all, rarely wrong. I handed them to her and she held them to her breast.

I placed the linden plank on which Mamka performed her marvels across her lap, then lit a lump of frankincense and watched smoke curl up through the rafters, past the dried herbs hanging there. She felt it encouraged the spirits. It encouraged the clients, too, since the scent covered the sweet odor of sickness. Why do people risk death just to peek at their future?

Taras, who took care of us in his own way, waited in the shed and watched it all through his favorite crack in the wall. He had lived there for as long as I could remember; sleeping among the tools Papa had taught him with, so clever, until he went away for two years to prison in Siberia, a place that had changed him in every bad way possible.

A jangle of bells, a coachman's *Whoa!*, and a woman's voice came all at once outside and I hurried to the door. I heaved it open and the candle flame grew brighter, as if it expected the guest, then settled. Outside our door the troika came to a stop and the two black horses pawed the ground. In the back of the open carriage sat a lady in a sable hat, up to her neck in a polar bear fur rug.

The countess.

The coachman threw off the rug and she stepped down and through the doorway, dabbing her handkerchief at the wet little dog in her arms. As she passed, I almost reached out to caress the thick fur of her sable *shuba*. What a coat it was, deep red, the beads of rain collected there glittering in the candlelight.

A servant in a green jacket took his place near the door as the countess stepped to the beautiful corner, the saw-toothed shelf in the eastern corner, which held Mamka's little village of icons painted on wood. The glow of the red oil lamp above caught the silver foil of the Madonna and child and St. Winnoc, who protected Mamka against fever. The countess made a little bow to the saints, and then made her way toward Mamka's bed, the heron feather in her hat bouncing as she walked.

The candle threw her shadow high along the wall and teased the diamonds at her ears and throat to life. And her *boots*. I watched the countess's hem closely for a glimpse now and then of them—pearl gray kid stitched with silver threads. The very ones Grand Duchess Tatiana wore, pictured in a magazine. I pulled at my skirt to cover my own woven birchbark shoes.

The countess forged ahead to Mamka's bedside, the tiny brown dog clutched to her bosom. As she passed me, I bent at the waist in a deep bow, clasping my apron to hide the holes.

I stepped to the head of Mamka's bed as she sat up straighter and extended one hand toward the countess, a ghost of her manners from her time at court, when she'd visited her cousin, a lady-in-waiting there. If she hadn't fallen for poor Papa she might still be there.

"Zina Glebova Kozlov Pushkinsky, Your Grace," Mamka said with a cautious smile. Of course, we were all named Pushkinsky, the lower classes living in that district.

The countess paused and then reached one pink-kid-gloved hand and shook Mamka's in the briefest way.

"I was not told I'd be attending a sickbed," the countess said, slowly, in Russian. She waved away wolf lard smoke from the candle.

"I'm sorry, Countess Streshnayva," Mamka said in her prettiest French. "I didn't know I'd be feeling so poorly."

The countess stared at Mamka for a second, then answered in French. "Certainly, you of all people should have seen it coming." She let out a funny little laugh.

"Please sit," Mamka said.

"I was told you're a crystal seer—have you no ball?"

She expected a dark woman with bells on her shoes?

Mamka smiled at her. "I cannot start until you sit, Countess."

The countess cast her gaze about the room and then, ever so slowly, lowered herself onto the edge of the chair. "No samovar?"

"No, Countess. Taken for taxes. We tried to get it back but it had already been sent to the city."

Mamka kept her voice steady but we had both ended up crying on that terrible day.

The countess brushed raindrops from her sleeve. "One must pay taxes after all."

Mamka nodded to the bed stand. "No tea, but the boiled milk is for you."

The countess plucked up the cup, held it to the dog's snout and he produced little lapping sounds as he drank.

My gaze went to the planked wall of Taras's shed where just a wisp of white breath escaped from the crack between the boards. *Please don't come out and ruin it all.*

"Do I know you?" asked the countess as she lifted the lorgnette she wore on a chain and looked Mamka over.

"Well, actually, Countess, my father taught in the city—you may have known of—"

The countess dropped her lorgnette. "Pardon my haste, but do get on with it."

Mamka gathered the neck of her nightdress in one pale-as-ivory fist. "Please. Before we start I would like to say that I ask for no money in payment."

"Well, *that* is a first."

"Instead, would you find a place on your staff for my daughter, Varinka, here? She is a hard worker."

I stood straighter.

The countess glanced at me. "Oh, this is most inappropriate."

"She's pretty, is she not?" Mamka asked. "And I've schooled her well. She has read widely and knows all the saints. Every Greek and Roman god and goddess. I taught her and my husband's young apprentice French. She took to the language well."

"I prefer men serving in the dining room."

"Kitchen help? A dairymaid? She has a way with children."

"How old?"

"Sixteen—"

"And unmarried?"

Mamka just looked down at her hands and the blood rushed to my cheeks. Every peasant girl in the village had been married by fifteen. My life would never be like theirs.

"Does she bathe on Saturday?" asked the countess.

"Every day. And she speaks good French. Taught her myself."

"*Really?* Well, I don't see why not. It's impossible to get good help out here in the wild."

Mamka reached out her hand to the countess. "You won't regret it, I promise."

Me? Work for the countess? What was this dining room? Would they let us have leftover food from that room? I would wear a uniform and see their clothes up close and maybe wear perfume?

"I'll send word when I need her," the countess said, ignoring Mamka's hand. "And I will pay five kopecks if this reading is good. I'm no miser."

Mamka smiled. "Good, then." With the burst of energy she always showed at the beginning of a reading, she pulled the cord from the deck, peeled off one card and smoothed it onto the plank. I stood on my toes to see it, for this was my favorite part.

"The first card tells your past." She set down the fish card, upon which a glistening pink carp jumped from a blue sea.

Mamka smiled and stole a quick glance at the countess. "The fish is a very good card. It is a strong symbol of wealth."

The countess frowned. "Wealth? A blind man could see that. My husband is a cousin to the imperial family, so of course you see wealth."

"The next card will tell the present," Mamka said. She pulled another card from her deck and slid it onto her plank. It was the child card. One of my favorites, it held a little boy in a feathered cap running with a hoop and stick.

"A new family member has joined you," Mamka said. "With you for two years now."

The countess breathed in a quick gasp of air and then pulled a fan from her sleeve and snapped it open with a crack. "This is true. Though he came too soon. What more?"

"Well . . ."

The countess shimmied her chair closer to the bed. "Out with it. I insist."

"It's a child, a boy."

A child! Envy curled around inside me. How lucky this countess's daughter was to have a baby boy.

The countess fanned herself vigorously, causing the candle flame to run away.

Mamka looked heavenward with a radiant smile, like one of her martyred saints painted on gilded board. "He was born on a bed of poppies under a silver sky."

"This is true," the countess said. "The bedsheets bore red flowers; the canopy of the bed was silver. You truly are gifted! Now tell me when there will be another birth."

Mamka set the deck of cards on the plank, her brow creased. "And that is all. I'm tired."

Was she getting one of her bad feelings?

The countess snapped her fan closed and tucked it back up her sleeve. "But I came all this way on flooded roads. A mangy wolf chased me half the way."

"The wolves are hungry. Your gamekeeper kills all the elk—"

"And I ruined my boots in your mud. You'll tell me *nothing* of the future?"

"I can't—"

"There's an extra ruble in it for you if you do," the countess said.

Mamka stared at her, rubbing the pack of cards with her fingers.

"Tell me what's to come or I won't find a place for your daughter after all."

Mamka stared at the wall, still as a painting, and then took up her cards once more. "If you insist, we will see the future." She placed one down with a little snap.

The fox killing the dove.

Mamka looked into the countess's eyes. "Four girls will fall on their stones."

"What girls?" the countess asked. "I have only two daughters. I don't understand."

"The big ones and the small."

"You make no sense at all."

Mamka turned another card onto the plank.

The ship.

"This card tells of travel," Mamka said, a furrow in her brow.

The countess smiled. "More travel? To Paris, I hope."

Mamka circled the water on the card with the tip of one finger and fixed her gaze on the countess. "It says the boy child will be cleaved from its mother."

The countess held her dog tighter. "I don't understand."

"It says the child will cross water four times before he can rest. He will only be safe when he is under the torch."

"There must be some mistake," the countess said. "What torch?"

Mamka's fingers trembled as she took the next card from the pack and placed it on the shadowed end of her plank. "The next card is most important, so heed it well." She lifted the candle from the bedside table and angled it downward, squinting at the card. The flame jumped and cried wax onto the board.

The scythe.

A shiver of dread ran down my back.

"Oh—" Mamka handed me the candle and pushed the plank away as if she'd been stung and the cards slid to the bed. She slumped back, one fist to her mouth and waved the countess away. "Go now."

I held the candle closer to the bed where the offending card lay faceup on the bedcovers. It looked innocent enough: a golden sheaf of wheat, the silver-bladed scythe resting at its base. But nothing good ever came from that card.

"What about the rest?" the countess asked.

Mamka waved the countess away. "I can see no more."

"But when will all this happen?"

Mamka turned her gaze to the candle in my hands, her eyes wide. "I've told all I know. Please go."

The countess gathered herself, stood, and strode to the door. "Well, this was a most unsatisfactory trip," she said in Russian. "Can't say you deserve five kopecks."

She nodded to the servant in the green jacket who tossed a coin onto the bed and they hastened out.

As the troika rumbled off I took Mamka's hand. She was shaking, her face toadstool white.

"Are you tired, Mamka?"

Taras burst from his room, dressed in his bearskin coat, and Mamka tightened her grip on my hand. He bounded to the bedside in four steps, the earflaps on his *ushanka* flapping like the ears of a dog. His shadow on the wall loomed over us.

Taras snatched the coin. "One kopeck? Parasite."

I hid my disappointed face from Mamka. One kopeck would not buy a piece of bread.

Mamka laid back, head on her pillow, staring ahead.

"What is it, Mamka? You did a good reading."

"No. I couldn't tell her."

"It was fine—"

"No. I saw it all, Inka. You don't know—"

Taras pocketed the coin. "It serves that pig right. I'll see her die a painful death."

CHAPTER

7

Eliza

1916

ONCE HENRY BOUGHT THE HAY, HE MADE A FEW SMALL repairs but became too busy with work to travel up there more than a few times. I put it out of my mind completely and focused on city life and my other two favorite things: my correspondence with Sofya and our trip abroad. Sofya wrote every weekday without fail and I sat in the same spot on the sofa in the living room of our Manhattan apartment waiting for the mail. The second Peg handed me the letter that day I slid my opener through the envelope.

Dear Eliza,

You won't believe what a terrible time we had of it getting out of the city for the country yesterday, like something out of a novel, really. We'd taken a carriage and were besieged by a savage mob, filled with the saddest cases, mothers and wasted babies, deserted soldiers. We are lucky we lived to tell of it. Poor Justine is in nervous fits and I'm afraid we will have to send her home, leaving us with no nursemaid for Max. . . .

She closed her letter with an elaborate signature and a photograph of little Max in Luba's arms, now a handsome toddler with a halo of light curls. How lovely to hear from her, as usual, but when would they take a savage mob seriously?

I turned my attention to our upcoming trip. The arrangements seemed endless, since the war in Europe made planning difficult, but that fall there were rumors of a cease-fire daily so I hoped for the best and threw myself into preparations. There were trunks to pack, and with Henry's mysteriousness about the destination I kept our dressmaker busy fashioning clothes for every climate.

It was a cool autumn afternoon, the threat of rain heavy in the air, as Peg and I threw all the clothing I owned about the enormous living room in our apartment. Peg, whose given name was Julia Smith, was a slender, doe-eyed Irish rose, often in need of tending. She had alabaster skin and an unruly headful of brown hair, which never knew its place, no matter the number of hairpins employed.

That apartment was a high-ceilinged place at 31 East Fiftieth Street in Manhattan, too big for the three of us really, with five bedrooms, maids' quarters, and a lovely library. I left the spacious living room untouched by a professional decorator's hand and evoked a dramatic Parisian scheme myself, furnishing it with a great many Louis XV sofas and chairs, etchings of French scenes, and Grandmother's soaring trumeau mirror over a gilt console table. A chinoiserie foldout bar stocked with liquors of the right sort and Father's Sarouk carpet added just enough flavor of the East.

Among it all Peg arranged our luggage in a circle about the room, a Stonehenge of Mother's Goyard wardrobe trunks, vanity cases, and hat trunks, each fixed with its own plaque: *Malles Goyard 233 Rue St-Honoré Paris—Monte-Carlo—Biarritz*.

The very sight of the trunks, heaved from the luggage room at Gin Lane, evoked all that is good about adventure. With their black-chevroned linen and cotton fabric linings, orange leather belting, and brass hardware dented by rough seas and even rougher cargo boys, they still bore the vestiges of my parents' last *voyage éclair*. Bits of dried lavender in the fabric-lined drawers. A stack of gauzy, vaguely mothball-scented saris in emerald and pink and orange. I smoothed one finger across the ghost of Mother's initials marked in red across the side of the hat trunk. CWM. Caroline Woolsey Mitchell.

I laid linen and a variety of gloves for hot zones in one drawer. Gabardines and wools for mountainous regions. Should we add oilskin coats in case of monsoon?

My daughter Caroline sat reading a book of Lord Byron's poems on one camelback sofa, surrounded by the dolls making the voyage with us, arranged by height, an unblinking, silent army.

Peg held out one stocking. "Put them on and you can read all you want."

Caroline kept her gaze on her book and extended one slender foot.

Peg rolled the stocking up Caroline's shin. "There you go."

For a girl who bought her hats in economy basements, Peg wore her street clothes well, but took the complete maid's uniform only as a general suggestion. She seldom forgot to wear the black dress with stiff white collar and cuffs, but the accessories were often missing, one black stocking loose and fallen to her ankle, her coronet cap of white muslin nowhere to be found.

Peg wouldn't have made it in any other reputable household in Manhattan at the time, for although the best maids to get were the Irish girls who had been in this country for some time, Peg showed only a dim recollection of how to draw a bath and certainly wouldn't have made it one day ironing the queen's newspapers.

It was a good sign, however, that she was up and about that day and had not retired to a closet to read gossip magazines and drink something other than tea.

Peg hovered a golden straw hat crowned with a wreath of hydrangea blossoms above Caroline's head. "This will keep the sun off."

Caroline batted it away. "I'd rather not go to India, Mother. May I stay with Betty? She wants me to join the Girl Scouts with her."

"What in the world is that?"

"It's a club. Girls wear homemade uniforms to meetings and learn to survive harsh conditions. Rub two sticks together to make a fire. Make a whole meal from one potato."

Peg tossed the hat into the trunk. "Sounds like why we left Ireland."

"Please, Mother. They're taking a field trip to a pond in New Jersey."

"We don't know for certain if Father has planned on India, dear, but wouldn't you like to meet a maharishi? Wear a shocking-pink sari?"

"Not in the least. I yearn to walk in the woods. Wrote a poem about it this morning."

Peg knelt to hook Caroline's shoe button. "I'd give my right arm to meet a maharishi."

Caroline pushed the hook away and drew her feet up under her. "Stratford-upon-Avon is the only town I'm interested in seeing."

Peg tossed the buttonhook on the sofa and scooped an armful of scarves into a trunk drawer. "He may've wrote good sonnets, but Shakespeare was not at all faithful to that poor Anne."

When Henry came home with his friend Merrill in tow there could not have been a more inconvenient time to chat. My Henry was not blessed with the coordination athletics require, which thankfully saved me from expeditions like birchbark canoeing and limited him to safer pursuits like reading. But that Saturday was different. He was to play tennis with Merrill.

The two bounded through the apartment door like college boys released from class. Mr. Richard Merrill, known in society simply as Merrill, was a friend of Henry's from St. Paul's boarding school. Full of a tremendous amount of "roll up your sleeves" energy, Henry had made his own fortune, while Merrill had inherited his seat on Wall Street. And while Henry was blessed with strawberry-blond hair and aquamarine eyes, Merrill was a bit taller, raven-haired. Merrill was considered the most eligible bachelor on the eastern seaboard, if one didn't count the handsome artist Albert Eugene Gallatin.

"Hi-ho!" Henry called.

Merrill stopped short when he saw me. "Hello, Eliza." He'd changed little since I'd seen him last, perhaps a few more lines around the eyes.

"I live here, actually."

Henry stepped to me, kissed me on the cheek, and I caught the scent of a mentholated lozenge.

I lay my hand against his cheek. Warm. "Still coughing?"

He kissed the top of Caroline's head and that of the closest doll. "Merrill has challenged me to a tennis match in the park. Just going to change."

"Please don't, Henry. It's chilly out."

Since the two had known each other at school, they'd fought with fists over a variety of issues, including me. Injuries were usually minor, though Merrill had once received Henry's ire in the shape of two black eyes. Henry quickly presented Merrill with two steaks to bring down the swelling, which Henry cooked and they ate that night, quite happily friends again.

Henry waved Caroline down the hall to his room. "Caroline will help me choose the proper clothes, won't you, my girl? And fix me a Dubonnet, Eliza?"

"Before tennis?"

"It is mostly quinine."

"It will protect you from malaria," Caroline said.

Henry held out his arms, palms up. "See? It's medicinal."

"May I come to tennis, Father?" Caroline asked.

"You have a German test to study for."

Caroline stood. "I hate the kaiser. He's rank mad."

Henry glanced at me with a wide smile. "I think we have an actress on our hands, Eliza."

"Let's not fan those flames, Henry."

He took Caroline by the hand and hurried down the hall to his room.

I called after Henry. "Please don't go, dear."

"Do offer Merrill a lemonade, Eliza," Henry called back.

Their steps receded down the hallway and Merrill turned to me with a smile. "It's been a while."

Peg cast us furtive glances from her spot at the trunk where she stood folding a sweater, glacially slowly as if practicing *furoshiki,* the ancient Japanese art of garment folding.

"I'm terribly busy, Merrill. Packing for a mystery trip. Hoping for India."

"The wilds of India? Hot as hell there." He pulled a gauzy, orange sari from the trunk and held it to the light. "You're wearing this? I prefer women in quiet, conservative clothes, carefully made."

Was it any wonder I chose Henry over Merrill? He had none of Henry's flexible, good humor. Though undeniably attractive, Merrill was almost too typically good-looking and lacked those flaws that make a face interesting. Like a curious scar or slight overbite.

I snatched the sari from him and handed it to Peg. "Of course you do, Merrill."

"Why anyone travels is a mystery—"

Merrill considered a trip to Staten Island risky.

"Must you take Henry for tennis, Merrill? You'll just run him around—and he may have a fever."

"Nothing wrong with friendly competition." Merrill held out one hand. "It's good to see you, Eliza."

I walked around him toward the trunk, which held my wraps, folding a scarlet piano shawl. One can never have too much outerwear when traveling.

He followed. "It would be nice to catch up sometime. Talk." He placed one hand on the small of my back. How many times had he done that when we'd stepped out together in the old days?

I stepped aside. "About what, Merrill dear? I need to fix Henry's drink."

"Just, well, old times, I suppose."

Though I had seen Merrill about town at social events, it had been twelve years since he and I had briefly seen each other socially.

I touched his sweater sleeve. "I hear you've been seeing the Jackson girl. She seems quite nice and would be willing to share your, well, simple lifestyle." I handed the shawl to Peg and she tossed it in the trunk drawer.

"What is that supposed to mean?"

"Oh, let's be honest, dear, when you're not working you're chasing a ball somewhere."

"You'd prefer I went on safari?"

"What I prefer doesn't matter any—"

Henry bounded back into the living room dressed in white duck trousers and a linen shirt, Caroline in tow twisting a peppermint candy from its cellophane.

Merrill stepped to the wall to examine a print.

"What are you two scheming?" Henry asked. "I'm off to teach old Merrill a lesson."

"Henry, stay home and make sure your trunks are packed properly. It's going to pour rain and there's no need to prove anything, dear. Not everyone is meant to be sporty."

Henry pulled a towel across the back of his neck and held it by both ends. "I played tennis at St. Paul's."

"So you claim," Merrill said.

Henry kissed me on the cheek, his mustache grazing it in a lovely way, and the two headed for the door with barely a glance back.

"Stay and have your Dubonnet, Henry."

They rushed out the door.

"We'll toast the winner, so don't wait up," Henry called back over his shoulder.

Peg closed the door behind them and their voices trailed off. I stepped to the window and watched Henry and Merrill emerge onto the street below. Henry lit a cigar and Merrill waved his tennis racquet as they walked, the sky darkening over the building tops.

Then I turned back to my packing. One cannot be too prepared for the wilds of India.

IT WAS PAST MIDNIGHT when Henry returned and stumbled to his room, no doubt having drowned the sorrows of his defeat in Dubonnet. I pretended to be asleep when he crept in to say good night, keeping my breathing deep and rhythmic. Henry stood by my bedside for a long moment and then made his way back to his room.

The next morning, I woke early for a ride. Henry did not emerge from his room so I slipped into my riding clothes and Thomas drove me to the Central Park stables. Caroline was visiting her friend Betty Stockwell for an overnight, so Betty's mother, Amelia—a friend since our debutante days—joined me for my morning ride.

It was a glorious, clear fall day, for the storm had swept through and left the sky cerulean. We rode north on the Bridle Path in Central Park, toward the reservoir. We were mostly alone up there since, at mid-morning, ladies formed the bulk of the civilian cavalry. Amelia had clearly spent most of the morning on her toilette, her chestnut hair pulled back in a snood. Her daughter Betty resembled her in every way, down to the mane of chestnut hair, widow's peak, and casual off-hand manner of speaking.

"Your Caroline is teacher's pet, Eliza. Miss Webb said if she had a daughter she'd like her to be like Caroline in every way. Who coaches her?"

"Really, Amelia. Caroline is simply like her father."

"I was having Betty tutored, but the young man resigned, claiming exhaustion. Young people are so delicate today. Maybe it's for the best. Latin never got a girl a husband. Men just want a warm body. Richard would just as soon have Cook in the bed as me. Wouldn't know the difference in the dark and he's always excited by cinnamon."

"Sometimes I think husbands complicate life."

"Try making your way in real society without one. Florence Schermerhorn's James ran off with the wife of a Bible peddler. Doors all over New York shut in her face, poor thing. She had to move out to Larchmont and the only suitor she has is an old parson in a tye wig."

We made our way along the reservoir and, though I longed for a good canter, kept the horses at a trot, well within the six-mile-per-hour speed limit. The trees laced their fingers above us and the horse's hooves gave a pleasing thump along the soft path.

I pictured Henry waking, chastened, and seeking strong coffee. It served him right that only Peg would be there to nurse his aching head and bruised ego. Perhaps that would teach him not to play tennis in the rain.

AFTER LUNCH WITH AMELIA and a shopping trip to pick up quinine tablets and other travel sundries, I arrived back at the apartment, brown paper bags in arms. By then I'd decided to forgive Henry. He was only showing off for me after all and would make it up to me on our trip.

Peg met me at the door, face splotched pink among the freckles.

"Mr. Ferriday's in a bad way, ma'am," she said, fists clenched under her chin.

"Bad way how?"

She patted her chest with one hand. "Havin' trouble in here."

A flash of dread ran through me. "Since when?" I dropped my bags.

"Since I brought 'is tray this morning, ma'am."

I started toward Henry's bedroom.

Peg followed. "He's usually sitting bolt upright on the stroke of seven sayin' 'Peg Smith, bring me a gallon o' coffee,' but today he's talking gibberish, the blinds not properly shut."

I arrived at his room, the door ajar, his breakfast tray in the hallway, untouched.

"You didn't bring his tray in, Peg?"

She stood in the hallway, arms wrapped around her waist. "Started to, ma'am, but what if I were to catch somethin'?"

I pushed into the room. Henry lay on the bed, curled on his side, on top of the still-made bed, one arm out of his sweater. I touched his hip and felt the wool, wet through.

"Close that window, Peg. You couldn't get him a blanket?"

Henry shivered and barked a wet cough.

Peg stood in the doorway. "My mam said Joanie Sullivan's cousin caught lung fever—"

"Help me get these wet clothes off—"

"—and was dead before dawn."

Peg stayed in the doorway, fingers to her lips. With great effort, I pulled Henry's sweater off over his head, and the shirt beneath clung to him. What would Mother do? Why had I not paid more attention to their nursing conversations? I pressed one hand to his forehead. Hot.

"I came to your room last night," Henry said, through chattering teeth. "Wanted to say—"

"Quiet, now."

"The tickets—"

"Which ones, Henry?"

"I want to go everywhere with you, but . . ." Henry drifted off.

"You'll be fine, won't you? Of course you will. It's just a fever."

I looked over my shoulder to Peg. She stared at us from the doorway, though her eyes flicked to the ceiling when my gaze met hers.

"At least get a basin, with warm water and a clean sponge. And the thermometer—in the kitchen."

She hesitated.

"*Now*. And call Dr. Forbes—tell him to *hurry*, and my mother, too. . . ."

Peg ran off.

By the time I stripped off Henry's shirt, his whole body was shaking terribly.

Peg returned with a basin and left it on the floor just inside the doorway.

I took the basin from the floor. Cold.

"Is Dr. Forbes coming?" I asked.

"The line is busy."

"Mother?"

"Called Gin Lane and they said your mother's down with the grippe herself just this morning."

Mother sick? How could she be when I needed her most?

"Where's the thermometer?"

Peg removed her cap and wrung it in her hands. "I looked in the kitchen and—"

"Peg Julia Smith, I will skin you alive if you do not run down to Dr. Forbes's office and bring him back here immediately."

Peg stood rooted to her spot.

"Did you hear me?"

"The doctor where I took Caroline?"

"No. Dr. *Forbes*. Down on Thirtieth Street."

"Near the bakery?"

"No. Next to the apothecary—"

"Where I picked up the cough syrup?"

"Yes—"

"But that's twenty blocks."

"Hail a cab, but *go*."

Peg bolted off and I searched every kitchen drawer for the thermometer, to no avail, and tore about the apartment, ripped blankets from beds and layered them atop Henry until only his head peeked out from the mound.

I closed all the windows, begged Henry to drink water, which he refused, but nothing would stop that terrible cough.

IT WAS LATE AFTERNOON before Dr. Forbes finally arrived. He hurried in toward the bed, shedding his jacket as Peg hovered in the doorway. My whole body relaxed at the sight of our distinguished doctor with his top hat and fat, black cowhide bag, worn rust-colored at the bottom corners. Dr. Forbes had been Mother's savior for years; sat by my bedside when I had scarlet fever; delivered Caroline and my godson Max, too, of course.

"I came as quickly as I could," he said. "Breech birth. And a fire down on Fifth Avenue snarled traffic."

Even under the layers of blankets, we saw Henry's whole body spasm as he let out a deep cough.

How had it worsened so quickly? "He's been coughing like that for hours, Doctor."

"Hours?" Dr. Forbes began throwing back Henry's blankets like a New Delhi rug merchant. "Last time he ate?"

"I'm not sure. Last night, I suppose."

He pulled a thermometer from his bag and shook it. "Take his temperature?"

"No thermometer."

He slid his thermometer under Henry's arm. "No thermometer in the house of Carry Woolsey's daughter?" Dr. Forbes scowled and pressed two fingers to Henry's wrist. "Why did you not call sooner? He's toxic."

A chill ran through me. Toxic?

"Peg called—"

Dr. Forbes touched the back of his hand to Henry's cheek then pulled the thermometer out and read it. "He's burning up, Eliza. Elevate his head."

"I gave him a cold bath."

"Tell me you did not give him a cold bath. It must be *tepid*. Boil water and cool it slightly. Cold bath sets the fever."

I lifted Henry's head, hot to my touch, and slipped in an extra pillow. "He played tennis yesterday. Slept in wet clothes."

"Why on earth? And all these blankets worsened the fever. For God's sake get him to drink water."

Henry clawed at his chest and laughed. "It's too hot, Mother. Why is it so hot?"

Dr. Forbes opened the window. "Keep these open. He needs oxygen in his lungs."

I held the glass to his lips. "It's Eliza, dear. You need to drink some water."

Henry slapped it away. "Where is my daughter, for God's sake?"

Dr. Forbes pulled at his beard and gazed down at Henry. "Has he been smoking?"

"Cigars."

"Could be lobar pneumonia. There are two possible types of pneumococcus responsible, though. It's anyone's guess which it is."

Henry set into a series of hacking coughs, which ended with a deep gasp as if he were drowning.

"*Do* something." I knelt next to Henry.

"Don't get too close, Eliza."

I smoothed Henry's forehead. "You must act, Doctor."

"There is a serum . . ."

"Send for it."

"But it is only useful against certain types of exudative material and must be ordered."

"What else?"

"We could try an arterial puncture but it is risky and quite new. X-ray treatment might lead to a resolution. A Murphy drip for hydration."

"We must get him to St. Luke's. Call an ambulance."

He reached for his bag. "They're all engaged—at the fire. He might not survive a move, anyway. If only we'd acted sooner . . ."

Voices echoed in the hallway. *Caroline.*

Taking deep breaths in through her mouth, she pushed past Peg into the room. "Father—I was at Betty's—"

"My girl—" Henry turned toward her voice.

She ran to him. "I came as soon as I heard."

Across the bed, Dr. Forbes shook his head at me. Of course, Caroline could not be near him. With her weak lungs, it was out of the question. But how could I deny my daughter her father?

I caught Caroline by the wrist, before she was halfway to the bed. "You can see him soon, darling. He just—"

Caroline broke free, rushed to the bed, and slipped her arms around Henry's neck. "I'm here, Father. I won't leave you."

Henry turned to her. "Where have you been? I've been calling—"

Dr. Forbes rushed around the bed. "This is no place for children, Caroline." He wrapped his hands about her waist and pulled her from Henry.

Caroline fought like a distempered cat, arms flailing, kicking Dr. Forbes. "He is my Father. I have the right to—"

Henry held out one hand. "Caroline—"

Dr. Forbes dragged her toward the door. "She must leave the premises immediately."

Caroline reached out as she passed me, eyes wild and pleading. "Mother, please. You must let me stay."

I looked away. "Take her, Peg. Have Thomas drive her to Southampton."

"No, Mother—"

Peg clamped onto Caroline's wrists, took her from Dr. Forbes, and pulled her out the door, closing it behind her with her foot.

The closed door muffled Caroline's last cry. "You have no right. He is my *father*."

Henry looked toward the door. "Where is she? Caroline?"

Dr. Forbes pressed one hand to Henry's forehead. "She'll be back. You must cool down first."

A most pitiful look came to Henry's face and tears pooled in his eyes. "I want my daughter, goddamnit."

I held his hand. "Soon, my darling."

Henry closed his eyes and grew quiet. Dr. Forbes pulled a canvas tourniquet from his bag, then looked up at me. "I suggest you pray like you've never prayed before, Eliza."

The world slowed.

All I could think was: *Take anything you want from me but not him.*

Sofya

1916

THE MORNING OF AGNESSA'S FIFTIETH NAME-DAY LUN-
cheon, the turtledoves cooed in the trees as we ate in the dining room.
It was the hottest autumn in recent memory in our woods and even the
ice in the icehouse had melted to a tepid pool. We all sat at the table,
Agnessa in a trumpet-sleeved dress of white linen.

"*Do* let some air in," Agnessa said.

Our gamekeeper Bogdan hurried to open the windows. Such a good
man, with his kind blue eyes and weathered skin. He was tanned dark
from years outside in every season with his team of beaters, men skilled
at shouting and waving their red cloths to flush prey from the forests
and steppe. At seven I'd been his worst student, though he patiently
taught me to shoot. He smelled of rum and worn leather, his arms
around me as I aimed, and was like a proud father years later when I
got my first elk.

Beads of sweat on his forehead, Cook set the traditional name-day
ring cake sprinkled with almonds on the table in front of Agnessa. The
cake perspired as well, a layer of dew forming along the ganache.
Where had he even found the sugar to make it? The black market, I
suspected, since even with a ration card, one seldom found a grocer
with sugar.

Cook stepped back and looked to me for approval.

Luba leaned closer to me. "He's in love with you, sister. Could it be more obvious?"

"You're mad," I said, though there was something sweet about the idea.

How lucky we all felt that Cook, known to most as Baron Yury Vanyovich Vasily-Argunov, a fine-looking bachelor with considerable land holdings, found happiness in our kitchen. Agnessa had invited him to a dinner party years ago and after he tasted an undercooked soufflé, he'd taken over the kitchen and never left, insisting we call him Cook.

The ring on his left hand caught the light. It was an old family ring, given to his great grandfather by Alexander II, a wide rose-gold band layered with a gold imperial eagle, a fat diamond in its belly. Agnessa told us he'd had many offers to buy it and even the tsar had admired it. I never cared for diamonds on men, but he clearly prized it.

Luba pulled her book of constellations from her lap and began to read.

"Manners, Luba," Agnessa said. "Put that away this instant. Stars. Such an empty pursuit."

Luba slid the book back to her lap. *"Damnant quod non intellegunt,"* she muttered.

Agnessa looked to Father. "What is she saying?"

" 'They condemn what they do not understand,' " he said.

Agnessa brushed a phantom crumb from the tablecloth. "I understand stars perfectly. I just wish they'd stay in one place. All that moving around. It's unsettling."

Luba looked to me, eyes heavy-lidded, as if to say, "Why argue with a person so happy in their ignorance?"

Raisa, one of our estate laundresses, a kind, big-boned girl who wore her hair in scrawny, strawberry-blond braids, stood behind Agnessa flapping a dingy gray ostrich-feather fan, keeping air moving through the rooms.

That house was an imposter of sorts, a commercial laundry turned country estate, in no way elegant, but the high ceilings made it appear so. While my mother was alive she'd put away the French dining room chairs and ancestral portraits and decorated it in a casual, Russian way.

She arranged pillows on the floor for seating, Russian folk paintings on the walls, and filled every receptacle in the house—teapots, drinking glasses, and pitchers—with wild roses she picked herself, the sweet scent perfuming the air.

Once Agnessa came to live with us, she had the French furniture dragged out of hiding and sent the pillows to the attic, probably hoping to wipe away any trace of Russia. And Mother.

Though Luba and I protested, Agnessa brought back the gold dining room furniture and dusted off the ancestral portraits, some most frightening, and hung them in the *zala*, the equivalent of an English drawing room, which ran along the front of the house.

Upstairs, Father's and Agnessa's rooms, Afon's and mine, and Luba's converged around the grand staircase. Mother's room had always been our favorite place to congregate, and we often arranged the featherbeds on the floor and stayed up late talking and reading poetry.

She allowed us full range of her closets, free to play there, slipping into her Worth sable coat, the lining cool as water against our sunburned arms. We ran our hands down the dresses of orange and emerald silk and held her velvet kimonos soft against our cheeks. Mother rarely wore the exquisite things and chose instead more comfortable clothes she could easily move in, peasant clothes and gardening trousers, black canvas Chinese slippers.

After Mother died the terrible finality of it set in, so quiet and unbending. Father kept her room locked, with a key kept on his person at all times. When Agnessa arrived, she had the room opened, Mother's coat cleaned and put away for herself, the linens and laces split between Luba and me. Thankfully, we had our holiday trip to Paris with Eliza to help dispel the sadness, but when we returned to Russia Agnessa did everything she could to erase Mother's memory.

Agnessa redecorated Mother's bedroom in the French style, the bed made with fine linen, Father's crest embroidered on every piece, the closet filled with new French couture, in grays and lavenders. Luba and I barely recognized our house once Agnessa whitewashed the brick, replaced the brightly painted Russian shutters with gray pairs in the French style, and had English ivy planted to grow up the facade.

I held Max on my lap, one arm around his belly as he ate kasha from a bowl with a spoon, the satin bow of his silver foil party hat tied near one ear. Afon made faces at him from across the table and Max's blond curls shook as he let out deep belly laughs.

The servants brought in baby Volga sturgeon and ironstone tureens filled with Father's favorite dishes, like the salty-sour *rassolnik*, cucumber soup with beef kidneys, which Luba refused to eat. Afon ate with great relish, perhaps thinking he would not see such food for a while, since the long-dreaded telegram had arrived and he was due to report soon at regimental headquarters in Petrograd.

Father sat straight in his chair, head to toe in country-wear: fawn-colored loose trousers and *rubaha*, the linen shirt peasant men wore, the placket unbuttoned at the neck, hanging down like a sow's ear. The headline on the newspaper in his hands read: BIG ADVANCE BY BRITISH. GERMAN LINES DRIVEN BACK. The news that day cheered us all. On top of a decisive Russian victory by General Brusilov on the southwestern front, the Allies were gaining ground at the Battle of Somme with their new secret weapon: the tank.

Agnessa leaned toward me, sending a wave of carnation and ylang-ylang my way, which put me off my *oeufs en cocotte*. "I visited that fortune seer last week, you know."

"So that's where you went. Such a waste of time—"

"Her name was Zina and she . . ." She pulled me closer. "She said little Max would cross water four times."

"Fortune-telling is the work of charlatans, Agnessa."

Afon reached for a piece of black bread. "Can she tell me what regiment I'll be assigned?"

"I know it's bad luck to try and see the future, but she is *quite* famous. The best people come from all over to see her. She told Roksana Petrovana she would pass a stone and it came out of her that very night."

"Let's talk about your name day, Agnessa," I said. "Father arranged quite a gift."

She leaned closer. "The way I look at it, little Max crossed water once in going to America when you were pregnant with him. The second time was when your water broke and he was born. And he crossed a third time sailing back."

"Do we really—"

"So that leaves one more crossing."

A cold shudder went through me, strange for such a warm day, and I gathered Max closer. I would get Maxwell in my arms where he would stay for the entire summer and not so much as look at a washbasin. I couldn't live through another accident. Max's hand had slipped out of mine when he was just learning to walk and he fell and cut his chin deeply. Agnessa ran about the house crying as Father sent for the doctor and I used my skirt to stem the flow of blood.

I felt Max's chin for the scar and felt, with a pit in my stomach, the ridge there.

"And then she looked like she'd seen the bowels of hell and refused to continue."

"I hope you paid her well," Father said with his gaze on his newspaper. "Sensitives can put a hex on you."

"Did you ask her if there will be another revolution?" Luba asked, exchanging smiles with Afon.

Agnessa smoothed the tablecloth. "The tsar's troops will put down any revolt. It's his divine right to rule, though he doesn't seem to be doing much of that."

I shifted in my seat. Such bad manners for Agnessa to mention the tsar's name at the table, but since she started it, I dove in. "It's terribly unfair the tsar keeps twenty-one palaces, when his people are starving."

Luba forked a beef kidney and eyed it. "The soldiers are hungry, too. Barely fed some days, isn't that right, Father?"

"Luba, go study your French, this instant," Agnessa said.

"Right away," Luba said. She stayed where she sat and read the book in her lap.

"Think the tsar will keep Fena's House open when we're gone?" I asked Father.

Agnessa sat up straighter. "Must we talk about that place on my name day?"

Though my home for impoverished women was widely considered a worthy cause, Agnessa loathed talking about it or anything else connected to my mother.

"I will write the Ministry and ask them to oversee it," Father said. "In the meantime we must take precautions here."

"True," Agnessa said. "The villagers love us, but one never knows. Watch them come take over this place and make us all corner tenants."

"Father has been kind to them," I said.

"Just hope the imperial forces guard the emerald mines," Agnessa said.

Afon stood. "Perhaps we should show Agnessa her gift?"

Luba sat up straighter, causing the little red bell, which hung from a cord about her neck, to issue a gay little jingle. "Time for the surprise?"

She must have been caught speaking Russian again, hence Agnessa's punishment: wearing the "devil's bell." Little did Agnessa know Luba liked the bell and considered it a badge of honor for, though French and English were more fashionable, Russian had been our Mother's language of choice.

Agnessa pulled Tum-Tum closer. "The only gift I want is a train straight to Paris."

Father stood and stepped to Agnessa's chair. "Just a few more days, my love. I am tying up loose ends with the Ministry. You should begin packing, only the most necessary items."

"And fold up our tent like Bedouins and leave with *nothing*?"

"Once Afon goes, we must move quickly. We can return once it's safe."

Agnessa held a cube of cheese under the dog's snout and he turned his head away. "Could we proceed with the gift? I have much to attend to. Six courses for Max's name-day dinner, alone."

"Do give a hint about the gift, Father," Luba said.

"Well . . . it's quite big."

"I hope it's an amethyst," Agnessa said.

"It's out in the far barn," Father said.

The estate boasted a whole collection of barns: the near barn, in which we stored sacks of grain, the twenty-stall horse barn, the dairy barn, and the empty far barn.

Agnessa looked about to cry. "You know I dislike barns, darling."

"Let's blindfold her!" Luba said.

"It's the manure," Agnessa said, a damask napkin to one nostril. "I can smell it from the house."

Father pulled the napkin from her hand, snapped it into a triangle like a bandit's kerchief, and tied it around Agnessa's eyes.

Luba ran to Agnessa and led her by the hand like a blind person. Agnessa clutched Tum-Tum to her chest as Luba led her toward the barns and we followed.

We walked in a group. Max was at my hip and he swayed in my arms, singing his favorite song, getting only about every third word right. It was a macabre little French nursery song Agnessa taught him about sailors at sea who decide to eat a little boy.

There was once a little boat
That never on the sea had sailed
Ahoy! Ahoy!
After five or six weeks rations began to wane
Ahoy! Ahoy!

The adults joined in and sang as we passed Agnessa's hothouse and the wind delivered a waft of the lazy, sweet scent of peach. What a pretty, glass-paned hothouse orangery it was, sent from Paris, the top edged in white scalloped metal; inside, even in autumn, the dwarf lemon trees were heavy with fruit. I cherished my time there under glass, little Max playing at my feet as I repotted plants and grafted roots, the watery breath of gardenias, Amazonian orchids, and Mr. Gardener's roses clinging to the windows. I admired his white rose so much I propagated a whole shelf of individual plants from it, each with its root ball secured in a burlap bulb bag tied with twine.

"There isn't anything I could possibly want out here," Agnessa said, one hand feeling the air in front of her.

"Just relax," I said.

Luba led Agnessa into the far barn, which no longer housed animals, but the smell of hay still lingered. Afon and I followed and he took my hand, our steps soft on cedar shavings. Father waved us in. Placed against one wall was a hulking, dull green metal box as tall and wide as a bull elk. It rumbled as if a small animal ran about inside it.

As we edged closer, Tum-Tum growled and Agnessa hugged him tighter.

Father took Agnessa's hand and placed it on the metal.

"Tell me this instant, Ivan."

He unknotted Agnessa's blindfold.

She scowled, blinking in the low light. "Dear God, what is it?"

Luba stepped to the metal thing and opened the hinged door on the front. "Can you not tell? It's an ice machine, Agnessa. It will make ice for you day and night."

"Afon's friend from the automobile club brought a generator to run it."

Agnessa handed Tum-Tum to Father and stood still, mouth agape. "Holy Fathers. Oh, Ivan, once we return from Paris I can have all the parties I want." She reached into the hole and ran her hands through the pale blue cubes. "And it's the clear ice I like, darling, not the cloudy kind."

Father kissed her cheek, a look of true love on his face. Hard as it was to deal with her sometimes, she made him happy.

Agnessa held two cubes in her palm, like a child at her name-day party, a few curls escaped from her upswept hair, as she went to each of us in turn, showing off her new gifts. She handed Max a cube, he stared at it in his palm and then dropped it to the cedar shavings with a shriek.

"Froid!" he said.

This sent us all into fits of laughter.

I held him close and felt his heart beat through his little vest. "Yes, it is very cold, my darling."

"I am the luckiest woman on earth," Agnessa said with a faraway smile, the cube forming a little puddle in her palm.

THE NEXT MORNING, I woke and nestled closer to Afon. He barely stirred as I pressed against him, my belly to his back, and felt his hip bone through his pajamas. How thin he'd become just from one week of a sore throat. Perhaps we could sneak away for a few hours alone before he left. Since Max's birth he'd all but ignored me in that way, perhaps fearing I'd suffer another difficult birth. Dr. Abushkin said I would not have another child, but why not prove him wrong?

I left the bed and, eager to see my horse, pinned up my hair, proud to do it with only five pins, as Mother taught me. I stepped to my wedding chest to consider my trousseau.

I ran my fingers down the silk of a powder blue camisole. According to Agnessa, men abhor blue on women, and like black underthings or nothing at all. I drew a lacey, beige corset cover from the drawer and slipped it on over bare skin. Once I pulled it tight across my chest and hooked it down the front, scandalous glimpses of skin showed through the glorious spiderwebs of open lacework. I slipped a blouse over it, pulled on my riding pants, and left Afon a note to follow me.

I made sure Raisa was stirring in case Max woke, and then stepped to Luba's room. She sat on the floor, legs crossed, scissoring something.

"Come for a ride?" I asked, one hand on her doorjamb.

Light flashed upon the silver scissors as she hid them behind her back. "I'm busy."

This was the secret project she'd been working on. Luba kept the details private, but I knew it involved silver paper, for the floor of her bedroom was littered with flecks of it.

"Don't go outside the gates, Sofya. It isn't safe."

"I can outride anyone."

"You'll be dead for sure if Agnessa catches you in those riding pants again."

"And what if she catches you with scissors? Where did you even find them?"

Luba was magpie-like with her ability to acquire things. "I did not steal them from Agnessa's sewing basket. I swear by God's stars."

"You only say that when you lie. Swear on Father's life."

Luba smiled. "Have a good ride, sister."

As I walked toward the barn my horse, Jarushka, snorted gently, expecting her petting and carrot. Of course, she knew I was coming, for she had a sixth sense. The product of an unplanned, midnight liaison between a hefty Cossack cavalry horse and one of the tsar's prize Arab mares, she was a sight to behold with her shaggy fetlocks, coarse mane and tail, and lop ears that hung down like a dog's. Though not handsome enough for Agnessa, Jarushka had superior wind, an angelic disposition, and an undying loyalty to her owner, for which cavalry horses are known. With her light chestnut coloring and silky-smooth canter, she was the perfect horse for me.

We rode out through the gates onto a path through the woods, the trees a glorious blaze of autumn color. I gave Jarushka her head and soon we jumped downed trees and crashed through the undergrowth, making new paths as we went, cool wind in my hair.

I lost track of time, grew terribly thirsty, and stopped near a thicket of raspberries to turn back.

That is when I spied the crude little cabin. I had almost missed it, for it was built into the side of a rock outcropping, the weathered wood walls the same color as the stone. I rode closer. It was a snug little place with one bare window, a front door fixed with a coarse rope pull.

"Anyone there?" I called out in Russian, my voice sounding harsh yet strangely muted there in the forest. Only larks answered.

I slid down off the warm leather saddle, tied Jarushka to a tree branch, and then, heart pounding, stood tall to peek through the window. I could see only part of the room, a rough-hewn table covered with tools.

I pushed the door open, walked in with the step of a trespasser, and, to my great relief, no person slept there. It was a homey little place, furnished with the table and an army cot, topped with a bearskin.

A wall of moist, blue stone served as the cabin's back wall and it shone in the dim light. There was no musty smell, only a pleasant peppermint scent. A small ax and several wood-handled tools lay on the table surrounded by tiny gold and silver shards. A knife lay there, half-finished, the blade still rough. I grasped it by the handle and ran my fingers down the smooth wood inlaid with sterling silver, the black letter "T" no bigger than my pinkie fingernail burned into the knife's flank.

I stepped to the window and scanned a collection of postcards impaled next to it by the nails of the unfinished wall. They were captioned in French and depicted young women in various stages of undress. I ran the tip of the knife down one, of a naked girl smiling at the camera from a shallow basin of bathwater. Another, completely nude, blew her flute to charm a snake from a basket. They were all blond, from top to bottom.

All at once a rustling sound came from the woods behind the cabin.

I crouched to the dirt floor near the table, barely able to breathe. My heart hammered against my knees as I strained to hear. The sound came closer and the knife handle grew slippery in my palm.

All at once the door swung open and in the morning darkness I could only see the silhouette against the light.

I stood. "I have a knife—"

"You aim to kill me before breakfast?" said the assailant, stepping back.

"Afon." The blood rushed back into my arms. *"Really."*

He stepped into the room, as if arriving at a fine hotel room, piece of bread in hand, canteen strapped across his chest. "I've never noticed this place before."

I slid the knife back onto the table. "How did I not hear you ride up?"

Afon came to me, still wearing his nightshirt, tucked into his trousers. He looked like a young boy that morning, his dark hair not yet combed.

He smiled. "Guess they should assign me to an army stealth unit." He took a deep breath in. "Can you believe the larch trees this year, Sofya? That pine scent is like medicine."

"You should be an arborist."

"And who would stand up to the German hordes who want our trees?" He glanced around the little house. "We left our son to the care of Agnessa, you know. Raisa had to go see her cousin in town."

How stupid I was. Max with Agnessa? "Oh no, Afon."

"Agnessa was at her vanity table, giving him free rein of her jewel case, but before long she'll be resting on her bed with boric acid pads on her eyes, letting him wander."

"You could have brought him."

"It's my last day as a free man, Sofya. I needed a good ride." His glance rested on the postcards on the wall. "Who lives here? Bogdan?"

I stepped to the postcards. "I don't think so."

He stood behind me. "Quite a collection."

I pulled the snake charmer postcard from the nail. "I've never been to India but I don't think it's done like this. . . ."

Afon took the card from me and tucked it in his pocket. "I may need to borrow this for future study of a scientific nature."

I wrapped my arms around his waist and lay my cheek at his chest. "I'll miss you."

He held me away from him. "Stay strong, darling. You mustn't cry."

I reached for the canteen strap and he helped me loop it over his head. As I raised it to my lips and drank, water fell to my blouse, revealing the lace below. He brushed the water away. I gathered courage and kissed him on the mouth.

He seemed surprised at first, but returned the kiss. He tasted of black bread and tea.

"Afon, let's find a better . . ."

He kissed the hollow of my cheek and worked his way to my neck. "I'm glad you're an early riser."

Afon slowly ran his lips down the length my neck, causing me to catch my breath.

He became quite serious as he unfastened the top button of my blouse. "You smell like a whole garden."

I pulled the pins from my hair and it fell down my back as he released two more of my shirt buttons and slid his hands down the sides of my corset cover.

"I love you in lingerie, Sofya."

"What if someone happens upon us?" I asked.

He gathered my hair in great handfuls and pressed soft kisses down my throat sending the scent of fresh air, pine, and wood—

All at once from the corner of my eye I spied something at the window. A blur at first. A glimpse of blue shirt.

I breathed in a sharp burst of air. "Afon. What was that?"

"Probably a bird," Afon said, working his lips down my neck.

"No. I saw something. A man. *Watching*—"

A shot rang out in the woods, not far from us, so loud I felt the vibration of it through the stone against my back.

Afon pulled me close enough to feel the thump of his chest. We barely breathed there in the darkened cabin.

"Don't move," Afon whispered in my ear. "I'll be right back."

Afon hurried out the door and ran toward the sound of the shot. I followed and soon we came upon old Bogdan lying on the forest floor, blood seeping through the shoulder of his shirt.

"Think it was a thirty-five. Went straight through."

"Did you see who did it?" Afon asked.

"I went for my gun but he got me from behind."

Afon and I exchanged glances. Perhaps Father was right about leaving for Paris right away.

CHAPTER
9

_____

Varinka

1916

WOKE EARLY THE DAY I WAS TO REPORT TO THE COUNT-
ess's home. I lay on my child-sized straw mattress-bed atop the massive, whitewashed Russian oven, in the snug place Papa fashioned for
me up there, close enough to Mamka to hear her breathe at night.

The autumn moon crept by the skylight Papa had cut through the
roof, the one he made so the man in the moon could visit me at night.
The moon was sharp, almost full; the old man up there was protecting
me, for that was where Papa was.

Would he see me grow up and marry and fill the house with children? Mamka had seen I would someday have a child. But that would
never happen. Certainly not with Taras.

I sat up on my mattress. Such thoughts were childish. I would never
leave our *izba*. I'd be stuck there in the woods forever, if Taras had his
say. Though I wore the same linen dress the village girls did, a long,
shapeless, high-waisted *sarafan,* and covered my hair with a kerchief,
he still wanted me. He would never put a child in my belly, of course.
That was the most important part of the arrangement.

At least Papa had fixed me a perfect world up there, my bed snug as
a ship, with a rope ladder down the side. Next to my bed I pinned up
pictures of the tsar's four daughters, the grand duchesses. I never tired

of studying their dresses, hair, and jewels. I kissed my fingertips and pressed them to each girl in turn. Olga, the eldest, who loved to read, and then Tatiana, who they called "The Governess." Maria, the sweet one. Anastasia, the clown. And the dark-haired boy, Alexei, their brother and the heir.

I ran a finger down the row of our books standing on the bookshelf that ran the length of my bed. Cervantes. Dostoyevsky. The Brothers Grimm. A whole book of famous paintings. Who needed the school-house when I had Mamka and all these teachers? Papa alone had taught me the history of the world.

I eased the ladder down the side of the oven and climbed down, quiet, to not disturb Mamka, and slipped my wrapper on over my che-mise and bloomers. I started Mamka's groats cooking. It was an impor-tant day, so I was quick about it all. I would walk to the village to sell my oil, then on to my first day working at the countess's estate.

A floorboard creaked behind me.

I stood with a jump to find Taras standing there. The calm of the morning vanished in a second, causing my temper to flare. He seemed especially large that morning. "Why do you *scare* me? You should be out—"

He shrugged. "Already shot a doe this morning." He kept his gaze on mine.

At twenty years old, four years my elder, Taras stood as tall as the doorway with legs like poplar trunks, his chestnut hair parted down the center and tucked behind his ears. How much I'd loved him before he went to prison. Before he'd come back so changed.

"Hunting in the tsar's woods? You'll hang for sure. Work at the linen factory."

"And put more money in that bourgeois pig's pocket?"

"Mamka needs bread. We have an agreement, Taras."

"Exactly."

I tried to step around him to the dustpan. "I'm busy. Maybe tomor-row."

He caught my wrist, thankfully my left, since my right was still healing after he'd broken it.

"Please, Taras."

"Did you make more oil?" he asked.

My free hand went to the vial in my wrapper pocket, cold and smooth. "I need to sell it."

My oil was prized in the village. Some said it was magical and cured the aches, but it was only linseed oil with a touch of peppermint.

He nodded toward the woodshed.

I tried to pull away but he held me fast. "During the day, Taras? But Mamka . . ."

He brought his face close to mine. "You made a promise and you need to keep it." I knew the signs that one of his black times was coming. Heavy breathing. A faraway look in his eye.

He released my wrist. "Your Papa himself said it. Men must desire their wives, wives must respect their husbands."

"We are not husband and wife and never will be."

He started toward the door to his shed. "I don't have to stay here and take this."

I followed and found him ramming a shirt into his rucksack on the bed. The room was warm but dark and his bed sat neatly made in one corner, a fire glowing in the little iron stove. A thin slant of light hit his collection affixed to the wall—my father's old knives, a scythe as tall as a young boy. The woodworking tools he'd crafted himself lay neatly arranged on the workbench: maple-handled awls and chisels, a tiny iron letter "T" that he used to brand his initial into the knife handles.

"I could have been halfway to Lake Baikal, but I'm here." Were those tears? He needed me to keep him calm, for Mamka couldn't take another one of his episodes. Plus, Mother and I were lucky he brought us food. Taras could live alone in his little hut in the woods and let us starve.

"Your friend isn't coming around?" I asked.

Vladi, Taras's fat little former cellmate, came to the *izba* at the most difficult times, expecting to be included in our meager meals.

"He called a meeting in town."

"All right." I closed the door. "Just this once."

We both knew the rules. I gave him massages and let him watch me undress in exchange for his protection. No mouth-kissing allowed. No touching below the waist.

Taras slipped his shirt over his head and stood, a shaft of light across his chest, his eyelashes spiky with unshed tears. I ran my fingertips through the haze of dark hair in the valley of his chest, down his smooth belly, like the underside of a turtle's shell, rippled and hard. Everything about Taras was large. Feet, arms, eyes, as if he'd been born of a giantess. I smoothed his front tattoos, a catalog of his time in Russian prisons. On one shoulder, a hand clenched around the stem of a tulip. On the other, a rose-entwisted dagger. I ran my thumb across my favorites, the two cherubs at flight on the smooth skin of his chest, fat, flying babies holding a banner, which said in blue script: ничего не верить. *Believe in nothing.* How different he'd looked before he went away to prison, softer and slender, his skin smooth and ink free. Back when he smiled and called me Pet.

"Hurry, now," I said. "On your belly."

Taras lay facedown on the bed. I pulled off my wrapper, straddled him, and felt the muscles in his back through my thin bloomers. I released the stopper from the vial and Taras breathed deep at the first smell of peppermint.

"Slowly . . ." he said.

"*Quiet.* Mamka is right outside."

I poured a pool onto the small of his back and spread out the oil, to his shoulder blades, over the most magnificent tattoo of the Virgin Mary and child in the heavens, two angels floating above them. My fingers kneaded his back, his skin chamois-leather soft, and rubbed the great clouds and the Virgin's dress. The peppermint oil grew warmer as my fingers found the knots in his back and glided over the mounded scars of bear claw wounds, thought to be good luck by many. The only good luck about those scars was that Taras stabbed that bear before it could maul him worse.

"You should have a tattoo, Inka."

A shudder ran through me. The thought of a needle piercing my skin made me sick.

"Maybe a tiny rose. Next to your eye?"

"On my face?" The horror of it. "Never."

After a few minutes of kneading the knots from his back I stood.

He swallowed hard. "Go ahead. Slowly, now."

Looking anywhere but at him, I undid the buttons of my chemise and slid it off. I didn't have to look to know he was rubbing the front of his pants.

"Keep going," he said.

I stepped out of my bloomers and stood as he watched. As he rubbed harder, I sent myself away, to Mount Olympus, to the entrance gate tended by the seasons. I floated through the clouds, over the gods in their crystal palaces, feasting on nectar and ambrosia to stay immortal.

All at once, I bent to retrieve my chemise. "That is all."

Taras sprang from the bed, wrapped his hand around my upper arm and squeezed. "Stop teasing me. You do it on purpose."

He squeezed tighter and I grew faint from the pain. "No marks. Remember?"

Taras released my arm, bit the stopper from the vial and poured it down my chest. He kissed my neck and pulled at my breasts with oily hands.

I shoved him away, but he returned, this time rougher still. Before long I was back on Mount Olympus as a god ran a hot peppermint tongue down my chest. My hands tangled in his hair and smoothed the blue angels on his shoulders. His hand smoothed down my side, toward the V between my legs.

I pushed him. "No, Taras. You promised."

He grabbed my hand, yanked me to him, and a familiar stab seared through my wrist.

The pain brought me to my knees and water came to my eyes at once. "You hurt it again."

Taras knelt and held my wrist as if it were one of the baby birds he rescued and ran his fingers up and down the bone. "It's just sprained."

I stood and stepped to the door, holding my wrist. Today of all days.

LATE THAT AFTERNOON I walked to the countess's estate, my wrist wrapped in a cold, soaked rag and it felt better. When Mamka asked how that happened, I said I tripped sweeping out the shed.

Cool darkness gathered as I gave my name to the guards at the gate and walked the road to the estate. Soon I heard music and saw a brick house lit up in a distant clearing. As I drew closer it seemed like a fairy's palace, the windows aglow, the figures inside shimmering in pale blues and white.

I stepped to the back door, took a deep breath, entered, and continued through to the kitchen, bright as day in there, with windows high as a tall tree. A tall, blond man in a long jacket the color of new snow called after black-uniformed servants as they rushed silver pots back and forth. It was hard to hear and my stomach complained at the smell of roast chicken and fresh bread.

"Get that chocolate off to cool!" the man in the white jacket shouted at someone in English. I said a little prayer thanking Mamka for making me learn English.

A big girl with skinny braids and cheeks flushed so red they looked slapped, hurried by and then stopped in her tracks. "Who in God's name are you?"

"Varinka. The countess sent for me." What a fine uniform she wore, a black dress, crisp white ruffled-edged apron, and black leather shoes.

"And you're here to do what?"

"Kitchen help?"

"I'm Raisa," she said, pulling me by the hand into the kitchen. Her hands were rough and red as her cheeks. She led me to the tall white-jacketed man who stood bent at the waist over a tray of fancy pies. "Cook, this is Varinka."

I bowed deeply from the waist in his direction as Mamka taught me.

He kept his eyes on his work. "Stand up, girl," he said. "Girls curtsey in this house."

I straightened, glad he didn't look at me for I trembled all over. How handsome he was up close, with his thick blond hair and eyes the color of cornflowers. This cook had the look of money about him. Why was he sweating in the kitchen? He placed a white chocolate ear, so thin you could see light through it, on the head of a little chocolate mouse no bigger than my thumb.

"You the girl the countess sent for?"

I nodded.

"*Est-ce que tu parles français?*"

"*Oui, monsieur.*"

"Good. They only speak French in the dining room." He set a tiny black tail on the mouse. "Ever serve in a dining room before?"

"Of course," I said. "At the seaside one summer."

He squinted up at me. "A white tablecloth restaurant?"

"Yes."

"What did they serve?" he asked, one eye narrowing more.

"Well, stews . . ." I stood taller. "And only the best venison and pork. The tsar himself ate there once. Asked for a second helping of the venison."

The cook shifted his gaze back to his work. "You're a terrible liar, Miss Varinka. The tsar doesn't care for venison and you've never stepped foot outside this forest."

My whole body grew warm. How could I have been so stupid? Would he send me home?

He picked up a silver spoon. "Haven't I seen you in the village? With that woodsman?"

"Taras. My guardian." Did he see my hands shake?

"Maybe you'd be better off in the laundry."

Raisa stepped closer. "But we're shorthanded in the dining room tonight."

He tossed the spoon into the sink with a clatter. "So you'll have to do. But just tonight."

Raisa led me down a hallway to a special room where the food was kept and I breathed out a big puff of air. "Your cook is handsome. And he speaks such good English."

"You would too if you went to Oxford. That's in England."

Raisa pushed a neatly folded pile into my arms, a pair of black tie-up shoes like hers atop it. "Hurry and put these on. The shoes may be too big. I'll be right back."

I undressed, shook out the black uniform dress and slipped it over my head, the fabric sliding down cool against my skin. I kicked off my woven shoes, unwound the length of rough linen, and smoothed one white stocking up and over my knee. I smiled as I fastened a fancy, white apron about my waist and set the black shoes on the floor.

I looked at all the food kept in that room, so much they could not eat it all at once and needed a special room to hold it. Boxes of flour and tins of fish. A whole crate of oranges sitting on crinkled paper that looked like birds' nests.

A knock came at the door and Raisa stood outside the waist-high window, the wavy glass making her just a moving shape. "Ready yet?" she called from the hallway.

"Going fast as I can." I stepped one foot into a shoe. She was right about the big fit.

Raisa talked through the door. "Stay aware tonight. Place the tureen on the sideboard and stand along the wall until you get the signal to serve. Remove the lid, leave it on the sideboard, and serve from the *left,* of course. She will speak French so you and the other servants won't be able to eavesdrop on her conversation, but she'll switch to Russian if she wants something from a servant. And whatever you do, don't look at her directly."

I laced both shoes tight to try to keep them from flopping about when I walked and emerged from the little room.

"Good," Raisa said, plucking at the ruffles of my apron.

"The shoes are too big," I said.

"Make do for tonight."

We stepped back to the kitchen and watched the cook spoon borscht into a white tureen.

My head buzzed with orders. *Place the tureen on the sideboard. What is a sideboard? Serve from the left. Don't look at them directly.*

I picked up the tureen with two hands, and relief washed over me, for my wrist did not hurt. Raisa held the dining room door open for me and I stepped through it, my feet wobbling about in my new shoes. I walked into the room, which held a big table, and almost fainted at the blur of colors there. A gold cloth on the table glowed like the sun itself was caught inside and a kind of tall pink flowers I'd never seen before stood in a shimmering bowl at the middle of the table. Above it all a lamp of shining glass pieces blazed as if on fire.

I shuffled toward what I guessed was the sideboard, a long, low brown chest. The countess sat at one end of the table, looking smaller somehow from the night I saw her at our *izba.* She wore a white dress, her hair piled atop her head, a sparkling comb stuck there. Mr. Streshnayva, who I recognized from the village since he ran the linen factory, sat at the other end of the table.

The countess's older daughter, who was almost the twin of the tsar's daughter Olga, sat with her younger sister on one side of the table, and a young, dark-haired officer, handsome as Rapunzel's prince, had a whole side of the table to himself. A young boy sat between the countess and her daughter, in a tall chair of his own, banging on the little table in front of him with open palms. My gaze stuck on him, with his golden curls and the face of a cherub.

I placed my tureen on the sideboard, stood at the wall, and surveyed the scene. Each person had their own china plate and clear glass cup on a high stem like a flower. As a servant tinkled ice-filled water from a silver pitcher into the countess's glass like a melting river in springtime, each person sat, backs perfectly straight, elbows back, their fingertips just so on each side of their plate. How could a person eat sitting this way?

The countess stood. "A toast to Maxwell Streshnayva Afonovich Stepanov, who, though his mother won't leave him properly in his own bed at night to sleep *alone,* is developing into a fine young man who does not suck his thumb as so many children do and has the vocabulary and intellect of a child twice his age."

I could not tear my gaze from the boy in the high chair. He turned to smile at the countess, his blue eyes shining in the candlelight. His skin was the color of an ermine's winter coat, like that of the baby on the Virgin's lap at the village church. On his feet he wore white leather moccasins tied with blue satin bows.

All at once the child began to cry and kick his chair. His mother offered him a biscuit but his howls grew louder. Did she not see he wanted to free himself of that chair?

From my place at the wall I crouched, screwed up my face in the child's direction, and he turned to me with a look of surprise. All at once a smile broke out on his face. I tried another face, this time stuck out my tongue.

The boy laughed outright. *"Plus! Plus! Le referais!"*

Of course, he wanted more. Did anyone there play with him or was he just their little pet?

The boy's mother raised her eyebrows and smiled at me.

Mr. Streshnayva held up his glass. "To Max!"

The countess leaned toward the younger girl. "Do try the borscht,

Luba. The tsarina herself gave me the recipe." She then waved in the direction of the tureen.

My signal. All at once my knees grew weak. I stood straighter and stepped to the sideboard, wiped my palms down the front of my apron, and removed the lid. The countess gestured toward the younger daughter and I carried the tureen to her side and set it on the table. I dipped the ladle and spooned enough borscht into her bowl to cover the bottom. She looked at me with a grimace and waved me off.

"Luba, really," the countess said and pointed to her own bowl.

My hands shook as I stepped toward her. I set the tureen on the table, pulled the ladle from the soup and hovered it over her bowl. Then all at once, in my wrist I felt a sharp pain, and my hand faltered and, as if in a dream, a fleck of purple no bigger than a pinhead flew to the countess's white sleeve.

The countess pushed back her chair as if stung. "What must it take to get decent help in the dining room?" she asked in Russian.

Breath stuck in my throat and I stood like an elk caught in a clearing. *What to do?*

I brushed at her sleeve with a napkin. "I can wash it—"

"This is *linen*, it's ruined. Out."

"But—"

"Do you not understand *out*? Out, out, out!"

The countess's older daughter stood and pushed her chair back. "Agnessa, it's just a *spot*."

I threw down the napkin and ran toward the kitchen, the blood pounding in my ears.

I stepped into the pantry and closed the door behind me, tears stinging my eyes. I pulled off my apron, ripping one of the ties, and kicked off the clunky shoes. They had money to burn in that house. Could they not provide their servants with proper shoes? I wrapped my legs and slipped into the woven shoes I came with. At least they fit.

A knock came at the door and it opened. It was the boy's mother, the child on her hip.

She held out her hand. "Don't mind Agnessa. I am Sofya."

I bowed deep before her. "Varinka Niscemi Kozlov Pushkinsky."

"No need to bow, Varinka."

"Your mother—"

"My *step*mother. Agnessa has trouble keeping her anger in check sometimes. We've all felt it, I'm afraid. Please don't be offended."

I held my tongue and studied the floor. I turned my head to hide my tears. "I'll be going now."

Sofya touched my sleeve. "Wait. What a lovely scent that is."

I stood, mute. Was she mocking me?

"Don't be afraid. Is it peppermint?"

"Yes. Make it myself."

"Reminds me of my childhood. Do you have any experience with children, Varinka? You certainly charmed young Max, here."

I paused. "Just village children. I try and teach them a little Latin. And French, which my Mamka taught me."

She smiled. "*Vraiment? Merveilleux.* This is Max. He is just over two years old." She swayed and cooed something in his ear and then walked out of the room, expecting me to follow.

Sofya turned to me as we walked. "Our Swiss nanny, Justine, left this morning for home. She cried every day she was here since she missed her family, so it was a relief to see her go, I'm afraid. We also had an English nanny but Luba left a lizard in her bed."

Sofya led me up the steep back stairs to a nursery as big as our whole *izba*, the walls covered floor to ceiling with yellow paper showing finely dressed men and women having picnics. A small fireplace sat on the far wall, a fire blazing there, and in one corner stood a basket on wooden legs, draped with white lace and ribbons.

"What is that?" I asked.

Sofya smiled. "Why, a bassinet. Where Max sleeps."

I just stared at this bassinet, a thing I'd never seen before. Mamka told me I'd slept in a drawer when I was a baby.

"I slept in it as a child. Luba, too, though she was tiny when she was born, had to sleep wrapped in cotton wool and packed with hot water bottles. It was a hard birth for my mother. She never fully recovered."

"I'm sorry."

"Here I am talking way too much about me and I should tell you about your new charge, if you accept the position, of course." Sofya touched one finger to Max's chin. "Max fell when he was just learning to walk and cut his chin just under here, very badly. Had a little black beard of stiches for weeks."

I tickled him under the chin. "He mended well."

The boy smiled and I caught my breath. Such perfect little baby teeth.

"Would you like to hold him?"

She handed the child to me and his weight surprised me. A good eater. I held him close to my side and he settled in. I thanked all the saints and Papa, too.

"He likes you already," Sofya said. "Must admit I could use the help."

I ran my fingers down the side of his leg, soft as milkweed silk.

Max looked up at me, smiled, and then jumped a little. I held him tighter and felt a pull in my belly. It was as if Papa himself had answered my prayers and dropped little Max into my arms.

Eliza

1916

THOUGH ONE WAS REPEATEDLY PROMISED, NO ambulance arrived for transport to the hospital so we alone worked to save Henry. Dr. Forbes ordered his serum and we applied plasters, compresses, and cool towels through the night. But no matter what we did Henry's skin turned grayer by the hour, his coughing spells lasted longer, and his eyes grew glassy, with an unsettling, fixed stare.

Then at nightfall Henry's temperature lowered. Hope. Doctor Forbes sent me to my room for a nap. Relieved, I fell into a fitful sleep only to be shaken by the shoulder soon thereafter.

"Eliza," Dr. Forbes said. "Wake up, dear. We've lost Henry."

My first thought was *Go* find *him, for goodness' sake*. But then, as I woke, I understood the horrible truth. I ran past him to the bedroom, heart beating wildly.

I stepped to Henry's bed and gathered him in my arms. He was still warm. "Why did you not call me sooner?"

I could not tear my gaze from Henry's face, calm as if he slept, grayer still, his lips bluish at the edges. It couldn't be. I smoothed his hair back from his forehead.

"I wouldn't do that, Eliza," Dr. Forbes said as he walked back to his hideous black bag coiling a length of rubber tubing. "I called someone to come."

"No one is taking him—"

"It's necessary, Eliza. Pneumonia is communicable. The household will—"

I took Henry's hand in mine. Already cooling. "How could this just *happen* when I wasn't here?" He'd robbed me of my chance to say goodbye.

"The dying often allow themselves to slip away when their loved ones are out of the room." Dr. Forbes turned to look down at Henry. "Even in his last moments, he was considerate."

Rage grew in my chest and cut off my breath. "We should have taken him to the hospital."

"There was nothing anyone could do. The rain, the cigars, a bug of some kind." With two hands, he held my shoulders and gently pulled me from Henry.

I swatted him away. "You are a *doctor*. You could have saved him. Or at least called me before he . . ."

The doctor stepped to his bag and clicked it shut. "When God calls, Eliza—"

"Don't talk to me of *God*, Dr. Forbes."

A knock came on the door and a young man entered. Hatless and brown-haired, with jug-handle ears, he introduced himself as Mr. Archibald Trymore. He had the kind yet deferential disposition of those in his unfortunate line of work.

My whole body began to quake.

"Mr. Henry Ferriday?" he said to no one in particular.

Dr. Forbes nodded.

Mr. Trymore entered and I held Henry tighter. "Please don't," I said, by then shaking as if doused with frigid water.

I struggled as Dr. Forbes pulled me back, more forcefully this time, and I left Henry lying on the bed. I stood, losing balance as if standing on shifting sands, while Mr. Trymore smoothed a linen bag up and over Henry.

I lunged toward Henry but Dr. Forbes held me back.

He slipped a bottle from his jacket pocket. "Take two of these at mealtime. It will help."

I accepted the vial as I watched Mr. Trymore pull the shroud over Henry's face.

Dr. Forbes rubbed my back. "Perhaps step outside, Eliza—"

Was this real? I pushed his hand away. "I will not. How could you give up on him so easily?"

Dr. Forbes went back to arranging his bag.

Poor Mr. Trymore barely slowed his business of packing Henry up. "May I ask if you prefer the deceased to be arranged in a slumber robe or a favorite suit?"

"Where are you taking him?"

He tied off the shroud and moved Henry onto his wheeled trolley, much as a grocer loads his cartons. How many times had he done this?

I grabbed Mr. Trymore's sleeve. "Please, no."

"Get hold of yourself, Eliza," Dr. Forbes said, pulling me back again. "Woolsey women are strong."

No we're not, I wanted to say, *this is too hard,* but I could only stand and watch him go.

Dr. Forbes restrained me by the hand as Mr. Trymore wheeled Henry out, and it was only then I realized my face was wet with tears.

I SENT CAROLINE TO STAY with relatives, as was the custom then. She sat in the entryway of our apartment rubbing a favorite pocket square of Henry's, ashen-faced, all cried out, as Peg gathered her luggage.

Peg took her by the hand and they walked toward the door.

Caroline sent a dark glance back at me. "I didn't get to say good-bye."

THE FUNERAL AT ST. THOMAS CHURCH was a blur, frail Mother at my side, still shaky from illness herself. We stood with Aunt Eliza in the front pew and they locked arms, the last of the Woolsey women, their chins held high. Dr. Forbes's pills helped dull the ache and I stood, numb, as we sang "Nearer My God to Thee" and an endless loop ran through my head. I should have worked harder to save him. It was Merrill's fault for running him around in the rain.

My gaze fixed on the satin ribbon of one floral arrangement as it fluttered ever so slightly, curling like a hand beckoning to the casket, Henry lying there in his best bespoke suit.

How did so many floral displays find their way into the church? I had requested an n.f.—*no flowers*—funeral, since bereavement flowers are so vulgar and such a hideous waste of blossoms. Yet so many floral emblems stood on stands around the casket. Dyed indigo roses and tinseled leaves in the shape of heaven's gates ajar. A pillow of monstrous white, waxed roses, *At Rest* lettered in burgundy chenille, a stuffed white dove lying there. It mocked Henry's life, for no one loved birds and fresh flowers more than he.

Mother and Aunt Eliza stood with me as I greeted a dark line of mourners. I was unable to say much as Julia and E.H. delivered heartfelt embraces. Merrill murmured condolences and moved on. Henry's Poor Brothers coworkers, faces blotched, kissed my cheek and whispered earnest comforts. I could not take my gaze from the black crape armbands that squeezed their jacket sleeves.

What did any of it matter? Henry was gone, and my one chance for happiness finished.

CHAPTER

I I

_____

Sofya

1916

THE MORNING AFON DROVE OFF TO THE REGIMENTAL
quarters in Petrograd Father started locking the doors. Perhaps it was
old Bogdan being shot in the woods. We'd found two iron bars of the
back fence pried loose, but no sign of the shooter.

I sat at the breakfast table with Agnessa and watched Bogdan, his
arm in a sling, supervise Cook and the male dining room staff as they
boarded up the house.

"We'll be imprisoned inside our own home?" Agnessa asked.

Cook helped Bogdan slide an oak panel over the window behind
Agnessa. Though a cool, fall day, the perspiration down the middle of
his back caused his shirt to cling there.

Agnessa lit a candle. "Well, if the Bolsheviks do come here to kill us
in the woods we'll already be dead from lack of air."

The men covered the glass parts of our doors with oak planks, affixed iron bars to the windows, and installed great, brass locks, which
opened by means of a key larger than my whole hand. It felt good to
finally do something to protect ourselves.

"It's as if we are being bricked up in 'The Cask of Amontillado,'"
Agnessa said, looking pleased she'd made a literary reference.

Thoughts of Afon plagued me after he left, for our bed still smelled of him. Max squirmed in my arms, a fussy toddler with a new tooth, and I felt the loneliness descend like a shroud. How would I raise Max alone?

THE FOLLOWING NIGHT I woke with a start from a dream about Afon to the sound of heavy footfalls downstairs and the hum of an idling motorcar. I sat up, heart pounding. Was it Afon, back on an unexpected leave? I rushed down the front stair, wrapping my dressing gown around me, with Agnessa, Father, and Luba close behind. Raisa, perfectly dressed, answered the door.

Every part of me sagged as Count von Orloff entered the vestibule and Bogdan and two pantry boys followed, heaving in his trunks, along with an enormous silver cage containing two peacocks, and set them on the tiled entry floor.

One bird screamed and my thoughts drifted to another peacock, the one at the tsar's Winter Palace, in the magnificent peacock clock. I'd come to the palace for my debut, lost interest in the pomp of it all, and stepped away to visit the oversized timepiece. It was the tsar's pride and joy, and we stood entranced by the golden woodland scene, as each metal forest creature, life-sized peacock, fox, rooster, and owl came to life.

As the clock began its show with an eerie chime and the little owl turned his head, a young man walked up behind me. As he passed I caught a wave of his scent, of motor oil and shave cream.

"You've found my favorite way to tell time," he said.

"Too bad it wouldn't fit on your wrist."

The golden peacock turned its head and slowly lifted its tail.

"I am Afon," he said.

I extended my hand. "Sofya Streshnayva."

He kissed my hand and lingered there, his lips soft on my skin.

"I must admit I saw you come in here," he said.

"How brave you are. Now you'll be stuck here talking with me even if you find no pleasure in it."

We turned our attention to the charming mechanized show and I gasped as the peacock turned and fanned out his golden plumes.

"What a burden such beauty would be," Afon said, his gaze fixed on the bird.

"You're handsome enough to be the peacock, you know, as I'm sure every female since birth has told you."

"And that makes you?"

"Please, not the squirrel."

"Choose the quick fox. No animal is more beautiful to my mind. It suits you well."

"Might the fox not devour the peacock?"

Afon smiled, with a trace of sadness that pinched my heart. "I fear the poor fellow may already be slain."

I felt a rush of—

Count von Orloff rushed about the vestibule tapping his cane on the floor.

"Take this thing *off* me," he called to Raisa as he shrugged off his traveling coat. Barely taller than Luba, his booming voice made up for his lack of stature. The last time I'd seen him he was wearing a turban, trembling on a St. Petersburg tram.

The Count rushed to Agnessa and clasped her hands in his. "Countess, I have most unfortunate news."

"Come in, Count. We can get Cook to—"

"Eat? Never, after what I've been through." His eyes had a wild look to them. He wore a patent leather–brimmed sailor's cap and double-breasted jacket.

Agnessa clenched the throat of her dressing gown. "I'm afraid the guest rooms are not aired out. We can put you in Luba's room."

He waved the suggestion away. "Sleep? Who can sleep when the whole world is going to hell with those dirty Bolsheviks? I carry three guns now."

Luba leaned toward me. "One to shoot with and the other two for the bandits to steal."

"I barely made it out alive tonight. We'd just finished packing up the car, hoping to join my wife in Moscow, and heard a terrible commotion outside. It was *rabble* come to invade the house. From upstairs I saw them running through the place, most with bottles in hand. They held my valet out the window by his feet. Though he begged for his life they dropped the poor man three *stories*."

Agnessa gasped. "Despicable."

"I escaped out the back door, thankfully the driver had stayed at the wheel, and we came here, with no hope of making Moscow safely. Things are beyond repair in the cities. A man was shot dead on our corner a week ago when he refused to give up his watch. We've *never* locked our doors and hardly lost the least thing. But now bandits come into any house on any excuse and walk away with lady's *cloaks*. My wife's friend visiting from Siberia had *two* sables stolen."

Agnessa led the count toward the *zala*. "Clearly, not everyone in Siberia is as poor as they'd have you believe."

"The *point*, Agnessa, is you can't trust a soul today. I would be dead if not for my quick thinking. No one is safe."

Agnessa settled the Count in a seat in the *zala* and one of the peacocks screamed, causing Agnessa to jump.

"Get those birds out to the poultry house," Father said to Bogdan. "Is there anything worse than that scream?"

Raisa lit the lamps and Father opened the brandy cabinet, starting the elaborate Kabuki dance of consolation.

The count looked to the ceiling and wiped away a tear. "The worst is that I cannot even appeal to the tsarina for help. She had always welcomed me at court, invited my counsel. The tsar as well. But no more."

Cook entered and stood near the doorway, his shirt unbuttoned at the throat, and sent me a quick glance.

The count took a crystal glass of brandy from Father and held it upon his knee. "Well I could not sit idly by any longer. With His Excellency away at the front the tsarina is surrounded by *despots*."

Agnessa leaned in. "Rasputin?"

"That dirty prophet is the least of it. Madame Wiroboff is the real snake. Has all those German spies at her beck and call."

Cook and I exchanged glances. Certainly round, clumsy Madame Wiroboff was not clever enough to instigate all this?

The count stood and paced the room. "How did we underestimate that woman's power over the empress? She sits at her mistress's feet, addressing her as 'The Sun and the Moon.' Now we are done for. She allows only her German friends access."

"What proof do we have there are Germans at court?" Father asked. "I've never met any."

"My own two eyes. They speak the language. Exchange German gold coins. They have removed the tsarina from everything of importance and spread poisonous stories. The latest is the tsarina and Rasputin are, well, *romantic*."

"Nowadays it seems the bigger the lie the better people swallow it," Father said.

The count sipped his brandy. "Well, she does write him flowery letters, Ivan. And with the tsar off at the front she does anything that madman says. It's a disaster. The kaiser will end up just waltzing in here."

"They may have her drugged," Agnessa said.

The count waved us closer, wide-eyed. "And here is the worst of it. They have been doing something *most* despicable and I caught them, red-handed."

Agnessa glanced at Father, sensitive to his limited tolerance for gossip, especially about the imperial family. "Perhaps we should talk later. You must be tired—"

"I called on Madame Wiroboff and being left waiting, happened to spy upon her writing table, whereupon sat a half-finished letter I just happened to glance upon and you will not believe me when I tell you what was written there. A faked letter, written in the false pen of Madame Wiroboff herself, but pretending to be a peasant, with misspellings and atrocious grammar, attesting to this supposed peasant's continued fidelity to the tsarina."

Agnessa frowned. "I don't understand."

"Madame Wiroboff is writing fake letters to the tsarina," I said.

"To what end?"

Cook stepped to my side, his shoulder against mine, so close I could smell the yeasty scent of bread in his hair. "So the tsarina will think the policies of those surrounding her are working. And to trick her into believing the people still love her despite the bad decisions her counselors force her into."

The count drained his glass. "There were *stacks* of letters, all written in the same counterfeit hand, faked to look like they were from different soldiers and peasants. I approached Madame Wiroboff's assistant about it and he so much as admitted agents post them from all parts of the country to make the ruse seem real."

"We must tell the tsarina," Agnessa said.

"I did, in a most delicate way. I told Her Highness that this entourage is not letting the truth through. She answered with such violence, defending Madame Wiroboff and Rasputin and their political program. And I am now banished to Siberia for my concern. Not to return under any circumstances. Anyone liberal is treated the same."

Father removed his spectacles and rubbed his eyes. "She will reconsider."

"The tsar has completely surrendered to his wife and her evil friends. Perhaps it will be better to have Germany overtake us. Teach us a lesson."

"Be that it happens quickly," Cook said. "And saves us from ourselves."

THE FOLLOWING NIGHT AFTER DINNER, while Agnessa let the count win a game of mahjong, Father waved Luba and me into his study with great urgency. We hurried into that wood-paneled room, our fortress, cool and dark even on the hottest summer days, more the den of a college professor than finance minister.

Luba and I took our seats in the worn leather chairs as Father lit a kerosene lamp and rushed about the room, pulling papers from a cabinet under the watchful eye of a red clay bust of Benjamin Franklin, who wore Father's Cambridge University mortarboard. How many nights had Mother sat with us in this room, as Father read aloud, her gazing at him in the lamplight, so in love.

We spoke in Russian, as Father always did when Agnessa was not with us.

Father walked behind his desk, his face serious "I must be quick— there is much to do for the Ministry before we go. You know I don't like to worry you with these things, but . . ."

He stopped. Tears shone in his eyes. Through the closed door came the muffled sound of the count and Agnessa talking and the distant clack of mahjong tiles.

Father crying? I'd only seen that twice. First, the happy day Luba was born. And second, the morning Mother died.

He reached into another drawer and pulled out the worn, chestnut leather holster for the revolver issued him by the Ministry and a paper box of bullet shells. He slid an ordinary-looking gun from the holster, one of his many Nagant pistols, standard military issue with a wooden handle.

"You two are smart girls. If anything happens—"

I sat up straighter. "We can put more guards at the gate."

Father kept his gaze on his work. "It may be too late for that." His hand shook as he reached into the box and removed one shell. Light grabbed the brass casing as he opened the loading gate and slipped the bullet into the chamber.

"You can tell us, Father," Luba said. "I've read the Ministry letters."

He turned to Luba with a weary look. "Is nothing private, Luba?"

I stepped to his desk and set my fingertips on his paper desk blotter. "It's bad, isn't it?" My gaze went to Father's paneled gun closet, his hunting rifles locked in there.

He replaced the gun in the drawer. "We are still safer here than in any of the big cities. I've moved up our timetable. You need to be prepared."

"And Agnessa?" Luba asked.

He looked down at his hands. "She'll be fine. But I want you two to have a plan in case we're separated."

Luba listened, her face looked drained of color but for two red spots on her cheekbones.

Father unlocked his desk drawer and lifted out his green metal box. "In my Ministry position I have great responsibility." He opened the lid and, like a priest handling a holy chalice, removed a deep blue ledger. "On a single page in here you will find the bank account numbers and passwords for the entities whose money I am entrusted with."

I swallowed hard. "What banks?"

"It is all noted here," Father said, two fingers on the leather volume. "Swiss. Italian. All over Europe."

Luba reached for the ledger. "I know the perfect hiding spot."

Father looked at her with a wan smile and handed her the book. "I have kept a copy hidden, as well. My colleagues in Petrograd have been instructed to destroy theirs if the Ministry is threatened. If anything happens to me, take it to Paris. There will be people there who need it, though bad people will want it, too."

"Who?" I asked.

"This growing unrest among the underclasses is not a new thing, but they are gaining traction. Bolsheviks. Mensheviks. Left-wingers. Their talk is increasingly negative about the ruling class, calling us the Whites and themselves the Reds. Referring to us as parasites."

"But that's not true," Luba said. "You built Fena's House for them, the linen factory—"

"Sadly, today authority, not truth, makes law," Father said. "They want to erase any trace of the tsar's bloodline—which includes us, of course. This list is the only access to the fortunes we'll need to fight the forces that want us gone. Guard it well."

"Should we gather personal things, too?" I asked.

"Only essentials for the trip to Paris. I'm working on details now. Travel documents are coming from the city. These days it's infinitely easier to get into Russia than out."

"Will we take Cook?" I asked.

Father nodded. "If he wishes."

"Servants?" Luba asked.

"We'll have to make do with hotel staff. I've written to Afon of our intentions." Father pulled off his spectacles and pinched the bridge of his nose. "Without Afon here, little Max will be . . ." He paused, overcome.

Luba went to him and smoothed his back. "We'll protect him, Father."

He took her hand in his. "While I breathe, I hope."

"I've been hiding some things in the perfect spot in case we must leave quickly," Luba said.

Father smiled up at her. "Of course you have. But we'll leave soon. Be packed and ready to go. Tell no one." He stood and opened his arms to us and held us close. "We are stronger as a unit and no one will harm you girls if I have a breath left."

LATER THAT NIGHT, BEFORE BED, Luba and I amused Max on the nursery floor. Varinka was home with her Mamka and it was wonderful to be alone with Max and Luba. We spread a few coverlets and featherbeds on the floor to do what Luba called "camping out," to sleep there, which Max enjoyed immensely. He lay between us paging through his picture books, every now and then straying to bring back a favorite toy. Luba lay on her belly, marking calculations in a tiny notebook. The room seemed smaller in the darkness, lit by a candle and a kerosene lamp.

"He's going to ruin his eyes in this low light," I said.

"So take them away. You're the parent."

"Sometimes I wonder what would have happened if Mother had lived and I'd been able to work with Professor Bartell."

"At Brillantmont? You'd be somewhere in Switzerland dressed in a white lab coat mating pea plants."

"She said I could be the next Gregor Mendel."

"It was a terrible thing having to come home to help Father after Mother died but you never would have met Afon. Or had Max. Or broken Cook's heart."

"I was fine until Agnessa started wearing Mother's coat."

"How could she? It still had Mother's name in it. Let's be honest, that woman is our hair shirt."

Luba was quiet for a moment. "Remember Mother's story about the two sisters bound by a silver thread so strong they could never be apart? Sometimes I feel like that's us." Luba took my hand in hers. "Promise we'll never be apart? Even if Afon wants to move away someday? I couldn't bear it."

I kissed the back of her hand. "Promise. So where is this perfect hiding spot of yours?"

"There," Luba pointed to the floor at the corner. "Under the floorboard."

"What is so perfect about that? Servants are in and out of here all day. We should put our supplies in my room. No one goes there. In a bottom drawer."

"Think, sister. If we are overrun by bandits—which is a high probability the more time we spend out here in the woods—what's the first place they'll look? The main bedrooms, of course. Under mattresses. In bureau drawers. No one will think to look under nursery floorboards."

"We should include money," I said.

"Jewelry is a better choice. If the tsar is overthrown—"

"Unlikely. He already beat down one revolution."

"Father said that if the tsar is overthrown, money may become worthless and that gold and gemstones are always good currency. I asked Agnessa for one of her brooches and she said she's taking them herself, so I took this instead." Luba pulled from her pocket a bracelet. It was one of Agnessa's favorites, a Moghul-era gold armlet, with two makara dragonhead terminals, which met at their ferocious-looking, toothy, open mouths. It was enameled in deep indigo and the dragon-heads set with ruby and onyx eyes.

"*Luba*. If she knew——"

"Agnessa will never miss it and we can hide Father's list in here."

Luba opened Father's ledger and ripped the first page from it.

I grasped her wrist. "Are you insane?"

Nimbly as a spider wraps her victim in silk, Luba rolled the paper tight and threaded it into one of the dragons' mouths. "There. Who would dream this was in here?"

"You should work for the secret police."

"I also packed my sextant, of course."

"If you get the sextant I want my rose clippers."

Luba tilted her head down and looked up at me as though I were a child. "With a sextant we can navigate. Flowers serve no purpose in survival."

"I would need my Montessori books——"

"You don't need a book to raise Max. Just get away from Agnessa and trust yourself. You were born a good mother, Sofya. Just like our own."

"Better than Varinka?"

"That doesn't deserve a reply."

"She seems to know his every thought even before he does. Puts me to shame."

"Keep an eye on her, Sofya."

"You sound like Cook and Agnessa. She's just a girl."

"A girl who carries Max everywhere. Barely lets him walk on his own."

"We're leaving and she's staying behind, problem solved. What else did you pack?"

"One of Father's old guns he'll never miss, *loaded* of course, a length of rope, scent-killing petroleum jelly to cover our skin with in case we're followed, and one week's worth of jerky. I've also added balls of cotton wool to dip in the petroleum jelly, which Bogdan says are good fire starters. It all fits in one bag, in case I must carry you, too."

"I'll not need carrying, thank you, and that sextant won't even fit in there."

"It does. I've already tried it." She stood and pulled up one board to reveal a hole the size of a small breadbox under the floor. "The sextant folds, you see? And it all fits in this canvas sack."

"Well, that leaves me no space."

"Your things take little room. A month's supply of biscuits for the baby, powdered milk, and a sheepskin cask for water. It's all in there. We'll use our jewelry to barter for things once we're there."

"And what of clothes?"

"I've hidden warm traveling clothing and boots for all three of us in the stable, deep in Jarushka's tack box. Pants for you, you'll be happy to know. We'll be headed south to Paris. Weather permitting, by horse that would take us just under three weeks, with stops for rest and recuperation."

"Recuperation from what?"

"Exhaustion. Possible starvation."

"Three weeks? Impossible."

"We'll do our best not to travel in winter, though we may have no say in the matter." She unfolded a map and smoothed it onto the floor. "The way I see it, we're 1,340 miles from Paris. On horseback at fifty miles per day, with three hours of grazing time it would take us—"

"Twenty-six-point-eight days to get there," I said.

"Very good, sister. Not accounting for travel, prohibitive weather, or an unusual number of wolves."

"This unrest will all blow over. You'll see we are worrying for nothing. We'll be on a train tomorrow night."

Luba stuffed the map and bracelet in the rucksack and tamped the floorboard down over it with the toe of her boot.

"I hope you're right, but now I have a surprise for you, Sofya—for Max as well."

"What, Luba?"

Luba stepped to the kerosene lamp. She blew out the flame, left one small candle burning, then rejoined us there on the floor.

My eyes adjusted and I reached for her hand, there in the inky darkness. "I don't see anything."

"Look up," she said, a smile in her voice.

I looked to the ceiling and saw the glow from points of silver light arranged in a familiar pattern. If we were not inside I would have sworn we lay under a constellation in the starry night sky.

The breath caught in my throat. "Luba." So, this was her secret project. "It's exquisite."

"It's Max's special constellation. I stood upon Bogdan's ladder and glued it up there."

"Oh, Luba—"

"It's Taurus—the bull, the sign under which he was born. If Max wakes at night he won't be afraid."

Luba rested her head on my shoulder. I held her close in the darkness and took in her young scent of glue and lavender toilet water and hope.

"Taurus sits in the sky right between your sign, Gemini, and Aries, which is Afon's."

Tears blurred my gaze and the silver stars swam above us.

"Do you like it?" Luba asked.

"It's the most precious gift, sister."

The three of us lay there in the darkness watching that sky and felt the enormous weight of the world slowly turning, as if there was some master plan for us. We would have to be ready, for it was stronger than any of us and would take us wherever it pleased.

Varinka

1916

I LEFT MAMKA AT THE *IZBA* AND TOOK MY NEW SHORTCUT to work at the estate, scanning the forest floor for mushrooms and herbs. Autumn had come to the forest and some of the best treasures hid under the bright leaves. I brushed them away as I walked, looking one way then the other for Cook's favorites, an old pillowcase for my finds tied at my waist.

I'd become an important part of things at the estate. If I stayed clear of the countess, most everyone else liked me very much. Raisa had a cake planned for me, for she'd asked me twice what flavor icing I liked and I said lemon. There was to be a grand dinner that night, celebrating the countess's friend's visit, and three geese were to be served. Goose was Mamka's favorite and there was bound to be some left over.

From the look in Mamka's eyes she liked hearing my stories of the estate, of the ladies' fine dresses and shoes—and of baby Max. I couldn't tell Taras, though. He would only say those pigs kept all the animals in the forest for themselves and how much better off we'd be without them. Was that true? It was just by accident of birth that we didn't have fine carriages and silk stockings, too.

I emerged from the forest onto the main dirt road, not far from the estate gates, and spied, nestled in the grass by the side of the road, something round and orange. I observed it for a moment, then picked it up and turned it in my fingers. It was an orange—a fruit I'd seen in Mamka's encyclopedia. Things like that happened to me a lot, especially on happy days like that one. Four-leaf clovers. Unexpected presents. It was a gift from Papa, I knew. I tucked it into my dress pocket.

"Hello, Inka."

I jumped at the sound of a voice behind me and turned. Taras and his friend Vladi. Taras was dressed in his hunting clothes, a sealskin vest and leather *brodni,* knee-length hunter's boots, covered in tar. No wonder they nicknamed those boots "stalkers," for they allowed hunters to silently follow their prey.

Vladi stood at his side, so much smaller, that terrible burn down his face shining in the sun.

"It isn't polite to sneak up on a person," I said.

I took a step backward and looked about. Where had they even come from? Taras had better trails than the deer, and certainly knew the woods as well. How many times had I watched Taras scanning the forest, head cocked sideways, reading animal tracks and looking for broken spiderwebs?

"Good to see you, Inka," Vladi said, his shiny, red tongue flicking to the sides of his mouth. I tried not to stare at his burn.

"We've been looking for you," Taras said.

"I need to get to the estate."

"Too fancy now to say hello to Vladi? He has moved to Malinov."

"Good for him."

"He has the villagers on his side. Things are changing quickly, Inka. Very good for the cause. We have friends in high places in Petrograd now."

"Good. Go there and stay."

Vladi tossed a pebble into the woods. "The city is full of the news. A movement to take back what's due us."

"Each week brings a new movement."

"This time we'll win. You should see the crowds."

"I must be going. I have the Streshnayvas—"

Taras grabbed my wrist, sending a jolt of fire up my arm. "You promised to tell me about them."

"Don't ruin this for me, Taras. I won't spy for you."

"I brought venison."

"Cook gives us pheasant." I pulled away and walked ahead. "I thought you were enlisting."

Taras followed me. "The whole army is deserting."

So, he hadn't enlisted after all. Mamka had predicted it, saying he was only going to Petrograd to watch films at the cinema.

"The people are starving in Petrograd. Growing angrier by the day. Our time has come and you need to help."

"The estate is boarded up tight," I said. "You'll never get in there."

Taras came at me from behind, spun me to him, his hands gripping my throat. "How many manservants in the house?"

I tried to answer but his fingers choked off my air.

"I want you to leave the kitchen door unlocked tonight."

"No," I whispered.

"We'll never be free with those parasites in charge." He squeezed harder and the blood pounded in my head. "Tonight, leave the rear door unlocked and wave a white towel through the nursery window as a sign you've done it."

A jolt of fear ran through me. How did he know the estate layout? He'd most likely been all over the grounds in his mysterious way. I grew dizzy, my air cut off, and nodded.

Vladi stepped to us. "Taras. Stop."

Taras released me. "If you care about me, you'll do it."

I bent at the waist, sucking in air.

How could I care about a person like him? I rubbed my throat. Would Taras's fingers leave bruises the countess would see? Would he hurt Sofya? Surely, he would not hurt the child.

I walked on. "Stay in the woods tonight, Taras," I called over my shoulder. "Mamka can't eat when you're at home."

I turned, but they were gone.

CHAPTER
13

Sofya

1916

FATHER PACED THE ENTRYWAY, WAITING EACH DAY FOR his documents from the Ministry, which would allow us to leave Malinov. I tried to stay busy packing and sent more letters to Eliza and Afon by Father's Ministry mail pickup.

Father decided to hold his weekly choir practice as usual, to avoid arousing suspicion that we were leaving. He also planned a stop at the general store, since his shipment of fresh tobacco had failed to arrive and I was low on ink.

I loved the general store. Through the wide front windows of the tidy place one could see walls stacked with soap powder and stationery, anything one could need. Mr. Astronavich, whom we called Mr. A., was Father's only tenor, a burly, doughy-faced former ploughman in charge of the tobacco, pipes, and cigars. He would lift the little glass doors for Luba and me to breathe in the heavenly scents of tobaccos from places like Sumatra and Malawi.

Mrs. A., thin as Mr. A. was stout, managed stationery and sweets. Pads of paper stacked in neat blocks. Fountain pens and nibs. Caramels of every flavor sorted in her prized Venetian glass jars. India ink in blues and blacks and red.

I stepped up into the carriage holding a potted geranium, Mrs. A.'s favorite. Dressed in his best linen sailor shorts and top and Venetian straw hat, little Max stood on his knees next to Father ready to watch the woods for animals.

"May we bring a rabbit home?" he asked.

"They are very fast," Father said. "We'd have to shoot it."

Max gasped at that, causing Father to throw his head back and laugh. How rare that was in those days.

I could have left Max with the peasant girl Varinka we'd hired for extra help. She was nice enough and seemed more skilled at the day-to-day mothering than I was, but I took no chances. Agnessa planted doubt about her, harping at me to speak to the laundry about reassigning her there. It was hard not to look at our attendants and wonder of their loyalty.

Though it was a cool fall day, Father chose the open carriage and the coachman, David, set off with a great deal of shouting, standing dressed in his country uniform, a long coat and flat cap topped with a circle of peacock feathers. Come winter he would wear so many coats he would have to be lifted up onto his seat. Not that we would still be in Russia to see it. We would be long gone by winter.

Jarushka pulled us at a nice trot as we left Aleks and Ulad at attention at the gates and we soon came over a small rise to see the distant village of Malinov, the trees splashed with oranges and reds. From afar the village looked as it always had, but as we drew closer, Jarushka's hooves beating a rhythm on the hard-packed road, it was clear something was wrong.

Father and I exchanged worried looks as we passed the *izbas*, their window frames ornately carved with the most charming flowers and animals shuttered up tight. And where was everyone? Usually women were out chattering to one another, carrying flax to Father's linen factory.

We rode by the Malinov Inn. The little school. The music store. All closed.

We passed the bakery, the shop's front window smashed out. The baker's wife paced out front. Jarushka slowed and stopped in front of the general store. Next door, the barn where army provisions were stored, usually locked up, lay open, the door smashed in. Hay and

LOST ROSES • 133

empty wooden crates trailed out of the gaping doorway and a chalk-white milk block sat melting in the sawdust.

Father jumped out of the carriage and bounded up the steps. I followed, leading Max by the hand, to find Father speaking with Mr. A. as his wife tried to sweep up her broken candy jars in the dark store. The place had been ransacked, crates overturned, glass shards glittered across the place, all colors of ink splashed about the walls and floor. The tobacco cases stood empty, their glass cracked.

Mrs. A. spotted Father and hurried to him, bowing at the waist. "Excellency, we knew you'd come."

"Only God knows why they did this," Mr. A. said.

Mrs. A. stood, resting on her broom handle, her hair bun down one side of her head like a fried egg that had slipped off a plate. "Everyone is hungry, that's why. And the tsar expects us to give all we have to the army?"

A food riot! In our little Malinov.

I set my geranium on the desk and stepped to Mrs. A. "You've been through a serious trauma. You must sit."

"How can I sit with this place such a mess?"

I took the broom from her and swept glass shards into a pile. "How did it start?"

"They got the warehouse first," Mr. A. said. "Imperial stores for troop provisions."

"Who?"

"Villagers, mostly. And some others from the city."

"Did they take the flax?" Father asked.

"Everything, Excellency. Milk blocks. Hams. It was all in there. Then they came here. The baker was up early heating the ovens."

"Knocked him senseless," Mrs. A. said. "Took every loaf he had. Then Lucya Popov came in here with a few of her ladies. Said the price of our flour must be lowered by sixty kopecks. When I said 'I pay twice as much myself,' she grabbed a sack and shouted, 'Drag it off, girls!'"

"Then the others helped themselves to our tobacco," Mr. A. said. "Nicked the wife's chinchilla hat, too, bastards."

Mrs. A. pulled a biscuit from a yellow tin of Max's favorite McVitie & Price biscuits, then knelt and handed it to him.

Max grasped the biscuit.

"Say thank you," I said.

He brought the biscuit to his mouth, with no reply at all. Mrs. A. raised her eyebrows and I felt my cheeks burn. Why did he not listen to his own mother?

"How could villagers do this?" Father asked.

"Some of my best customers, but one fellow has them worked up," Mr. A. said. "A criminal sort named Vladi. New to town."

"What of the police?" I asked.

"Old Jaska stepped in, but they took his gun and beat him up, though not too bad."

Father waved toward the telephone on the counter. "I can call Petrograd."

"Lines are down."

Mr. A. handed Father a pouch of tobacco. "Here's the last of it."

Father nodded a little bow and slipped the pouch in his pocket. He didn't mention the price, for that would be very bad taste and Father never carried money of any kind.

"Any word about the linen factory?" he asked.

"Some are talking about leaving their stations," Mr. A. said.

"I've heard nothing of this from my foreman."

Mr. A. shrugged. "Vladi makes a good speech. Spoke of low wages. 'The factory should belong to the people.' 'Down with the tsar.' The usual."

"I pay a good wage. Someone's always trying to raise trouble."

"Pardon me, Excellency, but this feels different. We are barely growing enough food now to feed ourselves. Half the village has been conscripted. I may be next."

Mrs. A. came to stand near her husband. "And if the government doesn't stop just printing more money we'll all starve."

Father glanced my way. "I think I know how the Ministry works, thank you. Let's not scare the girl."

I kissed Mrs. A. on both cheeks. "You're not alone. We'll catch those who did this."

"Of course," Mr. A. said. "Uprisings come and go. You two should get home now or God will have no way of helping. Who knows when they'll come back?"

Father shook Mr. A.'s hand. "Put the tobacco on my account."

"That account is mounting up, Excellency," Mrs. A. said.

Mr. A. sent her a pointed look.

Father turned to her. "My man of affairs will see to it. God will get us through this."

Mrs. A. looked down at her ink-stained floor and shook her head as Mr. A. spread his arms wide and shepherded Father and me out the shop door.

Father and I took Max and checked on a shaken Father Paul at the rectory, who blessed us all, then we hurried back to the estate. There would be no choir practice that day.

BACK AT THE ESTATE I helped Cook harvest what was left of the fall vegetables in the garden plot at the far part of the estate property, near the poultry houses. We tugged dusky, purple beets and bouquets of pink radishes from the earth as the count's peacocks paraded about the lawn pecking at the ground for bugs and discharging an unnerving scream now and then.

Cook wore his usual gardening uniform: an old flannel shirt and khaki trousers. Taller than Afon and broader across the chest, his long hair tied back with a piece of twine, he looked good tanned from his outdoor work. The sun caught the diamond in his ring and sent a shower of prisms across the dark earth. Why wasn't he married? Bogdan had whispered he might not like women at all.

"Are you packed?"

"For days now. I'm headed out for a ride soon."

"We should be gone already." He stopped digging, rested one arm on his spade handle, and surveyed the woods. "I have a bad feeling, Sofya."

"Father told the count he can only bring two trunks. He may take all day, repacking."

"From my kitchen help I hear things. The pantry boys say there's talk of another revolution."

"The tsar—"

"The tsar's a fool. He's handing this country to the Reds. And this time they're organized. Targeting the peasants with radio broadcasts.

They can't read but they can listen. Posters with no words, to sway the illiterate. If Lenin comes back the first thing he'll do is ban the newspapers that oppose him, mark my words."

"We're leaving tomorrow, for goodness' sake."

"It may already be too late."

"If you stop making them that apple cake we'll be on our way. The count lives for it."

"There's a bad element here now. I don't like it. I would have left a long time ago."

"What is stopping you?"

"You're not safe here. If the documents come today we should go tonight."

"They wouldn't have threatened my mother if she were still here. She threw a party for the villagers every year on her name day in June. They all slept out here and she held a lottery for them, baked them special cakes herself."

Cook scanned the distant forest. "You don't understand, Sofya. No one is safe anymore."

LATE THAT AFTERNOON I rode off the property, my last ride with Jarushka for some time. I needed to get away from Agnessa so I could sit in a bower, think, and tend to last-minute details. She interrupted me so often, barking at the servants to pack with care and sew jewels into the linings of our traveling coats. I was assigned the emerald necklace Father had given our mother on their honeymoon. I felt the hem of my jacket, the platinum heavy there.

All day Agnessa had sat in the *zala* trying to calm the count, plying him with Father's best brandy.

The count swirled the brandy in his glass. "The Bolsheviks hate us. How many revolutions do we need to understand that? I hope you're taking all the silver. It may not be here when you get back."

"Bogdan will watch the house while we're gone," Agnessa said.

Settled on a mossy mound in the woods, I ate some brown bread and cheese Cook gave me for the ride, wrote a letter to Eliza, and pulled Afon's latest, most precious letter from my rucksack. Mail service was spotty and even Father's couriered Ministry packets had dwindled to one per week.

Even if your parents are reluctant, Afon wrote, *take Luba and Max away from Malinov immediately.*

Afon wrote that the fighting was intense, but the details were censored in black ink. How I hated those black streaks. We knew from the newspapers that the worst fighting was in Verdun, France, on the western front, at the crossroads of Belgium, Luxemburg, and Germany. Where was Afon's regiment? He hinted they were close to Poland.

I willed him far from Verdun.

On the ride back to the house, I bent low over Jarushka's neck, tearing through the brush. Cook's five o'clock dinner bell tolled in the distance proclaiming my tardiness.

Darkness descended as I rode, my jacket unbuttoned, the cool wind dancing around the inside of my linen shirt. As I neared the house Jarushka slowed, then startled and sidled. Something moved near the far barn, darkened figures. Surely, I was imagining things. Without Afon at home, how I jumped at every little thing.

As the lights of the house came into view I calmed. Agnessa and Father would be worried about me, but I was ready to go, my trunks already reduced to necessities only.

Dismounting in the barn, I hugged Jarushka about the neck and she nuzzled my side. It was the last time I would ride until she was sent along to meet us in Paris. I left her with her nose in a bucket of oats and stepped to the back door of the house, brushing dust from my jodhpurs as I walked.

I barely tapped the back door with my crop and Raisa unlocked it and bobbed a little curtsey.

I held out my hand and Raisa removed my one glove, then the other. "What a ride that was. Is Varinka here?"

"Yes." Raisa leaned close and whispered. "And your father asked me three times where you were. I told him out for a walk, may God bless me." She crossed herself.

I hurried on toward the dining room and passed Cook, hands on hips, hair slicked back, his blue eyes deep with concern. His apron wore a world map of that night's dinner—a goose-greasy blotch of Africa, a raspberry compote North America, Europe a chocolate smear.

"Where have you been, Sofya? Your Father has been asking for you."

"*Quiet,*" I said as I passed. "Agnessa will hear."

"We're leaving tonight, no time for a proper dinner. The travel papers came. I packed you some flower seeds for the trip."

As he leaned close and handed me the little packet, I caught the scent of his French cologne mixed with the incense of turned soil.

"I took the hulls off," he said.

I hurried into the dining room to find Agnessa, Luba, Father, and the count, all dressed in traveling clothes, except for Agnessa who wore a beige lace dress, her idea of casual wear. They sat around the table, finishing a simple meal of breads and cheeses. A map lay extended among it all.

They all rushed to me.

"I thought you'd been kidnapped," Agnessa said.

"We leave tonight," Father said.

"Cook told me."

Luba stepped to my side, finishing the last of a buttered roll. "We only have room for two of the count's trunks."

"And what of my peacocks?" the count asked.

Father folded a map and tucked it in his breast pocket. "We'll ride second class from Petrograd to Paris and send for our heavier things."

The count dropped a sugar lump in his glass of tea. "Bedding down with every thief in Russia?"

"Second class will attract less attention," Father said.

"Let's not rouse suspicion by seeming *too* poor," Agnessa said. "I can't wait to see Paris, but it's outrageous we of all people should be forced to leave. Don't we treat our servants well, spread benefits to the miserable?"

Luba licked her finger. "Perhaps the miserable don't like being called that, Agnessa. And they have no opera at which to wear your cast-off gowns. They cut them up for household rags."

"French velvet is very durable."

Cook, dressed in a handsome brown traveling coat, rushed in and stepped to Father. "Ready?"

Father slipped his watch from his vest pocket. "As soon as we load the count's trunks we will be off."

All at once, a great commotion rang from the hallway, the sickening crunch of broken wood and brutish male voices.

Agnessa reached for Father. "My God, Ivan."

I pulled Luba close, her heart thumping against my chest, and time stood still as our world came crashing down.

Eliza

1916

CAROLINE RETURNED TO THE APARTMENT FOUR DAYS
after Henry died, the cold, rainy night of his burial, and sat alone in her
bedroom, refusing dinner. Pale and somber, she brought to mind an
egg with the contents blown out.

Peg placed the mourning wreath on our door, proof the dread visitor had borne away another prize. The seamstress so bent on sewing
our voyage ensembles sewed Caroline and me mourning frocks, four
of mine, almost identical, made of dull, black twilled silk bombazine
with stiff, black crape trim that scratched my wrists and throat, my
penance for not saving Henry.

Mother came to my bedroom one morning and left on my bedside
table the locket she'd always worn in memory of Father, his miniature
likeness pressed inside under glass. I stared at it there, the oval, gold
case inset with a jeweled spider. A fat old mine diamond made up the
spider's abdomen, his head and thorax rubies. It had been her mother's,
my grandmother Jane Eliza Woolsey's, which she had worn after her
husband had died at sea. Were we Woolsey women cursed to live in
heartbreak?

"The best cure for grief is to throw yourself into charity work like
a maiden into a volcano," Mother said.

"Not now, Mother," I said and pulled the quilt to my chin.

Numb with grief, it took me hours to complete the simplest task, but with manicure scissors I cut Henry's picture, the size of my thumbnail, from a wedding photo. I opened the gold locket and slid it under the glass opposite Father. Both men smiled up at me.

How could you both leave me? I slipped the chain over my head and it weighed heavy on my neck and chest.

I sorted through the condolence letters and pulled an envelope written in Sofya's hand from the pile. I sat for a moment soaking it in, the stamps double-ring-cancelled in Cyrillic letters, her lovely upright script, though it looked more rushed than usual. What a comfort it was that we wrote each other every single day without fail, the next best thing to having her with me, and it let me know she was safe for the moment.

I ran my fingers under the envelope flap and unfolded two sheets of creamy white stationery, with *Malen Koye Nebo,* "Little Heaven," engraved in black type at the top. Just seeing her handwriting sent a pang of longing for my dear friend. What a comfort she would be, here with me, to talk about Henry and that terrible day. How strange she didn't even know he'd died. I had written her about it. Were my letters still being received?

Dear Eliza,

I hope you are well. It seems like just last week we stood on your terrace in Southampton. We received your books, thank you. I've always wanted to read *Five Weeks in a Balloon* and Luba is over the moon, for she loves Jules Verne and is quite curious about Africa. I will tell you the day we start so we can all read together.

As you so aptly predicted, the situation deteriorates here, I'm afraid, with the working classes in an ever-worsening state of discontent, distracted by war for now but for how long? Germany is a most determined foe. Father grows more concerned about the mounting Bolshevik movement and the growing number of attacks on estates by bandits, and we are packing for a move. With Afon off with his regiment, we are increasingly vulnerable and Father has arranged for our departure via train.

I will send a telegram and write with more details immediately upon our arrival.

A kiss to your charming Henry, and one to Caroline, too.

Do say a prayer or two for us.

> Your most loving
> and devoted friend,
> Sofya

My whole body grew cold as I reread the letter. *The growing number of attacks on estates by bandits?* Why had I not followed through and sent Sofya my travel agent's name as I'd promised? They could have been safe here with me this very moment.

I ran through the names of Mother's friends at the State Department. Could one of them help the Streshnayvas? Ensure safe travel out of Russia? I pocketed her letter and stepped into Caroline's room.

I held on to one post of the canopy bed, and fought back tears at the sight of Peg, her dark hair piled up on her head, helping my daughter step into a mourning dress of her own. Since Caroline was only thirteen years old, not yet fourteen, the age at which children were sentenced to wear black, she wore a frock of dull, white linen, with an oversized, black crape sash as an awful reminder her father was gone.

Caroline's gaze came to me as I entered, a lilac crescent under each eye. "It's not fair that you have to wear heavy black when I wear white, Mother."

Why could I not embrace her, wash away her pain?

"White's a symbol of hope," Peg said, through the pins in her mouth.

While Peg had only a vague idea of how to mop a floor, she possessed an encyclopedic knowledge of mourning practices.

"I've baked the mourning biscuits, Mrs. Ferriday," Peg said, eyes on her work. She nodded to the morbid little ovals, which sat in a bowl on Caroline's desk, each wrapped in wax paper, with a black wax seal affixed.

"And I've covered the mirrors in crape." Peg wore a black dress, which I assumed got regular use since she spoke of funerals she'd attended as some speak of their favorite plays.

Caroline waved her hand in front of her face. "The crape smells terrible."

Made with a host of harmful chemicals, the fabric was unhealthy, but was the requisite item worn to show proper mourning. Clearly the deceased's family was obligated to risk their own health after their loved one died.

"No need to cover our mirrors, Peg."

"You don't want the spirits seeing themselves."

I was too tired to fight. Was it Dr. Forbes's pills?

"And please stop turning the pictures over." I returned every photo upright, only to find them turned over once more, all part of Peg's bereavement protocol, since she felt departed spirits would invade the photos.

"Yes, ma'am."

Thunder rumbled above us and shook the china dogs on Caroline's shelf. Peg stepped to the window, drew back the white-dotted Swiss curtain. "That thunder means Mr. Ferriday reached heaven—"

Caroline turned her face to me, eyes bright with tears.

"—and may come back tonight for a visit."

"That's enough, Peg."

"But, my uncle Pat—"

"I don't care about your uncle Pat, you are scaring my daughter and I want you to stop with this. The pictures and the predictions—"

Peg bowed her head and dabbed at her eyes with her black-trimmed handkerchief.

"Ridiculous Irish voodoo. Mr. Ferriday is dead and he's not coming back."

Peg wrapped her arms around Caroline and the two stood crying as one, black and white together. How had I been reduced to scolding poor Peg, grieving herself for Henry? A hot word had been almost unknown in our house.

I wrapped my arms around them both and felt their sobs in great heaving breaths against me.

How would we get through it all without him?

CHAPTER
15

Varinka

1916

I APPROACHED THE ESTATE GATES AND A CHILL WENT clean through me, as it always did, to see those sharp, black spikes atop there. Such a scary-looking fence for such a pretty house. Eager to get to work, I hurried by the guardhouse and Ulad and Aleks waved to me.

"You get prettier every day, Miss Varinka," the younger, Ulad, said.

"I seem to remember it's someone's name day," Aleks said.

"I'll bring you both some cake," I said, barely looking at him, and hurried by.

It was growing dark by the time I made it to the estate and climbed the back steps to the rear entrance. I knocked, listened for Raisa, no longer able to see through the pebbled glass, for old Bogdan had boarded up the glass of the doors.

A key scraped in the lock and the door swung wide to reveal Raisa.

"Come in quickly," she said, moving aside.

I stepped into the back hallway and breathed in the scent of vanilla cake.

"So, it's your special day?" Raisa asked as she closed the door behind me and locked it. "There's a surprise for you."

From the kitchen came the usual clank of cast iron against the porcelain sink, Cook shouting orders, the scent of fatty goose. Maybe I could live there one day and share the oak table downstairs in the servants' dining room. Sofya was close to offering it, I could tell.

"But go upstairs to work now," Raisa said.

I climbed the back stairs to the nursery, my fingers caressing the orange in my pocket. Mamka would love such a treasure. We would open it together.

I stepped into the nursery, once a rather plain room furnished only with a fancy bassinet and a white slatted crib. Sofya made it much more comfortable once Afon left. She'd moved a cot and some of her clothes into the room. I lifted one pillow and held it to my nose. She didn't allow the maids to launder her bed linens because they still smelled of him. Of palaces and hair pomade and love.

In the corner, a trunk stood open, hung with racks of small clothes. This was new. I had overheard Raisa say the family was leaving soon for Paris, but why had Sofya not told me? I clutched the crib rail, light-headed. Would I never see Max again?

I moved to the fireplace, tossed a birch log onto the grate, and put a match to it. Once the log caught, I wiped every bit of soot from my hands on a white towel.

I stepped to Max's crib, picked him up and he clung to me. "*Face hibou,* Inka!" he said, and I made one of my silliest wide-eyed owl faces. He shook with laughter.

What a good boy. I slipped him my special remedies, designed to induce love in a person, just small tastes when no one was about. They seemed to have done their job. What was the harm in this?

With his blond curls, I could pass for his mother, couldn't I? I brushed Max's soft cheek with my lips and he smiled up at me. Taras and I would never have a baby, so what was the harm in pretending Max was mine? Sofya had everything and all I wanted was him.

If only Mamka could see his little smile.

All at once a heavy gray smoke billowed out from the fireplace. I stepped toward it, waving it away with my hand.

How had I not seen it smoking so?

I opened the nursery window, grabbed the white towel, and swung it back and forth over my head to dispel the smoke.

Suddenly I heard shouting below us and the sound of footsteps on the back hallway floor.

My gut lurched. What had I done? The signal.

I froze in place.

Taras.

Sofya

1916

LUBA AND I CLUTCHED EACH OTHER, THERE IN THE dining room. Why could I not move? The bandits shouted orders to the servants and the sound of gunshots came from the direction of the back entryway. Who are these intruders? Would they attack my family? My *son*.

"*Max*—I must go—"

Luba whispered in my ear, "Quiet."

Father ran to Agnessa and stood between her and the door.

The bandits wasted no time making their way toward us in the dining room. It was all men, it seemed, from the sound of their voices.

"God help us," Agnessa said.

I could not think, the blood pounded in my head so.

All at once the dining room door burst open. "What is—" Father shouted.

A squat man entered, wearing a two-sizes-too-small, grimy kangaroo fur coat and a lady's chinchilla hat, in one hand a revolver, which he seemed quite comfortable with, and in the other, a white pillowcase.

"Welcome to a new world," he said.

He had the voice of a peasant but was supremely confident.

Another man entered after him, much taller and dark-haired. He wore a dirty lynx coat and held a length of coiled rope.

"On whose authority do you just come into a private home?" Agnessa asked.

I held Luba closer.

"Tie them up," said the one in the chinchilla hat. And then, to Agnessa, "If you don't shut up I'll cut out your tongue and serve it to you there on your plate."

I could barely tear my gaze from the shiny, scarred side of his face, partly grown over by his untidy beard. I'd seen him before.

I barely breathed. Was Varinka still with my son? And then all at once it came to me. The bandit from the tram. Would he recognize me?

"Guards!" Father called.

The men laughed.

"The guards will be going nowhere I'm afraid," the burned one said. "A bit under the weather."

The tall one stepped with his rope to Father and pulled his arms behind his back. Father struggled at first, then after one blow to the face, no longer resisted.

Count von Orloff piped up. "Please. I have money. I'm a great *fan* of the Bolsheviks. I have a whole warehouse full of vodka—"

The burned one pushed the count down onto a chair, his gun trained on Cook. "Empty those pockets. Slowly, now."

Cook pulled a silver cigarette case from one pocket and a money clip from the other.

The short bandit yanked the bills from the money clip and a photo fell from among the ruble notes.

"Oh, sweethearts?" the bandit said as he retrieved the photo and held it up to compare with my face.

Cook carried a photo of me?

My cheeks burned and Cook's gaze met mine with a silent apology, as the tall one finished tying his hands behind his back.

The tall one came to me next. I tried to run, but he grabbed me by the wrists and bound me tight, as a hunter binds a deer.

The burned one grabbed Luba next but she fought like a cat as he tied her hands.

"You won't get away with this," she said.

He slapped Luba hard across the face.

Father stood, hands bound. "For God's sake, she's just a *child*."

Luba persisted, her cheek crimson. "The Ministry will come—"

The burned one stuffed a napkin in Luba's mouth, pushed Father back into his seat, and then tied up the count last. As they shoved us out of the dining room, my knees felt about to give out. Where were they taking us?

We passed the kitchen, now silent, my whole body moving strangely slow and dull, thoughts tangled. Was that Max crying upstairs? How to reach him?

As we passed the back stairway, I turned, started up the stairs, and said in most basic Russian, "I need to get my coat. It's upstairs."

The bandit waved his gun toward the door. "Move along, all of you."

I continued up the stairs. "It has money in the pockets I can give you."

He pushed me along.

I bowed low to the ground. "Please, generous Father. I promise I will come right back."

He raised his gun and shot into the ceiling, which caused us all to jump and sent my heart racing. The plaster showered down on us in chunks.

He yanked me to standing, and set his face close to mine. "I said, move along."

Tears pooled in my eyes as he herded us out into the rear yard through the cold darkness toward the barn in the distance. It *was* Max crying upstairs, louder now. I pressed my arms across my belly, dizzy from the pain of not being able to go to him, and gulped the night air to calm myself. What if I just ran back to find him?

Being shot would not help my boy.

I turned and looked back at the house and choked back a cry. Up on the second floor, the nursery window stood, a dead, dark hole, lights extinguished except for the silver pinpricks of light shining on the ceiling—Luba's stars.

CHAPTER
17

Varinka

1916

I STOOD IN THE NURSERY WITH LITTLE MAX IN MY ARMS as gunshots erupted downstairs. A quake of fear ran through us both. This was Taras and his friends forcing their way into the estate? Max cried and I shut the light in the nursery and held him close, his body warm against mine. What to do? Run to Taras and stop him? He wouldn't listen. I might get shot and who would tend the baby?

Soon I heard heavy footsteps in the back hall and Vladi's voice, barking orders, drifted up. "Move along, all of you." A bullet shot up through the floor and tore clear through the ceiling. I cried out and little Max shrieked louder as plaster rained down on us.

"Hush," I told him, his little body wracked with sobs.

I pushed back the nursery window curtain and watched a line of people, with hands bound behind their backs, head out toward the fountain in the courtyard. Where were they taking them? I had to get home, but how? Raisa always lit me a kerosene rag–wrapped torch to light my way and fend off wolves. How would I make it in the dark?

The child calmed as I took his blanket and stepped down the back stairway and out the door. I wrapped his blanket about him against the cold air as the moon ducked in and out of clouds while I walked, guiding us down the road toward the gate.

I squinted at the gates in the darkness, the black spears shining in the moonlight and my foot hit something soft, yet heavy. The moon came out from behind a cloud and revealed the two guards on the ground. I gasped and bent to Ulad.

He lay on his back, a deep slash at his throat and a halo of seeped blood on the ground behind his head. Vladi's work, no doubt. I shook with fear and with anger, too, at Taras. Why had he ruined my good fortune? I fought the urge to retch, held the baby tighter, and hurried to the entrance of my shortcut trail.

Would wolves come to the scent of Alex's and Ulad's blood? The owls called when they spotted wolves on the forest floor. I clenched my teeth and willed Max not to cry. I would protect the child with my life, stand tall to intimidate a bear or climb a tree if I had to.

Less than a verst away, an owl called out and I picked up my pace. The moon disappeared behind a cloud, leaving me in inky darkness. *Please, Papa, not now.*

An owl called again, this time closer. I held Max to my chest as I ran.

I relaxed my jaw when I saw the candle in the window of our house and the blood tingled in my arms. In the house, I found Mamka sitting in a chair by the window, a shawl over her shoulders, the candle illuminating her tarot cards, laid out on the table, her dark eyes reflecting the candle flame. She looked at me with no expression, as if she expected to see me step into our house with a baby in my arms.

"What an ugly baby," she said.

Of course, this was what we all are careful to say when we see a baby for the first time, so as not to bring bad luck.

I stood for a moment, not sure what to say. "It's the gamekeeper's son. He needs taking care of tonight."

Mamka stared at me, unblinking.

"Just one night. He is a good sleeper." Why could I not stop talking?

"The truth," Mamka said.

"I swear it."

Mamka reached across her table, picked up a card and held it up. The Fool card, a gentleman carrying a pack on a stick, one foot over a precipice. Her liar's card.

Why was she so insistent? Max was a good thing. A gift from Papa.

"Well, yes. He belongs to the Streshnayva family. Something terrible has happened at the estate."

"Taras?"

"Yes." All at once my throat closed off and I tried to keep the shake from my voice. "He and his friends broke in."

"We must leave."

"Yes." But to where? I placed the baby in her arms and Mamka smiled for the first time in so long as she looked down at him. She stroked one finger under his chin and he returned that smile. I ran about gathering clothes and food for a journey: some dried groats, another orange I'd found, and stuffed them into a rucksack. "We will go to Petrograd. Someone will help us." How wonderful it would be to finally escape Taras.

Mamka looked up at me, her eyes wide.

"He's a good baby, is he not?" I asked.

Mamka nodded, her face serious in the candlelight. "The mother?"

"I don't know what happened to her." I stuffed Mamka's nightie into the bag. "That doesn't matter right now."

Mamka kept her gaze on my face.

Prickles rose on the back of my neck. "*Stop*, Mamka. There's nothing to be done to find the mother right now, so just let me pack."

Mamka clutched her shawl closer as the sound of thudding horses' hooves came at the front door.

Taras?

I ran to snatch the rucksack from the bed but stopped as the door was flung wide and Taras strode in, wearing a lynx coat, a pistol in one hand, in the other a pillowcase bulging with boxes, their sharp elbows poking against the linen.

He closed the door behind him and glanced at the rucksack on the bed. "Going somewhere?" he asked softly.

"Of course not."

In Mamka's arms little Max stirred and cooed.

Taras set his bundle down on the foot of the bed and directed his pistol toward the baby. "What's that?"

"It's the gamekeeper's child." The heat rose in my cheeks. Could Taras see it in the dim light? "Put the gun down, Taras."

He ran his fingers through his long hair. "Where did it come from?"

Mamka held the boy tighter.

I stepped closer to Taras and touched his sleeve. "What happened to the family?"

"We just wanted money, but Vladi got carried away. It will all be fine, though."

"They've been kind—"

"You need to help *me*, now, Inka. Vladi is coming to stay here tonight—late, after our meeting—to make sure you are safe while I guard the prisoners."

"We don't need his protection."

Taras pulled me closer and smiled. "Things are different now, but I'm not taking any chances. At least we'll have all the food we need."

Little Max cried and reached for me.

Taras pointed his gun toward the child. "That will not be staying. I don't care where you have to take it."

Mamka wrapped Max tighter in his blanket.

I held out the fruit to Taras. "Look—I've brought you an *orange*."

He waved it away and walked to the door. "I'm leaving." He stopped and turned. "And if you don't get rid of that child, Inka, believe me, I will."

Eliza

1916

ONE MONDAY SOFYA'S LETTERS JUST STOPPED COMING, adding an eerie emptiness to our post box. After several days of fretting and speculation I visited Mother's friend Eliot Blandmore at the New York Bureau of Immigration. She'd met him at a Southampton painting class and arranged a meeting at his office in the newly built, forty-story Equitable Building in lower Manhattan.

I found his office, a typical gray cube, every inch of it stuffed with people, all waiting in a pungent, cheese-scented haze of cigarette smoke. I pushed into the crowd, through heated Italian and German conversations, sidestepping a family picnicking on the floor and over-stuffed valises brimming with worldly possessions.

I made it to a man who sat behind a desk, deep in conversation with an elderly gentleman in a baggy tweed jacket, who turned his cap in his hands.

"I don't know where your bird is, Mr. Pirelli. Two doors down you'll find animal control."

Mr. Pirelli moved on.

"Mr. Blandmore? I am Eliza Ferriday. You're expecting me?"

He stood and offered his hand, a lanky man with an Adam's apple the size of a golf ball.

"Haven't much time, I'm afraid." He shuffled through some papers on his desk. "We're short-staffed and half the world wants into America's golden doors. The unfortunate half."

"My friend, Sofya Streshnayva, from Petrograd, I haven't heard from her. No letter in a week."

"A *week*, Mrs. Ferriday? Come back in a month. We attend to serious cases here."

"I understand, Mr. Blandmore, but Sofya writes every day."

"Ambassador Francis is barely able to get his own correspondence to us from Russia and says the tsar's on the ropes himself with the war going badly."

"Sofya told me there were bandits around her country estate. Could you help send an embassy message—"

"I'm sorry, I can't help you."

"Any bit of information would help me greatly."

"I see you're one of *those* women. Won't take no for an answer."

I stood straighter. "I am simply here on a mission of mercy for a dear friend, Mr. Blandmore. If you are implying entitlement—"

He dropped the papers onto his desk. "Yes, we *have* heard reports of Bolsheviks gaining traction in Russia and criminals under a red banner committing crimes and . . ."

"Please be frank, Mr. Blandmore."

"Well, the reports may not be one hundred percent accurate, but there have been mentions of criminal activity on some estates south of major cities."

"What kind of criminal activity?"

"I shouldn't have told you even that, Mrs. Ferriday. Just know we're watching it closely so our own borders are not infected with revolution. We're starting to see our first émigrés arrive from the fallout of it all. Whole bunch of them just made it through." He pulled a clipboard from under a pile and ran one finger down a list. "No Streshnayvas though."

"Where are they from in Russia?"

"Moscow mostly. But from all over Russia, and that's one big country. They've been left to me, I'm afraid, and I'm at my wits' end with what to do with them. All were rich." He leaned in. "Bet they practically lived on caviar. But they had to escape quickly, so no money, no passports. Better English than mine, but no skills. Mostly women and children."

"Can they sew?"

"Just fancy stuff, never used a machine, but they still may have to go to the mills. I'm not allowed to place children there, so the little ones may need to go to foster care."

"You can't take children from their mothers, Mr. Blandmore. Surely you can reach out to the Russian-American community here. . . ."

"Tried that, but most of the Russians already here are poor folks driven out by the tsar—told me they call these ladies 'White Russians' and I should let them starve since they supported that murderer."

"What about hotel jobs? Perhaps they could board there, too."

"I can't spend my day calling hotels. St. Luke's Hospital says they'll take them temporarily, but then they'll go to a lodging house down on Rivington Street."

"The *Bowery*, Mr. Blandmore? How could you?"

For misery, filth, and debauchery, the Lower East Side neighborhood had no equal.

"Look, Mrs. Ferriday, I didn't invite them here."

"May I speak to them?"

"You need to be a registered immigrant aid society."

"Well, Mr. Blandmore, that's just what I happen to be."

"Name?" He pulled a pad from his drawer.

"The, well . . . Central Committee . . . for . . ."

"Russian Relief?"

"That's it."

Mr. Blandmore wrote on his pad. "Surely it's American."

"Of course. The *American* Central Committee for Russian Relief. I like to call it ACCRR."

"Think twice before you go in there, Mrs. Ferriday. They're a needy bunch and there's more coming every day."

"Let me be the judge of that, Mr. Blandmore."

"Suit yourself. Consider yourself registered. Go talk all you want. Detention room seven, down that hall."

I made my way to number seven, an even smaller room, folding chairs lined up against the walls. I entered to find women sitting, several with children on their laps, a neat stack of valises in the corner. They stood as I came in. Even in their rumpled traveling clothes they were a refined group.

"Pleased to meet you all. I am Eliza Ferriday—I've come to offer help."

A woman with close-cropped light hair and aquamarine eyes stepped forward and held my hands in hers. "Thank you."

Another, holding a child on her hip, came closer. "We will work. Please don't let them take my girl."

"I'll do everything I can to help."

She handed me her sleepy baby and the child lay her head on my shoulder. So close to little Max's age.

I went from one woman to the next, murmuring gentle comforts as I hatched my plan, more than happy to throw myself into the volcano.

I SPENT HOURS SECURING positions for the White Russian women, happy to have a new mission. As I waited for their paperwork, Mother proposed a trip up to Bethlehem, Connecticut, to visit The Hay, thinking it would be good for Caroline. I dreaded the trip, knowing it would pour salt on the wound of losing Henry, but agreed to go. I braced for the worst, hoping it would heal the rift between my daughter and me.

The following Monday, sweet Thomas drove us five hours north of Manhattan to the old place. Mother and I sat in the backseat, Caroline and Betty Stockwell in the front, as he drove slowly along the town green.

Fall was in full color and the village of Bethlehem seemed frozen in time with its neat town green and the same sort of sensible, pre–Revolutionary War houses one sees in quaint New England towns.

"Nice town," Thomas said, a little too brightly. "All they need's a general store." Was he trying to smooth over the gaping hole of Henry's absence?

"One restaurant would be nice," I said.

The lonely hamlet made Southampton look like Indianapolis and it needed more than a general store. The only activity came from across the green at the old Bird Tavern. Carriages came and went from the dark, toaster-shaped inn, a vestige of colonial days, up on a grassy rise, a horseshoe toss from The Hay's front lawn.

"Any word from Sofya?" Mother asked.

"No. Something's terribly wrong, Mother."

"Perhaps the mail's been disrupted? There's a war on, not that this country recognizes it."

To our great distress, America was still officially neutral in the war, but the Battle of Verdun raged on, the line held valiantly by the French against the Germans.

"I'm out of my mind with worry, and here I am on a pleasant country trip."

"It is your obligation to your daughter, dear."

"Eliot wasn't much help but he introduced me to a group of lovely Russian women who've come here for asylum, suffered terrible things due to mob dissent. They left Russia with nothing."

"How many revolts have there been against the tsar? Perhaps this one will be his undoing."

"The women are all so like Sofya, Mother. Fine and gentle, many the wives of army officers. And the dearest children. I've decided to found a relief society to help them."

"Admirable, dear, but after Henry's . . . well . . . you need to rest. Focus on your daughter. She's in mourning, too, you know."

"If the women can be placed near hotels or restaurants they can be self-sufficient, earn their own living. The Grand Hotel near Julia's house in the Catskills would be the perfect place for as many as they'll take, and some with Julia, too, I hope. Could we employ a few up here?"

"This place may not even be habitable yet and we already have Peg and Thomas and six day maids."

"Perhaps we could host a few in Southampton?"

"You know how they are out there, Eliza, with their rules. Non-family visitors are limited. But we'll see. And I'm sure Sofya will send a telegram any day."

I reached into my skirt pocket, rubbed the little blue charm I kept there. *Please let it be soon.*

Betty turned to us from the front seat. "Telegram? My mother just sent one from their trip."

Though not as tall as Caroline, at fourteen years old Betty was already showing signs she would be a beauty and quite curvaceous. She wore a silver dress with a pink ribbon at the waist for our country trip, and her parents' footmen had piled more Goyard luggage into the boot of the car than Mother and I brought combined.

"How is your mother, Betty?" I asked.

"Well, thank you. She writes the longest letters. Says Palm Beach was blazing hot and she couldn't abide it there with Father playing golf in the raging sun each day. She told him she would not lay about in a bathing costume since there are enough alligators in Florida without her looking like one, too, and he said he rather likes alligators and she said the only good alligator is one found in the shape of an Italian-made purse—"

"Thank you, Betty dear," I said.

Caroline turned in her seat. "Mother, may Betty and I take supper in my bedroom?"

"I'm beginning to think you're avoiding me."

Caroline turned back around.

The two girls moved on to conversation with Thomas, and Mother leaned close and whispered, "You need to spend more time with Caroline, dear. Don't you feel the rift?"

"It will work itself out."

"Things of value seldom just work themselves *out*. You must put your shoulder to it. Henry would want you two to get on well. Plus, once I'm gone you'll only have each other."

I pushed the thought of Mother dying to a dark recess. "She avoids me. Just holes up with Betty or reads all day. Theater magazines, of course."

"Perhaps you avoid her, too. Don't you see, she is wounded, Eliza? You remind each other of Henry's—"

"She wants to become an actress just to anger me."

"Actresses will happen in the best regulated families, dear."

"And she's desperate to be a Trail Scout and tramp the woods."

"Girl Scout. And I think it's a good idea. I know you like to be in charge, but you can't control her every move."

How did Mother poke only the most exquisitely tender spots?

"Caroline needs to focus on school and college, Mother. Maybe study abroad and see the world."

"That's what you never got to do, but she's not you. Maybe she likes tramping the woods, and actresses today are well traveled. You could go with her on tour. Julia can cast her."

"Julia's a bad influence. Of course, Caroline prefers her to me. Barely talks to me, her own mother."

"Can't you see? Caroline isn't like you, dear. Acquiesce on something with Caroline and you'll see a change."

"I suppose, Mother."

"You asked my advice."

"I didn't, but—"

"She needs to be a *child*. Let her run free. Don't forget she is officially half owner of that old farm."

Thomas pulled the car through the opening in the stone wall to The Hay's gravel driveway and came to a stop at the side porch door. He helped us out and we stood looking up at the facade under gray skies. Any strength I'd gathered wilted as it all came rushing back. Henry's kiss in the barn. His love of that decrepit place. Terribly busy in the city, Henry had only done a few projects around the old place and in the weeks since his death, the house had fallen into deeper disrepair. The yellow paint peeled off the clapboard like giant pencil shavings and the lawn choked on its own crabgrass and dandelions.

"Is this the gardener's cottage?" Betty said.

"No, dear. It's the main house."

Hornets flew in and out of a dark gash under the eave overhead, the only signs of progress being made about the place. Where was Peg to greet us? She'd come up two days before and knew I expected three things from her upon my arrival: food on the table, fresh flowers, and a fresh cocktail, none of which were to be found.

We wandered to the back of the house, under the shade of a generous maple tree.

Caroline pointed across the meadow. "Oh, Mother, look. Father had the little house moved."

Mr. Gardener walked up the steep rise of lawn toward us. "Hello, ma'am. Misses. I mowed the hayfield, last time for the season. Got the remains of a great apple orchard out there. Some Sheep's Nose apples. Virginia Crabs. None better for pies. Great spot for a garden back here, too," he said with a rare smile. "Course this old maple would have to come down."

Caroline turned to me. "Oh please, Mother. I've always wanted a garden. With sweet musk roses and eglantine. I could look out my window every morning and see it."

I swatted away a tangled tornado of gnats hanging midair. "No tree shall be cut down, Mr. Gardener. I'll never take down what God has put here. We have bigger concerns inside the house, Lord knows."

Caroline and Betty ran off across the spiky, shorn hayfield toward the playhouse.

"No running," I called after them. "Dr. Forbes . . ."

Mother and I stepped inside the house to find a leak sprung from the faucet, gushing like a geyser. With scrub brushes strapped to her feet, Peg skated across the floor, working up a lather with the pooling water. Thomas stood leaning on the stove, in animated conversation with Peg, as he sprinkled soap powder on the floor. Half of the water ran off through the open floorboards to the cellar below.

"Oh, Peg, we must do something."

"Good to get this floor cleaned," she said.

"Call a plumber, for heaven's sake," Mother said.

"I did, ma'am. Called yesterday and no one's come."

Caroline came to the kitchen doorway, pressing one hand at her side. "You should see, Mother," she said, taking deep breaths.

"You were running—"

"Father had the little house moved and had someone make curtains for the windows and set it up with Shakespeare books."

How wonderful of Henry, ever thoughtful. A stab of longing shot through me. How tragic I could not bring him back for her; the one always able to fix everything suddenly could do nothing.

She held out one hand. "Come see."

I turned to the gushing sink. "Not right now, dear."

"At least come out to the hay barn. Father loved it so."

How could I tell her that was the last place I could visit, where Henry and I shared such tender moments? "Some other time, maybe."

Caroline stepped into the kitchen, a tremor in her voice. "You don't miss him at all."

"Don't cry, dear. And that's not true."

"You don't show it. Acting like all's well won't make it so. Betty says in Girl Scouts they talk about their—"

I wheeled to face her. "I don't want to hear another word about Girl Scouts."

"You don't let me do a thing I want to. If Father were here he'd be on my side. If I could, I'd live with Aunt Julia."

"Putting on plays and pretending you're accomplishing something worthwhile? Running around emoting all day, declaring your love to each other?"

"You might want to try it, Mother." Caroline rushed out of the kitchen, slammed the door behind her, and ran back out toward the playhouse.

I turned to find Peg frozen in place, soap bubbles rising around her, as Thomas clutched the soapbox to his chest.

Mother came to me and slid one arm across my shoulders. "Calm down, dear."

I shook off her arm.

Peg shuffled toward me on brushed feet. "It's just the grief talking. Children can't—"

"That's enough, Peg."

Suddenly it was all too much.

I turned to Thomas. "We will be going back to the city after all, Thomas. Right away."

"Yes, Mrs. Ferriday."

"And, Peg, have these windows shuttered up. We won't be coming back."

Sofya

1916

I DARED NOT CLOSE MY EYES THE NIGHT THE BANDITS locked us in the barn. Agnessa, Father, Luba, and I lay huddled, cold on the hay floor, and Cook kept watch near the door in case anyone returned unannounced.

They had shoved us in there for the night without a word of explanation, blankets, or food. The others somehow slept but I barely dozed, moonlight streaming through a high window, a jumble of questions in my head. Where was my son? Safe with Varinka? Guilt gnawed at me. I'd been out enjoying a good ride as outlaws surrounded our house, ready to attack my family.

Around midnight, male voices came from the courtyard, our captors, speaking too softly for me to hear what they said. I crawled to a crack in the barn siding and peeped at them standing there by the fountain, washing themselves.

Cook came to kneel by my side and looked through the crack. The scent of last night's dinner on him, of cinnamon and sage, made my stomach growl.

"Behold the new guardians of all Russia's culture and art," Cook whispered. "These are not run-of-the-mill Bolsheviks."

The tall one stripped off his shirt. A magnificent display of tattoos covered his powerful torso where winged angels carried a banner across his wide chest.

"Sailors?" I asked.

"Those are prison tattoos. The tall one is Taras, a woodsman Varinka knows. I think the other is named Vladi, a queer sort of bandit I've heard villagers talk about."

"I think I may have seen him in the city. He robbed the tram."

Taras turned and splashed water under his arms and onto his face. The moonlight hit his back, showing a blue Virgin Mary and child in the heavens.

"Prisoners made those tattoos? They're so elaborate."

"Some of our kitchen help have them, lesser versions. It is a sacred language of symbols that tells the story of a prisoner's life. The more tattoos, the more status."

Taras slid his shirt back on and the two wandered back toward the house together.

I turned from the crack in the wall and sat cross-legged next to Cook, his hair white in the moonlight, face in shadow. "How did this happen?" One tear fell onto the back of my hand in my lap. "I'm sorry to cry."

Cook wiped the tear off my hand with one finger. "Never apologize for feeling. That is what makes us Russian. Besides, crying only makes women more beautiful."

"I'm afraid for Max," I whispered.

He brushed his fingers along my chin. "We won't let anything happen to him."

"We should have left—"

Cook slid one arm around my waist and drew me to him. He hesitated a moment and then leaned in and his lips met mine. We lingered there and he kissed me harder, his mouth a lovely mélange of bread and tobacco and my own tears.

After some time, we pulled away from each other and I pressed the back of my hand against my lips. I seldom kissed Afon so vigorously.

I sat back, breath coming hard. "No one needs to know this happened."

Cook pulled farther away. "Of course."

What was his expression in the half darkness? A mixture of sadness and joy that stabbed at me.

What a wicked way to repay my good husband, at that moment probably risking his life in battle.

Cook returned to his place by the door. "Try to sleep, Sofya. We must keep our wits about us for tomorrow."

"If he lets us out, I can try and run," I said.

"Just distract him. I'll go for help."

...

CHAPTER
2 0

Varinka

1916

THE NEXT DAY I WOKE AT THE *IZBA* WITH TARAS'S WORDS
in my head: *Get rid of that child, Inka.* I would do no such thing, of
course. I would protect Max with my life.

I had slept the night with Mamka and Max, one eye open keeping
watch on Vladi asleep on a haystack in the corner.

I slipped from the warm bed, waking Mamka, who sat up and gathered sleepy Max closer, and stepped to watch Vladi as he slept. How
could a person become so cruel? Was he born that way, ripping his big
head through his mother, cursed at birth for killing her? Vladi would
do anything for Taras, their friendship forged by years of protecting
each other in prison.

Vladi slept with his face in the hay, the back of his balding head like
an abandoned robin's nest with a giant, fleshy egg in the center. He
turned onto his back, surprisingly innocent in sleep, the shiny scar on
his cheek facing up at me, the peaked shape of the iron's tip burned
there in his flesh.

How terrible to be burned on the face. At least that scar was better
than what Taras told me had been tattooed there. The image forced on
him in prison, the man's private parts tattooed in blue next to his mouth,
that terrible badge that told the world of his relationship with another
man.

Taras had started the fire so I heated water to make Max's favorite hot cereal while Taras chopped wood. Images of what I imagined the Streshnayvas were going through bubbled up in front of me. All of them bound and gagged. Had Taras and Vladi mistreated young Luba? The countess would not be enjoying her tea this morning.

I clanked the lid onto the pot.

Vladi roused, running his hand across the top of his fleshy egg. "Good morning."

"You should go sleep at the estate."

"Good to see you, too, Varinka." He stood and scratched his chest, suspenders looped down at his sides. As he lifted his arms to the roof and arched his back, his shirt lifted to reveal a blessedly quick view of his hairy belly. "I'm taking over the linen factory, you know."

"On whose orders?"

"*Orders?*" Vladi adjusted the red cloth tied about his upper sleeve. "This is all I need now."

"You know Mr. Streshnayva works for the Ministry. What if the tsar sends Cossacks?"

"How is anyone to know things are amiss? We're having the old man write letters to Petrograd as usual. Plus, the tsar's probably off sailing on the royal yacht. But if any of those imperial idiots send troops, we're ready to defend ourselves."

I poured the groats into the pot and watched them roil in the bubbling water. "What will happen to His Excellency and the Streshnayvas?"

Mamka turned to listen.

"Stop calling him that. That old pig means nothing now. They're just another group we need to eliminate."

Mamka sat up straighter in the bed. "They're good people."

"Good? Working their fellow Russians to death for low wages? We can only be free once all those *belaya kost* bloodlines are purged. White-boned, *ha*. They're already running like rats to Paris and Shanghai."

I tucked Max's blanket around him. "Just curious what's to become of them."

"They won't die, if that's what you're asking. Not right away anyway. Need the old man to tell us how to run the factory and to keep that

Ministry money coming. They'll stay in the barn closest to the house for now."

"You think you know it all, don't you?"

He ran a dirty finger down my hand. "One word from me and you'll be gutting fish in a work camp, so be nice to me, Inka."

He stepped closer, his cheek scar shining in the morning light. "Watch yourself, girl. Taras may throw you out and then you're left with me. There are worse things, you know." He pulled my hand to his crotch, the fabric hard and damp.

I snatched my hand away.

He glanced in Mamka's direction and kept his voice low. "And by the way, don't think I don't know about you and Taras. He told me all about your *arrangement*. . . ."

"*Quiet,* Vladi."

"I was surprised a nice girl like you would do that with him. Even dogs know better, don't you think? But I have to say I like the sound of it." His shiny red tongue darted to the side of his mouth. "I'll keep it to myself for now, but what would people think if they knew you two were—"

Max cried and startled us both. He sat up next to Mamka and took in his surroundings, his curls flattened down one side of his head from sleep.

Vladi stood. "Whose kid?"

I smoothed one hand down Max's cheek. "The gamekeeper's son."

"Gamekeeper was at least eighty years old with a pecker soft as those groats."

"His grandson maybe. Everything's in such a mess now over at the estate."

Vladi snapped his suspenders onto his shoulders. "You want freedom, you have to crack some eggs."

Taras rushed in the door, his linen shirt stuck to his chest with sweat. He grabbed his canvas bag and waved Vladi to him. "Hurry."

"Where are you going?" I asked.

Taras stopped at the door, turned, and fixed upon Max with a hard stare. "I meant what I said, Varinka. Get rid of the child or I will."

The two rushed out and Mamka and I stepped to the window and watched them ride off.

Mamka turned to me. "It's not safe here for the boy."

"Taras is all talk."

"He is unstable, Varinka, and when Vladi finds out who the child really is—"

I sat next to Max on the bed and smoothed one finger under his chin. "Who would touch a sweet child?"

Eliza

1916

SOON AFTER OUR DISASTROUS TRIP UP TO THE HAY, I visited Julia Marlowe and her husband E. H. Southern at their lovely home called Wildacres, in the better part of the Catskills. Still feeling Caroline's chill and barred from most public gatherings due to deep mourning, I was at my wits' end in the city and accepted the invitation at once. I'd already persuaded the Grand Hotel up in the Catskills near Julia to take six Russian women and hoped Julia would employ three more.

I rode the West Shore Railroad north along the Hudson River. Parties at Julia's Manhattan townhouse were always gay and brimming with exotic types. Would the country be equally festive? The gray hustle of the city gave way to unparalleled autumn scenery of the Hudson River Valley, the trees along the river splashed with scarlet and gold. Perhaps it was for the best that Caroline refused to come along. Maybe we needed time apart.

I unfolded *The New York Sun* from my bag and scanned the news. With the help of their new tanks the British had swept Germany, and German morale was flagging. Perhaps the war was turning in the Allies' favor? With any luck passenger ships would be sailing again soon and I could go abroad in search of Sofya.

Once I disembarked at Highmount Station, Julia's driver motored me up a steep mountain to a most attractive, grand cottage, painted top to toe in white. It was an extreme sort of bungalow, constructed half in wood, half in stone, with a pleasant confusion of roof lines and a spacious veranda facing a broad lawn. We pulled under the porte cochere and soon a multitude of servants emerged and pulled my luggage from the car.

Julia stepped down from the porch, arms outstretched. "Welcome, New Yorker!"

How wonderful it was to be embraced by her, all perfume and French silks, to be swept up in the arms that each night on Broadway welcomed throngs of theatergoers with ease. For once in so long, dark thoughts of Henry melted away.

"How are you today, darling?"

How good of Julia to add "today," making it easier somehow.

"It's a good day," I said.

Julia grabbed my hatbox from me. "We must hurry. We're planning a splendid dinner tonight with two other guests attending."

She led me through the living room, up the front stair, the stained-glass windows there ablaze in yellows and oranges. "I saved the best guest room for you, of course."

"I received a letter from Sofya—she said she feared they were in danger. And then no letters at all."

"I do hope she's gotten out, I've heard terrible stories."

"I've met some women, so like Sofya in every way. They had to flee hostilities there and left all their personal effects behind. Mother's friend at the Immigration Bureau says they need to move them to the Bowery if I can't place them soon."

"Not the Bowery, Eliza."

"Many with children. Forced to flee with only the clothes on their backs."

"They won't survive on the Lower East Side."

"Might you take a few here?"

"Of course, darling. Have them come at once."

Julia led me along the upstairs hall. "I can't wait to show you the house, Eliza. We entertain little up here, preferring the comparative solitude of the mountains, but we have a treat for you." She paused for dramatic effect. "Gareth Hapgood."

"Oh."

Gareth Hapgood needed no introduction, a household name to anyone at the time who followed Shakespearian theater. I'd never seen him perform but heard he kept a milk cow on his yacht.

"You're not happy."

"I'm not ready, Julia. Yesterday I forgot Henry was gone. Looked for him—"

"Gareth is just someone to chat with. He brought a friend who shall remain our mystery guest—all I can tell you is he's an early riser."

Julia famously eschewed morning people, perhaps from her years in theater. For her, breakfast started at the noon hour.

"I do think you'll like Gareth, such a dear man. *Quelle* handsome. He comes from Troy, New York, but don't worry, he seldom speaks of it."

We came to my room and Julia flung open the door. "*Voilà.*"

I followed her into a most charming guest room hung with Delft Blue wallpaper. The scent of anthracite, which lingered from the coal fires, lent a pleasant fireworks scent to the room. An enormous canopy bed stood against the far wall, but my favorite part was the wide porch, which I shared with the bedroom next door, accessed from my room by a handsome pair of wide French doors.

Julia took me by the hand out onto the porch.

"Oh, the view, Julia." I took in the long slope of lawn and the sweep of gentle mountains beyond, the upper elevations splashed with tangerine and vermillion. "It's like being in Switzerland."

Birds of all kinds sang in the trees and sailed and dipped in the sky above us. I turned my attention to the room next door, the draperies drawn back, a fire glowing in the fireplace. Which one of Julia's guests was my neighbor?

"I do love the fall up here." Julia linked an arm through mine. "Like my birds?"

"They're exquisite." Tears threatened and I felt for my handkerchief, my constant companion those days.

"Is the sadness any better, dear?"

"Some days. It helps to breathe mountain air, but I don't know if I'll ever be normal again."

"I know you're still in deep mourning, dear, so don't hate me for bringing it up, but you might want to start thinking about when you'll stop wearing your wedding ring. Might help you move on."

"So soon?" I clasped my right hand over my left. "It's all I have left of him."

Julia pointed to a brown bird circling above the treetops between the mountains and us. "That's an osprey, off to catch a fish in the river soon, no doubt. I could watch her all day."

I stemmed a wave of envy watching that bird. How good it must be to fly wherever one chose.

"See how she flies, and after the downward wing stroke, her wings pull up? That's called the recovery stroke. Isn't it lovely? That's all you need, Eliza. Time to take your recovery stroke."

Tears flooded my view, turning the trees on the mountain beyond to an orange blur.

Julia pulled me close and kissed my cheek. "Be patient, my darling. You really will feel better someday."

JULIA HURRIED OFF AND I dressed for dinner, changing from my traveling dress of black bombazine and crape to another, almost identical. How tired I was of black. Early Christians in the second century wore white in mourning. What misguided soul had turned society toward black?

I unpacked the room decorations I traveled with. Strung my length of tiny Tibetan prayer flags across the vanity mirror and flipped open the silver travel frame Father had given me so I could keep my loved ones close. Henry, Father, Mother, Caroline, Sofya, and little Max.

At least I wouldn't need the veil at dinner. I opened my locket and pressed my lips to Henry's picture. I caught my reflection in the window, lit by the fire, my skin so white against the black.

A widow.

The word pulled on me like a brick roped around my neck.

I stood taller, brushed lint from my skirt, and wrapped my Orenburg shawl about my shoulders. At least I was making headway placing the Russian women.

I stepped down the stairs and through the dining room, past Julia's massive birch Adirondack table set for five. In the center sat a silver bowl filled with autumn branches, the bowl large enough to bathe a baby. The table wore Julia's best silver brought up from their mansion at 377 Riverside Drive in Manhattan.

I followed voices out onto Julia's newly built, columned veranda, which ran along the front of the house to exploit the view. I stopped in the doorway and took in the group as Julia struck a theatrical pose and E.H. helped himself and a blond gentleman to drinks at a mirrored bar.

E.H. turned to me. "Oh, Eliza, you're here. Do come out. May I present Gareth Hapgood, direct from the stage in Philadelphia?"

Gareth stepped toward me at the doorway, chin held high, a frowsy, yellow chrysanthemum at his lapel. "*Enchanté*, Eliza," he said with a deep bow.

I extended my hand. "Lovely to meet you, Mr. Hapgood."

He took my hand and kissed it. "May I call you Eliza?"

Had he marinated himself in cologne?

"Julia's been telling us about your impressive family. To think you are descended from those fine Woolsey women."

"That's enough, Gareth," Julia said, handing him a glass of *Moët*.

"My deepest condolences about your husband. I myself have a lung condition. My doctor says the only form of exercise I may take is to be tossed gently in a blanket."

Gareth was clearly Julia's pick to replace Henry, but he was not my sort of man at all. While he no doubt cut a masculine enough figure onstage in his skirt of leather strips and plumed helmet, he couldn't hold a Roman scepter to my Henry.

Julia linked her arm in mine. "Let Eliza breathe a bit."

I felt a gaze upon me and turned.

"And please meet our mystery guest, dear Mr. Merrill. Gareth is his client."

Merrill took a step toward me, brow creased, amber liquid in his crystal tumbler. "Eliza. I had no idea you'd be here."

Merrill? I pulled at the collar of my dress. Could this dinner get any more uncomfortable? Perhaps the kaiser himself would like to join us?

"How nice to see you, Merrill."

Gareth stepped between us. "You two have met?" Something in his voice suggested jealousy.

Julia held my hand. "I thought it would be nice for you, dear; you and Merrill being old friends. You can never have too many handsome men at a dinner."

I looked to Julia. *Merrill?* And then instantly forgave her for inviting him. I'd never told her my objections.

I turned to Gareth. "My late husband, Henry, and Merrill were friends at St. Paul's."

Merrill sipped his drink, the ice cubes clacking. "I've known Eliza for quite some time."

Julia and I led the way to the dining room, a fire lit in the fireplace there, and I considered ways of falling and breaking an arm.

We took our seats.

"Not to brag, but I can identify any spice in a soup," Gareth said. "I've been educating my palate, as did the ancients. Did you know Roman epicures cultivated their tastes so perfectly they could tell me where in a river a fish was caught?"

"Oh, really?" I asked. *Is there anything more tedious than suffering a gourmand of brandy and plovers' eggs?*

"We'll have your favorite mincemeat pie, Gareth," Julia said.

Gareth smoothed his napkin onto his lap. "Europe laughs at our pies, you know."

"Europeans can be insensitive to others' feelings sometimes," I said.

Merrill finished his drink. "And you are sensitive to the feelings of others, Eliza? Some might say not."

That was all I needed: Merrill dredging old lakes in front of others.

I turned to Julia. "You have the most idyllic spot out here, darling."

"I much prefer the bustle of the city," Gareth said. "Have you been to Troy, New York, Eliza?"

"This is the perfect country retreat," Merrill said. "No need to board a ship."

Of course, he still hated to travel.

"Enjoy it," Julia said. "If there's a war, they'll call you young men up."

I sprinkled a pinch of salt on my soup. "Only a coward would wait to be called up. Good men enlist."

Gareth waved his spoon toward Merrill. "Merrill's new lady friend would most certainly not encourage him to enlist."

"Who's that?" E.H. asked.

Gareth touched his napkin to his lips. "Only *the* Anna Gabler."

"I know Anna," Julia said. "She's fresh off her success at the German Bazaar. Raised an obscene amount of money for German war relief."

"Every German in New York came out," Gareth said. "Opening night line was halfway around Madison Square Garden."

"I hear the shooting gallery was especially popular," I said. "Call me old-fashioned, but German Americans shooting effigies of French and Russian soldiers seems, well, unkind."

"Anna *who?*" asked E.H.

Gareth glanced at Merrill. "Gabler. A handsome woman of German extraction who has captured half of New York's bachelors in her thrall."

Julia leaned toward me and whispered, "As does the Indian cobra."

"Gareth, can you speak of nothing else?" Merrill asked.

Julia passed the breadbasket. "Beware the fortune hunter, Mr. Merrill. Women can be charmed by the silver music of the almighty dollar."

"No worry there," Gareth said with a little smile. "Her father owns Gabler Rubber. They're already in at the Meadow Club. Mr. Gabler is diversifying into oil and wants to bring Merrill on to his board, for his expertise in energy stocks."

Merrill tossed his napkin on the table.

"Oh, be a sport, Mr. Merrill," Julia said. "You mustn't deny us our fun."

Gareth leaned in, the spikes of his chrysanthemum almost grazing his soup. "Especially when there is sensational news to impart."

Merrill shifted in his chair. "Gareth—"

"Do spare us the suspense," Julia said.

"Well, as of yesterday evening, Mr. Merrill here is . . ." Gareth paused, lips pressed together.

"*Gareth*—" Julia said.

". . . officially engaged to Miss Anna Gabler."

"How wonderful," E.H. said and raised a glass.

"Is it?" Julia said under her breath to me.

Gareth drank to the good news and set down the glass. "The two plan to honeymoon on safari. At war's end, of course. Miss Gabler is quite a shot."

Though I'd never met her, a picture of Anna Gabler floated up in front of me, of her grinning, with one booted foot atop a dazed water buffalo. Was that a stab of jealousy, due to someone else planning a trip? We would all be free to travel once the war ended. No, it was more a vague sadness, for tears pricked at my eyes. Though I had no romantic interest in Merrill, perhaps I'd hoped he would pine for me indefinitely?

I held up my glass. "Here's to Merrill and Anna," I said with the brightest smile I could drum up, head high, careful not to let one tear breech those walls.

WE ALL RETIRED EARLY and I breathed a sigh upon closing the door to my room. Had Henry's death made me an old crab, unable to appreciate the kindness of a new acquaintance?

I left my dress and shawl on the chaise longue and slipped into my nightgown, which Julia's maid had laid out. The wind howled and rattled the windows so I slid the desk chair to the French doors and buttressed them closed. I turned down the kerosene lamp and slid between the duvet-topped cool sheets, the feather bed pillowing up, all fifty pounds of goose down surrounding me with warmth.

I listened to my neighbor making the usual bedtime noises, knocking about. It was Merrill, for I'd seen him enter his room when we all retired, no doubt fixing another drink. How irritating his behavior had been, bringing personal issues to the table.

Rain pelted the French doors as I fell off to sleep and reexamined the evening. While Gareth had displayed every kindness, Merrill remained aloof and focused on keeping his and E.H.'s brandy snifters filled. We could never be on friendly terms. He clearly harbored old grudges and how could I ever forgive him for running Henry to death? The more I considered the pair, he was a perfect match for a rich social climber like—

All at once a great crash came from the direction of the porch and I sat up in my bed, heart thumping. A cold gust had slammed the French doors open against the chair I had propped there, smashing out a windowpane. Rain flew into the room, soaking the rug.

I threw back the covers, ran to the doors, and forced one closed. I started to shut the other, but my old thumb injury barred me from applying enough pressure, and the wind pushed me back, my bare feet picking up shards of glass.

"My God, get back. What's wrong with you?" It was Merrill, arrived via our shared porch.

"I'm fine," I said, struggling with the door.

Merrill pushed me aside and closed the second door and stood, wet through, his back to the doors. He wore his white shirt from dinner with his tie undone and loose. The rain had drenched his hair, matting it down across his forehead.

I felt his eyes on me and remembered I was dressed only in my nightgown.

"Bring the fire screen," he said. "We'll push it up against the doors."

I stepped to the fire, picking up more glass shards in my feet as I walked. I grasped the screen in a hurry, knowing my nightgown showed my figure silhouetted against the fire's glow.

I handed Merrill the screen and he slid it under the door's knobs and then stepped to the chaise longue, grabbed my Orenburg shawl, and pushed it at me.

"Put that on."

"I could have handled this myself."

Merrill ran his fingers through his hair. "I should go. I'll use the hall door."

As he headed out I hobbled toward the love seat near the fire, the glass shards stabbing my feet.

Merrill stopped and turned. "You've stepped in glass, for God's sake. It's in your hair."

"I'm fine."

He hurried to the lavatory and returned with a towel and a basin. "Sit down." He stepped to the desk and threw open the drawers.

I sat and pulled my wrap tighter around me. "No need to be surly."

He returned, holding a sewing needle between thumb and forefinger. "In this country people say thank you."

"*Thank* you, but you could have left me to my own devices."

Merrill sat next to me on the love seat, wearing a rather worn look and a day's growth of beard on his face, both, of course, becoming on him. He lifted my foot upon his lap and examined it with all the concentration of a diamond cutter.

"Careful," I said. "You've been drinking."

"I didn't see you refusing the champagne."

He was right. And reclining there on the love seat, it was making me dizzy.

"But champagne is less lethal than brandy, certainly," I said.

"You live to argue."

"You've mistaken me for your fiancée."

He stopped his work and turned to me. "What's wrong with you, Eliza? Once, you were the model of kindness. But since Henry——"

"You really should lower your voice." What would Julia say finding us here? Gareth would certainly impale himself on his Roman sword.

"Suddenly, you can't even be civil. You're the one that wronged me, remember?"

How could I tell him I ached every day for the man he ran around the tennis courts so carelessly?

Merrill set the basin on my lap and went deep with his needle. I clenched my shawl to distract myself from the pain. "Let us just agree to live our lives."

The wind picked up, louder still, and whistled through the broken pane of glass, as he dropped each success into the metal basin with a little clink. It felt curiously good, that pain of the slivers sliding out. How serious he looked, checking my face now and then, his dark eyes catching the firelight.

"You're just angry I've moved on," he said. "Thought I'd pine for you forever."

"No." I tried to pull my foot away but he held it fast.

"That's it. You're regretting casting me aside so thoughtlessly—now that Henry's gone."

I set the basin aside and stood. "You should go—"

He pushed himself up off the love seat and turned to me. "How does it feel to be lonely, Eliza?"

He smelled of brandy and pipe tobacco and pine. How long had it been since I'd been that close to a man?

"No one asked you to come in here, Merrill."

"I'm sorry I did."

Was he sorry? He made no motion toward the door. How strange I wanted to lean in to Merrill. Feel his arms around me just for a moment. I swayed a bit, dizzy and hot near the fire. How disloyal that thought was to Henry.

"You should have left him home that night," I said.

Merrill leaned closer and pulled a glass shard from my hair. "You don't know the whole story." Was that shine in his eyes from tears? "Eliza. I never told you—"

A knock came at the door and Merrill and I hurried apart. Julia entered and Merrill stepped toward the door.

"What in heaven's name?" Julia asked.

I rushed to the wet part of the rug, my foot free of pain, the glass splinters gone. "The French doors blew open. Ruined the rug here, I'm afraid."

Julia followed me. "You poor dear. We'll move you down the hall this minute."

"I'm fine. Merrill came to the rescue. Pulled half a pane of glass out of my foot. Isn't that right, Merrill?"

I turned toward him, but found only the door closing behind him.

Sofya

1916

THE FOLLOWING AFTERNOON, AS A LIGHT RAIN FELL,
the barn door rolled open and the bandit Vladi appeared there.

"Get out here, pigs," he said. "It's your lucky day, for you won't be
dying, at least not today."

I helped Agnessa and Father to their feet. Father had spent the
morning in the house being interrogated by Taras and had just returned
with bruises on his face, telling us Taras had forced him to write to the
Ministry.

I prayed they would not find the rucksack Luba secreted under the
nursery floorboards.

Vladi waved his gun toward the barn door. "Line up outside. Let's
make this orderly, comrades."

He shoved us out into the courtyard and lined us up near the fountain, Cook at the end closest to the woods.

"If you haven't heard of me, I am Vladi, and I've come to liberate
this place." He cocked his gun. "Sorry to be distrustful but in case any
of you get any heroic ideas about escaping, remember I shoot to kill."

How to distract him? Perhaps he would engage in conversation?

"This is a great day," Vladi said, waving his gun toward the house.
"This estate now belongs to the people."

"So, you are the one all Malinov is talking about," I said.

He smiled, the burn on his face wrinkling. "The people need a leader." Vladi turned his face to one side, but kept his gaze on me. "I know you from somewhere."

How could he remember me from the tram, with all the Persian makeup I wore that night? "If we are all equal now, should we not be treated as any Russians, with a fair trial?"

Vladi stepped closer. "No trial for parasites. You must be cut at the root or the people will never be free."

A shiver ran through me. Did they know Max was my son? Would they kill a sweet child?

All at once Luba fell to the ground, clutching her belly. "The pain! Holy Fathers, it's back."

I knelt to her, almost believing it myself. "It's her appendix again."

Vladi watched her roll on the ground for a few moments. "She's fine."

I stepped to him. "We'll need the doctor."

"You'll heal on your own like the rest of us for a change."

"If she dies it's on your hands."

"You're all weak, you bourgeois. Get her up."

It wasn't until Luba stopped crying and I helped her stand that I realized Cook was gone. What a stealthy runner he'd been.

A few moments later Vladi called out. "Taras! One of them escaped."

Taras came at a run from the horse barn. "How?"

I turned and, deep in the forest, saw the brown of Cook's jacket blending with the dense trees and thick underbrush.

Taras ran into the barn for his rifle and shot into the woods. The burst of the shell echoed through the forest and sent a shudder through us all.

I held Luba. Had Cook fallen?

"You got him," Vladi said.

Luba took my hand. The horror of it, poor Cook shot.

"Just a wound." Taras mounted his horse and rode off down the road at great speed.

I prayed Cook would evade Taras and come back with imperial guards and defeat these thieves. Or else I would break out of that place myself.

Nothing would keep me from my son.

Part Three

Part
Three

KRISTIN HANNAH

CHAPTER
23

Sofya

1917

BY WINTER'S END THE MOB OF VILLAGERS WHO'D TAKEN the estate gathered out by the poultry houses and roasted and ate the peacocks. They captured the screaming birds, built a fire, and soon the scent of roasting bird wafted to us. Our stomachs growled at the smell of it as the villagers, some waving peacock feathers, vodka bottles in hand, shouted up threats to us until they wandered back to the house. I was sad for the poor birds, but happy for the blessed quiet.

After a long winter in captivity, spring finally dragged herself to Malinov. Once, spring held the promise of Easter celebrations and coming summer, but that year it held only another day of hoping Vladi didn't kill Father.

The morning things finally changed, we waited for Father in the room Vladi had moved us to, Bogdan's old room over the former servants' quarters, out near the horse barn. It contained one saggy cot and a cast-iron woodstove, which smoked badly; and there was an opening in the roof the size of a dinner plate, which leaked rain and sleet on us. Vladi had given us strict orders not to make a sound up there and nailed our one window shut, though Luba had pried it open.

On the walls hung framed photos of old Bogdan, standing, rifle in hand, next to a mound of dead birds, a sad reminder of our beloved gamekeeper whom Vladi often bragged about murdering the night we were attacked.

I paced the room as Luba sat next to Agnessa on the cot and rubbed her back. Tum-Tum lay curled near his mistress, a pitiful little sack of bones, ever faithful. How far poor Agnessa had fallen. Before we'd ended up here she'd never once laced her own shoes nor wore the same pair of white cotton gloves twice. Now it took all of us to help her to the filthy chamber pot.

The count slept in his usual spot on the floor near the stove, not well himself. He rarely spoke, a sharp contrast to his old self.

Would Father again come back bloodied and bruised? Vladi had kept him all night.

It had been a terrible winter, filled with constant snowfall, which often covered our one window. It was hard to know what was worse: the fear, the boredom, or the crushing longing for my son and husband.

Half the village of Malinov had moved into the estate, and Varinka, her mamka, and Taras were clearly living there as well, for we saw them from our window; and Luba had seen the briefest glimpse of Max. Did he wonder where his mother had gone? Did Afon know our fate? Why had he not sent help? All winter Luba and I had watched the door for our chance to escape and felt a glimmer of hope, for Vladi's vigilant ways had relaxed as time went on, as if he'd tired of dealing with us.

We fretted about Cook, too. Had Taras killed him?

All at once, the door banged open and Vladi pushed Father into the room.

"Shut *up*, old man. If we don't get replies from those letters soon, I have no reason to keep you all around."

Father fell onto the floor and Vladi closed the door and bolted it.

Luba and I rushed to Father and helped him to the cot. Dried blood splotched the front of his white shirt, the edges of his cuffs and collar black. How could I even look at his face, his cheek swollen and another tooth missing, his glasses cracked?

"Did they have you write more letters?" I asked.

Father massaged his knee, lost in thought. "Yes, but the Ministry no longer answers."

"Have they smelled foul play?" I asked.

Father removed his spectacles with a shaking hand. "Difficult to say. God only knows what's going on in the city."

I hurried to the window to retrieve the wet piece of Agnessa's underskirt we kept there frozen, brought it back, and held it cold to his cheek.

"Any sign of Max?" I asked.

Father looked up at me, water welling in his eyes. "No, my dear. There are many people living there in the house now. Thank the Holy Fathers your mother can't see it like this."

Luba loosened Father's collar. "They can't hold us here forever."

My sister had been our rock, more convinced every day that the Ministry would see through Vladi's scheme. His was a brilliant if devious one: First he had Father write the Ministry saying he no longer needed the travel documents, then had Father pen his usual monthly letters pretending all was well, to keep money coming. It had worked for almost seven months.

Father turned his attention to Agnessa and smoothed the hair back from her forehead. She wore the same beige lace dress she wore the night of our capture, now dirty and gray, loose all over, for as hope faded, she'd stopped eating. I touched her back, careful not to wake her, and felt the bones of her rib cage.

Still breathing.

Luba sat on the cot next to Agnessa and I joined her. "I want to fill you in on the progress of my project."

My sister had grown so thin herself, giving half of her bread to Father when I wasn't looking, claiming she was full.

How many escape plans had she been through? Start a fire as a diversion. Code Father's letters. Hunger strike. "They say one has to come up with at least fifty ideas before you get to the best ones," she said. "And this is number fifty."

But this time it was a more practical plan. All month, she'd been collecting lengths of material to make a rope we could use to slide down from the window. Father's coat lining. My holey sock. Part of Agnessa's petticoat. At night she tied them together with sturdy knots and lowered it down to see how much more length we needed. When not in use, Tum-Tum slept atop the coiled rope in the corner near the door.

"Our escape rope is almost long enough," Luba whispered. "And I've been watching through our hole in the roof here. Soon the Cassiopeia constellation will be directly overhead and there will be no moon that night. I will climb down our rope, come back up and release you all, and we'll be on our way."

"Certainly Taras will track us," Father said.

"Harder for him if we have a four-hour head start."

"But Agnessa can't be moved," Father said. He rested one hand on her back.

Once I'd thought he only married her to have a female in the house, but how wrong I was. Over our months in captivity I'd seen his true devotion to her.

"We can't just *accept* this, Father. It's only a matter of time before Vladi tires of all this and we're his next victims. We have to risk it. Agnessa is light as can be. Sofya and I can take her on our backs."

All at once the sound of a key in the door lock echoed around the little room, the door opened and Mrs. A. stood there, a tray in her hands. As she did every day, she set it down inside, next to the door, and then emptied the latrine bucket over the side of the steps.

"Hope you're not too attached to winter," she said. "Seems like spring is finally coming."

She picked up the tray and set it on our one table. "And look what the chef made specially for you all."

How I wished she would come up with something better to say every time she brought our tray, the same single tin bowl of groats we shared twice a day.

She took a book from the tray and tossed it into the room, where it landed with a dusty thump. "Here's that book you wanted. Don't let Vladi see it."

I hurried to the book and picked it up. Eliza's *Five Weeks in a Balloon*, a hot-air balloon basket on the cover. Jules Verne. I held it to my chest. How smart Luba had been to ask Mrs. A. for it.

Tum-Tum rose from his little bed in the corner to greet Mrs. A., dislodging the towel that covered Luba's rope. I stifled a gasp as Luba noted the problem and started toward the corner.

Mrs. A. reached down and picked up Luba's coiled rope. "Somebody thinks I'm stupid. After all the things I've done for this family."

She held our one hope in her hand and shook it. "I'm taking this out of here and lucky for you I'll not tell Vladi, for there'd be hell to pay for all of us."

The weight of the defeat was a crushing blow and as Mrs. A. left, bolting the door behind her, I glanced at Luba, expecting a tear perhaps, a downtrodden look. Instead, she pulled at her lower lip as she often did when thinking, already on to idea number fifty-one.

I WOKE AT DAYLIGHT the next morning to read my precious new book. How good Eliza had been to send it, back in the good times. I ran two fingers down the illustrated cover, which featured a castaway trapped in a hot-air balloon basket, tethered to a desert island. How good it would be to just float out of that terrible little room.

I opened the first page to find three four-leaf clovers, pressed flat, resting in the book's gutter.

Eliza.

Tears came to my eyes. Such a good friend. Did she fear the worst at this point? If only I could get word to her. Tell her how clearly the good-luck clovers were not working for us.

Luba woke, came, and sat next to me. "I have a new plan, sister."

I sat up on the cold floor and rubbed my back. "It's early, Luba."

"This one's foolproof. But it means giving up Mother's necklace."

I felt for it, still heavy there, sewn in my travel coat pocket lining. "We've been over this. Once Vladi knows we have it, he'll just take it."

"Yes, but what about Mrs. A.? She likes me, I can tell. She brought your book when I asked. And Father was good to her. What if I tell her she needs to release you, just temporarily? To get medicine for Agnessa. Offer her the necklace as payment for her kindness."

I felt for the hole in the silk lining and pulled out the necklace. Not exactly a model of thoroughness, Vladi had searched us that first day and missed it. Even in the dim light of Bogdan's room the emeralds glowed and diamonds shot prisms of light against the walls. I glanced toward Father as he pressed the cool cloth against Agnessa's forehead.

"Vladi would shoot her if he found out she let me go," I said.

"I can cover for you. I'll say you're still here, sick and resting there under the coats. Plus, she has all of us as hostages. I'll tell her she gets the necklace once you're on your way."

"What if she tells Vladi?"

"She's smart enough to know he'd take it from her."

I considered her plan. What could it hurt to try? I handed her the necklace. "And when I get out I will go to the house and retrieve Max."

"No," Luba said. "First you must go to Alexander Palace and get help from the tsarina. Then you can get him."

"I haven't walked more than six steps a day since last fall."

"Even with frequent rests you can walk there in one day—"

"Perhaps you've forgotten the snow is three feet deep."

"It's packed down on the roads and it'll get slushier by the day. Perhaps you've forgotten I put away winter clothes for you in the horse barn."

Though I was loath to tell her, she truly was a genius.

"So, if I make it to Alexander Palace, I just walk right in?"

"The chapel is always unlocked. Go. Tell the tsarina what is happening. Come back with imperial guards."

She made it all sound so simple, but we'd spent a year with no newspapers. Who knew the status of the monarchy? "I don't know, Luba. I have no food, money."

"Take our bread for today."

"How can I leave you here alone? What if another mob comes for you all? They would have killed Father if Taras hadn't stepped in. What if Taras leaves?"

"You have a better plan? The alternative is we die here. Besides, I have plans of my own."

Soon the door opened, letting in a freezing draft, and Mrs. A. stood silhouetted against the weak light of day. She set a tray down on the table, took our latrine bucket by the handle and tossed its contents.

As Mrs. A. replaced the bucket and started to close the door, Luba hurried to her and spoke in a hushed voice. "Thank you, Mrs. A. You are most kind. May I have a word? I have a proposition for you."

"What could you propose to me?"

"Agnessa needs medicine. My sister can get it for her if you let her go."

Mrs. A. sent a quick look my way. "I can do nothing of the sort."

"She knows where she can find it, but she must get out. She promises to come back as soon as she has it."

"Why should I do such a thing?"

"Father was always so good to you," I said.

"If you call not paying your bill good. Do you know how much pineapple and fancy sardines your cook ordered? The tobacco bill alone almost broke us. Your father's man of affairs never paid us close to the full amount."

"I'm sure he meant to settle up," Luba said. "I have a way to pay you now."

Mrs. A. continued to shut the door.

"Wait," Luba said. "Something valuable to give you."

Mrs. A. paused.

"It is a very fine emerald necklace. The tsarina herself admired it."

Through the door opening, Mrs. A. squinted an eye at Luba. "Let's see it."

"I'm afraid I can't do that, but as soon as you free Sofya it will be yours."

"Why should I trust you?"

"You have the rest of us as hostages. And my word. *And* you will soon have a Fabergé piece worth a fortune. Vladi is stealing anything of value from the estate. Why should he have all the reward while you toil as his servant?"

Mrs. A. craned her neck to look toward the house. "Be quick about it. And you better make it look like she's still here."

Luba smiled. "That won't be hard. Vladi seldom comes up here."

I stood, heart pounding, freedom on the other side of that door. I brushed the dust from my pants and smoothed my hair. Would the tsarina even recognize me in such a state? My whole body pulsed with something I hadn't felt in so long. Hope.

Eliza

1917

THE FOLLOWING SPRING AMERICA FINALLY ENTERED the World War to fight alongside France, England, and Russia. On April 6, 1917, planes zoomed over New York City and dropped two tons of confetti, which drifted down over the rooftops and buildings and covered the streets like late spring snow. Once Julia Marlow sang *The Star-Spangled Banner* at the Hudson Theatre, her coat on and a black hat down over one eye, the recruitment office was deluged with men of all ages and social strata enlisting. Would Merrill enlist? I had watched the society pages for news of their wedding, with no sign of it. I brushed away thoughts of him.

America entering the war didn't surprise me, really. After a German U-boat sank the British ocean liner *Lusitania,* killing 128 Americans, and the U.S. intercepted a secret telegram from Germany to Mexico proposing Mexico turn against the U.S. in exchange for the return of Texas, Arizona, and New Mexico, President Wilson asked Congress to declare war on Germany and got his wish.

That February in Russia, yet another revolution had broken out, a major one this time, and by March the tsar had abdicated his throne. Lenin was back in Russia, heading up the Bolshevik Party, and on his second day in power abolished the free press. Seemed he was bent on liquidating Russian civil society top to bottom. Could the world get any more chaotic?

How was it impacting Sofya? I found myself waking at night, mind racing with thoughts of her. I rubbed my little telegram charm that I wore around my neck, the only cure for the terrible worry.

In desperate attempts to learn her whereabouts, I sent letters and telegrams to Alexander Palace, where the royal family lived under house arrest, but heard nothing back. If only the war would end so I could travel abroad and find her.

ONE LOVELY SPRING DAY Caroline and I were in the kitchen of our apartment pitting plums, the pits to be delivered to the army's gas defense department to use in making carbon for gas masks, when Mother stepped into the kitchen.

"There's a Russian woman here, Eliza, claiming you invited her."

"I may have told Mr. Blandmore he could send a few over. It's just temporary, dear."

Mother drew herself up to her full six feet. "Without consulting me?"

"It's my apartment—"

"I don't like this."

"It's because she's Russian, isn't it?" Mother didn't like the tsar's treatment of his peasants, but she had another reason to dislike Russians. Though we seldom spoke of it, when Mother was a girl, her parents' Russian stableman disappeared along with her favorite pony, which caused her to hold a vicious grudge.

"You were fine with the Streshnayvas—"

"Ivan was Henry's *friend*."

"She's not an escaped convict, Mother."

The kitchen door swung open and a hunched woman poked her head around the corner. She brought to mind a coutured pullet as she stepped in, dressed in a velvet French coat and gloves, a beaded bag looped over her forearm.

Peg followed through the door. "Sorry, Miz Ferriday. She's a stubborn one."

"I'm possessing ears, you know," the woman said in a thick Russian accent.

I held out my hand. "I am Eliza Ferriday. This is my mother Caroline Woolsey Mitchell and daughter Caroline. How do you do?"

"How do I do? I do terribly. My leg has not stopped hurting since I left Russia and—"

I stood and pulled out a chair. "That was a rhetorical question, actually. In this country, we ask that as a courtesy."

"Strange to ask question when you don't care about answer. I am Princess Anna Yurynova Yesipov. From Kiev. You heard of Yesipovs?"

"Won't you sit down?" I asked.

The princess looked at the chair as if it were a live snake. "In kitchen?" The princess brushed off the chair seat and sat.

"Do you know a Russian family named Streshnayva?" I asked. "They're from Petrograd and Malinov."

"No," Princess Yesipov said.

"Would you inquire with the others back at the building?"

"Building?" Princess Yesipov asked. "That place is insult to buildings. Not fit for animals."

Peg set teacups on the table. "No self-respecting person will live down there in the Bowery. Smells like a dirty chamber pot most days."

"Thank you, Peg," I said. "Perhaps, see about some muffins?"

Mother poured tea into our cups, the steam clouding her spectacles.

"Well, I'm thinking of ways to help," I said. "Perhaps a party to benefit the Russian émigrés."

Princess Yesipov sent a dismissive wave my way. "American parties? All jokes and games. Russian parties are dignified, with sad music."

"How festive," Mother said.

"If there is an actor, he will recite a poem, maybe everyone's favorite, 'The Deep Grave Dug in the Deep Earth.' "

"Haven't heard that since the Civil War," Mother said.

"You haven't seen a civil war like the one happening in Russia."

"My Woolsey ancestors served as nurses at *Gettysburg*—"

"A few cannonballs? Nothing compared to what Russia is going through, Russian against Russian. Soldiers have turned on their officers."

A shiver ran through me. Afon?

Peg placed one of Mother's walnut muffins, the pride of her oven, in front of Princess Yesipov. The princess examined it and then began extracting the walnuts, collecting them in a triangular mound.

Mother stared at the princess as if she'd pulled a switchblade. The steward of good taste, Mother felt it better to ignore a baked good than to plumb its depths with finger and thumb.

"I'd like to ask the displaced in Paris to make dolls—lace, too—and sell them here, at bazaars, or some here at the apartment."

Mother turned from the stove. "Not sure how the Billingtons will feel about their neighbors opening a thrift shop."

"Of course, we'd make more money if we had something donated to sell," I said.

Mother poured the princess more tea. "Bath salts always do well."

Princess Yesipov tasted her tea, grimaced, and then pushed the cup away. "Bath salts?" She leaned in. "I tell you what really makes money." She paused. "Russian *vodka*."

Mother sat back in her chair. "I don't—"

"But there is prohibition in Russia," I said.

"Russians drink *samogon*. Made from home stills. From grain. Very rare here and not legal, but like drinking nectar."

Mother stirred her tea. "Some call alcohol 'the devil's friend.'"

The princess leaned in toward Mother. "Russian cigarettes, too. Very good. If you are *serious* about making money, this is how."

Mother barely looked at the princess. "Of course we are serious."

"Well, thank you for your help," I said. "We look forward to having you stay with us."

The princess gathered her bag. "We will go get my luggages. Please send your valet to assist."

Mother set her spoon on her saucer. "We don't keep a valet, Princess, but I suppose Peg can help you. And you are welcome for tonight, but I'm afraid we will be closing the apartment as we are on our way out to Southampton soon to our cottage on Gin Lane. The new roof is finally on."

"Where is Southampton?" Princess Yesipov asked.

"The eastern end of Long Island," Mother said.

Princess Yesipov leaned close to Mother. "How big is this cottage?"

Mother hesitated. "Why, twelve bedrooms."

"So you have room."

What to say? No one had ever invited themselves to Gin Lane before.

"Yes, you're more than welcome—" I said.

Princess Yesipov stood. "Your mother maybe not happy with that."

Mother brushed a speck of lint off her sleeve. "Well, the season doesn't fully open out there until June twenty-fifth and the cottage is quite a mess. From the roof and all."

Princess Yesipov shrugged. "It can be cleaned."

Mother sensed defeat but fell back to her favorite default. "We'll see."

THE FOLLOWING RAINY MORNING, Peg hurried off to the lodging house in the Bowery to fetch the princess's luggage and I stood in my bedroom amid a sea of tea-colored tissue, packing up our black silk and bombazine to go to Gin Lane.

Mother stopped by my open door, dressed like a longshoreman ready to confront a nor'easter. She wore Father's old galoshes, her Civil War–era caped black coat and a plaid, waxed-cotton Scottish fisherman's hat.

"I am going out to meet Auntie Eliza to go door-to-door for the St. Thomas rummage sale."

"In this weather?"

"Farmers who wait for the right weather never plant, dear. And this is the best time to catch people at home, after all."

Rain poured down the windows in sheets.

"Be careful out there, Mother. Can you imagine what the Bowery is like in this weather? It doesn't seem right all those poor women stuck there."

"Yes, it's terribly sad to see these people come down in the world," Mother said as she drew on her gray kid gloves. "But they were happy to benefit from the exploitation of the peasants. You reap what you sow, don't you agree?"

"Imagine the conditions in that lodging house, Mother. Gin Lane would do those women a world of good."

"St. Luke's Hospital does a world of good—saves a good many beds for charity cases. Perhaps they can go back there. But, of course, we'll do our Christian duty and find them all suitable homes."

Mother left and I picked up and folded a black crape veil. At times, Mother still wore hers, all these years after Father had died. Perhaps I would follow her and never wear color again.

I had barely folded three more dresses when the door burst open and Peg stood at the threshold, bent at the waist.

"Good heavens, Peg. Do knock, dear."

Peg inhaled deep breaths. "Miz Ferriday, we got to that lodging house and I had to come right back. One of those Russians is terrible sick and they say your mother needs to come quick."

"Come where, Peg? Settle down."

"The place in the Bowery they're all staying. Some Russian lady named Nancy just arrived and sick as can be and they need your mother. You should see where they're living, the poor things."

A shiver ran through me. Could I go? I couldn't possibly help anyone.

"What about Dr. Forbes?"

"He's sick, himself."

"Well, get Dr. Ferguson."

"No other doctor will set foot there. It's bad, Miz Ferriday. She's coughing something awful, just like . . ." Peg's gaze drifted to the carpet.

"You can say it, Peg."

"Where's your mother? I'll go find her."

I went to the window and saw small streams flooding the street below. Mother could be anywhere by now.

I stepped to the front hall, gathered my gloves, and Peg followed.

"I'll come," I said.

Peg raised an eyebrow. "You? I mean . . ."

"We'll never find Mother in time. Get my umbrella and Mother's black bag. And a canteen of cold water. Leave word for her in case she returns, but I am perfectly capable."

"Well—"

"Peg. I won't hear another word." I stepped into my galoshes. "I'm better than nothing."

PEG AND I HURRIED toward the lodging house on Rivington Street, second thoughts about my mission of mercy flooding my head. I clutched Mother's leather bag to my chest and looked up at the old brick place, which seemed about to fall over, chevrons of rain pouring off the roof, windowpanes missing or stuffed with newspapers.

Should I have waited for Mother? I'd done nothing but impede Henry's recovery, after all.

"Hurry," Peg said. "Through the back. Up to the attic."

I followed Peg along the side of the building, our shoes slippery on wooden planks, which floated atop a putrefying sludge of what looked like human waste and garbage. We made our way through a forest of wet, gray underclothes and shirts on clotheslines, past barefooted children playing in the mud among heaps of trash and broken bottles.

From above came the sound of a window opening.

"Careful," Peg called back to me as a slurry of garbage rained down on the plank before me.

We stepped through the back door and up steep stairs, the railing long gone. As we ascended, the stench hit me like a wall, of unwashed chamber pots and rancid meat.

The sound of terrible, distant coughing met us as we arrived on the third-floor attic landing and my own breath grew short. Peg was right.

It was just like Henry.

I followed her down a dark hallway to a windowless kitchen in which a gray stew pot steamed on a black iron stove, a rug below it so dirty and worn into the wood, as if being slowly digested by the floor. A tin basin on the stove caught a rivulet falling from the ceiling, which hit hot metal with a little hiss. Mounds of old overcoats, skirts, and stockings lay about the little room, topped by a coverlet here and there.

"The women sleep here?"

Peg turned as she walked. "Most of the mattresses were stolen."

We followed the hacking cough into a smaller, low-ceilinged room, no bigger than Mother's luggage closet at Gin Lane. An eyebrow window sat high on one wall, providing weak light, and rain seeped in through the eave encouraging speckled, black patches of mold on the wall. In the opposite corner sat a shelf with pictures of saints, their stretched faces pale in the candle glow.

Against the windowed wall lay a light-haired woman on a thin, blue-striped mattress, piled high with coverlets and heavy overcoats of all kinds. Several women huddled around the mattress, and two knelt in the corner at prayer.

I placed the back of my hand to the woman's forehead. "How long has she been this hot?"

Our patient looked up at me, face flushed.

Where had I seen that face? Those aquamarine eyes? The Immigration Bureau detention room that day.

A woman in the corner raised her hand. "She's been this way two hours or so."

"She shivered so bad, we covered her," said another.

"Please, everyone must leave," I said.

How many times had I seen Mother clear the room before she performed one of her medical miracles? I glanced at the girl on the mattress. This was our Russian Nancy? Such an American name.

The women hurried out and I crouched near Nancy's head. What to do?

Peg came to my side. "Well?"

Another terrible cough wracked the girl.

I froze. Was it pneumonia? I pulled a coat back to examine Nancy's face. The bluish lips. Just like Henry.

I stripped off my own coat and rolled up my shirtsleeves. "Take everything off her, Peg."

Peg hesitated. "But she's cold—"

"You must take off the coats and I'll open that window. She needs air in her lungs."

Peg pulled the coats off the girl as I stood on the chair and opened the eyebrow window a crack.

"Let's sit her up, take off that wet shirt, and tap her back."

Peg and I patted the girl's back and then Peg fetched hot water in a basin and laid it next to the mattress.

"Wait for the water to cool," I said. "Must be tepid. A cold bath sets the fever."

Soon I ripped a piece of my sleeve, dipped it in the cooling water, and ran it down Nancy's cheek and neck.

We repeated our system of back patting, bathing her in tepid water, and fanning clean air about her face; and before long the pink color started to come back to her lips.

Nancy mumbled something in Russian.

"Maybe she's thirsty," Peg said.

I held the canteen to her lips and she drank.

As the sun set and the room darkened, her terrible coughing lessened and we watched Nancy's chest move up and down, her breathing leveling off.

I opened Mother's black bag, pulled out a thermometer and slid it under Nancy's arm. As I waited for the silver ribbon of mercury to climb I tucked a lock of hair behind her ear. What a lovely young woman. Why had she come so far from her home? She wore a wedding ring. Where was her husband? Maybe she knew something about Sofya?

I slid the thermometer out and checked it: 100. "Her fever is coming down."

Peg crossed herself. "Thanks to God."

All at once I heard Mother's voice from the hallway and she rushed in.

"I came as soon as I heard," Mother said, unbuttoning her coat. "No wonder she's sick, here in this wretched place."

Peg turned to Mother. "Thank you for coming, but the crisis is done for. Eliza saved her."

Mother turned to me, the light from the window catching a glint of the tear in her eye. "Of course she did."

I smoothed the hair back from Nancy's forehead. "She will not properly recover here, I'm afraid."

Mother bent near to me. "Well, there's only one place for her, I'm afraid."

"St. Luke's?" I asked.

"Gin Lane," Mother said. "It will do her a world of good."

CHAPTER

25

Varinka

1917

MAMKA, MAX, TARAS, AND I HAD LIVED AT THE ESTATE all winter when the mob from the village came to take the Streshnayvas from their quarters and murder them that spring. Mamka and I stood in the countess's old bedroom watching it all. Vladi, pistol drawn, led men and women through the snow, many of them former workers at the linen factory, to the old servants' quarters out back near the barns. We kept Max away from the windows as always. Why risk a stray bullet or one of the mob seeing the young boy and asking questions about his parents?

Taras mounted on his horse, rifle pointed at the mob, and barred their way.

"Move aside, Taras," Vladi said.

"They're more useful to us alive," Taras said. "We must be patient."

If Taras was being the voice of reason we were all in trouble.

Vladi turned toward the hothouse to show his frustration, his breath coming in white fog. He took up a sledgehammer and crashed it through the glass panes and metal frame, the glass raining down in sheets around him. He passed the great hammer along and others in the mob took turns, swinging wildly at the glass that remained. Despite cuts to their faces and hands they drank vodka and sang patriotic songs and soon reduced the little glass house to ruin.

The mob retreated, but that afternoon Vladi led the same group back to the estate, dirty feather beds and bulging cloth sacks over their shoulders, a new swagger to their walks.

He stood at the front door and waved them in. "This is your new home."

How would the Streshnayvas feel about that? They were still living out in that one room, half dead. I kept an eye on them all. Snuck out there to watch them now and then.

How strange it was to see the whole village move into the estate, choosing rooms and making themselves comfortable under the crystal lights. It was their right, since the people deserved a fine place to live as much as the Streshnayvas did, but how terrible to see Peter Pavlinov from the hunting goods store spitting on the fine *zala* rug. Mrs. Astronavich wheeling her trunk into Mr. Streshnayva's room.

I tried not to look at the countess's hothouse, the once-beautiful home for fancy plants now a shattered, tangled mess of white metal and jagged glass. The emerald, swan-necked stem with one purple blossom, now lying on the heap. Roses the color of fresh cream tossed about, their feet still bound in little cloth bags.

The people of the house set about turning it into their trash heap, tossing their newspapers and milk bottles there. Tin cans. Old woven shoes. People scoured the Streshnayvas' pantry and ate all the fancy tinned sardines and caviar, but no one was working in the fields and ordinary food was scarce. Were we really better off now?

LATER THAT WEEK, ONE MORNING when Taras was away hunting, I took the key from his boot, stole a warm loaf of bread from the kitchen, wrapped it in a linen towel, and visited the family. My plan was to unbolt the door, leave the bread, see how they were doing, and re-bolt it.

The courtyard was quiet as I stepped up the stairs to the old gamekeeper's room and peeped through a crack in the door. The younger daughter Luba sat near the window and the others slept in the middle of the floor, under a mound of coats. Their tiny dog, little more than a skeleton, must have caught the scent of bread and came toward the door.

"I can see you, you know." It was Luba.

I stepped back from the crack, heart beating wildly, warm bread pressed to my chest.

She must have stood, for her voice came closer. "Why do you watch us?"

I said nothing and stomped the snow from my boots.

"Why do you not help us escape? You can't be happy with all this."

"It's not my fault."

"By doing nothing you condone it. How is little Max?"

I stood, quiet.

"If he's still alive, this isn't good for him, living with such evil men."

"What do you know?"

"You and your mamka must leave with him before it's too late." The little bell she wore tinkled.

"The guards would never let us pass the gate with you. Besides we have no money."

"I have a secret way out of the estate. Money, too."

"We would be lost the first day. The wolves would like that."

"I have many things hidden in the house. A gun. And a sextant to navigate by the stars."

"That isn't possible."

"I know latitude and longitude."

I grew quiet. It would help to know the way.

"Think how much better it will be for the child," Luba said. "We can go to Alexander Palace. They know my family—"

"The tsar stepped aside."

Luba stopped for a moment at that, and then continued. "They would still help us and our townhouse in Petrograd is full of things we can sell. I know where the townhouse key is hidden."

I clapped my hands over my ears. "Quiet, so I can think."

"Let me out now and I will gather everything and meet you anywhere you like. I will get you to safety and all I want is my freedom."

"I can't trust you."

"You have my parents, don't you, sleeping here—with Sofya there next to them?" Luba waved toward a mass of coats heaped on the floor near the woodstove. "Would I do anything to endanger them?"

I peered into the darkened room. "How many sleep there?"

"Everyone except me, of course. My parents. The count. Sofya."

"Why does it not look like so many?"

"We're all so thin, Varinka."

How to decide? What if Luba let Sofya out, too, and she took Max back? But if I stayed with Taras I might never be safe. With Vladi so powerful now, Max and Mamka were at risk, too. There was no better time to try it, with both Vladi and Taras away.

I sucked in one big breath. "All right. Meet me at my old *izba* in one hour."

"I will be there. Come with your mother and Max. Dress him in several layers and don't be late. I will have our route planned."

Was this a good idea? We needed the help. But could I really trust her? If only Mamka were there to ask.

I unlocked the door and pulled it open. The hinges screeched, causing a flock of blackbirds to take flight. Would the whole world hear?

Luba stepped out, I set the bread on the floor, and closed and locked the door.

"Make sure you bring plenty of food for Max," Luba said.

"If you're not at the *izba* in one hour your family will suffer."

"I will be there," Luba said. "I swear by God's stars."

CHAPTER

2 6

Sofya

1917

ONCE MRS. A. RELEASED ME I SLIPPED OFF OUR property undetected and hitched a ride with a goat farmer bound for Petrograd. I traveled much of the way in the back of his open *lineika*, surrounded by bristle-coated goats, who huddled near me like a litter of puppies, happy for another warm body. After twice proposing marriage, the farmer told me he heard the tsar had given up his crown and was being held under house arrest by a small band of guards appointed by the provisional government. With a smile, he drew one finger across his throat. So much for the tsar being the "little father," beloved by the people.

I arrived at Alexander Palace well past midnight. Distant gunshots echoed in the air as I disembarked at the edge of Tsar's Village. The park seemed oddly still and in the black night, with only a crescent moon to guide me, I made my way past the Chinese Village, the red pagoda roofs towering above a mob gathered in the courtyard there, brandishing torches and placards and shooting off their guns. Would they storm the residence and take the tsar?

I passed the Children's Island we had played upon as youngsters, the weak moonlight showing the arbors and blue-painted playhouse under the mounds of snow, the lilac and magnolia trees covered with boards to keep off the snow.

Once I made it to Alexander Palace I hid behind a tree, the grand, lemon-yellow facade rising above me. Guards stood at the front entrances stamping their boots in the snow, arguing about something and sharing cigarettes.

I stepped around the back of the palace and crept up the stone steps to the chapel. How many times had we worshipped there, the tsarina too ill to go out to the church in town? Was Luba right about the chapel being unlocked?

I hurried to the chapel door, my heart thumping in my ears, and reached for the brass knob.

Cold in my bare hand, the knob gave way and I opened the door.

Every part of me calmed as I stepped through the doorway and into the high-ceilinged chapel, my steps echoing on stone. We'd often sat in the front row, close to the royal family as they sat behind the screen, for the devoutly religious tsarina needed her privacy.

I stepped through the adjacent billiards room, careful to make not a sound, up the stairway and down the carpeted hallway to the private apartments.

I hurried toward the door of the tsarina's inner sanctum, her Lilac Room. How Alexandra's society critics had panned that room. Expecting her to entertain publicly as previous monarchs had, they chastised the quaint, homey sanctuary where she retreated with her family.

I followed Olga's voice, reading aloud from the Bible. Tears came to my eyes at the sound of her voice, so clear and direct.

I stood in the doorway for a moment taking in the scene. It was dark in the room, except for one candle near Olga. Olga and Tatiana, the two eldest sisters sat together in one chair, clothed in white dressing gowns, their heads shaved smooth. Next to them, their mother, the tsarina, lay upon a lilac silk chaise. The sweet scent of lilac branches, forced to bloom, from cuttings in the imperial hothouse, hung in the air. Clearly, their house arrest was not stripping every luxury from the family.

How I'd loved that room as a child, with the pale lavender silk walls, dyed to match a lilac sprig the tsarina had given her decorator. The soaring ceilings. The polished lemonwood furniture. Barely an inch of the walls at head height was left uncovered by some framed picture, treasure, or bibelot; and the dressers and tables held little villages of framed photographs and golden icons. But that night it suddenly seemed old-fashioned, maudlin even.

Tatiana noticed me first and stood as if stung. "Sofya."

Olga snapped closed her Bible and joined her. "How did you get in here? There are guards everywhere."

They ran to me and hugged me.

"Through the chapel."

"I thought only the front and kitchen doors were open," Tatiana said.

Olga took my hand in hers. "I prayed for this."

Tatiana smoothed one hand across her head. "What do you think of this? We've had the measles. It's much easier, actually, and has made us appreciate hats. The others are still sick with it, upstairs asleep. Papa is finally getting some rest, too. You've heard they made him resign? Each day they make him clear the snow down by the fence so the lower classes can stare and jeer."

I was conflicted hearing this. I had great affection for the tsar, pitied him as I did the blinkered horse at the mill forced to walk in endless circles, but the price we were all paying for his narrow-mindedness was so great. Did he not deserve his fate?

"Come see Mama," Olga said. "She's having a five. Not well, another headache."

Some things never changed. The girls still used a system of numbers to rate their mama's pain.

We stepped toward the tsarina, at rest on her favorite settee, much thinner since I'd seen her last and her eyes red-rimmed, a double shawl of lace lined with lilac-colored linen drawn to her knees. A vase of her flower of choice, Frau Druski white roses, sat by her side.

The tsarina held out one hand. "Sofya. What brings you here at such a time?"

I kissed her hand and received her embrace, catching the scent of her favorite perfume, Atkinson's Essence of White Rose. How quiet it was there, so different from before the tsar had abdicated. Even at night while the family slept, the palace had always been fully lit, humming with activity, visitors and servants milling about. But one got the feeling the tsarina rather liked the solitude, finally had what she wanted.

"I come from Malinov." Why, after so much hardship did I choose that time to want to cry? "Last fall bandits broke into the estate and took us all hostage." I unbuttoned my coat and let it slip down off my shoulders.

Olga gasped. "Sofya. You're so thin. Bandits kept you all that time?"

"It's happening everywhere," the tsarina said. "They set fire to Count Freedericz's house."

I lay my coat across a chair. "More bandits than Bolsheviks, we think. They've been forcing Father to write his Ministry correspondence as usual and stealing the money. He's beyond despair."

The tsarina watched me carefully. "Despicable. And your son?"

"A young peasant girl who was tending him at the time of the attack still has him."

"Can she not help you?" Olga asked. "Certainly, she wants to reunite you with your child."

"She shows no sign of it. We've seen only a glimpse of Max since the attack. I'm afraid he thinks of her as his mother and has forgotten me."

Olga and Tatiana came to me. "Don't cry, cousin."

How good it was to finally tell someone our troubles.

"God will help you," the tsarina said. "He knows a mother must be with her son." How could I tell her, lying there surrounded by gold-painted icons, that God had abandoned us long ago?

"How is Agnessa?" Tatiana asked.

"Near death and refuses to eat."

"Luba?" Olga asked.

"Stalwart as you can imagine, but we need help—"

"The letter, Tatiana," the tsarina said. "Where is it?"

Tatiana stepped to a desk in the shadows. I had forgotten how the tsarina treated Tatiana as her glorified maid, while strong-minded Olga often resisted her mother's requests.

"A letter arrived just last week," Olga said. "From Afon."

"I can't believe it."

"And a telegram and a letter from your friend Eliza. I hope you don't mind that Mama opened them, in case we could help."

Tatiana returned and handed me the ecru envelopes, both slit along the top. "Much has been censored in Afon's, but it is like hearing his wonderful voice to read it."

I held the envelopes to my chest. How long had it been with no word? Was he frantic? And what of Cook? Had he come to the palace for help?

"Have you seen Baron Vasily-Argunov?" I asked.

"Yury?" Olga asked.

"He escaped when we were first captured. This would have been his likely first stop. We think one of the bandits shot him though."

"No," the tsarina said. "We would remember such a handsome visitor. Perhaps he didn't make it. So many have fallen to the rabble."

The thought of Cook lying dead under the snow in the forest was too horrible to dwell on.

The tsarina sat up straighter, one hand to her back. "It is past midnight. You need a bath and fresh linen and a good rest. Olga, have Anna see to it. And have her bring a third cot to your room. We will see to the Malinov situation in the morning. I have a direct telephone line to the Winter Palace and can send a letter to the Ministry as well."

Every part of me calmed. "Thank you, Empress. You are too generous."

"Tatiana, stay and read a bit more. Olga, tend to Sofya." The tsarina slid a book from her table and opened it, our sign to repair to the children's quarters upstairs.

Olga and I hurried out into the hallway, a new lightness to my step. Imperial guards would have no problem taking on Vladi and Taras. Would they send Cossacks? I smoothed the envelope in my fingers. Word from Afon at last.

I turned to Olga. "I can't tell you how grateful I am. My parents—"

Olga stopped in the middle of the hallway, one hand on my arm. "I must tell you the truth, cousin. I am sorry Mama raised your hopes."

"I don't understand."

"My mother is delusional. The pain of her back and the worry over our increasingly tenuous situation frayed her mind, I'm afraid. She cries much of the day but pretends our house arrest is temporary. Claims we have running water and electricity, but both were shut off weeks ago, so the maids fetch well water. She knows little of the news for they keep the papers from her and our phones are disconnected. Truth is, Petrograd is entirely turned over to the revolutionaries."

"But this is Ministry business. These bandits are stealing from the government, holding a member of the Finance—"

"The provisional government is in chaos, my darling. The duma dissolved. The Ministry is reeling itself, infected with traitors, one step away from radicals cracking open their safes. Even Papa is not accepting the truth that his people no longer support him. Keeps blaming his troubles on the Jews. Says they hate him."

"He funded pogroms against them, Olga. Murdered thousands—"

"I know it all, Sofya, and God will punish us. But don't you see? *Everyone* has turned against him. Even if they wanted to send a brigade to Malinov, who would they send?"

"Imperial guards?"

"There are no more imperial guards. Since Papa abdicated last month there is no more imperial anything. Last week the Council of Workmen and Soldiers dismissed Papa's long-standing regiment and replaced them with a hideous mob. Those guarding us have become increasingly hostile and we must lock our doors to keep them from walking into our *most* private spaces. They walk in as we dine simply and rant about our meals being too extravagant."

Olga pulled me closer. "They took our dear Madame Wiroboff from here in March—to Peter and Paul prison where she has been tortured, all just for her connection to us. We must hide you, for if they find you here they may do the same."

"I cannot just stay here with my family at risk."

"We must think quickly then, or else I'm afraid you will not be leaving here, at least not in time to help your family."

CHAPTER
27

Eliza

1917

A N AMBULANCE BROUGHT NANCY FROM THE BOWERY
to Southampton Hospital, where she received expert care. I still rested
on my medical laurels, happy with the idea I helped save her. The plan
was to host her at Gin Lane once she recovered. Would she offer clues
to Sofya's whereabouts? I yearned for her to mend so I could broach
the question.

Mother finally gave in and allowed us to bring Princess Yesipov,
too, mostly to stop her from pushing the issue each morning at breakfast. Mother's only admonition to us was, "Just don't let things get
rowdy." She was worried about the Southampton colony, the Pink and
Greens, reacting poorly to our guests. The season was not yet fully
open, but I vowed to do my best not to ruffle local feathers.

ONCE THE DOCTORS DISCHARGED Nancy she came home to Gin
Lane and one unseasonably warm, breezy April Tuesday, Mother
deemed her well enough to talk with me. Our goal, set by Mother, was
to have her well enough to walk to the wood-and-iron bench in the
backyard, which overlooked the ocean. The salt air was one of Mother's favorite cure-alls.

We started slowly, arm in arm, and walked about Mr. Gardener's garden, green-and-white-striped crocus shoots had just started to emerge from the dark earth. I hoped to hear some encouraging news about Sofya.

We started out toward the bench, waves crashing below us in the distance.

"How can I ever repay you?" Nancy asked.

"I have so many questions. If you don't mind me asking, Nancy is such an American name . . ."

"Just a precaution. Some think the Reds will not rest until they've done us all in, no matter where we are, to make sure we don't come back and overthrow them. I read a book called *Pollyanna* on the ship over and thought Nancy was a pretty name. Much easier to say than Yelizaveta."

"I know you may not be well enough yet to talk to me about it, but where is your husband?"

"You are kind to ask. I'm fine talking about Russia, but just not that. Not yet. I hope you understand."

"Of course, dear. Only when you're ready. I had a friend in Russia I wanted to inquire of. In Malinov."

"We used to visit my aunt at her estate near there."

"Sofya Streshnayva."

"Of course. Her father is with the Ministry."

"Yes, that's the one."

We made it to the bench. Only a bit winded, Nancy gripped the wooden back of it and looked out over the ocean.

"She was one of tsarina Alexandra's ladies-in-waiting. I was always so envious of her, so kind and refined, with the most handsome husband."

"Have you heard any news of her?"

Nancy stepped to the front of the bench and sat. "I hate to say . . ."

"Please, anything."

"Well, bad things were happening south of Petrograd before I left. Bandits raiding estates. Whole families, well . . ."

"I must know, Nancy."

"My aunt sent a letter. Said Little Heaven had been attacked."

I sat next to Nancy on the bench, light-headed. "By whom?"

"She said there was a terrible new element in town. . . ."

"Criminals?"

"Yes, but also some disgruntled factory workers and deserted soldiers, too. Ordinary town folk. But with newfound courage. Call themselves Reds. Seems once they wear a red armband they fear nothing
and simply take what they want."

"Where are the police?"

"She said there was a big change happening with the police. In Moscow she'd seen a terrible thing. People were holding a meeting in one
of the squares and the police shot sideways to dispel the crowd, but
then shot into them. People rose up, grabbed one policeman, and
dragged him away in his long greatcoat and gray fur hat. Took him
around the corner and shot him. After that, many policemen just disappeared or joined the ranks of the Reds."

"Could you write your aunt again—"

"She had to leave the estate, all her beautiful things. She said the
servants cried the night she left. And that's the only letter I have. I
don't know where she is. All I can do is wait."

What we'd suspected was true. The thought of the Streshnayvas
overrun by criminals was too terrible to bear. What of little Max? "I
should have done more when I could."

I handed Nancy my extra handkerchief and we both dabbed our
eyes.

"You mustn't blame yourself. Who could foresee all of this? Sofya
is a smart woman."

"Can you ask the others if they know her?"

"Of course."

We sat in silence watching the waves crash upon the beach.

"I feel bad staying here so comfortable, with the rest of the Russian
girls living in that terrible boarding house."

I touched her arm. "We call that guilt, dear. It's the foundation of
some of our most popular religions."

"I must go back and help them."

"You're barely recovered and bound to catch something new. But
rest assured they'll be fine, for I've arranged to bring them all here.
The community won't like it but that's too bad. I'm planning a party,
too, a gala to benefit Russian émigrés. All through my committee."

Nancy stood straighter. "May I help?"

"Of course. It's the American Central Committee for Russian Relief. I wrote to a woman my aunt told me about named Mrs. Zaronova, in Paris, who has organized a workshop and is employing displaced émigrés to make all sorts of Russian handmade items. I asked her if we could sell her things here in the U.S. We're now expecting the first shipment any day."

"Will you sell them in stores?"

"At our apartment in the city on Wednesdays this fall; and I've spoken to the Plaza Hotel about special sales there. Part of the proceeds will help the women here in New York. The remainder we'll send to Paris to support the women who make the items."

"I'm happy we can help," Nancy said.

She returned to the house, ready to nap, and I continued to the beach for a walk, wondering if I could keep my promises to bring all the Russian women to Gin Lane. The Pink and Greens would have me in stocks at Lake Agawam if I didn't watch my step. But how could I leave the women living in squalor?

For the first time in so long I felt a warm glow of sixth sense, an unexplained certainty. That somehow it all brought me closer to Sofya.

WE CHOSE THE WRONG time to venture into town to Hildreth's to pick up more cleaning supplies. Though the cottage had been scrubbed top to bottom, we needed to prepare for the additional Russian guests we expected any day; and Mother also wanted to show Nancy and Princess Yesipov Hildreth's, the oldest, largest, and most reliable Southampton store devoted to the sale of general merchandise.

We piled into the carriage, which we used for short trips into town. Southampton at the time embraced the new automobile, but couldn't give up its horses. It was a short ride from Gin Lane, along wide streets arched with elms, the horses' hooves falling soft on dirt roads. Was it the sea air that was helping Nancy? She already had new color in her cheeks.

"What a lovely town," Nancy said from the rear seat.

"Founded in 1640," Mother said.

Princess Yesipov leaned forward. "My town Kiev was founded in sixth century. Withstood Mongol hoards."

Mother turned in her seat. "Well, we've weathered our own challenges. The Vagabond Hurricane of 1903."

"And the Pink and Greens," I said.

"They are dangerous?" Nancy asked.

"Very," Mother said. "You don't want to poke that wasps' nest."

I laughed but it was true. My Henry used to call them "the Mink and Means," a force to be reckoned with.

"They run the colony here," I said. "Mostly the more mature ladies in town. They dictate what to wear. What kind of tea to drink."

"They wear these colors, pink and green?" Princess Yesipov asked.

"Yes. And they grow pink roses and green plants."

We arrived at Hildreth's, a wide, well-kept building with two peaked roofs and a long, striped awning that hung over the picture windows.

Caroline ran into the store and we followed.

Inside the wide shop the floors creaked with every step and I breathed in the essence of the old place, of soap flakes and fresh-cut hay. How satisfying it was to see those two floors packed with staples and fancy groceries, furniture, crockery, carpets, and horse feed stacked to the beadboard ceiling.

The fat, green cash register commanded the oak counter, which ran down the length of the place, and the stairs stood at our left. The Regulator clock on the wall behind the counter, brass pendulum swinging, kept time as it had since I'd come in as a child with Mother.

"Carry Mitchell. Back so soon?" Mr. Hildreth greeted us, a slim, bespectacled gentleman with a businesslike air. "Tried to get more sugar but I'm on a wait list. And no more plungers until rubber's back."

"We'll make do, Mr. Hildreth."

The princess pulled a jar of fancy gherkins down off a carefully stacked pyramid. "Six kinds of pickles? Very good."

Mother called out items from her list and we scurried to find them.

"Gayetty's Medicated Paper. One mop. Waterthin crackers."

Mr. Hildreth slipped Caroline two cellophaned root-beer candies and she pocketed them with a smile.

Soon Electra Whitney and her Pink and Green Garden Society friends stepped down the stairs, dressed almost identically in full shopping regalia, celadon silk dresses and rose-colored hats. Each carried a rake in one hand.

"How do you do, Carry?" Electra asked.

Mother sent her a curt nod. "Very well."

Electra stepped to me. "Good to see you, Eliza."

Proud of her small feet, Electra held her skirt hem high to show them off. Her granddaughter Jinx followed behind her, a square, humorless child who'd inherited Electra's entitled air and sour disposition.

Electra stopped at the base of the stairs and the other secure and leisured ladies stood on the stairs like debutantes posing for a picture.

"We are just picking up a few things."

Mother stepped aside, chin high. "Don't let us keep you. We're just browsing."

"What?" Electra asked. "Shopping? Not out carrying jars of soup to the sick?"

"And where are you off to, Electra? An anti-suffrage meeting?"

"If you came to one, you'd realize that giving women the right to vote would threaten the family."

"Women know so little beyond the home," a blond woman added, from her spot on the stairs.

"May I introduce Anna Gabler?" Electra asked.

So, this was the famous Anna. I stepped closer for a better look and was strangely satisfied to find her more plain than pretty, her features on their own quite good—a nice nose, ice-blue eyes, and golden hair—but put together were not what I'd call beautiful.

Anna nodded toward me. "Anna Gabler. One B like Ibsen's Hedda."

I nodded in return. "Eliza Ferriday. I hope the similarities end there. Things didn't go well for poor Hedda Gabler, did they?"

Even at first glance, the similarities between Anna and Hedda were hard to ignore. Aristocratic. Hard to please. Hopefully not pregnant, for Merrill's sake.

"Eliza, Anna's family has joined the Meadow Club."

I brushed a speck of dirt from my sleeve and tried to smile. "How wonderful."

"Anna is coming up to the camp next week," Electra said.

By "the camp" Electra meant her second country house on two hundred acres of Maine coast in Bar Harbor, where Mother's people often summered but Father had always refused to go, finding the women there vulgar and rowdy, since they swung their arms when they walked.

Anna smiled. "Electra wants me to see the place and has invited a whole houseful."

"Richard Merrill too, of course," Electra said.

I conjured an image of Electra holding court from a striped cabana at their heated swimming pool, Anna and Merrill frolicking in the shallow end. That pool had been a first in Bar Harbor and won Electra a great many friends since, though some may protest otherwise, a human body cannot survive Maine's coastal waters even in August.

"What important work are you off to?" I asked Electra.

"Planting salvia around the cannon in front of Daughters of the American Revolution headquarters."

"How *very* important, and you not even a DAR member."

"One does what one can," Electra said. "And you? Preparing for guests, I hear. Already? With the season not fully opened yet?"

"A few Russian friends," I said.

"That kind of thing is common in Slavic countries, isn't it? Crowding into houses? You never used to see such a thing on Gin Lane."

The rest of Electra's acolytes stepped down and stood behind her.

"You can always drop your Russians at the new hospital," Anna Gabler said. "They're taking in roomers."

Another woman spoke up. "Take them to Quogue. Plenty of boarding houses there."

Little Jinx addressed Mother. "Next thing you know, they'll all be on the relief."

Electra clasped her hands at her waist. "Reverend Dunmore says, 'Do not worship false idols,' and there's a lot of that going on in Russia, praying to shiny, false gods."

"I saw it in *National Geographic*," Anna said. "They hang pictures of them on every wall."

Caroline stepped toward the group. "In the Russian Orthodox Church, Mrs. Whitney, they pray to *icons* not idols, the faces of Jesus and Mary painted on board, some covered in metal. Mother brought one home from her trip."

Electra stood straighter and looked at Caroline as if seeing her for the first time. "Well, don't you offer opinions freely for a young girl?"

Caroline stepped closer to her. "These people are our guests. My mother is working hard to help them, and if you cannot issue them an apology we must ask you to leave, is that not right, Mr. Hildreth?"

Mr. Hildreth shrugged. "You're the boss, Miss Ferriday."

Electra paused a moment, clearly having never been thrown out of anywhere, and then waved her ladies onward. "Well, we need to be on our way, anyway. Anna is meeting Richard Merrill at the Meadow Club. But I know we won't be shopping here again anytime soon."

They swept past Caroline and out the door.

Merrill? In Southampton? My gaze swept the scene outside the picture windows. Perhaps I would see him?

I stepped to Mr. Hildreth. "I hope this doesn't hurt your business."

"Oh, no. Electra can't stay away. No one else has her favorite fertilizer. And it was worth it to see that daughter of yours stand up for herself. I like that."

"Good job, Caroline," I said, never prouder of my daughter, but I knew we'd poked the wrong wasps' nest.

Varinka

1917

ONCE I FREED LUBA I RETURNED TO THE ESTATE TO
pack for our escape, one eye open for Taras. He and Vladi were out
hunting, their feud forgotten for the moment. Since the tsar's woods
had become fair game to anyone with a red armband, the two were off
on a hunters' holiday. What would Taras do if he caught us running
away? Vladi? A shudder went through me. Would he track us on our
first day, walking to Petrograd?

I pulled Sofya's valise from the armoire, smoothed one hand down
the black-and-white fabric side of it and touched the fancy "S" marked
on the leather strap. How was she doing without her son? I forced my
mind on to the task at hand. Mamka, Max, and I were to meet Luba at
our old *izba*. What to pack?

In the armoire, Sofya's clothes still hung there by color. We were a
similar size. Why did it still feel so strange to wear her clothes?

I pulled out lavender silk slippers with silver beading and lay them
in the valise. A dove gray organza dress for Mamka and a tangerine
shawl. From the lingerie chest I grabbed handfuls of pantalets, che-
mises, and stockings and tossed them in. Max's *valenok*, little felt boots.
How small they were. He was growing out of them. We would get new
ones in Petrograd.

A silver frame sat atop the chest, a blurry group photo of the whole

Streshnayva family. Such a fine-looking group of people and such a sad end. Maybe they should have listened to the needs of the people?

I snuck down the back stairs to the kitchen, the once-bright room empty and cold with Cook long gone. Only two black bread loaves sat cooling on the wire rack. The people cooked for themselves now, ate their simple meals in their quarters, their makeshift stoves scorching the fine rugs and moiré silk walls.

I wrapped a loaf in a clean dishtowel and held it warm to my chest. Little Max would love the big city. The fine shops and the sweets.

Once back in the bedroom, I pulled the valise from the bed and gasped at the weight of it. I hauled it down the hallway to Mamka's bedroom and entered to find her sewing.

"Sewing in low light again, Mamka?"

"Where have you been all day?" she asked, without looking up.

"We need to change Max into outdoor clothes," I said.

"It is too late for him to play outside."

"We're leaving, Mamka. I will tell you the plan as we go. Wake him up now."

She set her work aside. "Isn't he with you?"

My body went cold. "Me? I've been packing. He was with you." I ran to the window and looked out over the garden.

"He was gone from his bed after his nap," Mamka said. "I thought you'd taken him."

Rage bubbled up in me. How careless of her. "You could have asked me. You were sewing all this time, weren't you?"

"He is your responsibility, Inka."

Luba. If she'd taken little Max should I tell Taras? Then he'd know I planned to escape. But if he found out himself it would be just as bad.

"Perhaps he's with the laundry girls?" Mamka asked.

"No. I freed Luba from their room."

"So, she took him." Mamka crossed herself. "It is God's will."

"Perhaps I got it all mixed up. I'm sure she will meet us at the *izba* after all. Either way, we must leave at once."

Mamka scowled at me.

"She will be there," I said. "She swore on God's stars."

"Don't be so sure, Inka."

I breathed deep, trying to stay calm. "Can you be positive for once?" I took up the valise. "Come. Help me carry this."

Mamka and I wore our felt boots and carried the valise through the woods to our old *izba*, on our secret pathway through the snow, stopping once or twice to rest, but soon glimpsed the cabin roof through the trees. How good it was to see that homey place again.

We heaved the valise through the cabin door and breathed a sigh. *Home.* The great hulking white oven, my old mattress above it. Mamka's sweet bed.

But no Luba.

Mamka crossed her arms across her chest. "I don't like it, Inka. We may have to leave without the boy."

"I won't."

We lit two fires for warmth, one in the big oven, one in Taras's woodstove, and waited for what felt like an hour, just sitting, listening to the crack and pop of the wood. Having no watch, did Luba get the time wrong? She was such a capable girl, but mistakes happen.

The sound of footsteps came outside and Mamka turned to the door.

"She's come with him," I said, pulling the valise from the bed.

"Thanks be to God," Mamka said.

Soon we'd see Petrograd and would be free.

Mamka and I rushed toward the *izba* door.

The door opened and Taras walked in, leaving the door wide open, the dark woods behind him. "Well now, look who's here."

He wore his sealskin jacket, stalker boots, and that expression dark as the sky over the steppe when a storm is coming.

Mamka went to the door, one hand to the wood to close it, but Taras grabbed her by the arm and flung her back.

I stepped to the bed and grasped the valise handle. "We're just gathering some old clothes to share with the people."

"Where's the boy?"

"I don't know," I said.

He gave Mamka a penetrating look and she turned away.

"What a good liar you are, Inka."

Taras pulled the valise from my hand, ripped the strap open and shook it upside down. Out tumbled a horrible upchuck of pale pink satins and lace and shoes, the loaf of bread in the middle of it all. Like a punctuation mark, Papa's picture fell on top of the pile.

"Your old tattered clothes look a lot like your best things."

"Hurry up, girl," came a voice outside.

Vladi.

He came to the cabin door, pulling behind him by the shoulder a shaken Luba, chin high, Max in her arms. My heart beat faster. Would she tell that I let her escape?

"We heard Father Paul had given some girl with a child some money to run away," Vladi said. "Then look who we found." He pushed Luba in the door, Max in her arms.

She tripped over the doorsill and almost fell.

"Guess you never know what will turn up when you're hunting elk. We almost shot them."

Luba turned to Vladi with a cool look. "Maybe that would have been preferable."

Max hid his face in the crook of her neck as Vladi leaned close to her. "You'll be getting your wish, insect. But let's start with Varinka. This one says you let her out of the quarters."

I felt Taras's eyes bore into me. "I know nothing of this."

"*And* I went to their quarters and found her sister gone. The liars said she was asleep there on the floor under some coats but *someone* let her out, too."

"I didn't do it," I said.

Mamka tried to gently pull Max from Luba but he held fast to her. "My Luba."

Luba pulled him away and handed him to Mamka, a pained look on her face. As Max left her arms Luba placed her hands over her face, shoulders shaking.

Mamka walked by and shot me a hot glance, her lips pressed together so hard they were practically white.

Taras turned to me, fists balled like stones. "You let this little pig out?"

"But I didn't think—"

"How many times have I *told* you?"

Vladi pulled Luba out the door. "This one outlived her usefulness a long time ago. Finally going to get their due and don't try and stop me, Taras."

"*Savages,* "Luba called back to us.

Taras took me by the arm. "Come."

I pulled away. "Where?"

"You helped her escape. You must be punished."

"I pitied the poor girl, Taras. Cooped up in one room."

"She double-crossed you and still you support her?"

"No, Taras. I was stupid."

"And now her sister's gone, too. This could ruin everything."

He dragged me toward the door to his woodshed.

I turned and reached for Max. "Give me my boy. Please, Taras."

Taras grabbed a handful of my hair and yanked me toward the shed, my hair on fire at the roots.

"Don't let Max see this," I said over my shoulder.

Mamka followed, Max crying in her arms. "If you hurt her, Taras—"

"*What,* crone?" He dragged me into the shed, slammed the door, and hooked the latch.

Mamka pounded the door. "Taras!"

He pushed me onto his bed, his scent wafting up from the linens, of sweat and gunpowder and peppermint. The iron oven sat beside the bed and cast blessed warmth, an orange glow in its belly. I scanned the tools on the wall. Would he use one on me?

"You can't depend on your Mamka to solve every problem."

How was he so remarkably calm? "You don't understand—"

Taras pulled birch kindling from a basket, crouched in front of the stove and added it to the fire.

He leaned over me, pulled up the hem of my *sarafan,* and ran his hand up my thigh.

I swatted his hand away. "No, Taras. The arrangement . . ."

"I never agreed to that." He flipped me onto my stomach and with two hands ripped the back of my *sarafan* in one motion, pulled the torn dress out from under me, and threw it in the corner, leaving me cold in blouse and bloomers.

I tried to crawl off the bed, but he pushed me down and pinned me by my shoulders.

"You're sick to want this, Taras."

He fumbled with his trouser buttons. "You started it. Showing yourself to me like a slut."

"By taking a bath?"

With one hand he wrestled my bloomers down and pressed his hardness against me. Every part of me shook.

I screamed for my mother and right away regretted it. What could Mamka do against Taras? She would try and kill him if she saw this and he would hurt her. Maybe Max, too.

He slapped his hand over my mouth, cutting off my air. I bit down on the soft part of it with all my strength, and tasted blood. Taras reared back like a stuck bear and then removed his belt with one motion.

Mamka pounded on the door. "I'll go for the police, Taras—"

Taras laughed to himself. Of course our one old policeman would never act. He was probably sleeping off the drink.

He cinched one end of the belt around my wrist, the other to the iron headboard, and tethered me like a dog.

"I know it was hard for you in prison, Taras—"

Taras stepped to the workbench and considered his tools, as if choosing a cabbage at the market. "Your Papa spoiled you, Inka."

"My arm is numb, Taras, can—"

"Actions have consequences. We are going to Petrograd soon, you and me. The Committee sent word. Vladi gave my name, can you imagine? And I need to trust you there, my girl."

He chose a small, wooden-handled tool, opened the door of the stove, and laid the metal tip of it in the flames.

"What are you doing, Taras?"

He sat next to me on the bed and the springs groaned. With two hands, he gently brought my head to his knee and held it there.

My whole body shook. "Not my face."

"What else do you care about, vain girl?"

He pulled the tool from the fire, the tiny T brand he marked his knives with. I could barely look at it as he blew on the metal tip, causing it to turn deep red.

"Please, no, Taras."

"You should have thought twice before you helped that girl."

From the corner of my eye I saw the brand come closer to my left cheek, a blurry red-orange glow, and felt the warmth near my skin. "Please, Taras."

"The more you struggle, the longer this will take."

"I promise I won't . . ."

He stroked my hair. "Hold still. It will be over quickly."

All at once came the sting of the hot metal on the top of my cheek near my eye, the smell of burning flesh.

A great pounding came to the shed door, Mamka's wails, and then a scream as the searing-hot metal pressed deeper into my skin.

Only after a while did I know the scream was mine.

Sofya

1917

T HE NEXT MORNING I WOKE WITH A START ON A COT in Olga and Tatiana's room, to see a black wrinkled face staring down at me, tongue drooping out of her mouth.

"Come here, Ortipo," I said and pulled the French bulldog from the adjacent chair onto my stomach. She made herself at home on my chest, panting meaty little breaths in my face. How good it had been to sleep in a bed, even just a camp cot. I stroked Ortipo's soft back and admired the room, a pretty, if a bit messy, extension of Olga and Tatiana. Framed pictures of happier days hung on the walls: with their father aboard the imperial yacht, the family posed on the tennis court. Flowered drapes flanked the tall windows, painted ribbons and birds flew along the tops of the walls, and books and little standing frames covered the desks and dressing tables.

Just the thought of my family back in Malinov sent my stomach aching. How were Agnessa and Father getting along? Had Luba succeeded in hiding my absence? Though Olga and Tatiana seemed dedicated to planning my escape, they had their own problems.

I reached for the letters under my pillow. After a cold sponge bath, I'd stayed up reading Eliza's letter from New York.

Dear Empress Alexandra,

It is with heavy heart I write to you, fearing the worst for my dearest friend Sofya Streshnayva Stepanov. I understand you know and love the family. Can you share any news of their situation in Malinov? I am at your disposal in any way I can be of help . . .

How like Eliza to go straight to the top and reach out to the tsarina. She seemed frantic with worry. I longed to be with her, to provide the same comfort she'd given me countless times.

I reread Afon's letter to the tsarina, the return address blacked out:

My dear Empress,

I hope you and yours are well, but write today fearing the worst has happened to my wife, Sofya, and family, after hearing rumors of trouble in Malinov. Six letters have gone unanswered and I seek any information you can provide. Would you find it in your kind heart to send a company to check on them? I am with the _____ regiment now fighting in _____, and expect no leave for _____due to _____. If you do contact Sofya please deliver my most ardent good wishes and love and tell her I will come home as soon as we_____.

Your most obedient servant,
Afon

I smoothed one finger across the envelope front, along Afon's looping script. He'd heard of our troubles. Where was he fighting? Was he even still alive?

All at once came the sound one floor below of the servant's silver hammer hitting the tsarina's bedroom door, their daily invitation to rise. Eight-thirty already?

I left my cot and found Olga and Tatiana, awake and seated side by side on a love seat in their dressing room, sewing the white linen in their laps. A bowl of what looked like diamonds sat between them. They were dressed in dark skirts and white shirtwaists, with knitted berets covering their shorn heads.

Olga looked up from her work. "How did you sleep?"

Tatiana set her sewing aside as Ortipo jumped into her lap. "She is a very bad dog for waking you."

How pretty Tatiana was, with her wide-set light brown eyes, and so like her mother, with the same slender figure and reserved manner. Called "The Governess" by her siblings for her doting way with them, Tatiana was unflaggingly positive and, in sharp contrast to Olga, rarely questioned their parents' ways.

"We are almost done sewing," Olga said. "Mama has us work on this project one hour every morning."

"Making ourselves armor," Tatiana said.

I sat in a nearby chair. "I don't understand."

"Mama's idea. Sewing our jewels to our vests." Tatiana held up her camisole, part of the bodice covered in a solid, glittering sheet. "See? Our maid Emilia pulls the stones from their settings and we sew them tight together here."

"There are rumors we're to be moved soon," Olga said. "And we'll wear these. In case we are shot, the bullets will bounce off."

Olga bit off a thread, her teeth as white as her favorite little pearls around her neck. "Sofya, if we rely on my parents to help you escape, it may never happen."

"Papa has just heard King George has denied us asylum in England, so they are preoccupied," Tatiana said.

"His own cousin?" I asked.

"Last night I dreamed of a way to help you escape," Olga said. "What if we dress you as a maid, in Emilia's clothes, and tell the guards you must take Ortipo to the veterinarian?"

Tatiana held her little bulldog tighter. "Ortipo is perfectly healthy."

"But what if we fake an illness?" Olga asked. "Put chili powder under her nose."

Tatiana smoothed the dog's head. "I couldn't live without her."

"Sofya can deliver Ortipo to the vet and make her way back to Malinov. Emilia will pack Sofya food for the trip and I will contribute all the pocket money I have."

"Is the staff still loyal to you?" I asked.

"Mostly, but we never know who is on duty—they come and go to see their families. The new guards hate it, never able to establish a firm roster."

"So, they wouldn't recognize my face as new?"

Olga smiled. "It's bound to work."

Once Olga and Tatiana dressed me in their maid Emilia's black dress and white apron, complete with round, tortoiseshell spectacles and black sealskin boots, they stepped back to admire their work.

Olga pinned the regulation white organdy cap on my head. "Hurry, now. Paul the guard is on until noon. Tatiana is his favorite."

Tatiana helped me into a black cloth uniform coat and shrugged. "He's cute and kind and sneaks us the most delicious rum balls from the village."

"You make a perfect maid."

Tatiana handed me a canvas kit bag, which held a feast of black bread and cheeses, my folded trousers and coat, an ostrich-skin coin purse stuffed with her pocket money, and a flask of water.

"They will search you as you leave," Tatiana said. "Sometimes in a most roguish way, looking for smuggled letters or jewels they can confiscate. But even if they didn't, we have no weapons to give you. I slipped your letters under the bag's lining."

"They deny us even butter knives," Olga said. She reached both hands behind her neck and unclasped her pearls. "But these may help."

"No, Olga," I said.

"It will make me happy and you might use them better than I. The guards won't see them as valuable."

Tears filled my eyes as Olga clasped the pearls around my neck and tucked them inside the collar of my dress.

"We must hurry, now. Don't say a word—"

"I speak good Russian."

"Too good, I'm afraid," Olga said. "He'll know you're not a maid the minute you open your mouth. Let us deal with the guards. You'll see Tatiana's great skill as an actress."

Tatiana slid Ortipo into my arms. "You will find the veterinarian next to the sweetshop in the village. They know her there. Tell them she has been sneezing and ask them to deliver her back here. Then be on your way."

Olga smiled and kissed my cheek. "A kiss for Luba." She kissed the other cheek. "And may God help you, cousin."

OLGA AND TATIANA LED me to the servants' entrance, just off the kitchen on the lower level, and Tatiana began her theatrics before we even arrived, hollering at me. "And if you are not back with her by noon, I will report you to the commander."

As we walked, Olga waved a vial of something under the dog's nose. "Remember, don't speak."

We stepped into the kitchen where a brutish-looking guard sat at the table, hat on. He chatted with a maid dressed as I was, as she served him a bowl of groats, steam rising from it. There was nothing cute or kind about this guard.

"Where is Paul?" Tatiana asked.

He raised his spoon, ready to eat. "On holiday. I'm Stas."

Tatiana led the way toward the door. "Stas, Ortipo has to go to Dr. Tartello right away."

The guard stood and hurried to stand between the door and us. "On whose orders?"

Ortipo convulsed with a wet, little sneeze.

"Can't you see she's sick?" Tatiana asked.

"I see it's eating food that could go to the people." Stas glanced at his bowl on the table and then turned to me. "Hurry up then, turn around."

I turned as he patted me about the waist and down my legs.

"You servants in your fancy uniforms and livery. You no longer work for your old masters. The people pay you now."

"Do hurry, Stas," Tatiana said. "The doctor is only open until noon."

Stas pulled my jaw open and took a long look inside.

Ortipo sneezed again, spraying us both.

Stas wiped his hand on his trousers. "Get moving."

I said a silent thank-you and, with one glance back at my cousins, stepped out the door.

"Hey, you," Stas called out to me as I stepped down the path. "Where's the doctor, anyway?"

I turned, silent.

"Since when does the palace hire mutes?" he asked.

How could I not answer? "Next to the sweetshop," I said.

Tatiana reached for Olga's hand, her face ashen. Why had I spoken?

"Hold it right there," Stas said. "Get back here this minute."

Eliza

1917

B Y MAY OF 1917 THE POLIO EPIDEMIC SLOWED FOR the time being, the daily newspaper updates showing a few cases per month. Many young Southampton men enlisted as the war raged on but somehow the colony felt immune to the struggle and resumed their favorite time-worn, daily cycle: golf, lunch, tennis, and a dip in the ocean. It seemed selfish to ignore the suffering overseas and while Mother worked for Belgian war relief I plunged into my Russian committee efforts and helped Princess Yesipov gather food and small comforts for those Russian women not yet placed, still living at the boarding house.

One Sunday evening I said goodbye to Mother and Caroline as Thomas drove them to the train, city-bound, Caroline laden with a book bag full of Chapin schoolbooks. When he returned I asked him to drive me to the Meadow Club, one of the few remaining clubs to which Mother and I still belonged, which advertised itself as "A place for manly exercise and innocent recreation, with twenty-five tennis courts and telephones in every room." Perhaps they could find a way to employ a few White Russian women? With Henry gone, my standing at the club was certainly diminished since he was the member, but surely I still had some pull there. Father, who built our cottage in 1890, had been one of the first and most devoted members. Though neither Mother nor I said it, as widows the club was our lifeline.

It was always casual at the club on Sundays and Joseph, the cook whom I'd known since I was a child, would fix me a plate. Would he think it funny that, due to the war, suddenly anything German was being renamed? Sauerkraut was "Liberty cabbage." Even dachshunds were renamed "Liberty pups."

What harm would it do to step out and see some of Henry's and my old set? Maybe talk about the war news, stir the membership to support my Russian émigrés? Of course, there was the danger that Electra, terribly fond of racquet sports, might be there, but as much as I hated to admit it, I was lonely.

I dressed quickly to get it over with, still wearing black. How I ached to wear soft fabric, in any color but black. With war deaths mounting, mourning rules had been relaxed to spare the families of the dead the additional sorrow of seeing so many in black. Many women in mourning wore no sign of it at all. But giving up black meant giving up Henry.

Young Thomas drove me to the club, his chestnut hair smoothed under his chauffeur's cap. His scent of shaving cream wafted to me in the backseat of Mother's car. Had it really been five years since Henry had hired him? The sun set as we drove along the beach road.

"I'm signing up tomorrow," Thomas said, smiling at me in the rear-view mirror.

"Oh, I'm so proud of you, Thomas. But what will we do without you?" Tears stung my eyes when I thought of him in uniform and of his mother, probably worried sick about her only son leaving.

"You need to learn how to drive, Miz Ferriday."

I smiled at that and settled in for the short trip. My stomach growled. What would life have been like if Henry had been alive and the war had never started? Sofya and Luba would be safe and we'd still be on our trip. In India? I relived it so often in my mind, shopping the bright Bombay markets, the sultry air ripe with cumin and saffron, Caroline and I wrapped in soft saris of turquoise and lime green. I imagined lunching with Henry on crimson curry and fried flatbread in the dining car of a Himalayan Railway locomotive car. We'd thrust our heads from the window as we climbed higher into the emerald mountains, headed for the fragrant tea fields of Darjeeling.

Thomas turned into the Meadow Club, tires crunching the crushed-shell drive, the place understated as always, bearing no sign. The clubhouse with its weathered gray shingles and crisp linen white trim loomed large in the dusk.

I wandered through the dining room, the dull thud of distant waves crashing on the shore mixed with the sounds of cocktail hour on the porch, the tinkle of ice and laughter of people without a care. I stepped close to the round tables set with white gladioli and hand-scripted place cards. Place cards? That was different, but then again, the club was changing as new members were admitted, becoming more formal. Why do people think place cards will improve a party? It removes all free will from a gathering.

I stepped to the porch doorway and took it all in, the neatly matched couples, cocktails in hand, arranged among the wicker furniture, dressed in a whole spectrum of what passed for white: men in creamy tennis sweaters and flannel trousers, some yellow-creased, newly released from their winter trunks, and women in ivory dresses and ecru stockings. It was like something out of one of Henry's favorite John Singer Sargent paintings. The green-and-white-striped porch awning framed the grass tennis courts and beige Japanese paper globes strung aglow along the porch's beadboard ceiling.

Merrill sat in a wicker chair in the thick of it all, his tennis racquet and a silver cup at his feet, Anna Gabler arranged on the arm of his chair, a vision in cream, a string of golf ball–sized South Sea pearls at her throat.

I was somehow surprised at the number of people there, most familiar, some not; that other lives went on while mine, eight months after Henry's death, still felt stunted.

From snips of conversation about close calls and ribbing about unfair advantages, it was clear Merrill had won the tournament. I suddenly felt out of place in my plain widow's weeds, with not even a spot of rouge on my cheeks. My stomach complained at the smell of roast lamb and I suddenly missed Henry terribly. He would have broken the ice. Said something funny to make everyone laugh.

I stepped onto the porch, a pebble in the pond. The gorgeous people, senses dulled by rum, slowly turned their gaze to me and drew quiet.

Anna stood. "Eliza Ferriday," she said, eyebrows raised, as if she'd spotted a woolly mammoth at the natural history museum.

Merrill stood, along with the rest of the men, his white trousers stained grass-green at the knees like a child's. Anna linked her arm through his and the diamond on her left hand caught the porch light.

Why had I come? It was still too soon to be social.

"Please sit," I said. "A little chilly for tennis, isn't it?"

"Merrill and I won first flight doubles," Anna said.

"Congratulations," I said. "I just came by for a bit of dinner and to talk to someone about employing some Russian friends of mine."

"More Russians?" Anna asked. "I think we're fully staffed here at the moment." She disengaged herself and stepped toward me. "And this is all so embarrassing, dear, but we haven't a place for you at dinner. It's a club function tonight."

"Oh, I didn't get the notice."

Anna exchanged a glance with a woman I didn't know, who bit the inside of her cheek and looked away.

I motioned toward the kitchen. "I'll just ask Joseph for a bite—"

"The cook took ill last week," Anna said. "Passed away, sad to say. Heart trouble."

"Has anyone called on his family?"

The group shifted about, not meeting my gaze.

"How did I not get the word?"

"I'm afraid you're no longer on the mailing list."

"Are you saying I'm no longer welcome here?"

"We're all so terribly sad about your husband, but the social secretary told me . . ."

Merrill came toward us. "Eliza—"

I took a step back. "My father headed the admissions committee for ten years. Henry was a member in good standing, too." Mother's people had been on Long Island since the eighteenth century. Did tradition count for nothing anymore?

Anna laced her fingers at her waist. "This is all so sordid, but you're no longer part of the club, dear. Bylaw number three. If the member predeceases the spousal member, said spouse shall be removed from the club roster."

"I know the bylaws, Anna. When my father died my mother was never turned away."

Merrill paced, swinging his tennis racquet.

"It's the rule, dear. We had to let old Mrs. Parker go, too, poor thing. If we made an exception for you—"

"For years my parents helped so many of you get in here and this is your thanks? Shame on you all."

Anna took a step back. "No need to be a hothead, dear."

"Decency and kindness were the pillars of the club then, but no more."

I turned and walked with a deliberate step back through the clubhouse. Footsteps echoed behind me.

Merrill.

"Eliza—" He pulled me by the arm into the darkened trophy room, the only light the glow from the underlit glass cabinets filled with sterling silver Revere bowls of different sizes, identical except for the names engraved on them.

"Leave me alone, Merrill."

He closed the door. "Will you listen for once?"

I turned to the cabinet. "How many of these trophies have your name on them?" I moved on to a large bowl atop a wooden plinth and read: *Anna Gabler and Richard Merrill, first flight doubles winners.* "You won last year, too? How lovely, you two forever enshrined together in tennis history. Did her father pay for that, too?"

"It's a good match, Eliza."

"You only care about appearances. Silver trophies. The Gabler money. Their Diamond Horseshoe opera box."

"You iced me out of your life long ago. Why shouldn't I be happy?"

"With Anna Gabler? It takes a certain kind of man—"

Merrill took me by the shoulders. "You're *jealous.*"

"Don't be ridiculous. I just hate to see a good person commit to a lifetime of pain."

"You never asked how it happened that day. Henry and I never played tennis."

"Don't be ridiculous." I tried to turn away from him, but he held me fast.

"We spent the day with a woman friend of mine, a Miss Angelica Vandermeer."

"The travel booker?"

"Ask her yourself if you like. Henry's cover story was that we were playing tennis but we actually went to see her to plan your trip."

I looked for a place to sit down, light-headed.

"Henry swore me to secrecy. Wanted to plan it to the last detail. He felt, with war brewing, India should wait and booked South America instead. We discussed the itinerary for two hours. Rio or Patagonia?"

I could only stare at him.

"A puppet theater in Lima for Caroline. Candlelight dinner in the ruins of a sugar plantation for you two. A trip to some literary place for your mother. I offered to drive him home, but he said he needed the exercise and wanted to walk. It hadn't started raining."

"I'm sorry, Merrill."

"Well, that's long overdue. I loved him, too, Eliza."

"You should have told me." I touched his sleeve.

He brushed my hand away. "It's too late for that. You can't just one day decide to invite me back into your life. I'm about to be *married*."

"I'm sorry, Merrill."

"Are you? I loved you, Eliza. Do you know what it was like having Henry come along and take you from me?"

"I didn't . . ."

"You thought only of yourself as usual. Engaged to him a week later with just a brief note to me. You could have at least said it to my face."

I shrugged. "You seemed apathetic."

"I was *shattered*, Eliza." He pulled me to him.

Someone switched on the globe of liver-colored glass above us and Anna entered, a battalion of her white-clad acolytes in her wake, craning their necks for a better view of us.

"It didn't take the grieving widow long to cast aside her sorrow, now did it, Eliza?" Anna asked. "I'll have your car brought around."

The humiliation of all of them staring at us wide-eyed sent my cheeks ablaze. I turned to leave and pushed through the crowd of Anna's friends clogging the doorway, a black-clothed widow forging through a sea of white. I picked up speed in the dining room and ran out to meet Thomas.

It would be the last time I set foot in the Meadow Club for quite some time.

I RETURNED TO GIN Lane, stepped into the vestibule, and slammed the front door shut.

Peg came from the study, a detective novelette in hand. "Mother of God, you're gray as dishwater."

"Don't ask," I said and ran up the stairs, down the hallway to my bedroom, and shut the door with a satisfying thud.

What a comfort that room was, with its low ceiling and faded wall-paper, strewn with once-scarlet cabbage roses, now just pale pink clouds. Mother's silver loving cup on the fireplace mantel. The sturdy little table on which Mother's family had rolled Civil War bandages, with the depression in the wood still there where a bandage roller had been clamped. How soothing to be there surrounded by the objects from family travels. A stone chunk from the Parthenon. Coins from around the world piled into an old night cream jar. A stack of travel magazines high as my waist.

How many crises had I faced from Grandmother Woolsey's hand-some four-poster bed? When Henry died and I retreated under that quilt to recover?

I ripped open the front of my dress, launching jet buttons about the room. What would Father have said about it all? A model of friendship to all, he probably would have supported Merrill, pointed out my hostile attitude toward him. How was I to know Henry had hatched a secret plan? I yanked my nightgown out from beneath the pillow.

I lay in my bed, staring out the dormered window to the moonlit, shimmering sea. The breeze nudged the ruffled edges of the white, muslin curtains there. Mother had sewn those herself for my sixteenth birthday.

Mother. She would be ripping mad about the whole affair, of course. The Meadow Club board better get ready for a tidal wave of angry letters from her club friends.

Why had I even come out to Gin Lane? The war. The club. Sofya. The world was spinning out of control.

I dozed and woke to the sound of tires on shell and an automobile engine repeating and then turning off. I glanced at the glow in the dark arms of the bedside table clock.

Five o'clock.

Soon the sound of a muted door knocker and a conversation in the entryway drifted up the stairs. I sat up, suddenly wide awake.

Peg rapped lightly on my door and entered. "Ma'am? There's someone here to see you." Her hair was tied up in a mass of white rags, like moths fluttering about her head.

"At this hour? Send them away, Peg. Really."

"I would've, ma'am, but he used some words I can't repeat and sets down on the front stairs and says even if Teddy Roosevelt himself comes to remove him, he won't budge."

He? I groaned. "Peg, can't you——"

"Sorry, but he says he has something to show you and if you don't come down he'll come up here to your bedroom, and if you ask me, he means it."

All at once, Merrill burst into the room and brushed by Peg.

She stood, stunned, one hand to her throat. "Jesus. Shall I call the police?"

I sat up in bed. "You can leave us, Peg."

Peg walked backward out of the room, her gaze trained on Merrill.

He pushed the door closed and stepped to my bed, eyes red-rimmed, one arm curled around a silver bowl.

"Couldn't this wait until——" I reached for my dressing gown and he handed it to me.

I eased myself from under the covers and stepped into my slippers. "It's late and Peg will broadcast your presence here in all forty-eight states by daybreak."

"This isn't easy, Eliza."

"Does Anna know you're here?" I tied my dressing gown at the waist.

"I deserved to lose you to Henry. He was the better man certainly."

"Merrill, please. We need to calm——"

He stepped to the window, and with one hand threw up the sash and opened it wide.

Merrill turned to face me and held the silver bowl with two hands. "Eliza, I regret the day I competed for this cup."

"You have every right to be sporty, Merrill."

"What you said before is true. I do care too much about appearances. But all that is changing tonight."

Merrill reached out the window and sent the silver bowl flying. It caught the moonlight for a second as it sailed out over Mr. Gardener's potager garden and then plunged with a distant thud onto the back lawn.

I smiled. "The trophy committee will want to be reimbursed."

"Damn the trophy committee. Damn the whole club. I won't be going back until they reinstate you. And Mrs. Parker. I'm tired of it, Eliza. The catty talk, the gossip."

"Merrill—"

"Just *listen* for once. I don't love Anna Gabler. I'd convinced myself I did, but seeing you tonight . . . You may not return my affection, Eliza, but I won't marry someone else just to go through the motions. If I can't have you I'll have no one. I'm leaving today. Enlisting."

A chill ran through me. "Oh no, Merrill."

"I thought you'd be happy."

"But—"

"I'm finally doing what's right, Eliza. After all, it's you who said, 'Only a coward would wait to be called up. Good men enlist.'"

"That was just casual conversation."

"I'll tell Anna on my way to get my physical exam. I hear there might be a group going to France to learn to fly according to French methods."

Merrill voluntarily traveling to France?

"An aviator, Merrill? Couldn't you drive an ambulance, far back from the front?"

He laughed. "It's much safer in the air. Don't know a word of French, but I'll learn. The training is top drawer. Need to make it through exercises at Newport News first."

"Virginia? Must you this moment?"

"I've never been more energized, Eliza. I feel like I'm finally doing the right thing."

Merrill stood transformed, cheeks flushed. "I love you, Eliza. I knew it the first time I saw you on the steps of St. Thomas Church."

"This is so—"

"Please don't say no. Just give me a chance."

Merrill pulled me to him and the delicious scent of sweat and salt air surrounded us and for once I forgot everything wrong with the world.

He whispered in my ear. "All I need is hope."

Varinka

1917

THE MORNING AFTER TARAS BRANDED ME I LAY UNDER the satin coverlet on the countess's bed and thought of ways to kill myself. How else to escape? Hang myself from the countess's chandelier? Throw myself from her balcony?

How could I live this way? Every day was worse, with no freedom, Taras watching me in the bath, ready to blow up at the smallest thing. But how could I leave little Max? At three years old, he was more aware than ever. How much did the child take in?

Max climbed up onto my bed, and I smoothed back his blond curls. I tried not to flinch as he ran his finger down the burn just under the edge of my right eye, gentle as a buttercup's kiss.

"*Fait mal,*" he said with a serious look.

"Yes, your Mummy hurts."

Mummy. Though I used the word he never did. It had been months since Taras and Vladi took over the estate and the boy still showed signs of stress. Purple smudges under his eyes from restless sleep. He insisted on spreading blankets on Mamka's bedroom floor and sleeping there, what he called "camping out." He stood by the window of his bedroom most days watching. Waiting for Sofya? He spoke mostly Russian but Mamka and I kept up his French.

At least Taras had called a truce on Max for now.

"We will get away from Taras," Mamka had said. But how? What would Papa have done about it all?

Papa. Just the thought of him brought tears, which spilled over, stinging my burn. Somehow the pain felt good. I had my own sins to atone for.

The door opened and Taras stepped partway into the room.

"Close your eyes, Varinka."

Max clung to me, arms about my neck.

"You're scaring him," I said.

Taras stepped to the foot of the bed. "I have something for you."

"I've had enough of your gifts."

Taras looked at the carpet and fell silent for a moment. "I have tried to find your Papa's samovar and cannot, but this is something you might like as well. Max, cover Varinka's eyes."

Max directed his gaze at me and I nodded. He sat up on his knees and placed his small hands over my eyes. I waited with a pit in my belly as the sound of Taras's footsteps on carpet came closer.

"Oh, dear," Max said.

"What is it?" I asked.

"A surprise," Max whispered, his soft lips tickling my ear.

Something lay cold and hard against the spot where Taras branded me, the cold metal soothing my burn. Then I felt cold metal across the top of my hand.

"Open your eyes," Taras said.

I found resting atop my hand a most incredible necklace, of diamonds so clear you could see through them and smooth, green stones like humps of moss.

"They're emeralds," Taras said. "I convinced Mrs. A. it was a fake and she offered it to me in exchange for the *izba*. She's going to store her supplies there."

"How could you? Papa built that place with his two hands." Oddly all cried out, I could not summon even one tear.

"It was the countess's and not a fake at all. Mrs. A. says blondes look best in emeralds. You like it?" With his free hand Taras smoothed a lock of my hair behind my ear.

I flinched at his touch.

"Ungrateful girl. But you'll need fine things for we are going to Paris."

"When?"

"Soon as I have a meeting in Petrograd. They chose me to go since Vladi will serve as district commissioner here."

Paris. Just the thought of it warmed me. Mamka had told me so many stories of it. The shops and the clothes. Could Mamka and Max and I escape Taras in Paris? Surely it would be easier there.

I tossed the necklace on the bed. "That is good news, I guess."

"You guess?"

"You sold my *home*, Taras. Mamka will never forgive you."

"You're never happy." Taras pulled a valise from the armoire and heaved it onto the bed. "I am taking you with me to Petrograd."

It was a sour thought, the idea of being with Taras for a whole trip, but my blood raced at the thought of visiting the city. I'd been there only once with Mamka and it was the most beautiful place, the streets lined with pretty shops.

I tried to brush away the bad thoughts that buzzed around me. How could I leave Mamka and Max alone? Would Vladi hurt Max while I was gone? Kill the Streshnayvas? Vladi said Sofya had escaped. Would she take Max? Did Max even remember Sofya? Mamka often brought up the subject that she was his rightful mother, but I just walked away. Papa had given the child to me and it was too late to change things.

Mamka stepped into the room. "My daughter is not going anywhere. The city is too dangerous right now."

"This is just a brief trip. The committee wants to speak with me and they are sending a motorcar and driver. It will do her good to get out of this place."

"I don't like it. Since the February madness every bandit in Russia is there. Telegraph service and post are cut off. How will you reach us if there is a problem?"

"Stay out of it, if you know what's good for you. Go pack now, Varinka. The car is coming."

Taras left the room and Mamka watched as I tossed clothes into the valise.

"We need to get away from him," Mamka said.

Images of Petrograd flitted through my head. Would I have a chance to escape? Why even think that way? Taras would keep Mamka and Max as hostages.

I tickled Max's chin. Just a look into his blue eyes made my troubles dim. Would he ever be safe with Taras in his life?

"When I return we are going to Paris. Taras has been sent there by the Reds."

"Saints be praised," Mamka said. "Everything will be better in Paris."

ONCE I CHANGED INTO one of Sofya's nicest dresses of pale pink satin, we put our bags in the motorcar and set off. I watched Mamka and Max grow smaller from the back window, nervous at every bump since I had never ridden in an auto before.

We passed through the gates, now staffed by a young man from town, and I tried not to think of Aleks and Ulad. I pressed my hands to my face.

Taras rubbed my thigh. "Don't cry, you'll see Max and Zina soon."

I pushed his hand away. "I'm afraid Vladi will hurt Max. What if he kills the family?"

"It's not your business."

"They are good people, Taras."

Taras turned to me, grabbed my wrist. "Would you *stop*? Things are different now."

The driver looked at him in his rearview mirror and Taras lowered his voice.

"It's our turn, don't you see? And the party needs me."

"To do what?"

"The less you know, the better."

I looked out the window at the deep forest passing by. Would Vladi shoot the family? More than once the villagers had come to take them away, stopped by Taras. Maybe it would be best for them to die, rather than continue living like dirty animals. I wished for a quick death for them all, even the countess.

WE ARRIVED IN PETROGRAD that afternoon and Mamka was right about the city being in chaos. Our fancy motorcar drew hostile glances until Taras raised his arm, tied round with a red cloth, to the window. One soldier lifted his bottle in salute. "Good day, comrade!"

246 • MARTHA HALL KELLY

It was sad to see our capital in such disrepair; the pavement pried up on so many roads, market women calling out their wares right on the fanciest streets; even on the best one, Nevsky Prospekt, thick crowds were shoving and shouting.

I was relieved as we slowed and approached Hotel Evropeiskaya.

"Tsar's gone now, 'course," the driver said. "Under arrest in Alexander Palace, whole family."

All at once Mamka's little portrait of the royal family, which she kept on her beautiful corner shelf came to mind. The "little father" with his neatly trimmed beard, the wistful tsarina, their four daughters and young son.

I tried to keep the shake from my voice. "But the tsar——"

"Don't waste a tear on that group."

"But he was appointed by God," I said.

"And I'm the Queen of England. Wake up. They cared little for us, miss. Only themselves. The tsar mowed down his own people in the streets. Taxed us to death."

My thoughts went to the terrible day the taxman came to the *izba*. Anything was better than that.

The driver smiled and waved in the direction of the Winter Palace. "The *Bolsheviki* had a good time raiding that palace. The fools passed right by the treasures there and cut the leather seats off the chairs instead. Chopped the gilded plaster from the tsar's walls, sure it must be real gold."

"Is no one stopping them?" I asked.

"The provisional government is on its last leg."

"So, the fighting is over?"

"Ha!" the driver said. "Just begun, if you ask me."

I stepped out of the auto and looked up at the hotel, a stately stone palace four stories tall. If only Mamka could see it. What looked like bands of criminals let loose from the prisons and soldiers in ragged uniforms roamed the sidewalk. Others encamped in the street, unfurling their packs and sleeping there. Some sold leather-covered books and paintings from their new outdoor homes. One soldier walked by bumping his gun along the street as a fine gentleman uses a walking stick.

We hurried into the hotel lobby, the grand place overrun with men resting on the velvet couches.

Taras grabbed me by the arm as we walked. "Stop giving your opinion so freely to strangers. You never know who is your friend here."

The hotel manager, a squinting mole of a man, showed us to our rooms, adjusting his wire-rimmed spectacles as he walked. As we rushed through the hallways I tried to peep at the rich furnishings in those rooms with open doors, many looking as if they'd been hacked open with the force of an ax and ransacked.

We stopped in front of a closed door and the manager turned a key in the lock.

"This is our best suite for now, I'm afraid. In better days Igor Stravinsky stayed here."

The suite held two rooms put together, a door between, each bigger than my *izba*, the ceiling three times Taras's height. I touched the keys of the grand piano and ran my hand down one wall, velvety as the fur on an elk's antlers.

"Have you never seen wallpaper?" the manager asked, clasping his mole hands together. "That is velvet damask. And the white lamps at either end of the sofa are wired to electricity. Not that we'll have power much longer."

He kept his overcoat on. Was he cold due to the lack of coal or just planning for a hasty retreat in case of attack?

"No maid service now," the manager said as he showed us to our adjoining rooms. "Servants are all on strike. Probably just out having fun in the streets. Washerwomen, too, so don't expect food or clean linen."

Taras turned and stared at the manager.

"Not that it isn't their right to work as they please, of course, comrades. Who am *I* to judge a fellow worker?"

We walked about the rooms, the furnishings dirty and topsy-turvy. Soiled water stood in the washbasins and the balcony doors had been left open, curtains fluttering in the light wind. A trunk almost my height stood near the balcony, open and violated, traveling clothes and cosmetics trailing out of every little drawer.

He handed Taras the key. "The *Bolsheviki* barge into the hotel's rooms at all hours to requisition goods and arms from anyone of any wealth. They carry off whatever they please, so sleep when you can."

Machine-gun fire erupted on the street below, sending the manager into a little spasm, one hand to his chest.

He swallowed hard. "This suite was once occupied by a princess who, well, won't be returning."

Taras handed the manager some paper money. "We'll lock our door."

The man pocketed it. "Locks mean nothing to them. They do as they please. The princess's trunks are still here—rifled through, of course—but will be removed soon."

The manager rushed off with a series of deep bows and Taras hurried to the balcony doors and shut them.

"I'm late for my meeting." Taras handed me the key. "Lock this door when I go. Do not set foot on the balcony. Do not let anyone in and don't go anywhere. Understand?"

I nodded.

He came to me, smoothed his thumb across my burn, and I willed myself not to flinch.

"I'm tired of the arrangement, Varinka. This is an opportunity for us tonight. No child. No Zina. I don't care what the priests say." He pulled me to him, close enough to feel the hardness in his pants, and kissed my neck.

I pushed him away. How could I risk having a baby with him?

His face darkened. "I'll be back at eight and you had better be here, Inka. I will not be so charitable next time you disobey me."

Of course, I would obey him. Where would I go? Join the mobs?

He hurried out. I turned the key in the lock and slipped it in my dress pocket.

I listened for Taras's retreating footsteps and then stepped to the balcony and opened the doors wider. What a relief to have him gone. My stomach grumbled. How to get food?

As it grew dark thousands of people filled the square, sailors lit fires and sang military songs. A thrill ran through me as sounds came from the direction of the shops on Nevsky Prospekt: young people's voices laughing and singing, and the shifting grind of the motor trucks passing below, their running boards filled with what sounded like drunken men shouting Russian songs.

I closed the doors, stepped to the bathroom, turned on the tap, and let the water run over my fingers into the big white tub. Such a wonderful thing, warm water from the tap.

As the water ran, I wandered the room and stopped at the ravaged trunk, such a sad sight. Perhaps that princess should have been more concerned about the people.

I eased the lacey underthings back in their little drawers and pulled a French magazine from one drawer. *La Vie Parisienne*. The cover showed a woman lifting her skirt high enough to show her shoes, four other pairs scattered around her. I stood and flipped through the pages, past pictures of half-naked girls wearing the newest hats and dresses. A store called Superior Lingerie showed pictures of stockings and "Corsets for even the curviest girls."

I stopped at one article titled "Do You Know How to Kiss?"

The article showed pictures of a couple embracing, the captions calling out the right and wrong ways to kiss. The right way was standing just the right distance apart, but not too close. The woman must lift her chin, close her eyes, and turn her head all in that order. I tried it, lifting my chin.

I tossed the magazine back in the trunk. For all Taras's romantic interest in me we'd never kissed mouth to mouth and I would die unkissed.

I checked the other compartments. A silver *kokoshnik* studded with gems lay in the bottom of one. I lifted it out of the drawer and ran one finger down the peaked crown, heavy with the kind of paste gems Mamka often sewed with. I rushed to the lavatory, looked in the mirror, and placed it on my head. It was just like one I'd seen the tsar's daughters wear.

A black thought struck me. Would it bring bad luck to wear the clothing of a dead person?

Soon there came a great commotion in the hallway. I stayed very still and barely breathed.

"Let us in, by order of the Red Army. We have come to check for guns."

I ran to the bedroom and froze there next to the great piano, fingers

250 • MARTHA HALL KELLY

laced at my chest, my heart thumping against them. Taras said not to let them in. But could they break down the door?

"We know you are in there," called one. "If we have to break the door down we will show no mercy."

Should I hide in the armoire? Under the bed? I felt my pocket for the key, cold and heavy there.

I stepped to the door and placed one hand on the cold wood. "Go away." Did I sound strong?

"We're not leaving until we check this room." Something hard hit the outside of the door.

"There are sick in here. Typhus."

Their answer was another slam at the door. Then another. The wood splintered at the edges.

"Stop!" I called out. I tried to put the key in the keyhole but my hands shook so.

"This is the last warning," a woman's voice called from the hallway.

I finally unlocked the door and six or seven men and one woman rushed in, all dressed in the kind of drab clothes we'd seen on the street. All stank of sweet wine.

The woman came toward me. "Your travel papers?"

"I have none. I came from Malinov on official party business."

The men laughed and the woman stepped closer. "Party business? You in your bourgeois dress and jewels."

"The headpiece came from the princess's trunk."

"Good story," one of the men said. He grabbed my backside and I jumped away from him.

"You'll have to come outside with us while we check the room," the woman said.

A little man wearing a white sailor's shirt stained about the neck with splotches of red wine pulled my arms behind me. He whispered in my ear, "I may just take one for myself tonight."

"Taras Pushkinsky. You may know him. He works for the party. I have rights as a citizen."

The woman stepped to the piano and ran the back of her hand down the keys. "No papers, no rights."

Suddenly the ruffians turned and looked at something behind me.

"Who authorized this?" a man's voice asked.

I turned to find a nice-looking young man, wearing a green coat like the ones the others wore and the same sort of gray cap.

The woman recognized him. "I'm sorry, Commissioner."

"Go check another room, if that is what you're really doing. You seem to be looting for your own purposes. This will not help the people."

The group filed out, the excitement of their little raid passed.

The man closed the door behind them and nodded his head. "I'm Radimir Solomakhin. What are you doing here alone?"

"Taras thought it would be a good time to visit—"

"Taras?"

I held my breath. What to say? How could I tell a stranger the truth?

"Taras Pushkinsky. My guardian. I am Varinka from Malinov. He is here for a party meeting and thought I would like to see the sights. Those people thought I was wealthy."

"Those people are *Bolsheviki* and a dangerous bunch. Lend you a helping hand one minute and put a bullet in your head the next."

Radimir smiled and held out one hand. "Come, Varinka. You're safe with me. Let's have some fun."

CHAPTER

3 2

Sofya

1917

I TURNED, THERE ON THE SERVANTS' ENTRANCE PATH. Why did I speak to the guard? I'd been so close to freedom. I clutched Ortipo closer, her little heart pounding against my palm. Did she sense my fear?

"I'm sorry—"

"How many times must I say it?" Stas asked. "Get *over* here."

I stepped back toward the servants' entrance.

Stas tossed a coin toward me. "Bring me back two peppermints."

I caught the coin with my free hand and glanced at Olga and Tatiana, relief on their faces.

"Of course," I said, the coin warm in my cold hand, and headed off toward town.

I HURRIED PAST A drunken mob that had vandalized the little wine shop in town, dropped Ortipo at the veterinarian's office, and headed out of Tsar's Village for the road back to Malinov. I removed my white maid's cap and apron, in case Stas had a sudden ray of insight and reported me missing. I wished thanks to my cousins for the warm boots, happy the tsarina shod her maids well and ordered them French-made uniforms.

The trek back to Malinov seemed interminable. I walked all day, hungry, but vowed to save the food in my kit bag for my family, and finally hitched a ride with another farmer who took pity on me. We had to stop over and sleep with his family in one room for the night before he dropped me near Malinov.

I trudged through the night energized by thoughts of seeing the estate again. I fixed little Max's sweet face in my mind. Would he remember his mama after so many months apart?

Near morning, lit only by the moon, I approached the estate, keeping to the ruts a troika had left in the slushy spring snow.

I rehearsed my plan. I would first get Max from his nursery, wait for the right moment, and then set my family free.

I stepped to the back of the house and at the sound of shuffling footsteps near the back door pressed myself close to a tree. A woman emerged and flung a box onto what looked like a massive refuse pile and then hurried back into the house. Could there be food there? My stomach complained at the thought.

I inched closer and saw Agnessa's greenhouse, somehow imploded, the glass and metal crushed and lying at odd angles in the snow, household refuse dumped there. Laundry soapboxes and tin cans. A funny little breathy grunting met my ears and I made out two hairy bodies among the trash, two wild boars nosing about.

I waited for the pair to move on, stepped to the pile, pulled out the closest box, and almost fainted from what I found there. Could it be? A package of Agnessa's French meringue dessert shells. I ripped open the bag and bit one, rock hard, and then slid it into my pocket. Just the taste of sugar helped me stand taller.

Something white caught my eye and I turned to find one white rose growing out of it all, a Katharina Zeimet. Mr. Gardener's rose. A true survivor. I pulled the plant out, root ball still intact and covered with burlap, and slid it into my bag, careful not to crush the leaves. Could I keep such a delicate thing alive?

I walked to the back steps, the oak panel Bogdan had nailed there so many months before pried off. It smelled of urine and boiled cabbage as I entered the hallway, the house hushed.

I climbed the back stair to Max's nursery, my hands clasped to stop the shaking. I would take him and go. To the village. I reached the top

of the stairs and halted, listening to the muted voices coming from behind the nursery door. Inka? Her mother? No. They didn't sound familiar, like those who would recognize me, so I took a deep breath and
entered.

The room was brightly lit with new hanging petrol lamps and an-
chored in the center by a typically Russian wooden desk big enough to
spread a picnic on, a man sitting on one of Agnessa's dining room
chairs there. Near the window sat a table heaped with ledgers. I stood
in the doorway, eyes adjusting to the light, watching a woman walk
about the room straightening up. I stood, rooted to the spot. It was dear
Raisa.

"You're late," the man said without looking up, hunched over a
glass of tea. Everything about him was round and porcine, his little
eyes lost in the folds of his fat, pink face. At least I'd never seen him
before. No chance he would recognize me.

"Late?" I asked. I walked toward the desk and read a crudely written cardboard sign there. *The People's Rope and Laundry, Laundry Division.*

"You'll have to fly to get to Kolpino by six. Where is your husband
to drive?"

Raisa and I met eyes. Would she expose me?

"Taken ill?" I asked.

"You are asking me? Ill with what? The drink, that's what. Am I the
only one willing to work around here anymore?"

"I can drive the wagon."

"You'll have to."

Raisa stepped to the desk and bent toward the man. "Commissioner, I must tell you—"

A chill ran through me. *Please, Raisa, don't expose me. I've come so
far.*

Eliza

1917

IT WAS A WARM LATE SPRING MORNING, THE NIGHT BEFORE our fund-raiser for the Russian women, when Merrill's first letter arrived.

Peg delivered it to me as I stood in the driveway at the front of the house. I hurried the envelope open and took in Merrill's lovely script.

NEWPORT NEWS, VIRGINIA

Dearest Eliza,

Had my first trip up this morning, with an instructor. Fairly simple getting up to 3,200 feet, some pockets of rough air but a glorious harbor view. We made a pretty landing having been up only 18 minutes. Other than knowing my life will officially start when I come home to you, the only other thing I know is that flying is something I want to stay with for some time. I head out for France soon, eager to see their machines there . . .

He closed the letter with a lovely colored pencil sketch, an aerial view of the harbor so detailed, down to the sailors on the boats in the harbor. Was this Merrill's artistic work? How unlike him, but what a lovely surprise to see that hidden talent. Had I made a tremendous mistake, shaming him to enlist? How good it would be to see him again.

As I refolded the letter and slid it back into its envelope, Officer Maddox rode into our driveway on his motorbike.

"Afternoon," he said, one hand at his uniform hat brim.

Everything about Billy Maddox, his gentle way, his slight frame and bland, Midwestern good looks made him wholly unsuited to police work. But what he lacked in authority he made up for with his affable way.

"Here on official business, I'm afraid."

I folded my arms across my waist. He was there to enforce zoning laws no doubt.

All at once Mother drove her car into the driveway, sending crushed quahog shells flying. She was due to pick up most of our household to see Mary Pickford in *Little Pal* at the Crescent Theatre. She sounded her horn and out of the house came Peg, Princess Yesipov, Caroline, and three women from the boarding house in the Bowery visiting for the day to meet with the Irving Hotel about possible work. They all piled into the car. Why had Billy picked that moment to visit us?

"Good day, Officer Maddox," Mother said.

"Good day, Mrs. Mitchell. Afraid I have bad news."

"The mean turkey is loose again?" Mother asked.

Billy kicked at the shells with the toe of his boot. "Yes, but there's more bad news. Electra Whitney has filed an official complaint against you."

Mother sent me her best stern look.

He held out a paper and read. "In Southampton proper, a one-family detached residence, unless a church or similar place of worship, seminary, parish house, convent—"

Princess Yesipov turned in the backseat and said in her thick accent, "Sir, we are missing our cinema."

Officer Maddox continued. "Unless dwelling is a camping grounds, multiple dwelling for three or more families, and is a country residence over two hundred thousand square feet—"

"Summarize, Billy." Mother stepped down from her auto.

Officer Maddox rolled up his paper and shook the little tube in Mother's direction. "Complaint says you can't have more than four guests staying here permanent unless they are family, Mrs. Mitchell. And from the sound of this group you've got a problem."

Electra wasn't the only one who'd noticed the increased activity at our house. I hadn't told Mother, but we'd received a letter from a New Jersey couple asking to rent rooms with us for the weekend, thinking it was a hotel.

"But Peg is a registered worker. Caroline is my granddaughter."

"And the rest? Mrs. Whitney says at least one's been working without a permit."

Mother stepped toward Officer Maddox. "How long have we known each other, dear? Since you were sick at the hospital?"

Billy removed his hat, licked his palm, and smoothed down his blond hair, suddenly looking younger than his nineteen years. Deferred from war by a diphtheria-related inner ear issue, Billy earned the top law enforcement job in town when the former police chief enlisted. His sweet nature and penchant for motorbikes made him especially vulnerable to Electra Whitney's demands.

He stuffed the letter in his pocket. "Lived there almost a month."

"You know me, Billy. I would never violate the law."

He stepped closer to Mother and lowered his voice. "I'm getting it from all Miss Electra's pals, too. Saying they will have me canned. Told me the town's overrun with folks talking foreign languages and they just don't like it. Said you're the problem, harboring so many aliens."

"Electra bought that motorcycle, correct?" I asked.

"Threatened to make me walk everywhere if I don't get you to comply. Said they talked to the hospital, too, askin' the board to have you removed, Mrs. Mitchell."

Mother stepped up into her auto and swatted the air with the back of her hand. "Oh, let them try, Billy. In the meantime, we will do everything in our power to relocate the ladies and make sure they are legal."

Billy replaced his cap. "Good thing. Have it done by tomorrow? Or else I will have to start arrests. Hate to do it, because they seem like good folks. Not sure where they'd be sent. Maybe back to Ukrainia."

"They are from Petrograd, Officer Maddox," I said. *"Russians."*

Mother backed up her vehicle. "Don't give it another thought, Billy. The problem will be solved tomorrow, isn't that right, Eliza?"

"Of course," I said.

I STEPPED INTO THE DARKENING kitchen to make final preparations for the next day's party, glassware arranged on the counters, a crystal ziggurat of *samogon* bottles stacked on the kitchen table. I seized a crudités platter from the icebox, sat near the window, and opened the newspaper.

I found an article about Vladimir Lenin, which said he was encouraging the wholesale slaughter of monarchists and anti-Bolsheviks and eliminated dissent through the Cheka, the new secret police. I looked past the dark lawn out to sea, the lights from the fishing boats on the distant horizon. Lenin's rise made the situation even more perilous for those like Sofya. How terrible it was to hear nothing from her. Was she even alive to see Lenin come to power?

Nancy stepped into the kitchen, cradling a dark rectangle in one arm, and picked up a bottle of *samogon*.

"Hello, dear," I said.

She turned, startled. "I hope you don't mind that I helped myself to a taste." She wore an old flannel robe Mother had given her. "Care to join me in a drink?"

"You're still recovering, dear—"

She held out the bottle and the light glinted off the glass. "This is good medicine."

More than a little curious about the vodka Princess Yesipov claimed tasted like nectar, I took a glass from the counter and held it out. "Perhaps a touch."

Nancy splashed clear liquid into my glass. It tasted not exactly like nectar, but it was smooth and crisp and sent glorious warmth through me.

"You are supposed to throw it back with one shot." She drank the contents of her glass in one swallow.

I did the same. For homemade alcohol, it was remarkably smooth.

Nancy pulled out a chair.

She took a stalk of celery from the platter and bit into it. "This is a surprise. No Russian likes this vegetable. Too noisy. There are so many surprises here. Like the kindness of Americans. Your daughter has been so good to me. Brings me tea every morning."

"Caroline loves you all. It's the first time I've seen her happy since her father died."

"If you don't mind me asking how?"

"Pneumonia." At least I could talk of it without feeling like the world was made of blown glass and about to shatter.

"You still wear black."

"Can't seem to give it up. It's all I have left of him."

Nancy poured me another glass and I drank it in one gulp. The warmth grew in my belly. "I should have been able to save him. I'm still not quite right."

"A natural death is a gift."

"It has caused me nothing but pain."

"I would have given the world for a natural death for my boy. A pneumonia germ. A death in the night." Nancy poured us both more *samogon* and tossed back her third. "You want to hear the story?"

"Of course," I said, setting my glass on Mother's kitchen table.

Nancy looked out the window at the surf pounding in the darkness. "Well, at first I thought it was a parade of some sort coming down the road in Kiev, but it was the Reds looking for us, a large rabble from town. My husband had been gone, at the front, for several weeks and our son Dreshnik, a cadet in military school, stood watch, his blue uniform pants a little too long, for I'd forgotten to hem them. At twelve, he was only allowed a child's rifle, though it shot real bullets. I held under my skirt my mother's icon of the Virgin Mary, covered in silver, her most prized possession."

Nancy played with the base of her glass.

"The men came about the house looking for money and watches. They laughed at Dreshnik guarding my ten-year-old daughter Sasha and me, but when a gang of them surrounded his sister and tried to take her off to the next room he shot and grazed one of them in the neck. At first Dreshnik stood astonished his gun had worked, but the mob surrounded him and took him away, as he screamed for me. They held Sasha and me in the house until they'd taken everything of value and we found Dreshnik later. Near the train station."

I covered Nancy's hand with mine. "My dear."

"They'd stripped off his uniform and hung him by the neck from a tree, and written in grease pencil on his chest: *Former Person*. The sight of him, so young and slim hanging there, his neck broken . . . Sasha cried for me to take him down. I tried but the rope was too high. We had to leave him there, for we heard the mob returning."

Nancy took another drink.

"Sasha and I were lucky to secure passage here but halfway on the trip she grew sick and they said it was typhus. I had the choice to return to Russia and have her buried there or continue on and do it here."

"I don't know how you went on."

"Is it fair my husband went to war never to return? That my boy died terrified and without me? That my daughter died in my arms in the belly of a ship? That I miss them every moment? No. But this is my life now. Every woman at the boarding house has stories similar. So I translate letters for them and help others best I can and try and accept things the way they are."

We were silent for a long moment. How brave she was. And she was right. I was lucky Henry died in his own bed, taken naturally, with me by his side.

"How are you doing today?" I asked.

She smiled. "There was a time when I couldn't remember my name. But today is good, thank you. You know, in Russia we have a name for a friend you make while drinking vodka."

"'Very drunk,' as I am now?"

Nancy laughed, her eyes bright with tears. "No. *'Sobutylnik'* is the word. You know, I have been trying to work up the courage to give you something."

"Oh, that's not necessary—"

She pulled from her lap a rectangular piece of wood the size of a cereal box, depicting the Virgin Mary and child painted there, covered in silver, the metal trimmed to show their faces. "This is my mother's icon. I would like you to have it."

"Oh, no, I couldn't, Nancy."

"Please. You are our champion and savior and I have nothing else. If my mother were still alive I know she would be happy if you took it."

She handed me the icon and I held it in two hands. It was surprisingly light, and I smoothed one finger down the cool silver.

"Hang it in a special place. Best if it's an eastern wall."

"My deepest thanks, Nancy. It is lovely and I have just the spot for it."

DESPITE DRINKING MULTIPLE GLASSES of *samogon* with Nancy, I woke the next morning clearheaded and free. At first I took tentative steps. Perhaps this new state of deep gratitude was temporary and would fade away like smoke rings in the air?

I stood in my bedroom, folded all seven of my black, bombazine dresses, and tucked them away in a trunk, tossing in the black jet jewelry. From the closet I pulled a white silk and chiffon dress I'd never worn and slid it over my head, the silk cascading down my shoulders, slipping along my skin like water. I stepped into sturdy, outdated pearl-colored kid shoes, wound three lengths of crystal beads around my neck, and hurried out to summon the troops.

Our Russian guests were already busying themselves about the house and the balalaika quartet Nancy had organized tuned their instruments in the living room. Princess Cantacuzène, visiting for the day to help, came dressed in full princess regalia, a tasteful diamond hairpin fixed in her velvet hat. We quickly revisited our last meeting on a tram in Petrograd and she inquired after my thumb and, finding it quite recovered, went to staff the *samogon* table.

Would Southamptonites come?

Caroline and Betty helped Princess Yesipov to a chair across the dining room and, seeing me, rushed to my side.

Caroline ran her hand down my sleeve. "Mother, you've given up your black."

I squeezed her hand. "It was about time, don't you think?"

"You look radiant, Mrs. Ferriday," Betty said.

"How would you two like to be in charge of the raffle? You could earn a Girl Scout badge for it."

"Do you mean it, Mother? I can be a Scout?"

"If you stick to the task."

I pulled her close, held her tight, and for once in so long she returned the embrace.

"Go now, before I change my mind," I said.

The girls ran off and I pulled back the curtain on a living room window and surveyed the driveway, expecting ten more women from the boarding house. If only we could encourage the whole community to rally round the cause and provide homes. The Irving Hotel had promised jobs for all if we could accommodate them.

I stepped to the living room, where we'd rolled back the rug and paraffin-waxed the floor. I sprinkled a light dusting of cornmeal across it and took a little slide across. The perfect floor for the dancing planned for later.

Mother fetched a newspaper and read us the headlines in town-crier fashion. "Squadron of German airships attack England. Germans conquer the Baltic Islands."

Would Germany never tire? The thought of Merrill flying over Germany made my stomach lurch.

Caroline and Betty positioned the Paris-made dolls for sale and I displayed an exquisite jeweled sword Princess Cantacuzène lent us to open the champagne in a grand way, once used in battle by her Russian husband's grandfather.

As we prepared the house my thoughts flashed to Sofya and Afon. Were they still alive? I had already sent more than two hundred dollars of profit from our handicraft sales, along with some of our own funds, to our contact in Paris to be distributed among the displaced Russians.

From the front vestibule Caroline shouted, "Look, Mother. A whole troop of women has arrived."

Mother came from the kitchen. "Eliza?"

I hurried to the driveway, Mother close behind, and found women, two six-year-old girls among them, disembarking from a small, white bus.

The driver came to me. "Got twelve suitcases. Where do you want 'em?"

"Welcome," I called to them. "Do come inside. We need every hand on deck."

Mother came to my side. "Luggage? Today of all *days*, Eliza. Billy Maddox is serious about arresting them."

"It will all work out, Mother."

"We'll be in handcuffs beside them, Eliza."

I waved the women in. "Come in, everyone; leave your things in the study."

"Join us in the dining room," Caroline called out as she led the way, holding the two young girls by the hand.

They were a handsome group and had dressed in the best they had, most in traveling clothes, many with scuffed shoes worn down at the heels. One got the impression in better circumstances they would have dressed in silks and lace, but they still wore the expectant looks universal to those looking forward to a party.

"Don't worry your English is not good enough," I said. "Let's show the people of Southampton what upstanding citizens they have living among them."

"Though at least twelve persons over the zoning limit," Mother said under her breath.

Mother's grandfather clock struck noon and Southamptonites trickled in, looking about the house, vaguely uncomfortable until Peg made sure they had a sample of our Russian vodka in hand. How could aristocratic Princess Cantacuzène, our very own White House royalty not impress them? The Josiah Copley Thaws from Windbreak. The William Douglases from Over Dune. The Sidney Harrises from Happy Go Lucky lined up to be introduced.

Julia Marlowe and E.H. arrived, drew quite a crowd, and Julia launched into a brisk autograph business. A reporter from the *New York American* circulated about, lending the air of excitement the press brings to any affair.

I stepped to the front hall amid the crowd, which had separated into two distinct sides, parted as perfectly as Moses's Red Sea. To the dining room side stood the Russian women, to the side closest the vestibule stood the Southampton guests, instinctively close to the door.

"Gather round," I called out, hurried halfway up the stairs, and addressed the crowd.

"Thank you for coming out today to honor these good women of Russian birth, who have been forced to flee their native country. Innocent women, mothers and children, targeted by the Bolsheviks. You will have the opportunity to purchase handicrafts to benefit the displaced émigrés—"

The front door slammed and Electra Whitney and Anna Gabler walked into the foyer. They made their way to the foot of the stairs.

Electra looked up at me. "Things really have gotten out of hand here, with every sort of vagabond hanging about. The zoning laws could not be clearer: Other than servants, no more than four unrelated individuals allowed permanent residence. I hear there are more than ten living here now, but it looks like we need to revise that number up. And don't tell me these are servants." She looked at Nancy, next to her, and spoke slowly. "Do you understand?"

I clenched my hands. "These are quality human beings who speak better English than you do, Electra, so please watch yourself."

"The mayor has been informed and Officer Maddox is standing by, ready to make arrests. Several of your Russians were drinking vodka at The Tavern and speaking quite loudly in Russian. How are we to know what they are saying? Our own twenty-sixth President of the United States, Theodore Roosevelt, insisted aliens must assimilate. I quote: 'We have room for but one language here and that is the *English* language.' And now you are peddling illegal foreign alcohol from your home? Southampton will not tolerate this."

The guests shifted in their shoes.

Mother, watching it all from the foyer below, pushed through the crowd and climbed the stairs. The room quieted as she took her place next to me and surveyed the crowd.

"Most of you know me, but for those who don't: My name is Caroline Woolsey Mitchell," Mother said, in her special Woolsey combination of cool voice and warm words.

Electra raised one hand. "You don't need to—"

"Keep your mouth shut for once, Electra, and listen."

Those in the crowd murmured and then settled.

"I never thought I'd say this, but I know how you feel, Electra. I didn't accept all this at first, either. My daughter had to show me the way—humbling for an old lady who thinks she knows everything. But then I got to know these women." Mother waved a hand toward Nancy, below. "Nancy. Raised in Russia but speaks better French than I. She lost her husband to war, daughter to typhus, and saw her son brutally murdered, and now cleans the bathrooms at the club. Princess Yesipov, who takes our leftovers to those living in tenements in the city."

Anna Gabler moved a few steps away from Electra.

"I'm not here to shame you, but to help you understand. To ask for your patience and a drop of the milk of humankindness. Yes, change is hard. Hearing Russian spoken at The Tavern may feel wrong to you, but for God's sake rise above it, dear friends. Extend the same hand others gave your forebears. They are eager to work in any way they can.

"As a young boy, President Roosevelt's own grandfather, newly arrived from Holland, once rode a pig through the streets of New York after church, which carried him full speed through the enraged congregation. How did his fellow Americans feel he was assimilating?"

Mother waved a hand in Archie Somerdyke's direction.

"Archie, people talked when your grandmother wore her Dutch cap to church each Sunday. Said she wasn't trying hard enough to fit in. Priscilla, your father refused to speak a word of English when he first came, only pointed his cane at what he wanted at Hildreth's. My own English great-grandfather called America 'the colonies' until the day he died. Electra, you're right, these Russian women are not our kind. They're our salvation. For if we stick to just 'our kind' we'll simply exist in this insular, petty world. A world that may be safe and predictable but with the life wrung out of it. Hang on to your grudges, if you must. Stoke your fear. Call in the authorities. But I will support these good people to my dying day, and if the police drag them out of here, I swear to the Almighty, they will have to take me, too."

Mother finished and the crowd stood silent, her last words hanging in the air, and then, all at once, the crowd erupted with heartfelt applause, which echoed through the hall.

Emma Baker pulled her husband by the hand and walked to join the Russian side. "You'll have to arrest us, too."

"We'll take four émigrés at The Clovers," Dudley Olcott said.

Mother and I smiled and waved to those who called out.

Chester Griswold raised one arm. "I can fit four at Crosswaves."

Electra took her leave in a huff and her Pink and Greens crossed the great divide to the vodka table.

Soon, all our Russian visitors had new accommodations and Mother and Princess Cantacuzène brandished their three cigar box cash registers bulging with bills. What a sum we'd have to send over to help the women here and in Paris. Now all I had to do was find Sofya.

Varinka

1917

Radimir stood in the hotel room doorway, his hand outstretched, a sweet-sad smile on his lips. How lucky I was to have such a handsome young man be so kind.

He held out his hand farther. "Don't be afraid."

It would be wonderful to go with him. To run through the darkened streets and get lost in the crowds. I felt the smooth burn next to my eye. Taras's next punishment would be worse.

"Come with me. I'm meeting friends."

I glanced at the clock on the mantel. Six P.M. What if I only went for a short while? Taras would never know.

I nodded. "Yes."

"Well, do you have something else to wear? Anything dark-colored, that hides your figure."

He blushed a bit after saying that.

I smiled. "I think there are some things in that trunk."

I rifled through the drawers and found some thick, brownish-green ladies' hunting clothes. Radimir stepped into Taras's room and turned his back while I dressed. Such a kind action, something Taras would never do.

We made it to the street and the crowds surrounded us. Radimir pulled a gun from inside his jacket and held my elbow tight. "Stay close, Varinka. We are not going far. Just to Literaturnoe Kafe. We must walk. The trams have stopped."

We fought our way along Nevsky Prospekt, jostled and knocked by the great sea of people. A well-dressed couple hurried by, looking anxious as a rabble of men with liquor bottles in their hands laughed and called after them. "Run, former people!"

We passed a soldier in uniform, lying on the sidewalk, a pool of dark blood under his head. The crowd around the man celebrated, shooting rifles into the air. I tried to stop and look, but Radimir rushed me along the darkened sidewalk.

We soon entered a restaurant with low ceilings, the scent of roast chicken and cigarette smoke thick in the air. It was very loud in there, packed with people pushing to get to the bar. Radimir pulled me by the hand to the back of the place and stopped at a couple who stood kissing, locked in a tight embrace.

"Varinka, these are my friends Dina and Erik. And apparently, they like each other very much."

The two released each other and Dina shook my hand. "Good to meet you, comrade." Dina made me think of a lion, her hair loose and full around her face. She dressed in pants and a jacket like Radimir's, but with the opposite figure of mine. What had the magazine called it? Curvy.

"When they are not kissing they both work for the newspaper *The People*."

"We are looking for staff at the paper if you are interested," Dina said.

"Oh, me? I'm just visiting. From Malinov. Need to get back—"

Erik poured a glass of vodka. "How did you have the bad fortune to meet our Radimir?"

I drew my hair down across the burn on my face. "He helped me. At the hotel."

Radimir put his arm around my shoulders. "A group of creeps. Looking for weapons—about to spirit her away."

"Some take things too far," Dina said. She touched my hand. "We're glad you're safe. Just don't make eye contact on the street."

"Why worry?" Erik asked. He nodded toward Radimir. "The commissioner here is issued bullets."

"Commissioner?" I asked.

"Since the Bolsheviks took power there are already hundreds of new committees," Dina said. "Too many for my taste. But a commissioner is the person who heads one."

Erik pulled me close. "In Radi's case he was the most brilliant one at the museum so they made him Commissioner of Art and Historic Objects of the People. And, at not yet twenty, chosen over more senior men. Feel free to genuflect."

Radimir smiled. "It's no great honor. They are just firing the entire old regime and hiring any comrade willing to serve. Trotsky made a waiter from a restaurant the head of one department since he spoke a little French."

"You only studied art since you could walk," Dina said.

Radimir turned to me. "My parents died when I was a baby and a museum curator and his wife adopted me. Lucky number thirteen child. So, museums babysat me a lot growing up."

"Who knew staring at naked people in museums could get you a cushy job?" Dina said.

"It requires a lot of travel."

"How terrible, having to go to Paris and Venice," Erik said.

"And it is not easy keeping the rabble from destroying the paintings. They almost burned *David and Jonathan*." He turned to me. "It shows Prince Jonathan and King David parting."

"King David?" I asked.

"You don't know King David?" Dina asked. "He was King of the Jews."

"I've not seen that icon."

Dina threw back her head and laughed. "We don't have icons, Varinka. Have you never met Jews before? You do realize all three of us are Jewish?"

I looked at the floor, my face hot.

"Leave her alone, Dina," Radimir said.

"Don't be embarrassed," Dina said. "It's understandable, you being from a small village."

Radimir linked his arm with mine. "Only those in the Russian Orthodox Church worship their saints via icons. You should see the old ones in the tsar's collection."

"I'm not religious, really," I said. "But my Mamka has the tsar on an icon."

Erik finished his vodka in one gulp. "Well, he's no saint, and we're finally done with that limp prick, happy to say. Done with the tsarina, too, and Rasputin, the whole mess. No more murdering us in the streets and no more *samogon*. We'll get our real vodka back."

"What if the Germans win the war and we all become German?" I asked.

Erik laughed. "Might be preferable. Butter is up to ten rubles a pound. But hopefully we'll fix our own wages now."

"I heard we'll all have pensions if the Bolsheviks win?"

"Lenin's promising us the moon, of course," Radimir said.

"At least the wealthy are feeling what it's like to be hungry," Dina said. "Don't we deserve to eat?"

My thoughts went to serving dinner at the estate, the Streshnayvas' tea table piled with enough food for the whole village. "It is true. But confusing."

How good it was to talk about the state of affairs with someone honest, instead of Taras, who told me nothing.

Dina handed me a pamphlet. "You should come with us, Varinka, to hear Lenin lecture from his balcony opposite Peter and Paul Fortress. You will understand then. He's speaking tonight—"

"No, I must get back." The clock behind the bar read 6:45.

Radimir pulled me closer. "By eight o'clock. That's a world of time. Come, sit with me."

Dina handed me a pamphlet. "Just a little something I wrote." *Red Russia: Triumph of the Bolsheviks.*

Radimir and I walked to a booth and sat side by side, so close our thighs touched.

"You have such an important job."

"Never would have happened under the tsar. He employed his rich friends. And hated Jews of course."

"Because they're taking all of Russia's money?"

"That's his sick propaganda, don't you see? For years, he has spread lies about us. He's not the great 'little father' he pretended to be, using his pretty family to curry favor with the people. Putting them on every postcard and picture book to distract from his evil ways."

"But his daughters were good people."

"Maybe so, but their parents used them to promote an image of goodness and piety that was not true. So many innocent Jews died at his hand." Radimir shrugged. "I suppose he had to have someone to blame for his failures. But I'm just happy we're preserving Russia's great art. Poetry and art are the first things to perish in times like these."

How smart he was. Surely, he would find me dull.

A waiter lit our candle and Radimir ordered us boiled eggs, black bread, and two vodkas.

"I've never had a drink of that," I said.

"Time to start."

"I cannot stay long."

"Don't worry. I'll have you back soon."

Radimir played with his glass. "I have a confession to make. I saw you come into the hotel lobby."

I tried to hide my smile.

"I went to every floor looking for you. Glad I came along when I did." He slid closer to me and brushed a stray lock of hair back off my cheek. "What happened to your face here?"

"I had an accident. Ironing."

He kissed the tips of his fingers and touched my burn just as Max had, with such care.

"Dangerous pursuit, ironing."

My eyes watered at his kindness.

The waiter came with the vodka bottle and two glasses and set them on the table.

Radimir leaned closer. "You have a pretty smile, you know. Makes me want to kiss you."

"I've never kissed a boy."

"Really? I don't believe it. But that's good for me. Nothing to compare me to."

Radimir poured vodka into both glasses. "Few girls have let me kiss them, of course, but I've studied the art from books and at the cinema."

I smiled. It was my turn not to believe him.

"Seems there are three things to remember." He threw back his vodka.

I looked at the clear liquid in my glass, took a breath, and swallowed it all.

"Very good, Varinka. You have promise."

I set my empty glass on the table. "Tell me the three things."

He smiled and looked away for a moment. "Well, number one is never go in cold. You must warm up." He touched the side of my neck with his fingers. "The great ones tease a bit. Maybe brush your lips across this spot just here." He sent his fingers along the curve of my jaw. "Or here."

I tingled all over. Was it the vodka?

"And then?"

He moved closer and took my chin in his hand to bring my gaze to his. "Part two is a good one. You must look deep into the other person's eyes. Maybe you'll see vulnerability. Or fear. Love, if you're lucky."

His eyes shone in the candlelight. What a nice color they were, green as his jacket.

He kept his gaze locked on mine. "Take your time here because that makes part three even better."

I swallowed hard.

He dipped a finger in his glass and ran it wet down my lips. "The final phase. The actual moment of pressing lips against lips. Soft and sweet if you do it right. The key here is to let it come to you."

Time stood still as I breathed in his scent, of leather books and hair tonic and smoke.

All at once, the waiter set a plate on the table, the boiled eggs rolling on it, white and smooth. I let out a long sigh. I would not get my kiss. Had I been holding my breath that whole time?

We talked about how good it would be once the Red Army won, until I checked the clock on the wall. 7:45. A spasm went through me and I grabbed Radimir's hand. How could a whole hour have passed?

"I must go."

He stood, tossed money on the table, and slipped the eggs and bread into his pocket. We laughed as we ran, on backstreets back to the hotel, trying to eat our slippery eggs.

Just before eight we stood outside the lobby doors in the shadows. I scanned the lobby for Taras.

"Open your mouth," Radimir said.

I opened it wide.

I could feel him smile in the dark. "You are a trusting one." His fingers traced my face, feeling for my open mouth, and a thick piece of black bread came gently pushed through my lips.

Had bread ever tasted so good?

"I would like to see you again," he said.

"I'm leaving Malinov soon."

"Me, too. Off to Paris."

I gasped a little breath. "We may all go soon, as well. Taras has an assignment there."

Something strange flickered across Radimir's face. "Well, then I'll see you in Paris."

He pulled me to him.

I pressed one hand to his chest. "I can't remember all the steps."

Would he hate me for rejecting him? Taras would break a wrist for less.

Radimir laughed and brushed the hair back from my forehead. "You're right, Varinka. I've made my kissing tutorial too complicated. And besides, you barely know me."

"Thank you for dinner."

"Go now. I will wait until you get in."

I RAN UP THE STAIRS, considering the elevator too slow, back to the suite and stood at the open door, heart pounding. Taras stood in the bedroom packing, tossing his clothes into a valise on the bed.

There would be no time to bathe away Radimir's scent.

In three paces across the giant rug Taras was at my side. "Where were you?"

After Radimir, everything about Taras seemed so horribly large and wrong.

I stepped into the suite. "I was in the lobby. I had to look for something to eat."

"I knew I couldn't trust you."

"I'm starving, Taras."

"Get packed. We're leaving."

"So late?"

"I have an assignment and must go. I'm putting you in a car to Malinov."

I turned away to hide my smile. I would not have to spend that night with Taras. I would glide through the night in the backseat of a motorcar, enjoy that musky scent on me and dream.

Of the boy I would see in Paris.

Sofya

1917

THE COMMISSIONER STOOD AT HIS DESK, THERE IN Max's old nursery. "*What* for God's sake? Out with it."

My knees turned to jelly standing there. What if I fell?

Raisa stepped toward his desk. "Just wanted to remind you to have her papers stamped by the transport office, comrade."

I breathed a quiet sigh. Thank you, dear Raisa.

The commissioner stood. "Of course, I remembered. Stay here. I will be back." He left the room and closed the door with a slam.

Raisa rushed to me and took both my hands in hers. "Sofya. We must hurry."

I held her hands tighter. "My family. How are they?"

"Varinka's mother, a good woman, helps Varinka care for little Max. They've taken over your parents' suite. Varinka is away—"

"I must go to him."

Raisa held my hands fast. "Wait. The estate has been nationalized. There are villagers living here now, in every room. If you're recognized you'll be done for."

"Has Afon returned?"

"No, but a letter came." A smile lit up her face and I could have kissed her right there. She rushed to the table, pushed it aside, and drew up the floorboards.

So Luba's secret place was not so impossible to find after all.

"I put it here, with your things." She pulled out Luba's rucksack. "Take it. And leave when the commissioner returns. Do not go to Max."

"I can't just leave my *son*, Raisa."

Raisa leaned closer. "I heard them talking. Varinka, her mother, and Taras are moving to Paris soon, little Max, too. You can get him back there. Here, you'll be caught for sure." She handed me the rucksack and Luba's sextant poked my side.

"Luba. How is she? My parents?"

Something dark flickered across Raisa's face. "The laundry wagon is waiting in the near barn. Ride on through those gates and don't look back until you reach—"

The door opened and the commissioner strode toward me. "Here," he said, handing me a trifolded paper. "Be off with you and make it quick or I'll have hell to pay."

With a quick look back at Raisa I stepped toward the doorway, the rucksack and kit bag over my shoulder.

"Wait," the commissioner called out.

I stopped, my whole body cold.

"That second sack."

I turned. "Yes, Commissioner?"

"You didn't come in with it."

I clasped my hands together to stop the shaking. Would he demand to inspect the contents? Find the bracelet with the codes?

"Don't you remember, Commissioner?" Raisa asked. "We now provide lunch for the drivers."

"What is that metal sticking out?"

"My sextant," I said. "I use it to chart my course."

"Well, you'd better hurry up or there'll be no course to chart."

I stepped out the door.

"And don't stop to eat that lunch—" he called after me.

I HURRIED DOWN THE back stairs, my boots heavy on the carpeted steps, and reached the back entry. How could I leave without Max? Once I found him I would release my family and take them all in the laundry wagon.

I stood there, numbed by indecision. But what if a villager recognized me? Vladi would have new plans for me, certainly.

I crept past the dining room, where the bandits had seized us a year ago, where a group of villagers now lay snoring on blankets on the dining table under the dimmed crystal chandelier. It stank of rotting meat and filth.

As I passed the *zala,* where a group of men sat playing cards and drinking vodka, my back tensed to see one of them wore Father's university mortarboard, the tassel swaying as he sang a folk song. I stemmed a wave of nausea as one leaned over and spat onto Agnessa's silk carpet. It was too dangerous to confront them. I had to find Max.

I snuck into Father's office, braced for the worst, and found it looted, the gun cabinet and desk drawers open and empty. The bookshelves stood bare and books lay in a massive pile on the floor. The Benjamin Franklin bust lay on the floor, shattered.

Making my way up the front stairs, the walls pockmarked with bullet holes, I stopped at Father's portrait, slashed, the eyes gouged with knife holes. How could the people hate him so, a man who taught their choir? Employed them at the linen factory?

I came to Agnessa's bedroom door, closed. I steadied myself, one hand on the wallpapered hallway wall, dizzy, my heart hammering so.

There would be no turning back once I entered.

I twisted the knob, stepped into the dark room, and closed the door. In the near darkness Agnessa's bed looked the same, made perfectly, the boudoir pillows arranged just so.

I walked carefully along the carpeted floor and was almost on top of little Max before I saw him, arranged on his back upon a cloud of coverlets, asleep in his pajamas. I choked back a sob. How he'd grown. I set down my rucksack, crouched next to him, ran two fingers across the top of his curls. He'd become a bit leggier, yes, but at three years old, still chubby with baby fat.

"He sleeps in his coat."

I stood and turned, heart racing, to find a woman with the Madonna's face standing in the shadows. Varinka's mother? One hand holding fast to the neck of her homespun dressing gown, she stepped to Agnessa's armoire and pulled out a pair of small felt boots.

"He won't sleep in a bed," she said, handing me the boots. "Says he wants to camp out so you will come back."

Tears came to my eyes.

"Take him and go now," she said.

"Thank—"

"Hurry. Through the back entrance. My daughter will be back—"

I touched her arm. "I can't thank you enough for taking such good care of him."

Behind me, the door to the hallway opened.

I turned to find Varinka standing there. I barely recognized her at first, dressed in one of my traveling ensembles.

"Varinka. Thank you for—"

"Move away from him," Varinka said.

"What are you doing?" I walked toward her.

"You need to leave. *Now*."

"How have you become so cold? He's my child. Think of all we did for—"

"I owe you nothing."

Varinka's mamka came to my side. "Inka, this is the child's *mother*."

She sent her mamka a hateful look. "And you, dear Mamka, would have sent these two off with a lunch pail."

I glanced at Max asleep on the floor.

Varinka narrowed her eyes. "I will count to three and you had better be gone or I will call for the commissioner."

"Varinka, think how you would feel—"

"Things are different now. The people make the rules."

"Have your own child, Varinka. Thank you for taking such good care of him, but Max will always wonder—"

"*One.*"

I looked down at Max, sleeping there, and tears stung my eyes. How could I leave him? "Varinka, please, I beg you. He's everything to me."

Varinka crossed her arms over her chest. "*Two.*"

What if I just ran with him? Could I make it to the wagon? I bent to gather him in my arms.

"Commissioner!" Varinka screamed, shrill and long.

The sound of steps came from another part of the house.

"They're on their way," Varinka said.

Max woke and tried to sit up, still half asleep.

Varinka's mamka came to me. "He'll be safer with us for now. . . ."

I hoisted my rucksack over my shoulder and stepped to the door with a glance back at my boy. "May God punish you, Varinka. I'll get him back."

I stepped out the bedroom door and rushed down the front stair, past the family having breakfast in our front parlor, the father scratching his belly through his long underwear.

Was the commissioner right behind me?

Vibrating with anger, I ran out into the back courtyard, dawn's first light just showing, to the apartment over the laundry to find my family. When the air met my wet face, I realized I'd been crying and wiped away the tears with both hands. She would not triumph. I would rescue my son in Paris.

I reached Bogdan's apartment and found it empty, my family gone, the door open and floor swept clean.

In the distance, the laundry wagon waited in the far barn courtyard. Even from afar I knew it was Jarushka harnessed there. The shaggy fetlocks. The lopped ears. As I drew closer she tossed her head against the reins. I ran across the cobblestones and flung my arms about her neck and she turned with a slight neigh.

I ran to the horse barn and burrowed under layers of horse blankets into Jarushka's tack box and pulled out the package of clothes Luba had hidden there, hurried up into the wagon seat, my rucksack by my side. I turned to see a full cart of linens neatly bundled in brown paper packages marked *Sheets* and *Pillow Covers*.

I checked back over my shoulder. It was better to escape and come back later than to be caught.

Jarushka set off with the lightest touch of the reins and I turned and watched the estate grow smaller as we headed toward the gate. Were Varinka's comrades following me? Surely, she'd told them by now.

Perhaps my parents had already taken Luba and fled to France? Our old townhouse in Petrograd? At least I was free. I would reunite with Max in Paris. With hard work and cleverness, I could do anything.

Jarushka picked up her pace along the road toward the guardhouse, through a tunnel of trees arched across the road. In the early dawn darkness, I could barely make out the gate up ahead. Suddenly Jarushka stopped. I bid her forward and she refused.

So strange for her. What was wrong?

I again asked her to move and she walked on, slowly.

As we drew closer I saw what might have concerned her.

"Go on, girl." What was it there on top of the fence?

As we neared the guardhouse and the trees gave way, the darkness slowly lifted and I saw the forms atop the fence. Confused, I stood, unable to take in the horror of it all.

I saw Agnessa first, her charred body impaled on two fence spikes above, still wearing the lace dress I'd last seen her in, seared to her skin, one lace-sleeved arm dangling, as if reaching to me. There was a crude sign written in Russian and tied with twine around her neck. *Parasite.*

Time slowed as I stepped down from the wagon and my whole body shook as I stepped to Father hanging there, his eyeglasses gone, eyes empty holes. His naked body was seared black in patches, small spots of flesh color here and there, his back arched, head thrown back and mouth open with a silent scream.

My gaze continued down the line and could barely look at my dear Luba, burned to the bone, her head hanging like a charred sunflower. My precious sister, so young, with so much promise, impaled there.

I fell to my knees in the road and retched up the little food left in me and then forced myself to stand. In the distance from the estate came a rider on horseback. I would have to escape or else join my family there on that fence. But how would they all have a proper burial?

I glanced at the approaching rider. There was no time.

Numb with the horror of it all, I stepped back up onto the wagon and urged Jarushka on, the tears on my face drying in the air as we picked up speed. I looked back. My dear family. I would have to grieve for them all later. Now it was more important to escape and live to tell of it all. To find Max and Afon.

And seek my revenge in Paris.

Part
Four

CHAPTER

36

Sofya

1918

IT TOOK ME MORE THAN A YEAR TO MAKE MY WAY SOUTH from Malinov toward Ukraine in hopes of finding Afon. By December Jarushka and I were almost to Krasnodar, a town where Afon and I had spent our first year of marriage. According to his letter he and the last of his regiment were in the area. I pulled from my pocket Afon's letter, which somehow missed the censors.

> My Beloved,
>
> Happy to say Pyotr Wrangel leads us now, more determined than ever. We continue on our way to where our first house was. Hope to rest there a while and regroup. Many good memories of that place.

Where our first house was. He meant Krasnodar of course, where we lived as a newly married couple, while Afon trained for the army.

I pictured our reunion, him picking me up as he always did, squeezing me so tight I could barely breathe. He'd request a temporary furlough and we'd travel on to Paris to find Max. I hoped the army might even provide food and extra guards for protection.

Nothing could stop the two of us together.

Throughout the whole journey Jarushka seemed to understand our mission as we'd hurried south before the commissioner could find his laundry cart missing. I had covered myself in the petroleum jelly, hoping my scent could not be followed if he sent his dogs after us, which must have given me the appearance of a dirty, greased pig. We'd evaded capture, but it was slow going since we avoided main roads for fear of meeting Bolsheviks. Half starved and waylaid by a bad storm, we'd found work in a village south of Moscow until the Red Army came too close and Jarushka and I fled.

Once we moved on, starvation was a constant threat. The baby biscuits, jerky, and powdered milk Luba had so smartly provided had run out, along with the provisions Olga had given me.

We made our way through dense virgin forest, the boughs of the pine trees like green-sleeved arms dusted with diamond-crusted snow. Father's old Nagant proved a faithful friend for hunting game and I had two bullets left, having shot at a wild pig that morning and missed. I had foraged food for both of us: some red clover I'd found crusted with frost, an unexpected gift, full of protein and vitamins. And delicious nettles.

My nose felt about to freeze off and I massaged it with thumb and forefinger as our nurse always urged us to do when we were children to fight frostbite.

After we left Moscow we slept in a network of barns along the way, where we met fellow travelers willing to barter. Olga's pearls proved excellent currency and the sheets and blankets in the cart provided warmth for us both and additional goods to haggle with. I even traded my lovely but impractical black maid's coat for a hideous but warm white dog fur hat and coat, which doubled as bedding at night.

From my pocket I pulled a cashmere baby sweater of Max's, which Luba had left in the barn with our traveling clothes, and held it to my face. It still held my son's baby scent of talcum powder and little boy and I breathed it in. He'd worn it his first name day, when Afon gave him the little present he'd wrapped himself.

How eager Afon had been to share a book he'd cherished in his own childhood. *Trees Every Child Should Know*. A charming book written in English, its green cover worn with use.

"Your papa read this as a boy," Afon said, showing Max the pages. "Larch and birch are my favorites."

What a good father. How happy Max would be to see him again.

I lifted the rose plant from under my coat. Though no longer blooming, the leaves were green and producing enough chlorophyll to live and even thrive, bearing two buds. During overcast days, I rode with the stem against my skin, the thorns pricking me with every jolt of the wagon, forcing me awake and aware. In bright sun, I opened my coat just long enough to provide the plant with energy. At night, it lay warm, next to me, the little burlap bag tied around its roots at my belly.

I opened the pouches I'd made from a pillowcase and spread dinner out on my lap: Mushrooms. Nettle leaves. Frozen wild plums.

I'd taken Cook's food for granted. The pigeon and baby eggplant sent in from Paris, much of which went uneaten, sent to the pigs. The baby carrots and tender haricot vert just like the ones I grew in the garden of our first house as a married couple. Afon and me newly married in Krasnodar, living in the guest house of a charming estate.

Darkness comes early in the forest, so it was still afternoon when we followed tracks in the light snow and stopped at a house and barn. The house was dark and the barn had no sign of livestock. If the tracks were an indication, there'd been many visitors to this place. I wasn't the only one forced to travel south fleeing the new government.

Stepping down from the cart, I cocked my gun at my side, opened the barn door. It was a small barn with a low ceiling and just enough hay on the floor to afford a night's sleep. We would have a private room for the night.

Jarushka nuzzled my neck as I unhitched her from the wagon and offered her a favorite dessert, a chilly pool of birch sap, which she licked from my palm.

I led her into the barn, tin pot under one arm, a few pieces of dry kindling inside, and smoothed a wool blanket over her. In the hay I created my bed, sat and arranged my dinner.

I'd found a surprising array of edible winter plants in the woods: velvet shank mushrooms and Russian olives and plums still frozen on their branches. I said a silent thanks for my foraging class at Brillantmont, one we'd all laughed about at the time. Why would we ever want to eat wild plants?

Jarushka stood and dozed, though I tried to persuade her to bed down in the hay with me, perhaps somehow knowing we were not safe that night.

I cracked off two icicles from the eave outside and set them in my tin pot. I'd stolen that pot from a farm where we'd stayed. How far I'd fallen, now a thief.

Once I arranged the kindling into a teepee and started the fire with Luba's cotton balls, I warmed the icicles for drinking water. I drank first and then set the pot down for Jarushka to finish.

My head hit the rucksack and I fell asleep in no time.

Afon came to me as I slept. We were living in our new home in Krasnodar and walked through our glorious back garden, overflowing with foxglove and narcissus. Afon stood next to me on the bridge, leaning on the rail, with his hands in the pockets of his army breeches, his skin suntanned. He teased me, saying hunting and drinking were superior pursuits to botany and books.

"I think you're more in love with your plants than you are with me," he said, his smile wide.

"I would only trade you for a pink Lady's Slipper orchid."

He pressed the full strength of his leg against my hip and brushed the hair back from my cheek. "Now that we're married you can't be rid of me." He kissed my neck and—

The low moan of the barn door opening tore me from my dream. I sat up in the darkness, heart racing, and Jarushka stirred. I felt for Father's gun, cold next to me on the hay. Could the intruder see me there on the floor?

"Good girl," a man's voice said.

In the darkness the moonlight caught his hand smoothing down Jarushka's flank. He stepped to the wall. Feeling for her bridle? He forced the bit on her and tried to pull her out. She refused, of course.

As he worked to persuade her, the sun must have breached the horizon for it filled the barn with the first light of day. The man wore a long coat, dirty felt boots, and a week's growth of beard.

"Walk on, nag," he said.

I stood, legs shaking. "Leave her and go," I said, trying to sound tough.

He turned.

"You Red Army?" I asked.

"Do I look idealistic to you? Just on my way to France."

"Any news of the tsar's family?" In my travels I'd heard bits and pieces about the tsar's execution at Yekaterinburg the previous summer but little of the family's fate.

He snorted a laugh. "There's a new rumor every day. But let's face it, they all died."

My thoughts went to Olga and her sisters sewing at Alexander Palace.

The man stepped closer. "The children had sewn their diamonds and jewels into their vests so they lived through the shooting. Bayonets had to finish them, the little dog, too."

I blinked away tears but they froze on my eyelashes. "Enough."

"Bet you don't know the Reds signed a peace treaty with Germany, either."

"Of course I know." The Bolsheviks were now even more entrenched as the legitimate government.

He squinted at me. "Oh, you're a *woman*. Any jewels on you? I know you all carry them. Close to your skin."

I stepped back, grabbed my rucksack and held it close. What if he got the bracelet with the codes? "I have a gun."

"Let's see it." He stepped closer. "Once you get yourself a bath we might have some fun." He rubbed the front of his coat. "It's been a while."

I waved my gun at him, the wood handle slippery in my grasp. "I'm warning you."

"I have a gun, too, but you know as well as I do there are no bullets to be had from here to Moscow. Even the soldiers don't have them."

"Come no closer."

He extended one hand. "Let's go on together. My friends are right behind me. We'll all take that cart of yours. Four can survive better than one in this world. Fight off the wolves."

He was right about that, though Jarushka and I had become experts at outrunning the cunning beasts and I'd killed one the night we found no barn to rest in. It would be harder once I ran out of bullets.

"My husband is a cavalry officer." My hand shook. Could I even fire upon a fellow human?

"Could be your late husband, now. I hear Reds are killing White officers all over."

All at once my breath seemed cut off. Afon? "There's a new rumor every day."

He stepped closer and the light from the window shone on the dark wool of his coat, a uniform overcoat I knew so well, of the army.

"You're right. Probably all made up. But, he's not here, is he? Must be staying warm with a new ladylove himself. You know soldiers." He smiled. "Cocks hard at all times."

"I'd rather sleep with a pig than a deserter."

His smile faded. "I'm not stupid enough to end up as one of the glorious dead."

"You're a coward."

He lunged at me and I fired. Jarushka screamed and skittered as the bullet grazed the man's hand. How hasty and stupid that shot.

"Jesus Christ," he said, clutching his palm.

He lunged toward me again.

I took a deep breath and fired once more, this time taking careful aim at his chest.

My whole body went cold as the man fell back on the barn floor and I stood, barely breathing, two fingers to my lips.

Crows cackled outside and the scent of gunpowder hung in the air. Was he dead? I stood there, strangely numb, and watched the blood pool out from under him and seep into the hay like a dark nest. I knelt by his side and placed my hand on his chest, where my fingers met sticky blood. Felt his neck. No pulse. He was already cooling, there in the cold morning air.

Had I really killed someone? The worst sin there was. He might have killed me if I hadn't acted and who would save Max?

Trying to step around the blood, I unbuttoned his coat, pulled the gun from the waistband of his trousers and checked the chamber. He was right about not having bullets. I pocketed the gun, searched his coat pockets, and found a handful of white-paper-wrapped sugar cubes. I considered taking his boots, but they were much too big and my stomach lurched at the thought of touching him again.

Should I say a prayer? Why? God had stopped listening to me long ago.

I led Jarushka out into the bright morning, and we were soon on our way. Still vibrating with the aftershocks of the encounter, I brushed away thoughts of the man's cooling body. Who would make that grim discovery? Had he been right about the White officers captured? I would have to soldier on for Max no matter what.

As we rode, enjoying the morning sun, I felt the sugar cubes in my pocket and sat a little straighter in my seat. Now not only a thief, but a cold-blooded killer as well.

TWO WEEKS AFTER I killed the man in the barn, Jarushka and I came to the outskirts of Krasnodar. Though a bitter wind greeted us, I urged my horse along, we were *home*.

I could feel Afon's presence there as we rode past the magnificent St. Catherine's Cathedral with its golden dome and seven altars. I urged Jarushka down side roads in case Red Army soldiers were in town. Were Mr. and Mrs. Zaitz still running their apothecary?

We passed the bridge Afon and I had stood on as newlyweds and approached Main Street. We rode by many new shops and restaurants and shuttered storefronts as well, but my whole body warmed when I saw the old pharmacy still there, wedged between newer shops. The green-and-white sign hung out front as it always had: *Zaitz Apothecary*.

I entered and found the place unchanged, the glass apothecary jars lined up behind the counter with mortar and pestles of all sizes. The old cash register sat on the counter, still polished bright. An upright piano on the far wall. A table holding a green blotter stood in the middle of the room, with all the necessities of correspondence.

I stepped to the counter and found Mr. Zaitz pouring powder through a funnel into a glass bottle. Would he remember me? It had been over five years and my appearance had changed markedly. They would remember Afon, certainly. Though we'd left shortly after it happened, Afon had helped them through a massive pogrom, when railway men and sailors and even some fellow merchants terrorized the Jewish families in town. Afon had called down his fellow teachers and his best cadets from the academy to guard the Zaitzes' home and store to prevent looting or worse.

"Mr. Zaitz?"

"I'm almost ready with it," he said without looking up.

"I don't need a remedy."

He looked at me, set down his funnel, and looked closer. "Sofya Stepanov?"

How long had it been since I'd smiled? "Yes." I almost reached out for Mr. Zaitz's hand but held back. Who knew what terrible germs I carried?

"Yeda!" he called toward the back room.

Mrs. Zaitz stepped from the back room, pushing a linen curtain aside. She carried a tray, which held two glasses of tea and a plate of biscuits.

"I'm here. I'm here. What is it for goodness' sake, you'd think the world is ending."

A trim woman with a mass of dark hair elaborately pinned up, Mrs. Zaitz was not blessed with tall stature, but what she lacked in height she made up for with her kind way and strong opinions. She set her tray on the counter.

Mr. Zaitz held out both arms as if presenting the tsarina. "Look who's here."

"Sofya Stepanov?" Mrs. Zaitz hurried around the counter to me. "What brings you here? What perfect timing you have. The water's hot. I have some good biscuits."

How I wanted that hot tea and English biscuits. I marveled at how, with some people, time apart never matters.

"I can't stay long. On my way to Paris."

"You're taking the long way?" Mr. Zaitz asked. "Traveling by yourself?"

"I hope to find Afon. He may be close by here. With the White Army."

The two exchanged a glance.

I took a biscuit from the tray, tasted one, and drank a sip of warm tea. I stuffed the whole thing in my mouth and reached for another.

Mrs. Zaitz brushed something off my jacket shoulder. "You must be tired, dear. Stay with us tonight."

Mr. Zaitz tossed a newspaper onto the counter. "This is an important town to the Reds now that this is happening." The newspaper headline read: FRENCH OCCUPY ODESSA. "The Allies are coming to help us."

Suddenly everything lightened. At last, outside help to beat the Bolsheviks.

"Stay with us for a while," Mr. Zaitz said. "You're not safe traveling alone."

I laughed to myself. If only they knew.

"We never thanked you properly back when you lived here. For Afon keeping watch here two nights during the troubles. No sleep."

"That's what you do for friends," I said. "But there are a few things I need. Three really. The first is matches. I'm almost out."

Mr. Zaitz reached under the counter and then slapped a carton of matches onto the counter. "Done."

I pulled the serpent bracelet from my rucksack and removed the cotton wool. "Can you post this for me? To my friend Eliza Ferriday in the U.S.?"

Mr. Zaitz took the bracelet. "We can try. Haven't lost a package yet, though that may change soon."

"To America?" Mrs. Zaitz asked. She took the bracelet from her husband and held it in her palm. "I have the perfect box for it."

"And the third thing. Do you have any vinegar? Molasses, too, and a bowl to mix them in?"

Mrs. Zaitz nodded. "Of course." She stepped into the back room with a worried look back at me.

I hurried to the desk and wrote a quick message on a sheet of paper, the penmanship like chicken scratch, my hand not yet thawed from the ride. How I'd missed ink and pen.

I handed the note to Mr. Zaitz. "I'm afraid I have no money to pay you."

Mrs. Zaitz emerged from the back room with molasses and cider bottles and a china bowl. "What are you doing with this?"

I pulled my rose plant from beneath my shirt and sat it on the counter.

"What in the world?" Mr. Zaitz said.

I splashed vinegar into the bowl, dripped in some molasses, removed the burlap from the root ball and soaked it in the mixture. I stroked one leaf. "Can you believe it has two buds?"

"Must be a special plant," Mrs. Zaitz said. "Some people trying to survive might put all their effort into finding food."

"It came all the way from America." I tied the burlap back onto the root ball and tucked the rose back inside my shirt. Surely, they thought me a confirmed lunatic.

Mr. Zaitz slid a pair of sheep's wool mittens along the counter. "We only have men's, but they're guaranteed warm."

Tears in my eyes, I slipped them on my hands and looked down at the coffee brown suede with a blurry gaze. Such kind people. The perfect gift.

Mrs. Zaitz leaned in. "I must insist you rest here for a while, Sofya. Take a nice bath."

I smiled. "I would like to look nice for Afon when I see him."

Mrs. Zaitz took my hand. "I'm sorry to be the one, but I need to tell you something, Sofya."

"Mrs. Zaitz, just say it."

"You don't know how it hurts me to tell you this, Sofya, but we heard something about Afon—"

"Just *tell* me."

"He came by here—"

I pressed one hand to my chest. "Afon, here?" I laughed. "Why did you not say so?"

"He didn't stay long."

"He was on his way back to find you," Mr. Zaitz said. "Heard there was trouble at the estate." He hung his head, unable to continue.

"What did he say?" I asked. "Who was he with?"

"He was alone," Mrs. Zaitz said. "Said he'd left his fellow officers at the bridge. They were headed up to Malinov."

So Afon had known of our situation after all. "But why did he not come?"

Mrs. Zaitz placed one hand on my sleeve. "They say the Reds got them."

I stepped back from her. "They?"

"Mrs. Osinov's friend—"

I turned away. "Mrs. Osinov's *friend*? How can you believe hearsay?"

Mrs. Zaitz rubbed one hand down my back. "I'm sorry, Sofya."

I shook my head. "No. Afon would never let that happen."

I hurried toward the door. Could it be true? Afon dead? It was too horrible to consider. But whether he was alive or dead, Afon was not in Malinov and I knew I must leave for Paris immediately to find Max.

"I have to leave," I said. "Thank you both."

"Send us a letter when you get there," Mrs. Zaitz said.

I stepped up onto the seat of the laundry cart. Was it possible Afon really had been ambushed by Reds? One thing was certain: He'd been on his way to help us. If only he'd arrived in time. If he'd indeed been captured, perhaps the Reds kept him prisoner still? Thoughts of Afon made me dizzy and I forced myself to think instead of Max's sweet face.

I took my gun and map from my pocket, set them next to me on the wooden bench, pulled my dog fur coat tight around my chest and urged Jarushka on without a look back.

Off, the two of us, to Paris to find my son.

Varinka

1918

IT TOOK US A YEAR AND A HALF TO GET TO PARIS. WITH the constant changes of plans from Taras's bosses in Petrograd, Mamka and I felt lucky to get there at all. When we arrived on that freezing December day, we brought our bags to 24 Rue de Serene, a tall building on a backstreet across from a café. Taras kept us on a short leash and watched our every move, but had approved a brief trip to the Lanvin shop at 22 Rue du Faubourg, the richest part of town. I took some money from Taras's boot, his bank of sorts, just enough to buy a hat. I had no idea how he earned his money. He was so secretive about it, it had to be bad.

I held Max's hand. What a good-looking young man he'd become, at four and one half years old, so handsome in the little woolen suit Mamka had made for him.

I wore the countess's sable coat, a bit too large for me in the shoulders, and ran one hand down the sleeve. The countess. How many times had she stood here at Lanvin? Perhaps it was better she was released from her suffering, but how terrible it had been to see the family die such painful deaths. Mamka said Vladi would burn in eternal fire for that.

I turned my attention to the front of the corner shop, *Jeanne Lanvin* spelled out in fat, gold letters above the facade. I barely felt the cold as I peeked into the white-curtained windows.

"I'm buying a hat," I said.

"It will cost more than our *izba*," she said. "Not that it's ours anymore."

Though Mamka's health had improved after almost two years of good food and the pink was back in her cheeks, she was still so thin and stuck to her plain ways and wardrobe.

Mamka, Max, and I stepped into the blond-paneled showroom, the famous wooden spiral staircase curling up at one side. We passed an army of mannequins draped in fine dresses, one more exquisite than the next. It was just as it looked in Mamka's dressmaking magazines.

Two women stepped to greet us, the older one tall and white-haired, dressed in a suit the color of fresh cream, with matching kid boots, the second a mousy girl in a gray silk dress, the sash glittering with embroidered beads.

"May I assist you?" the tall one asked. "I am Madame Devereux." Her gaze drifted to the burn on my cheek.

I felt my cheeks warm, brushed my hair down across my face, and stepped to the mannequin, which stood clothed in a pale green, silk dress with a tight, cropped velvet jacket, the white-quilted lapels embroidered with Madame Lanvin's signature floral beads and tiny mirrors. "Yes, I'd like to see a hat. Something in this color."

"Madame Lanvin makes her hats to order," Madame Devereux said. "For her best customers."

I swallowed hard. "A dress, then. Something in this fabric." I felt the silk, like a cold river through my fingers.

Madame Devereux pulled the fabric from my hand and smoothed it down the front of the mannequin. "Perhaps come back another time." She turned and walked toward the stairs.

Mamka stepped after the woman. "May I see Madame Lanvin, please?"

She turned and looked Mamka over. "What about?"

Mamka pulled a belt from her bag. "I do needlework."

The two women came closer and inspected the belt. It was one of Mamka's finest gold workpieces, with a magnificent beaded squirrel, his fur most lifelike, wild roses and vines curled between leaves and pinecones.

The mousy one took the belt from Mamka and ran a finger down the back of the squirrel. "*C'est merveilleux*. Perhaps I can show Madame Lanvin."

Mamka stepped to the mannequin outfitted in the green dress, flipped up the jacket hem, examined the buttonholes, and then shook her head. "Machine done."

Madame Devereux hurried to the mannequin. "No one hand-sews buttonholes anymore."

Mamka pulled back the satin lining. "Seams are skimpy, too."

My cheeks burned. How could she be so critical?

The mousy one could not take her eyes from the belt in her hands. "Are you available on Wednesdays?"

I stepped forward. "No, she takes care of my son—"

"Yes," Mamka said. "Any weekday, but I charge extra on Saturdays."

The girl smiled. "Come back tomorrow and we'll see. We do most sewing on premises but you may be allowed to take work home."

Mamka nodded at the woman and we stepped out onto the street.

"Did you see the hat with fur fringe around the brim?" she asked. "*Skunk* trim? Heavenly Father. We did it better in the forest."

"You want to sew for them? Why didn't you tell me? You are already half blind—"

"Would you stop, Varinka? We both know my eyesight is fine. Did you see their buttons? Not even reinforced. They need me. *And* I bet I can make five hundred francs a month."

"You will leave me every day?"

"This makes me happy and money buys freedom, Varinka. What we need more than anything."

"I need help with Max."

"So that's it. I'm your nanny? Suddenly you don't want to take care of the child you insisted on keeping?"

"I met a boy. In Petrograd. He said he would try and find me here."

"If you want to go out on dates, find Max's mother and give him back."

"How can you say that? You know how much I love him."

"Give him up, Varinka."

I picked Max up, barely able to carry him, his legs dangling long, and buried my face in his hair, breathing in the scent of little boy.

"I'm so sleepy," he said as he wrapped his arms around my neck and laid his head on my shoulder.

I ran my hand down his back. "You just rest, my love."

Give him up? That I could never do.

MAMKA AND I WALKED back to our new home. It was a three-story building, the front covered in wide windows, which let in the light but gave no privacy. I asked Taras for money for curtains but he refused, saying he needed to save funds for other things. Like prostitutes and drink? We'd only been there one night when he'd come home smelling of opium and toilet water. At least the townhouse had a second entrance, through the back garden, so we could come and go undetected.

We were almost home, Max holding Mamka's hand, when I spied him, walking toward us.

Radimir.

A nice little shiver ran through me. He looked good, his long hair loose and blowing back as he walked, carefree, looking in shopwindows as he went. Had he filled out a bit since I last saw him or was it just the heavier coat? Suddenly I was afraid to talk with him.

I walked by without even a glance at him.

Radimir stopped on the sidewalk as we passed. "Varinka? Is that you?"

I turned. "Oh, Radimir, hello. I didn't see you."

He stepped closer and smiled at me, blowing hot breath on his gloved hands. How good to see him, his cheeks flushed red from the cold. He was so different from Taras. Slender and kind.

"This is my mamka."

He made a little bow in Mamka's direction. "Pleased to meet you, my name is Radimir Solomakhin. I know your daughter a little."

Mamka nodded. "Zina Kozlov Pushkinsky."

"We were just about home," I said.

Radimir patted Max's back. "And who is this little man?"

I stopped short. "We're watching him while his mother works. On our way home now for his nap."

"May I accompany you?"

"That won't be necessary," Mamka said.

Radimir sent me a cautious look. "All right. I am off then. To Gare de Lyon. The restaurant there, right in the station."

I smiled at him. "Good to see you again."

"And you as well," he said. "Just off to wait at the bakery here at the corner for a bit before I'm off to the restaurant. Probably be there until one o'clock."

How obvious he was, but it made me smile. It was good to be wanted.

Mamka and I parted ways with Radimir and soon stepped in through the front door of our townhouse.

I held my hands out for the manservant to remove my gloves. How odd it was to have someone else dress and undress me, but Taras insisted on it. "Radimir is very nice, Mamka. No need to be rude to him."

"You may be sophisticated all of a sudden, Inka, but you have no business with him."

"Because he's Jewish?"

"You'd have a hard life together. People—"

"Who cares what people think? The world is changing."

"You have a *child* to focus on. A child you just had to lie about."

I felt my cheeks flush at that. "I'll take Max to the school and enroll him."

"Now that's a good mother."

Would she say that if she knew where I would go on the way back?

TARAS DID NOT WANT to come to L'Ecole Cygne Royal, the best elementary school in our arrondissement, but the school required two parents at the interview. At least it was not far from our new home.

I bundled Max up and we hurried there, fighting the wind. I had made Taras slick his hair back and wear his best shoes. I would have to get rid of Taras quickly thereafter to meet Radimir by one o'clock.

We stopped outside the prim stone building, the black-fenced side yard full of toddlers and teachers calling out to each other in French. Max knew a little French, but spoke mostly Russian. I checked my bag for the extra photos we'd had taken for our passports. Everything was lining up.

Of course the school would want him, the sweetest child alive.

I took Max by the hand and entered the school vestibule, our foot-steps echoing on the tile, Taras close behind. What a fine place this was. We approached a woman sitting behind a desk. She wore her hair close-cropped.

"Do you speak Russian?" I asked.

"A little," she said. "I teach languages."

"I, *we*, would like to enroll my son in school," I said.

She eyed my sable coat. "Fill out a form. The school year started in September. Next enrollment for the petite section will be summer session."

I pulled a form from the pile on the desk and began filling in the spaces.

"There is already a long waiting list." She looked the three of us up and down.

"My son is very smart and knows some French."

Her gaze flicked to my ringless finger.

"I'm teaching him to read." Why could I not stop talking?

"My hands are tied," she said.

"I would like to speak to the headmistress," I said.

"You are speaking to her. Madame Fournier."

"We came from Petrograd," I said. "He needs friends his own age."

"I'm afraid we cannot help you." Madame Fournier stood and walked back down the hall.

Taras stepped after her. "I don't suppose it will help your school if word gets out the headmistress has, well, had a little accident on the way to class one day."

Madame stopped and turned, a quizzical look on her face. Afraid? Astonished?

I continued to complete the enrollment form. *Varinka Pushkinsky. Taras Pushkinsky.*

Taras went on. Would he push her too far?

"Maybe let me tell you what I do for a living. Perhaps you've heard about people meeting a bad end . . ."

Madame waved the thought away. "Stop."

Taras smiled. "Surely you can find room for one more child in your ranks."

"That is blackmail."

"You learn so much at school," he said.

"I will call the police."

Taras frowned. "The poor police. Overwhelmed. Some of them are already my friends."

He was a brute, but at that moment I was grateful for it.

I handed my completed application to Madame Fournier.

Her hand shook as she took it. "By law I need to have your photographs for the application."

I pulled the white envelope out of my bag. "Right here."

"Well, we require a trial visit day," she said.

"I knew you would see it my way," Taras said with a smile.

Moments later, Taras and I stepped out of the building, having left Max behind for his half day of getting acquainted, his test to see if he would get along well enough there to join the class. How happy he'd been to see the other children.

I said goodbye to Taras, told him I was off to buy bread, and smiled as I pulled on my gloves. There was no question Max would pass the test.

I MET RADIMIR AT the bakery on the corner.

"Clever girl, Varinka," he said. "You understood my cryptic message."

We took a quick train ride to Gare de Lyon station. The restaurant there was part of the station so we walked only steps up to the entrance. I would have my first date in Paris and then be back in time to pick up Max.

Radimir linked one arm in mine and hurried me into the restaurant. "Look up."

I brought my gaze to the ceiling. "So beautiful." The whole thing was covered with paintings of country scenes, in fanciful golden frames. In the middle of it all sat a giant gold chandelier.

"Isn't it incredible? Since I first saw it I wanted to show you."

A waiter sat us on two leather seats facing each other, a table between us. I slipped my arms out of my sable coat and let it fall back, the label there for all to see, *Worth*, printed in script, the "h" swooped back across the word. I made a note not to slurp my tea from the saucer.

Radimir looked good, his dark green cap matching his eyes. He tossed his cigarette pack onto the table; I slid a cigarette from it, brought it to my mouth, and waited. "How long have you been in Paris?"

He hesitated, a slight smile on his lips, and then lit a match. "About a week now. You?"

"A few weeks." I coughed a bit. What was the attraction to smoking?

Radimir smiled. "You've become quite sophisticated, Varinka."

I smiled and looked about the place. A *date*. In Paris. How exciting it all was. Meeting at the bakery, coming to such a fancy place full of rich Parisians.

A waiter handed us a sheet with the restaurant's few offerings printed on it, but I could not tear my gaze from the ceiling.

"They're all landscapes," Radimir said. "I knew you'd like them. It seems crazy eating dinner at the train station but the food is good."

I closed my eyes and breathed in the scents of the kitchen. Beef and onions.

"These paintings were done by the rail company, each is a different scene one might see on a trip on their trains, through places like Lyon, Marseille. Forty-one paintings altogether. By twenty-seven artists."

"I like them all. But the one straight above is the best."

He looked straight up and his wool cap almost fell off the back of his head. "You have a good eye. René Billotte painted that. France's best. Perhaps we will travel by train together one day. Bring your mother. If she ever warms up to me."

"She's just very religious. She likes good people, though, so you have no worries."

"I'll blind her with my charms."

"Why do you never take off your hat?"

"I'm afraid you won't like me."

302 • MARTHA HALL KELLY

He pulled off his cap to reveal his hair, deep red as my sable coat. I couldn't help but stare.

"You hate it. Since I was a baby old ladies have been coming up to me and touching my red hair." He tried to replace his cap.

I reached across the table and stopped him. "It's beautiful. Not red like a sunset but deeper."

Radimir sat up a little straighter. "They tell me my father had this hair as well. Titian the painter made it his signature."

"Well, I like it very much."

The menu was limited, no eggs or sugar and little bread, but they did have the famous bouillon soup they were known for so we ordered a bowl to split. My mouth watered at the thought. I'd had no French food since we'd arrived, cooking Russian food for Taras at home, unable to go out with Max anyway.

"I worked at the Louvre yesterday and found a painting I must show you."

So he was planning another date?

"There is a word in Hebrew *beshert*. It means 'meant to be fated.' And that is how I feel about us. How else would I have met you in Petrograd?"

"And here on the street?"

"Well, I must admit I have been keeping one eye out for you here. But it seems God keeps throwing things in my path. Sitting here, it's hard to imagine there's a revolution going on at home."

"I hope it all ends up good for us."

"It's going to be better than you can imagine, Varinka. Finally, no more taxes. Everyone equal. No more tsar turning on his own people when we strike. Common people will finally own land. The art will be brought out from the big estates, free for all to enjoy."

Radimir took a drink of his water, cheeks flushed. How deeply he felt about—

All at once came a hard squeeze on my arm.

"Buying bread?"

I looked up to find Taras standing at our table.

"Get up."

I yanked my arm away, causing a water glass to fall over, sending water across the table. "We're in the middle—"

Radimir threw his napkin on the table. "Let her go."

Taras stared at Radimir as if memorizing him.

"How did you know I was here?" I asked.

Taras shifted in his hunter's boots. "I won't tell you again, Inka."

The hot stares of the other patrons lingered on us.

I stood and Taras shoved me toward the restaurant door.

Radimir scrambled to his feet. "Stay, Varinka."

Our waiter hurried toward the table. "No fighting in here."

"I'm sorry," I called back to Radimir.

Taras pulled me roughly by my arm toward the door, causing more patrons to gape at us. I knew I would be punished more, later, in private. Would Radimir see the results? I would use extra powder to cover the bruises.

I turned back as Radimir stood looking like he wanted to follow, our bouillon steaming on the table.

CHAPTER
38

Eliza

1918

N EW YORK CITY WENT MAD WITH JOY AT THE NEWS
the war ended that November. Mayor Hylan led what can only loosely
be called a parade, of city employees, in a delirious march up Fifth Avenue as New Yorkers choked the streets and almost drowned in confetti.

But no parade could hide the fact that the war had left nine million
soldiers dead, 125,000 of them Americans, and 21 million wounded.
Was Merrill among them? I'd had no letter for a full year and had written to every hospital in France with no word back. If I was lucky
enough to find him alive, there was no guarantee he'd still care for me.

I planned to sail later that month in search of him. What would I
find on my passage to France? Certainly, a country ravaged by war, but
I had American Central Committee for Russian Relief business and a
long-promised meeting with Nonna Zaronova to attend to.

And perhaps I'd find some clues about Sofya. The papers said the
number of Russian émigrés in Paris soared that year to over five thousand. Surely someone there knew more of her whereabouts.

THE DAY OF OUR third bazaar to benefit the Committee for Russian
Relief, held at our New York apartment, an unexpected, though most
welcome, guest arrived.

It seemed the whole city waited for our sales of handmade Russian gifts, a line forming around the block, and this pre-Christmas event proved larger than ever. In the vast living room, Mother and I had set up every table we had, upon which we artfully arranged our Russian goods. Guests hurried from one table to the next, gathering the hand-made, lace-edged sheets and pillow covers, dolls and painted boxes to their chests, knowing we sold out quickly. Caroline and her fellow debutante friends dressed in Russian dress for the day and milled through the crowd attending the shoppers.

A good-looking, blond gentleman with excellent posture stepped into the room, clearly not interested in shopping, and Mother and I went to him.

"I am looking for Eliza Ferriday?"

He stood tall, dressed in a wool suit, high white collar, and thin tie. His clothes were of the finest quality, though clearly worn, but he was perfectly groomed.

"Whom may I say is calling?" Mother asked.

He removed his gloves and extended one hand. "Baron Yury Van-yovich Vasily-Argunov, madame. But please call me Cook. Everyone does."

Mother reached out her hand to shake his, and he raised her hand to his lips and kissed it. She turned away, color high in her cheeks. The last time I'd seen her blush was when she'd worn a new pair of heels and Father had called her his "Amazonian princess."

I extended my hand. "I'm Eliza Ferriday."

"I know Sofya Stepanov. She spoke of you often."

Sofya. How I yearned to grill him on Sofya's status. "We must hear about Russia. There are so many questions."

"Let the man settle in," Mother said with a warning glance at me.

"I just sailed from France. Been in Paris several months."

"How is it?" I asked.

He spread his feet wide and folded his arms across his chest. "Dangerous for Russians. The Bolsheviks already have agents there, London now, too. Assassins to finish off the wealthy who flee, take the money they feel is Russia's. I had a few close calls."

"Murder?" A chill ran through me. Sofya.

"There have been a few killings. It's not uncommon for Russian aristocrats, 'former people' they now call us, to disappear in the night, sent back to Russia to stand trial. Some get poison in their meal. I was followed more than once."

"Have you heard news of the Streshnayvas?" I asked.

"Two years ago, I was with them when the estate was seized by thieves."

My stomach lurched. "So it's true?"

Mother pulled a chair over and sat.

"We've been frantic for news," I said.

"Sofya helped me escape, but one of their captors, a woodsman named Taras, shot me in the side."

"You poor man," Mother said.

"I was lucky it was nightfall and raining. I buried my boots in leaves so as not to leave tracks and somehow evaded him, but on the second day, half frozen, I lost consciousness in the woods. Next thing I knew, foragers had dragged me back to their *izba*."

"Did they have medicine?" Mother asked.

"They did what they could with herbs and poultices. Once the snow came it was impossible to get me out to a hospital—I had to wait for spring and by then Petrograd was in absolute chaos. The couple brought me, bound to a sledge, to my friend in the provisional government. He was packing his office, leaving on a diplomatic transport, and he secured a doctor and offered to bring me with him. I was too weak to stay on my own and my papers marked me as a 'former person,' so I had to leave. I begged my friend to send help back to the Streshnayvas, but the government had fallen. We barely made it out ourselves."

"With a bullet still lodged in your side?" Mother asked. "You must have had blood poisoning."

"Yes. The doctor couldn't believe I'd lived with the bullet inside me for months. Removed it on the train. Long recovery in Paris. My friend was good to keep me hidden at the embassy, but he was being transferred to New York and, after a close call with a Cheka kidnapper, I knew I had to join him here."

"Do you know what happened to Sofya?" I asked, almost afraid to know the answer.

Cook ran his fingers through his hair. "I looked for her every day in Paris. Checked the lists of émigrés at Rue Daru, where so many Russians have settled, but found not one Streshnayva or Stepanov. I did hear things about what happened to the family. Just rumors. That they'd met a horrible end." He pulled a handkerchief from his pocket and dabbed one eye.

I sat on the piano bench. "Oh, no."

"But I've also heard that Sofya's body was not among the dead, so I still hope."

"Where would she be if she survived?" I asked.

"Hard to say. She may have gone to the tsarina for assistance, but once the tsar abdicated he could be of no help. Ivan's townhouse in the city has been nationalized so there's no going back there."

I stood. "I'm traveling to Europe soon on a host of missions and hope to find her."

"Back before the attack the family was headed to France."

"Yes," I said.

"The first place she'd go would be Paris."

MOTHER AND I STOOD in the living room of my Manhattan apartment unpacking another shipment of handmade items from Paris when Peg burst into the room.

"Mail, Miz Ferriday." She reached out with a crocheted bag, stuffed with envelopes and packages. "There's a package there, ma'am. Return address says Russia."

I dug into the net bag and pulled out a pale blue, square cardboard box, the kind sewing supplies like bobbins came packaged in. It was not much bigger than two cigarette packs lashed together and wrapped with enough twine to truss a turkey.

I unwrapped the twine and pulled off the lid to find a bracelet lying on a bed of cotton wool. It was quite a nice enameled bracelet with two dragonheads, whose gaping mouths met where the bracelet opened. The beasts stared each other down, their eyes set with red jewels.

"I've never seen anything like it."

"It's from a Viking design," Mother said. "In Norse mythology, a giant serpent encircles the world, growing larger each day until it is big enough to devour itself. They believed that moment would trigger the end of the world."

"Cheery," I said.

I read the note, scribbled in a messy hand, harder to read than the hieroglyphics on the Pyramid of Cheops.

Sofya's? But no one had more beautiful script than she.

Please guard this well. It is all we have.
See you in our favorite city. Much love, S.

"My God, it *is* Sofya." I grabbed the box. "The address?"

Peg shrugged. "Just says Krasnodar. Odd name for a town, if you ask me. But then again 'K' words always sound harsh, don't they?"

"Not now, Peg." I reread the words. *See you in our favorite city.* That was Paris, of course. Cook was right.

I slid the bracelet onto my wrist.

Mother bent for a closer look. "I think those rubies are paste, but it's a handsome piece."

How good it looked on my wrist, as if born to live with my charm bracelet, which featured the Seven Wonders of the World, including a pyramid whose top opened to reveal a jiggling cobra.

And it was from Sofya. She was alive and well and at least near enough to civilization to send a package. But why such a gift? I ran one finger down the cool enamel of the bracelet. Why had she sent it all the way to me?

Just two of one thousand questions I would ask my beloved friend in Paris.

CHAPTER
39

Sofya

1919

O NE FRIGID JANUARY TUESDAY I FINALLY REACHED
the outskirts of Paris. I'd taken the southern route to avoid both winter
and war, west along the coast and up through France. On the way, I
bartered my starched Russian sheets and pillowcases for bread and
overnights in barns.

Many times each day the image of my family impaled on that fence
floated up in front of me as good Jarushka pulled the wagon along. I
did not swat them away, but steeped myself in every horrifying detail,
stoking my hunger for justice. I considered ending my life, thoughts of
Afon's disappearance swirling in my head. But nothing would stop me
from reclaiming my son.

I was eager to get to the city and start my search for Max, but our
progress was slow, trapped on the narrow, poplar-flanked roads, which
were clogged with traffic, mostly horse-drawn. Though the war had
been over for months, there were still a few ambulances among us, bandaged casualties sitting next to the driver or sitting in the back of the
cart.

As we drew closer to the city, Jarushka picked up speed and soon I
could scarcely look anywhere without seeing remnants of the war. Re-
minders of the bravery and ingenuity of the French people and what
they had done to survive were everywhere. I urged Jarushka along,

past the captured German cannon proudly displayed in the Place de la Concorde and the Champs-Élysées and drove along the grand boulevards where the once majestic chestnut trees, thinning now, had been cut for firewood.

How smart Parisians had been to remove the great stained-glass windows of the cathedral of Notre-Dame and store them for safety, replacing them with pale yellow panes. Victory flags fluttered in the harsh wind from every streetlamp and window.

But it was horrible to see the endless piles of rubble and boarded-up windows where German bombs had fallen. Though the enemy did not occupy Paris, destruction was everywhere. We passed refugees from the ruined northern regions as they roamed the parks and streets and soldiers who suffered lost limbs and horrible facial injuries as they reached up to me, begging piteously for change.

Jarushka slowed. I rubbed my hands to warm them and inventoried my wealth, such as it was: One map. Two guns. One pair of well-worn shearling mittens. One dog fur coat and hat. A few Russian pillowcases and Luba's sextant. How could I ever sell that, her pride and joy?

We headed off toward Eliza's apartment on Rue Saint-Roch in the first arrondissement, cruel wind at our backs hurrying us along. I rehearsed my plan to appeal to her housekeeper, young Madame Solange whom I'd known well, for asylum and a warm bed. I would house Jarushka in the stables the Ferridays employed and go about finding Max.

Once I found Eliza's building I left Jarushka on the street and rang the bell. The building had survived the war years well; the paper tape artistically arranged on its windowpanes to prevent breakage was the only sign of conflict. How wonderful a real bed would feel at last.

A white-haired man came to the door, wearing a blue smock and a sour expression. "The servants' entrance is round back," he said and started to close the door.

"I am a friend of Eliza Ferriday's."

He pulled his smock closer. "The Ferridays are not at home."

"Please, I have been here before. I know Madame Solange."

He eyed my clothes and for the first time I realized what a fright I must look, in my grimy dog fur coat and filthy face.

"Everyone knows my daughter. She is not here."

"I had the pleasure of staying at this apartment with Eliza many times when I was at boarding school in Switzerland, monsieur."

"My hearing is not good. Come back when my daughter is here."

"I've come all the way from Petrograd. The Bolsheviks are killing—"

"Yes, yes. People come here with all sorts of stories." He dug into his smock pocket and pulled out two coins. "Here. Take this. That is all I can do for you. All the Russians stay over behind the Grand Palais. You'll find a room there. Or on Rue Daru. Off with you now."

He closed the door and the lock clicked shut.

I rapped on the glass. "Please tell Eliza I was here?"

The man pulled down the little window shade.

I made my way back to Jarushka and realized I had not left my name. I examined the coins. Just two francs but what a gift. With more money I could telegram Eliza back in New York. She would make sure I had access to her apartment.

Jarushka was hungry and needed rest so we rode to the stables the Ferridays had used, just around the corner from their apartment. Every muscle relaxed when I saw the place there still open and I drove the cart into the brick building. The war had taken a toll on the old livery stable, the barrel ceiling caved in at the rear so you could see the sky. It was not exactly the stables of Versailles but Jarushka could rest there after her long trip and eat as she should.

A woman came from a stall, a bucket in each hand. "What is this?"

"The Ferridays sent me. Said you would board this horse on their account."

"They are not in Paris. Haven't been for years."

"Madame Solange sent me."

The woman eyed Jarushka. "She's a big thing. Probably eats her weight in hay. Board will be five francs a week, cash up front."

"Could you keep her for free if she worked?"

The woman walked around Jarushka, smoothed one hand down her flank. "Pretty skinny. Might be worth more for the meat."

A chill ran through me. "She's a fine workhorse."

"If the wagon stays I will try it. For one week. After that, no promises."

"Do you have a position for me? I know a lot about horses. I can sleep in the stall with her."

"We are full up now. I've taken on too many returning soldiers. There isn't a decent place to stay in the whole city right now."

I agreed to our deal with a handshake and stepped to Jarushka. I encircled her neck with my arms, my cheek against her warmth, and she nudged her velvet nose against my side. What a good friend she'd been to me.

"Please take good care of her. She will do her very best for you."

The woman took her buckets to the next stall. "One week," she said over her shoulder.

I hurried out, without a look back, holding back the tears. One week was an eternity after all. I would find Max and be back to fetch her well before then.

I walked along the Rue de Rivoli and passed by Agnessa's favorite spot in Paris, the Tuileries rose garden, reduced to a gaping crater by an enemy bomb. I took my rose from my rucksack and sprinkled it with water from the fountain there. It had grown half as much bigger and was prettier than any rose that grew there in summer, with her velvety white petals and golden heart.

I pulled an old newspaper from the trash and read: DEFEATED GER-MANY SURRENDERS.

At the 11th hour on the 11th day of the 11th month of 1918, what would become known as the Great War, had finally concluded. Germany, out of manpower and supplies, signed an agreement with the Allies in a railroad car outside Compiègne, France.

Where to look for lodging? Certainly not in this high-rent neighborhood.

I headed away from the Seine, toward the theater district. After a day of inquiring about available rooms with no luck, I stopped on a side street and watched the crowd, half the women in black mourning dress. How France had suffered.

I passed an unassuming building at 6 Rue Chabanais, with a neatly printed sign in the window. *Beds to let one franc per night.*

Finding that well within my means I stepped into the place to inquire. It was a clean, well-lit lobby, and I warmed my hands in the glow of the coal fire in the fireplace. Many well-dressed young women sat there talking among themselves. An older woman sat behind the hotel desk, her dark hair caught up in a half turban the color of her vivid blue eyes.

She stood and slapped open the hotel register. "And who do we have here?" She spoke in my favorite accent of all, Irish.

"I am Sofya."

The woman smiled. "Mary Melange."

"It is a pleasure to meet you," I said. I tried to neaten my hair and hid my rough, red hands in my pockets. "I've just come from Petrograd."

"Long trip."

"I'm looking to rent a bed."

"Well, you have come to the right place, my dear. I hope you don't mind me saying but you have the look of aristocracy."

I brushed a lump of crusted mud from my sleeve. "Perhaps, under all this dirt."

"For seven francs I will assign you a bed for one week, guaranteed no bedbugs, access to the bath, and one towel. We are a female-only establishment with very strict rules. Along with the bed comes a floor custodian you must sign in with every day."

"I can only afford one night." I found one franc and placed it on the counter. What a relief to finally have a bed of my own.

She tossed it in the cash register with a satisfying little clink.

"Can I trouble you for a telephone book?"

She pulled one from behind the counter and held it to her chest. "What do you want with it?"

"I'm looking for a man."

"We have plenty of those."

"Named Taras Pushkinsky."

"Boyfriend?"

"Certainly not."

She opened the book to the "P" page and turned it toward me.

I ran one finger down the long column, with not one Pushkinsky. He was here, no doubt, on nefarious business. Why would he even list himself in the directory? A wave of exhaustion crashed over me and I closed the book.

"Any idea where I can find work, madame?"

"There's always need for hardworking girls here. Just talk to your custodian, Oxana. Third floor."

"Thank you," I said over my shoulder as I headed for the stairs.

I made it up the steep stairs to my floor: one large, open, dormitory-style room, fitted with what must have been fifty beds, pushed next to each other with a bedside table here and there. Most of the beds were occupied with two or more sleeping girls. As I passed, I knew many were Russian, since they had taped to their iron headboards magazine pictures of the royal family, many of the tsar's daughters, the grand duchesses.

I found Oxana, a tall girl, who looked to be about twenty-one, with jaggedly close-cropped brown hair that looked like she'd cut it herself. She lay on a bed atop the chenille bedcover, reading a tattered movie magazine. There was something familiar about her as she ate beans from a can with a spoon, the lid still attached. Ordinarily not a fan of beans, I suddenly longed for them more than any dish Cook had ever made.

"I'm here to see Oxana," I said in French.

She sat up. "Shhhh. Can't you see girls are sleeping?"

Oxana was clearly Russian, but her French was good.

I lowered my voice. "Madame Melange sent me up. She said she assigned me a bed and I could take a bath."

"Good luck getting a bath. The line is always too long and all beds are all taken. But you can bunk in with me for one franc."

"She said—"

"Onetime offer."

"You would gouge a fellow Russian? I hope you realize I will have only one franc left to my name."

"I hope you realize you're not on Nevsky Prospekt anymore. A lot of the girls on this floor are Russian. One princess, a ballerina. Some eat out of trash cans at Jardin du Luxembourg. Best one is near the marionette theater, if you're interested."

"I'm happy to work."

She set the can on her nightstand. "Well, that's good news since it's required. You may have paid for your bed, but to keep it you must put in your hours."

"I don't understand."

"You are slow, aren't you? The girls here make their living on their backs. This is the dormitory for 12 Rue Chabanais just next door. Quite a fancy place. You won't believe the murals."

A brothel? My lips could not form the words.

Oxana pressed her face closer, eyes wide. "Yes, a *maison close*. You can tell by the numbers on the street above the door. Always bigger and more colorful."

She slid her spoon under my jacket front, lifted it, and let it flop closed. "You're a bit old for the best gentlemen and awfully skinny, but with the lights down low your tits are still good enough to keep your bed. For some of the men that come to *Les Chabanais*, just being seen with a Russian aristocrat on their arm is enough. And get rid of those trousers for goodness' sake. On the rare occasions when they wear clothes, girls here wear dresses and black stockings."

"I must leave right away." All at once my temple throbbed.

"Good luck getting your money back from Madame. Strict no-refund policy. The sooner you start the better."

All at once Oxana sat back and squinted at me. "You know I cannot shake the feeling I've met you before."

"I thought so, too, when we first met."

"Moscow Cotillion?"

"No. I debuted in Petrograd." I thought for a moment. "The Vienna Opera Ball?"

"I don't think so."

"My goodness. *Brillantmont*."

Oxana breathed a sharp intake of air. "Sofya Streshnayva."

"You were a first year when I graduated. Didn't you have long braids?"

Oxana ran her fingers through her short hair. "Sold them first thing when I got here. To the peddler on the way to Rue Daru. Paid me two hundred francs but I could make a lot more money if I still had them."

She considered me for a moment. "There are a few jobs for girls who sew. Good with a needle?"

I shook my head no.

"Every Russian in Paris flocks to the cathedral at Rue Daru. There's a workshop there, down in the basement, where you can earn a few centimes making dolls if you can tat lace. But don't tell them you saw me here?"

"Of course not."

"Wait. How did I forget? Don't tell her I told you, but there may be a job for you in Madame's office, since her collections girl just quit. She was stupid, with no sense for numbers. I would take it but I don't know the city well enough. Plead your case to her and see if she brings it up."

I waved to Oxana and hurried down the stairs.

"Hold out for eight francs a week," she called after me.

FOUR DOORS DOWN, 12 Rue Chabanais was just as Oxana promised, a gaudy lobby, the walls filled with sensual murals. The gilded mirror over the white marble fireplace reflected a group of breathtakingly lovely girls, most foreigners, sitting about in couture dresses as if at a good party, waiting for their husbands off smoking cigars.

I spotted Madame Melange as she twisted a young woman's hair into a chignon and secured it with hairpins. "I hope you don't mind me saying so, dear, but you have the look of aristocracy," she said to the woman.

I hurried to her. "I need my money back."

Madame took me by the arm and led me to the corner. "I don't know what you're talking about. We made a deal. Besides, this is the best you'll do in all of Paris."

"I can read. There must be some sort of job—"

"Half the women here can quote Aristotle, my dear. Unless you have a taxi license, no one is hiring Russian women, even to clean toilets."

I hugged my waist and paced the silk carpet.

"Look," Madame said. "There are two things people will always pay for. Food and sex. I don't know about you but I'm no chef."

Overwhelmed, I covered my face with my hands. What would Father think of me here in this place? Luba would surely figure out some sort of plan. Afon? How I ached for them. How could I find Max all by myself? Where to even start?

Madame Melange wrapped her arm around me, releasing a wave of gardenia and spice.

"There, there. Think of it as a new experience. Our customers are some of the richest in Paris and once you freshen up and put on some rouge you'll be in the mood. We have twenty-one theme rooms here. It can be fun, you know."

"I am related to the tsar. My father was finance minister—"

"An accountant?"

"Yes. Seems I inherited his way with math. One of my best subjects in school. Too bad there's no need for such skills here in Paris."

"Well, actually I do need a collection agent."

"Oh, really?" I asked.

"You can spare me the act. It's obvious Oxana told you. But I do need someone *reliable*. To call on our customers' homes and fetch monies due. My last agent disappeared with a whole day's envelopes."

At least I would not be the one providing services to the clients.

Madame counted on her fingers. "It requires a good knowledge of the city . . ."

"I have been summering here since boarding school."

"And, well, incredible discretion."

"I can be the soul of discretion for a price."

"You *must* be here each night before sundown to deliver the envelopes and it pays five francs per week."

"Room included?"

Madame nodded.

"For nine francs I will balance your books as well. And I would like a bonus if the work is good."

"No to the bonus, but I will pay eight francs and no more. We'll try it one week and see. Start today and you'll be paid in one week."

I shook her hand. "Happy to be your new collection agent, madame."

THE NEXT MORNING, I set off from the brothel armed with a list of Madame's clients and two francs of advanced salary. I soon settled into a pattern of constant collection work, sun up to sundown, resting only to grab a quick bite and scan the crowds and school playgrounds for Max. I was proud of my one hundred percent collection rate, mostly from maids who met me at the door and, when I mentioned Madame's name, paid quickly, eager to be rid of me. I even collected from one woman, who propositioned me, too. I politely declined. How could anyone, man or woman, find me attractive, so thin and haggard?

On the third day, I made a record number of collections and then treated myself to a warm roll. I was turning out to be a good business-person. Just like Father. He would be proud of my ability to survive.

The sun was setting as I arrived at the last home on the list, Rue de Serene, a nice neighborhood, home to many of the ambassadors and politicians who represented a good chunk of Madame's clients.

I rapped on the door and waited. The lively café across the street was doing a good business, amber light inside lit up the patrons, a few at café tables still arranged in the cobblestoned courtyard despite the cold.

A man dressed in a white jacket answered the townhouse door. A butler? How odd to see servants again.

"Yes?" the butler asked.

A figure stood in the long dark hallway behind him.

"I'm here to collect a charge."

He leaned toward me and whispered, "Madame Melange?"

I nodded.

"Wait here."

The man in the hallway counted out some bills and the servant walked by him, toward the back of the house.

I stepped just inside the door and found the man tall and broad across the shoulders, his shirt unbuttoned and open, his chest exposed. My eyes adjusted to the low light and then I saw the face was familiar. Wasn't he the man who'd attacked us at the estate? One of the group who kept us prisoner?

Taras.

I pulled my dog fur hat lower on my forehead. My knees shook. What if I fell right there?

He stopped counting and turned to me. "What are you looking at?" he asked in Russian.

Up close his power was immense. It was the tattoos that almost made me drop my envelope. Every inch of skin went cold to see them. The distinctive cherubs inked into the honey gold of his skin. My breath came fast as I watched him so casually count his money. Had he murdered my loved ones himself? Helped Vladi?

This was Varinka's house. I craned my neck closer to see if there was any sign of Max.

Taras slowed his counting. "Come in. Close the door. It's cold out there."

I looked at the floor and tried to keep the shake from my voice. "I'll stay right here, thank you."

"You Russian?"

I nodded.

He tilted his head. "Haven't seen you at Madame's."

"I handle the accounts." Didn't he know my face? My heart hammered my ribs. Of course, I was unrecognizable in my current state.

"That's a waste of assets." He leaned against the hall table, arms folded across his chest, the money in one hand. "Why not stay?"

"Can you just give me the money?"

"Why in such a hurry?" He waved me closer. "You drink vodka?"

"I have to deliver to Madame by sundown. Or else she—"

He stepped closer and handed me the bills. "Here."

I snatched the money and hurried out, stuffing the fat stack in my envelope, numb with my discovery. I was halfway across the street when the door slammed closed and I turned to see the black door shining in what was left of the day's sunlight. A cold shiver of relief went through me and I hurried on to meet Madame.

It wasn't until I delivered the proceeds that evening, relieved I'd done the job well, that I fully reveled in it all. I had earned an incredible bonus after all.

At last I knew where to find my son.

Varinka

1919

ONE JANUARY DAY, MAMKA AND I HURRIED ABOUT THE outdoor market in the afternoon while Max was in school. It was the typical bazaar one sees all over Paris, with fishmongers and fruit sellers, their winter wares on display in coarse baskets. Though the war was over, the offerings were still meager and prices high.

"Can you take care of Max tomorrow, Mamka? I have plans."

"No. I have plans as well."

I bent over a rotten fish. "Five francs," the fishmonger said.

I moved on. "Can you please cancel them?"

"Lanvin has asked me—"

I stopped walking and turned to her. "You're already working there?"

"Started last week."

"Without telling me?"

"Madame Lanvin herself gave me her best dresses to work on."

"So, you'll not help me with Max anymore?"

"He was your choice. Madame hinted I might someday oversee a *department*. Can you believe it? How quickly I've been recognized. You should hear what they say about my gold work."

We left the market and headed for home, with only dirty potatoes in my net bag.

"Please. They want to work you to death. I love being with Max—

I spent all day at the park yesterday helping him roller skate. But I'm finally making friends here in Paris. I need help with the boy."

"What friends? Radimir?"

I was silent for a moment and breathed deep to stuff down my anger. "I'm almost twenty years old, Mamka, should I not be able to do as I choose?"

"Yes. And I choose not to take care of the child you stole, Varinka. You could be working, too, you know, while Max is in school. We'll need rent money when we leave Taras."

A familiar-looking woman in a gray cloth coat approached us. "Zina Kozlov? Do you remember me from Malinov? Faina from the music store."

Mamka nodded.

"I hear you are sewing now at Lanvin?"

"Yes."

"I cut patterns there on Tuesdays. Madame Lanvin herself told us a woman of immense talent joined us and here it is *you*."

Mamka bit her lip to hold back a smile.

"Come join me for tea," Faina said. "I will tell you everything about the place."

"Now?" Mamka asked.

"Why not?" Faina said.

Mamka waved goodbye to me, the two walked on and just like that my mamka was gone.

"Enjoy your tea," I called after her, but she was too busy talking to her new friend to notice.

LATER THAT WEEK MAMKA and I sat at the kitchen table while she sewed and I tried to coax Max to eat his cereal. Taras was out for the evening and we reveled in the freedom. Was he visiting a brothel? Opium den? Though he still kept us under tight watch and often watched me through a crack in the bathroom wall, he seemed a bit distracted and had started pomading his hair and smoking cigars.

Wind rattled the windows as Mamka held a satin gown the color of spring grass in her lap. Another home project. It seemed all she did was sew, with no time to step out with Max and me.

With her quick needle, she finished the beading on the neckline of the dress, skewering the tiny silver tubes and filling in the shimmering background of the roses. She'd learned her skills sewing the faces of saints with silver and gold threads for the church. Learned the method of using silk floss of one shade and, simply through the direction of the stitch, showing light and shade upon a face.

Next to her sat a folded newspaper, a photo of the tsar and his family on the front page. Since the tsar had been executed the summer before, stories abounded about whether the whole family had been killed and all of Paris was fascinated with each new rumor. Had the whole family really been brutally murdered? I could barely look at the girls there in their white dresses.

I offered Max a spoonful of cereal. "Can't you eat, my good boy?"

He stared down at his bowl, his pale face blank, and barked a little cough. What was he thinking? He barely spoke lately, lost in his own world.

"This is the third time this month he's been sick," Mamka said.

"It's not my fault he eats only croissants and cereal."

Mamka kept her gaze on the dress. "It's the sadness."

I bent toward her, voice low. "He certainly doesn't remember, well, *before*."

"Of course, he does. The child won't sleep in a bed."

I smoothed one hand down his back. What had I done to him? "He'll grow out of it."

Mamka kept her gaze on her sewing, lips tight.

All at once I longed to step out for a movie with Radimir. Or just sit in the park and talk. Maybe share a kiss? But Mamka would not take care of Max.

"Why don't we go to a bistro tonight? Bring Max with us?"

Mamka's needle glinted in the electric light overhead. "I have too much work. Must deliver this to Madame Lanvin by tonight." She glanced at the little brass watch pinned at her waist with bright, Lanvin-blue ribbon, a gift from Madame Lanvin herself. How quickly she had recognized Mamka's value. "I've been made deputy chief seamstress."

"So soon? Of course you have. Who else works such long hours?"

"Can you imagine my good luck? Madame says that with all the material shortages, dress trimmings have become most important. With a band of needlework at the hem and cuffs one can stretch the amount of fabric needed. I showed her a *kokoshnik* I'd made and she wants to do a whole line of them. Russian fashion is becoming very popular, Inka. All the best Parisians are collecting the old Russian costumes of aristocrats and wearing them to balls. Can you imagine? Madame says—"

"Could you not say 'Madame says' one more time, Mamka? My head is about to explode."

"Oh, and I made my first hire. She was a princess back before—"

"How could you, Mamka? Those people held us down for so long."

"She was starving. Hadn't eaten in days and does good work."

"Finally we're making progress with the revolution and you are helping the Whites?"

"When did you become so cruel, Varinka? I will never become unkind just to serve a cause."

A knock came at the front door and I hurried to the front of the townhouse. Was Taras back? He said he'd be gone all night.

I opened the door to find Radimir standing there.

"Sorry to come unannounced but I'm on my way back to work and thought you might like to step out."

I checked the street and the bar across the street for signs of Taras and, finding none, invited Radimir in.

"How kind of you," I said.

He shrugged out of his coat, looking good in his dark green jacket. He'd left his chin unshaved in a good way, his hair tucked behind his ears.

I led Radimir into the kitchen. Mamka looked up from her sewing. "What is he doing here?"

"Just checking to see if I want to step out."

Mamka speared a silver bead with her needle.

"Radimir is working at the museum, Mamka. Meeting with—"

"I'm busy, Inka. I have to deliver this to Madame Lanvin by six."

Radimir removed his hat and stepped farther into the room. "I am happy to deliver it for you, madame."

Mamka sewed the last bead in place and cut the thread. "Oh, no. Lanvin is all the way—"

"I know where it is and I am going that way. And besides, it will free you up to do other things."

Mamka held the dress out and inspected the beading.

"Such beautiful work," Radimir said. "My grandmother was a seamstress but never made anything like that. Corsets mostly."

Mamka stuffed the sleeves of the dress with tissue paper and folded it into a perfect rectangle. "Corsets are the true test of a needlewoman's skill. Only the most accomplished can do them well."

"She was a very nice woman. Dragged me to every museum in Russia. Taught me all I know about art. Wouldn't have my present job without her."

Mamka wrapped the dress in white muslin and tied it with her signature ribbon. "Doing what?"

"Working with those very museums to make sure the Russian people's art is protected. I'm here consulting with the Louvre on a restoration."

Mamka barely looked at him. "I've been there three times. I find inspiration for my beadwork in the Dutch paintings."

Radimir bent a bit from the waist. "It is a secret, but there is to be a new exhibition there of textiles. Some from the seventh century. Exquisite beadwork never shown before."

"Madame Lanvin is a great fan of fancy work."

"Perhaps I can arrange to have you both take a private tour."

Mamka stole a glance at him. "I would not trouble you."

"Consider it done." Radimir held out his hand. "And it would be an honor to deliver your package, Mrs. Pushkinsky."

Mamka shook his hand. "Zina. And why don't you join him, Inka? Go enjoy yourselves. Max and I will spend the evening together."

IT WAS AS IF Radimir and I were shot out of a cannon that night when Mamka offered to take care of Max. Once we delivered the package to Madame Lanvin I said, "Let's not sit at a restaurant. I want to run all over Paris."

How he'd charmed Mamka. My cheeks hurt from smiling, my burn now fading. How good it was to be young and free.

Radimir smiled and took my hand. "I need to show you something first."

He pulled me by the hand to the metro and after a short ride and a chat with a sleepy guard we stood in a dark room at the Louvre, in front of a painting almost as tall as me, a fat, golden frame around it.

"The paintings just hang here in this one place?" I asked.

"Sometimes they travel to other museums, but mostly they are just here and for a price, people come and look at them. I spent too much time here myself today, slacking off. How much she looks like you."

The picture showed blond Psyche, her dress pulled down to reveal her naked body, and handsome, winged Cupid about to embrace her.

"She does resemble me. The face, even the . . ."

I broke off, my face growing hot.

Radimir smiled. "You can say it. The body. She is very beautiful. See the butterfly just above her head? In ancient Greek 'butterfly' is the same word for 'psyche' and represents the soul."

I could have listened to Radimir talk all night there in the darkened room, lit only by pools of light from the paintings, his hushed voice in the near darkness. How Papa would have liked him.

I reached out to touch the paint. "Cupid's wings seem real."

Radimir held my hand back. "Touching the paintings hurts them. But you can look all you want. See the expression on her face? The young princess has just had her first kiss. Do you think she liked it?"

Psyche looked surprised but seemed to want more.

I shifted in my shoes and the wooden floor groaned. "I think so."

Radimir looked at me in his serious way and then pulled me closer. "That was the first sign of their love."

I pushed him away.

"What's wrong?" He held my hands.

"It's just that I don't know . . ."

"How to *kiss*?" Radimir threw back his head and laughed, sending an echo about the room. "You worry too much, Varinka. Cupid kissed Psyche just so." He pulled me to him and pressed his lips to my forehead. "Nothing to worry about."

I lifted my face to his and kissed him on the mouth. I could feel him smile as he kissed me back, his lips warm. I held back and let him come to me, soft and sweet.

He pulled away, a broad smile on his face. "You're a good pupil, Varinka. Looks like I taught you well."

RADIMIR AND I DID run all over Paris that night, barely feeling the cold. Up and down the Champs-Élysées, Pont Alexandre, Place de la Concorde until he left me at the townhouse door.

He smoothed one hand down my cheek. "Next time, Luna Park. I can't wait to show you the roller coaster and it's shutting up soon for the season."

"I'd be most honored."

"You've become quite a Parisian, Miss Varinka." He kissed my cheek and walked off.

I stood on the step and watched him go. How lucky was I?

A light caught my eye as I turned to unlock the door. The glow of a cigar across the street. I searched the darkness and found the shape of Taras's head, the wide shoulders. He was back? Surely, he had seen Radimir walk me home. The kiss on the cheek. Would he lash out at me?

I hurried inside. I would lock my bedroom door and keep Max with me. And from now on I would meet Radi anywhere but at our home.

Eliza

1919

ONCE I DISEMBARKED IN LE HAVRE AND MADE IT to a devastated Paris, I watched, through the window of the hired car, neighborhoods filled with caved-in apartment buildings and shops. Parisians braved January cold and sidestepped bomb craters by the side of the road as if it were normal.

The driver looked at us in the rearview mirror. "Your president is here. Woodrow Wilson."

"Yes, I know who our president is."

"Here for peace negotiations at Versailles."

"Yes, it was in the papers, thank you."

"You should have seen the crowds cheering for him. Stayed at Hotel de Ville."

We passed a pyramid of stacked cannons on the Champs-Élysées.

"Each one dragged home from the land of the dead," the driver said.

France had lost over two million men to the war at that point, so most of those on the streets were female, many dressed in mourning black.

What a comfort it would be to arrive at the apartment on Rue Saint-Roch. There was so much to do to find Merrill and Sofya.

When I arrived, our housekeeper, elegant Madame Solange, met me at the door with a warm embrace. "A thousand welcomes, my dear Eliza. How is your mother?" Barely Peg's age, Madame Solange was already married, to our caretaker, and cherished our home as if it were her own.

It was wonderful to arrive in that handsome apartment, which Henry and I had bought just after our wedding. I breathed deep that lovely scent of lemon and floor wax particular to France. The old place was full of light streaming in through the floor-to-ceiling windows, bouncing off the polished hornbeam parquet floors.

I stepped to the living room and took in the pastel boiserie walls, and the pieces Mother and I had found at the *marchés aux puces* and other *antiquaires,* my Louis Seize desk and commode, the toile drapes, a bit faded perhaps but perfectly serviceable.

"Very well, thank you. She's happy you came through the war unhurt."

I handed Madame Mother's gift.

"I have been needing more bath salts," Madame said with a smile. "Thank you."

"The place looks well-loved, Madame." The windows shone, only one pane cracked.

"Thank you. There are shortages of everything. Soap. No *Savon de la Tulipe* in the whole city."

"How do you do the wash?"

"Beg for a scrap of hand soap." Madame stepped closer and placed one hand on my sleeve. "I must tell you, when my father was visiting he said a Russian woman came looking for you—"

A shiver ran through me. Sofya?

"What did she look like?"

"He just said she was dirty, a beggar, perhaps. She left no name and he thought she was up to no good. I pressed him for more. Her age? Hair color? But his eyes are failing."

"It could have been my friend Sofya." I sat on the sofa, eyes burning, the time difference catching up with me, deflated at the thought of missing her. How close I may have come to seeing her again.

"From Brillantmont?" Madame Solange asked. "I remember her."

"Of course she would look disheveled, having come all the way from Russia."

"I am so very sorry."

I gathered myself. "I have business to attend to—locating a friend. In the meantime, if she comes by here—"

"I doubt that. My father was terribly rude to her. I am so sorry."

"If she *does* appear please offer her every comfort. If it's not Sofya it may be someone with news of her."

I went to my room to dress for the hunt to find both Merrill and Sofya. They were both here in Paris, I could feel it. The only question was where.

I SET OUT ON my search for Merrill, dressed in as much scarlet as good taste would allow, barely able to contain myself, exhilarated to be back on the streets of Paris. Was my hunch right? Would Merrill be there at the Grand Palais? In my exhaustive research, it seemed the obvious place to go, where the wounded had been tended since shortly after the war began. I braced for the worst.

The Grand Palais, that lovely Beaux-Arts exhibition hall left over from the Universal Exposition of 1900, stood on the Champs-Élysées close to Mother's apartment. I hurried toward the massive building, with its soaring, glass barrel-vaulted roof, a tattered tricolor atop it flapping in the punishing wind.

I entered the main hall and stood, stunned by the vastness of the place where Mother and I had once seen a horse show, now an immensely busy hospital. Doctors, nurses, and visitors rushed about as recovering soldiers milled through the crowd.

A brown stockade fence, the top saw-toothed as if cut with giant pinking shears, ran around an entire village of canvas-tented buildings, of which I could only see the tops. A sign high above read: *Atelier du Blessé Franco-Américain*. "Wounded workshop." What a lovely way to describe this tragic yet wondrous place.

I followed a few patients toward the galleries, past rooms of recuperating soldiers lying in iron hospital beds lined up under the soaring ceilings and rooms where doctors helped patients work their bodies on a system of pulleys along a wall. I passed long tables of women, heads bent over their sewing, stitching bedsheets and pillowcases. Everywhere I looked for Merrill's dark hair and searched the faces of the wounded.

A woman in a high-necked white dress and a leather bag across her chest hurried by, clipboard in hand.

"Excuse me, Nurse. I know you are terribly busy but I am looking for an American flier—"

"I am a therapist, not a nurse," she said, still walking. "The Americans are no longer here. Shipped out by ambulance weeks ago."

I hurried alongside her. "But the sign says Franco-*Américain*."

"There were many Americans here during active combat but now the war is over they have been transferred. Only a few British men left and they are leaving today."

"Could he be behind that fence?"

"That is the operating area. In process of being shut down. This is now a rehabilitation center."

"Can you check your records?"

"We only record French patients now. American wounded passed through here to other centers and eventually home, or to, well, the American Cemetery. If I may say so you are looking for a needle in a haystack."

"I have come so far to find—"

"I am sorry, madame. We are very busy. This place needs to be vacated so that companies can hold their exhibitions once again. Try the Red Cross. Or the American Hospital up in Neuilly."

Though only a little past noon, my spirits sank, the needle in a haystack growing smaller still.

THOUGH TAXIS WERE SCARCE, I eventually flagged a decrepit one down and we rode up the Champs-Élysées, past the Arc de Triomphe, through the gate to the suburb of Neuilly, officially out of Paris, to the American Hospital, housed in an old school.

I exited the cab and was bowled over by the scale of the building. It rose five stories up from the gravel courtyard where rows of Ford motor ambulances stood, red-crossed on their doors, drivers tinkering under their hoods. How to find Merrill in this immense place?

I entered and a round-faced nurse dressed in a white dress and headpiece came to greet me.

"May I help you?"

How strange to hear French spoken with a Midwestern accent.

"I am here to see if you have a patient by the name of Richard Merrill."

The nurse scanned her list and I stepped aside as an attendant led a line of patients by. Each man wore bandages wound around his eyes and held on to the shoulder of the patient before him.

She looked up. "I am sorry, no."

"Can you check again? I've come a long way. Based in Aford, Cher France?"

"We have over six hundred men here, madame."

"A flier. Richard Merrill—"

"Oh, you said Merrill Richards."

"No, I did not, but—"

"Yes. Merrill. Here it is. He's a popular one. Of course, many of the men here have visitors. Sometimes the girls from town come out here and say hello to the men. Make them little—"

"Are you sure it is the right Merrill? Richard Merrill from New York?"

"Yes, shot down near Saint-Souplet but survived, poor thing. Think he was the one picked up by the Boche and came to us in a prisoner exchange. I hope you are not expecting to speak with him. He's had a bad time of it. Of course, he's not the only one who's suffered. We have whole rooms of *gueule cassées,* severe facial injuries." She held one hand to the side of her mouth and whispered. "We warn visitors to bring their own basin in case they, well, you know . . ."

Why did I have the misfortune to run into such a chatterbox, what Mother would have called a *moulins à paroles?*

"I'm sorry to interrupt but can you take me to Mr. Merrill?"

"Wish I could, but visiting hour is almost over. The men need their sleep. Most of them could sleep for days if we didn't have to wake them for their medications and to eat, of course. Come back tomorrow."

I started toward the wards. "I won't be long. I've come all the way from New York, after all."

The nurse blocked my way. "I do love New York. The people there are a little pushy for my taste, though. I'm from Wisconsin, myself——"

All at once a contingent of ten or so khaki-clad workers, a nurse in starched white hospital dress at the helm, entered and swept by.

The nurse abruptly stopped and held out one hand to me, causing her group to stand and wait.

"Eliza?" Though I scarcely recognized her at first, it was Mother's friend Mrs. Belmont, the former Mrs. William K. Vanderbilt, who had divorced and remarried.

"Mrs. Belmont. How do you do?"

"How is your dear mother?" She spoke quietly, in a firm and dignified way, such a long way from New York and her famous costume balls.

"Well. She——"

"Who are you here to visit?"

"A flier friend——"

She looked to the nurse. "What room?"

The nurse checked her clipboard. "Philadelphia."

"Come with us," Mrs. Vanderbilt said. "We are going that way."

I followed Mrs. Belmont at a fast clip, her entourage in her wake. "The wards are maintained by donations from the various cities and states, hence you see their names over the doors. Boston. Chicago. Rhode Island."

I struggled to keep up, trying to see each high-ceilinged ward we passed with their rows of crisply made white beds, spotless floors and walls.

"Terribly sorry about your flier, Eliza. You'll be happy to know he can't get better nursing. Our nurses are all Americans from excellent families. Angels. Two to a ward with one male attendant."

I could barely contain myself.

As we passed wards, patients well combed and washed smiled at us from afar.

"I am just president of the auxiliaries but we are staffed with Americans from every walk of life. Bank managers rolling bandages. The man glorifies the job, so they say."

"What kinds of injuries do you treat?"

"Every sort of injury and ailment one can imagine. Gas poisoning, with the terrible blindness. Gangrene, trench foot, and our share of shrapnel and bullet wounds."

Mrs. Belmont dropped me at the Philadelphia ward. "Here it is, dear," she called over her shoulder and continued on her way. "Don't hesitate to contact me if you need anything."

The ward seemed immense, with iron beds lined up along the walls, some equipped with tentlike wooden structures, suspending injured arms and legs in the air by pulleys. Several of the lovely, long narrow tables particular to France sat down the middle of the ward, topped with a few wine bottles, a tureen, and the remnants of lunch. Clearly any patient able to bring himself to the table could enjoy the customary long French lunch, no doubt the best medicine any hospital could pro- vide.

One had the general impression of restful beige, for the walls and patients' pajamas were all the same color, of lovely worn French linen and hazy light filtered in through the tall windows. Visitors clustered around some beds and the nurses, both animated and serene, watched over the men. Most were newly shaved, a clipboard of records attached to the foot of each bed, with the patient's name written in fat block let- ters.

A nurse walked through the ward, hitting the little box of chimes in her hand with a small rubber-tipped mallet, tolling the end of visiting hours.

I scanned the room for Merrill. A mustached man dressed in white, his rumpled linen vest buttoned down the front, stood near the table.

"Could you help me, Doctor?"

"Doctor? I am the chef."

I smiled. Only in France. "I'm looking for a man named Richard Merrill."

He pursed his lips. "Hmmm. Infantry?"

"No. A flier."

"That's right. Merrill." He waved toward the end of the vast hall. "The very end of the ward, there. Straight back. His friends hung an American flag over his bed."

I stepped down the ward with an increasingly quick step, thrilled to finally see Merrill again, flapping my hands at my sides to dry my wet palms.

I came to the end of the great hall and saw in the distance a bed against the far wall, the stars and stripes draped above it.

Merrill.

I hurried toward it. How wonderful it would be to see him.

But as I stepped closer my air felt cut off. Why had my feet stopped working? I stopped in the middle of the ward, visitors milling around me, taking a second to digest what I saw.

Not in my wildest dreams had I expected such a dreadful sight.

Sofya

1919

AFTER WORK EACH NIGHT, I WAITED NEAR THE TOWN-house where I'd seen Taras, hoping to see my son, but ending up with no sign of Max, only frostbitten toes. Perhaps they were already home at that time of day? Surely he and Varinka left each morning if he went to school, but my mornings I had to devote to my collections, the prime time to find people at home.

But even if I got Max, would he be safe? I needed a secure place to live and enough money to buy him food. Would I get more help from the White Russian community on Rue Daru? Maybe someone there could help.

I left for Rue Daru one late afternoon after delivering my receipts to Madame Melange. I was eager to see the place where so many Russians gathered and happy reunions took place. I had so little money still and hoped to make connections there, for a better job and my own bed in the community.

I took a longer route than necessary to pass my favorite sweetshop, À la Mère de Famille, Paris's oldest candy store. Not that I had any money to buy candy, but nostalgia drew me there. How many times had Mother and I shopped there and left laden with bags heavy with chocolates and bonbons?

I stopped in front of the dark green–painted corner shop and took in the sweets in the window. Though the war drastically reduced the usually bountiful offerings, my favorite oval-tinned candies, *les Anis de Flavigny,* sat there in pretty little stacks. Produced since 1591 these satiny smooth little candies, made by patiently covering an anise seed, layer by layer, with sugar syrup, were Mother's favorite and mine, too.

I stepped inside the shop and the most delicious scent of butter and sugar and peppermint wrapped around me. The place hadn't changed a bit: at the back, the glass booth where the owner rang up the purchase on his old cash register, the black-and-white tile floor with the name of the shop written there, shelves and tables arranged with small displays of bonbons and marzipan flowers.

There were a few shoppers near the glass cases, the candy women in their white smocks helping them choose their chocolates just as Mother and I once had. Would the owner even remember me? Certainly not in my disheveled state.

I found the little tins of *les Anis de Flavigny* stacked with care and lifted one to my nose. While faint, the scent of licorice made my mouth—

"Hey, you there," one of the candy women called. She hurried to me as a policeman apprehends a thief, a cross look on her face. "What are you doing? Those are for customers."

"I am just looking, madame."

"Just look from outside." She plucked the tin from my hand.

"Where is monsieur?"

"None of your affair. Leave now."

She pushed me out the door, barely touching my dog fur coat, and banged the door shut behind me.

I rushed away from the shop, tears burning my eyes, head down in the wind, missing my mother. What would her advice be, after losing everything? My son. My family. My fortune. She certainly would not stand for self-pity. Probably would tell me to stand up tall, one of her favorite cure-alls, and would quote one of her Japanese proverbs, like: *Better to be a crystal and be broken than to be a tile upon the housetop.*

I smiled at that and walked on, broken crystal that I was.

IT WAS A LONG, cold walk to Rue Daru and I regretted leaving my fur hat at home. On the way I passed a tent set up on a side street with the sign *Marchand de Cheveux* tacked on the outside.

Hair merchant.

The one Oxana had used?

The little tent was warm inside, heated by a portable stove, with a low stool and small desk on which the owner kept a black cosmetic case full of the accoutrements of his work. He met me as I entered, a white-haired peddler dressed in a belted, blue smock, chamois-colored trousers, and a wide-brimmed black felt hat. An enormous pair of brass shears hung by a ribbon dangled from his belt.

"*Bonsoir, madame.* Buying or selling?"

"Just looking."

"I am René Carville. If selling, you can be paid in cloth or silver."

I stepped to the tent walls to examine the hanks of tethered hair of all colors and lengths, and elaborate women's hair additions in every shape and size pinned there. On the little desk, three wooden mannequin heads wore men's toupees. A basket of balls of hair of all shades sat next to the stool.

I warmed my hands by the stove and the peddler pulled a hank of smooth, black hair from the wall. "If you need a hairnet Chinese hair is perfect." He pulled an auburn sample from the wall and held it to his nose. "Can always tell Scottish hair from the whiskey smell."

He offered me a whiff and I turned away.

"The fake chignon is popular now. The gentlemen prefer long hair, but with shorter hair in fashion everyone wants a false chignon to add." He leaned in. "We buy comb hair as well—the extra hair you find in your brush. I never buy the hair of the dead."

"That's a comfort."

I started on my way out.

The peddler followed. "Madame, wait. Would you unpin your hair? I could give a price, no obligation."

I stopped, curious about how much it would fetch. I pulled the five pins from my hair and let it drop to my waist. What a strange sense of pride came over me there with that old man admiring my hair. How far I'd fallen.

He unfolded his wooden measuring stick and gathered my hair in his fist at the nape of my neck. "Thick as a horse's tail—good texture. Almost ninety centimeters. Not as good as the best—the virgin hair of young Italian girls. That gets top dollar."

A fine-looking man stepped into the tent, pushing up the flap with his silver-tipped cane. He stood dressed in a vicuña coat and top hat, his starched collar and cuffs crackling as he walked.

The peddler snatched off his own hat and bowed low. "Monsieur."

The man waved toward the toupees. "I would like the usual," he said in Belgian-accented French. "Nothing skimpy this time."

He stepped to me and fixed his gaze on my hair. "How much for this?" He reached for a piece of my hair and rubbed it between his thumb and forefinger. "Just like my mother's. Same color exactly."

What could he pay? Surely quite a lot given the fancy walking stick.

The peddler ran his hand down my hair. "Oh, this is very special. Russian hair is some of the best."

"I'll pay seven hundred francs. Not a centime more."

I took a little step backward, dizzy at the sound of it. A fortune! I could resign my job at the brothel and spend all my time searching for Max. Eat a real meal. But I had never cut my hair, only trimmed it. What would it be like without it?

The peddler seemed as surprised as I was at the offer. "Well, madame, what do you say?"

The man removed his hat, leaned toward me, cognac on his breath, and whispered, "I've seen you at Rue Chabanais."

I stepped away. "No, monsieur."

He followed. "Are you a princess? Seems like every Russian woman in this town claims to be royalty."

I assessed his toupee, the deep brown color of a robin's wing, flecked with gray. But despite René's obvious skill, the hair splayed atop the man's head like a dead animal.

The peddler untied his shears. "Shall we?"

The man sent me an unpleasant glance. "Just make sure it's not lousey."

I turned. *"Lousey?"* My face burned.

"From the smell of it you've not changed your clothes in a month."
The man came closer and ran his hand along the hair down my back.
"But I prefer a ripe scent, really."

"Monsieur—" the peddler said.

"Quiet, René. I'm making a transaction."

I pushed the man's chest with both hands and sent him backward,
his toupee the tiniest bit askew. "Vile man. I would walk to the cemetery and die rather than sell my hair to you."

I stepped out of the tent onto the street, pulling my dog fur coat
close, loose hair streaming behind me.

The man called after me. "Russian *whore*."

"Bald *pig*," I called back to him over my shoulder. Even to my own
ear the words sounded pathetic.

Vibrating with anger, I hurried off toward Rue Daru. Why had I let
my temper get the best of me? Such a fortune I'd let slip through my
fingers. I'd just have to work hard and find cheaper ways to find my son.

SOON, I SMELLED THE SCENTS of Rue Daru. Beef and cabbage
and dill. Warm black bread, my mother's favorite. My stomach con-
tracted at the yeasty smell of it. I turned onto Rue Daru, a short street,
and all at once, so many people I passed spoke not French but Russian.

As the golden-domed spires of Saint Alexandre Nevsky Cathedral
appeared above me, I stopped on the sidewalk overcome with a heavy
sense of home. I pinned my hair back up, searching the faces of those
coming and going on the street. Russian faces.

I rushed toward the soaring cathedral, its three towers topped with
gold onion domes shining in the sun. Tsar Alexander, Nicholas II's
grandfather, had helped build it. My blood.

I hurried up the steps and through the open cathedral doors, warm
and safe and at home. The scent of incense particular to the Russian
churches met me, flowery and sweet, and the great altar rose up below
a six-tiered chandelier hung from the magnificent painted dome above.
I listened for sounds of the doll factory below. If there was an operation
going on down there it was a quiet one.

I stepped outside and down the steps to the basement of the cathedral, the crypt, and knocked on the door.

A woman opened the door a crack. "Yes?"

"My name is Sofya—"

"Who sent you?"

"A girl named Oxana."

She pushed the door. "Come back another time."

I thrust my boot across the jamb to keep it from closing. "I'm a friend."

"All right for Father's sake." The woman waved me in. "Come. Quickly."

My eyes adjusted to the darkness to find a crypt with a central pillar, fanning out with vaults, all painted with the muted scenes of saints. Rows of tables filled every part of the room and women sat crowded in at benches, each working at tasks. Their faces glowed in candlelight as they sewed and dabbed at wood with their paintbrushes. Some bent over mats pinned to masses of wooden bobbins making lace. It smelled of candle wax and turpentine and perspiration.

We walked the room and passed a young boy of no older than six, sitting barefoot at a bench, holding a simpler version of the wooden bobbins, attached to cotton threads, a woman bent over him.

"I am Mrs. Zaronova. Are you here to work? We only pay a few centimes." She was a tall, dark-haired woman with an abrupt way about her.

"Such a large operation," I said.

Mrs. Zaronova puffed out her chest. "We now have over one hundred workers."

"And so quiet."

"No talking allowed. Hurts productivity."

I stepped toward the benches. Women sat, busy at their work, most terribly thin and dressed in dirty coats.

"It is freezing in here."

"A fire costs money."

"Do you feed them?"

"When I can find food they eat once they make their quota. Fifty dolls. Three pillowcases of lace."

"*Fifty* dolls? For five centimes? That will not buy a piece of bread. You have children working here?"

"Who are you to question me? Here, at least they stay dry and have a place where they can be productive. With so many French men killed in the war, Russian men can find work, but for women it is harder."

We walked along the tables, past a row of lace makers, juggling their wooden bobbins, barely stopping to insert a silver pin every now and then. Here and there women slept on their benches.

"Can you not afford to install electric lights? Take the black paper off the windows? Their eyes will be ruined working by candlelight."

"You don't get it, do you? We cannot turn on the lights for fear of discovery. The Reds monitor any home or workplace carpentry and improvements. They have infiltrated every organization that helps us White Russians. Could be spies here right now. We're all afraid."

"Of what?"

She ran her fingers through her hair. "Don't you read the papers? Just last week another Russian woman was found in the park. Throat slit. At least now we have the money to bury the victims, at night, in secret. Always we are targets for them."

"But you're just making crafts."

"Crafts that provide money and help for us from America. The Reds want us gone, no matter where we are. Afraid we'll come back and restore the monarchy."

"But this place is inhumane, madame. The restaurant across the street. Could they provide food?"

"Make yourself useful and ask. I have begged so much everywhere they close the doors when they see me coming."

I HURRIED TO THE RESTAURANT across the street from the cathedral. Such a rustic-looking place right in the middle of Paris, A la Ville de Petrograd, lettered in red on black over the heavily curtained windows. The siding on the outside was made of real logs to look like a country *izba*, the outside painted with gay pictures of Russian countryside. My stomach groaned as I read the menu posted in the window in French: *Blinis. Pirozhki. Stroganoff.*

I entered and found one large, low-ceilinged room, the air thick with the scent of cooked beets and Sappho cigarettes. Groups of people sat at small tables and a cherry-red piano stood in one corner. I stepped to the kerchiefed older woman at the hostess table. "I am Sofya Streshnayva. My father worked for the Ministry."

"In Petrograd? Hold on."

She stepped through a door and came back with a gentleman dressed in a white apron holding a glass, wiping it with a striped cloth.

"Dr. Abushkin?"

"Sofya." He came around the bar and kissed me on both cheeks. "What a happy surprise. I cannot talk long. I need to get back to my duties." He leaned in. "I am a very important part of this operation— dishwasher. It's terrible getting jobs here. To continue as a physician they want me to go back to medical school. Start all over. Countess Pechesky is a washroom attendant now, dressed in her old gown, passing hand towels to the same women who once curtsied to her."

I smiled. "You're still the same."

"Just sitting on my suitcases here, waiting to go back as soon as this whole mess is ironed out. I heard about your family." He wrapped his arms around me and kissed the top of my head.

How good his arms felt. For all his old-fashioned thinking, he was still the man who'd birthed me.

"To think such fine people died that way. Thank God your mother was not here to witness."

"It's like medicine to see this place."

"Just don't breathe."

"I was across the street and in the crypt—"

"Be careful." He leaned in. "Checka guards are infiltrating such places."

Could I trust the doctor with the news of my son? No matter how well intentioned he was, a word to the wrong person would no doubt spread like disease here in this community.

"Don't tell people your name so freely, Sofya. You must stay aware at all times. As a woman you are more prone to spilling secrets. They could be in this room right now."

"Men spill secrets as often as women, Doctor. I can take care of myself."

"Take it seriously. They are using all tricks to lure aristocrats out of the safety of the community. To be kidnapped and sent back to hard labor or worse. A count was poisoned here, right there at that table."

"I will be careful. In the meantime can you spare some food for the women across the street? They're starving—children with bowed legs."

"Rickets. There is so little food now in Paris—farmers want a fortune for a cabbage. But as dishwasher, I can save scraps and see about some soup."

All at once a rousing piano chorus began, as it so often did in Russia, and the doctor nodded toward the pianist. "Your cousin."

The breath caught in my throat. *"Karina?"* I craned my neck above the crowd to see her back to me at the piano bench.

"I will send some pirozhki out for you two," he said as he hurried off to the kitchen.

I could barely stop smiling as I drew closer and saw Karina dressed in a white satin gown and playing the upright piano; atop it was a glass jar with a few coins at the bottom. She played the Tarantella finale of Brahms's first piano concerto, his greatest compositional triumph. It was one of the first I'd watched her learn as a child, as she sat on a stack of encyclopedias at the Dowager Empress Marie's.

Water filled my eyes. How did she end up here in a room of émigrés without the basic manners to listen to such greatness? How good it would be to see my cousin, have a friend with whom to talk over everything.

I waited for the song to end and touched her arm, trembling a bit with the anticipation of her reaction upon seeing me. "Good to hear you play again, Karina."

She stood, clapped her hands in front of her, kissed me on both cheeks and held me tight. "I prayed I would see you here."

We moved to a small table and a waiter set two pirozhki and a bottle of vodka with glasses down between us. The scent of the little buns, their brown, egg-washed tops toasted dark, made me realize how hungry I was.

"I heard about your family, Sofya. It hurts every time I think of it."

"They are with God now." It was a pat statement but was at least something to say to help others feel better about such a horrible tragedy. "But Max is still alive and I think I know where he's living."

"Here in Paris? Just go take him."

"It's not that easy. I haven't seen him there."

"Why not visit the schools in that area? Talk to the headmistresses and inquire."

"You're a genius, Karina." Why had I not thought of that?

"Let me help. I'm not working on Tuesday, I'll come with you." She covered my hand with hers. "You'll find him, I know it, but now you must eat."

I took one pirozhki from the plate and bit into the cabbage center, perfectly salty and warm. "Why are you so dressed up, wearing your golden party shoes? Isn't this a dress you wore to play for the tsar?"

"I'm saving my more practical clothes for my next life. I sewed some underwear from the bags in which they deliver the liver to the kitchen here. So now I attract only dogs."

I smiled. "How did you get so funny, Karina?"

"I've only a few minutes to talk—the owner doesn't like me taking breaks."

"Know where I can find a bed close by?"

"It's close to impossible right now, but I can get you on a list. I would invite you to sleep with me but I share my bed with two nasty sisters and one snores like something out of the zoo."

A young blond man came in the door and walked through the crowd with a stack of newspapers on his shoulder, selling them as he went. He stopped near us and handed a paper to Karina with a smile. "No charge."

With no comment to the young man, Karina grabbed the paper, LATEST NEWS printed across the front page, and opened it.

As the man wandered off I leaned in to Karina. "I think he likes you."

Karina kept her gaze on the paper. "They're talking about holding a beauty pageant. Miss Russia. Should we enter?"

"You should. They might not look kindly on my dirty fingernails."

Karina drew me closer. "Ilya sent me a letter. We'll finally be to-gether after all this time, can you believe it?"

"Be careful. Dr. Abushkin says—"

Karina spread open the paper. "The doctor sees conspiracy in every-thing. Ilya is smart. He's going to leave me a message in the Letters from

Home section—just here. Have you seen it? It comes out every day and it's how Russian people reconnect now."

"Those letters may be traps."

"I understand, Sofya. But my life without him is so hard. I have to take a chance."

"Just let me come with you to meet him."

"Of course," she said, running one finger down the column. "No word from Ilya. But look, a letter for you. Can you believe it? The very last one here. It says: *Sofya Streshnayva, You have a sum of money wired to your name. Please collect at this address.* It gives an address in the third arrondissement. *With tender affection, your loving family.*"

Karina turned to me, her face drained of color. "But you have no family."

A chill went through me.

Someone knew I was in Paris.

Eliza

1919

I STEPPED CLOSER TO MERRILL'S BEDSIDE AND BLINKED to change the image before me. He lay on his side, the length of his leg exposed, his skin a deep shade of purple, covered with hideous, shiny, blue-black bubbles.

A young man in a white smock stepped toward me. "Visiting time is over."

"Please, Doctor."

"I'm sorry, but we have much to do here. I have no time for transfer requests."

"I've come all the way from New York to see him. Could you just share your prognosis? I promise I'll let you get to your work."

He looked at me for a long moment and then down at Merrill. "Two serious issues. The first is gas blindness. Mustard gas most likely. He landed through a cloud of it. Lucky to be here."

Merrill stirred and turned toward me, thick strips of lace wound around his head, covering his eyes. Had they run out of bandages?

"Will he regain his sight?"

"Most likely, but there's no guarantee. The second issue is gas gangrene. He went down in farm country, where the soil contains a large amount of horse manure, which harbors bacillus bacteria. Once he crash-landed his clothing became saturated with the bacteria, it lodged in his wounds, and this is the result."

"Should you not cover them with gauze?"

"Best to leave them open to the air. There was a time when we covered these wounds up, left them alone, but now know they can infect major organs. So we've been watching that leg."

"Oh no, Doctor. Amputate?"

"I've seen the infection spread quickly to systemwide sepsis. But, believe it or not, he's on the mend now. Fever's gone, blister size reduced. We've actually had a few conversations and he's aware of what's happened. Has one bang-up headache and blistering in the lungs."

"At risk for pneumonia?"

"Yes, madame. Ten percent die and the others resume their lives, though can't say they're all what you'd call normal."

"Where was his gas mask?"

"Not issued to fliers. Odds of them successfully crash-landing are so low they don't waste a gas mask on a pilot. But he got it worse than most, flying right through the cloud."

"So much necrotic damage. Will he walk?"

"Pardon me, madame, but are you a nurse? We could use the help here."

I smiled. "No, just nurses in my family, but I'm happy to help."

"Well, I can tell you have the gift." He smoothed the sheet, which covered Merrill's unaffected leg. "It's hard to predict the extent of the muscle damage. May be a long recuperation."

"I know just the place for him to recover. And I have experience with pneumonia, Doctor. We're old friends."

I looked down at Merrill lying there in such terrible shape. The man who never wanted to travel. The man I'd shamed into battle.

He stirred and I bent to whisper in his ear. "With any luck you're going home soon, dearest."

"Eliza." He felt for my hand and I took his in mine.

"Once you land, you'll stay up in Bethlehem to recover."

"No. It's too much—"

"They do need a general store up there very badly. I know it may seem far-fetched to you right now but you're going to be well again one day and you could do us all a favor and run it."

Merrill smiled.

"And we'll start a baseball league. In the back meadow. We'll pass the hat for the umpire. Call them the Bethlehem Farmers."

"Ploughboys," Merrill said.

"Yes, that's better, dear. See? You're adapting quite well to country life already."

Dr. Martin felt for Merrill's pulse. "There is a troop ship leaving next week for New York. No promises but we can try."

Merrill held fast to my hand.

"Consider it done, Merrill. You're going home."

Varinka

1919

ONE COLD, RAINY MORNING, WHILE MAMKA SEWED, I tried to teach Max his letters by reading him the newspaper. He paid little attention as I ran one finger under the headline and read it aloud: OUSTED KAISER ENJOYS HOLLAND.

Max just looked to his lap with longing at his two thumbs, which I had covered in pepper and petroleum jelly to stop his thumb-sucking.

Since the war had ended and Germany's kaiser had fled in disgrace, he was often in the news. But the front-page photo that day was not of the kaiser. It was of the former tsar and tsarina and their children, for nothing kept the public's attention like that family, even months after they were rumored dead. The photo showed the tsar's daughters aboard the royal yacht in better times, the eldest, Olga, closest to the camera, squinting in the sun.

Max leaned over and looked closer at the picture. "Maman," he said, pointing to Olga.

I gasped a little breath and Mamka's gaze met mine.

"*I* am your Maman, Max." I flipped the newspaper over. "Does he still remember what she looked like?" I whispered to Mamka. "He was so little last time he saw her."

Mamka tied a thread and clipped it with tiny, silver scissors, a far cry from when she used to use her teeth to cut threads. "My first memory,

I was two. My mother going to a dance. She died soon after but I remember her face."

I pulled my shawl closer. After everything I'd done for Max he'd still not forgotten her. Would he ever think of me as his mother?

MAX NAPPED ON THE FLOOR of my bedroom and I read a stack of French magazines Mamka had brought home from Lanvin. Hems were shorter and white kid shoes with patent leather toes seemed to be the newest footwear to have. Perhaps I would take more money from Taras's boot and buy some.

Rain hit the windows making me drowsy there under the blankets. Where was Radimir on that messy day? We were supposed to see Luna Park together.

"Varinka, come quickly," Mamka called from the front of the house.

I ran to the vestibule to find Mamka there with a French policeman, a tall woman shaking off her umbrella, and little Max between them, dripping water on the marble floor.

"You the mother?" the policeman asked, brushing rain from his navy blue cape.

I nodded.

"Madame LaBlanc here found this child, wet to the skin, in the middle of the street."

"I had no idea—"

Madame LaBlanc brushed rain from her coat. "What kind of a parent doesn't know her own child is missing?"

"I was just reading—"

"Ran away from home." The policeman handed Mamka a lumpy pillowcase. "Wouldn't get far with a stuffed owl and a towel."

He tossed the newspaper we'd read earlier, now soaked through, on the front table. "Young man had this newspaper with him. Headed for the docks to find that ship. Says he's looking for his mother."

Madame LaBlanc turned to face Mamka. "Don't I know you?"

"Yes, madame. I work for Madame Lanvin."

"I thought so. If your daughter cannot keep constant watch on this boy, maybe keep him on a leash? He will end up crushed by a horse or worse."

"Of course, madame," Mamka said.

The policeman held the door open for Madame LaBlanc and the two hurried off.

I pulled Max by the hand, in from the vestibule. "You were a very bad boy."

Mamka pulled the towel from the pillowcase and dried Max's hair.

"Do you hear me?" I asked.

Max picked up his pillowcase and headed back to his room, sucking his thumb as he walked.

RADIMIR COULD BARELY CONTAIN himself the day he was to show me Luna Park, an amusement park in Porte Maillot, on the western edge of Paris. We came by metro to the park gates, French flags fluttering above us atop the stone crowns. How pretty the entrance looked, strung with foil bells and spiky tinsel. I smiled as Radimir paid my one-franc admission. This was a *date,* far from anywhere Taras would see us, and Mamka had agreed to watch Max. And best of all, my lips itched, which everyone knows is a sign a person is about to be kissed.

Radimir hurried us into the park, under the great arch, through the crowd.

"Come along," he said. "We need to get to Shoot-the-Chutes before the line forms."

It was half-price day since the park was closing for the winter and, as a result, much of Paris was there. Well-dressed people from all walks of life lined up for the rides. Women in their good coats and muffs, men in dark coats and bowler hats. Since admission was free to those in the military, men in uniform peppered the crowd.

Radimir had dressed up, too, in a dark blue coat, and his tie matched the color of his pond-bottom eyes. He had left his hat at home so his auburn hair shone in the little sun struggling through the clouds.

"This is the Theater of Flames," he said as we passed a tall, white stucco building. I arched back my head to read *Theatre de Flamme* spelled out in bamboo letters across the facade.

"They eat fire there," Radimir said. "We'll come back later."

Why would someone eat flames?

I didn't want to go on the Shoot-the-Chutes ride in which brave people rode in boats down a steep chute and splashed into the water below, but I did it for Radimir. We rode in a boat with the name *Gaston* painted on its rear and I hid my face in his coat as we hit the water and great plumes shot into the air.

We rode the romantic, scenic railway in little connected train cars, high above Paris, and could see much of the city. Radimir wrapped his arm around me as we went higher and watched the lights of Paris coming on, the Tour Eiffel in the distance.

Radimir looked about to kiss me at the very top but just brushed something off my face.

I gathered my courage and whispered, "I have not been completely truthful with you. You may hate me."

"I could never."

"Max is not a child Mamka and I were watching. He's mine."

Radimir turned to face me. *"Yours?"*

"I mean I have sole care of him. The mother fell under unfortunate circumstances and I ended up with him. Mamka and I protected him. He would have died without me."

"Well, certainly she wants her child back."

I turned my gaze to Paris in the distance. "Perhaps. She is a cousin to the tsar. I am afraid she may come here to Paris for him."

"Then, of course, you should return him to her, Varinka."

"But I'm the only mother he knows."

Radimir took my hand. "You were good to help him, but it's wrong to keep them apart. I grew up without my own parents. You cannot rob the boy of his mother."

"You don't understand."

"Come back to Russia with me, Varinka, and have all the babies you like."

"It's hard to explain how much I love him. He is so smart. I am teaching him to read. He sits on my lap when I read to him and burrows in close. . . ."

"If you loved him you would put his happiness first. Come back to Petrograd with me, Varinka. We'll travel. To Italy. Bring your Mamka. I've looked into that guardian of yours. He's a dangerous man, Varinka. All the more reason to send the child away."

"You could protect Max."

"Not only should he be with his mother, he has imperial blood. I would be kicked out of the party or worse if that became known. Come back with me to Petrograd. I leave in two days."

"So soon?"

Radimir pulled me close. "Have a child with me, Varinka. Of our own."

"Max *is* my own. Besides, what could I do with him at this point?"

Radimir looked out toward the city, lights coming on here and there as darkness came. "You'd solve this problem if you wanted to. Find the mother. There are Red Cross services. . . ."

"I'm not giving him up."

I shivered as night settled upon us, tired of the amusements.

Radimir took me home by the metro and we rode in silence.

It was clear a second kiss would not happen.

Not that night. Maybe never.

CHAPTER

45

Sofya

1919

THE DAY AFTER MEETING KARINA, AROUND THE TIME
Max might be returning from school, I waited down the street from Taras's
townhouse on Rue de Serene, alert for any sign of my son. I walked the
sidewalk in front of the house, pretending to be headed somewhere, head
tilted against the winter wind. What if I saw Varinka? Would she recognize
me? Would Max? What if they had not enrolled him in school? Varinka
was a peasant after all and perhaps didn't believe in formal education.

All at once the front door opened and Taras stepped out. Walking
toward him at that point, I could scarcely turn on my heel. My heart
beat faster as he passed me and I turned to watch him walk on. Off to
his brothel so early in the day? Or maybe attack another innocent family as he had mine?

My breath caught in my throat as he turned as well and with a
pointed look watched me go. How could he not recognize me as the
one who'd escaped? Before he was a Cheka agent, he'd been a woodsman. And everyone knows a Russian woodsman will hunt their prey
until they die themselves.

THE NEXT MORNING, back at Les Chabanais I woke to the sound
of crying. I rose and stepped to a group huddled near the window. Blue

ice covered the windows and gave them the look of stained glass as the young Russian women knelt, crying as they prayed. A newspaper lay on the bed and I drew closer. Some part of me already knew what was printed there. The front page held a black border, a sign of mourning, of course, and the photo of a body facedown in water, a woman's white satin dress cinched up above her garters, long hair fanned out in the water.

"When?" I asked one of the girls.

She turned to me with a tear-swollen face. "Just yesterday."

I leaned closer and read the caption: *Petrograd émigré Karina Shoumatoff found slain Monday night, afloat in the Seine.*

THE NEXT DAY AFTER I turned in my work receipts I ran most of the way to Rue Daru for Karina's funeral mass, through the sleet, hoping to somehow make peace with her death. How was it possible? Perhaps it was a mistake? Why was everything I loved taken from me?

There was a great crowd at the cathedral that day. Mourners circled the casket, stopping to lay flowers at her feet or kiss her lying there. Sweet incense filled the air, just as it had at my mother's service. That was the last funeral I'd been to and standing by Mother's casket I could barely look at her there.

Is that why I had such an unshakable fear of the dead? Father had never spoken of Mother's death, just kept a glass of water and a towel on his bedroom windowsill for forty days, a Russian tradition, since the dead were thought to travel the earth for forty days before they left this world.

Terrible images flashed before me. Mother laid out in our *zala*, paper crown on her head. The dead peasant girl in the snow and her frozen grimace. Father's charred body. I pushed my hands into my pockets, they shook so. But didn't I owe it to Karina to stay strong and say goodbye?

My throat closed off as I arrived at the casket, Karina lying there dressed in her white dress, roses and other hothouse flowers arranged in bunches at her feet. I avoided looking at Karina's face and bent to kiss her cheek, cold against my lips through smooth cloth.

She held a long, golden cross in her clasped hands and someone had stitched the slash at her throat with coarse, black thread, a piece of sheer black cloth placed over her face to hide it. Mrs. Zaronova stood at the foot of the casket. Had the doll factory paid for the funeral?

I forced myself to look at Karina's face. Even through the cloth I saw the gray pallor of her cheek, the paper crown across her forehead. It was Karina, of course. There was no mistake. It had been a bad death.

Those in line pressed me along and I left my cousin lying there, rage growing in my chest. No church could keep us safe. We'd lost our homeland and now no one was safe. God was not going to save us. Nor the French police.

I left the cathedral, ran down the steps and through the gates. There was only one way to keep us all safe.

"YOU'RE BACK," RENÉ SAID as I entered the tent.

I walked toward the stool and pulled the pins from my hair. "I want four hundred francs or I will go elsewhere. Do it quickly."

René waved toward the stool. "Sit, madame."

I tucked the pins in his smock pocket. "And more for the pins. I won't be needing them anymore."

"Of course." René untied the scissors from his belt and I held my breath.

I flinched as he tied my hair tight at the nape with a blue ribbon.

"Some wine to make it easier?" he asked.

"No. Just do it, please."

"No husband to object?"

"If you don't hurry up, sir—"

The sound of the cutting was the worst part, the brass of his shears cold against my neck. But in ten seconds it was over and I was left with a sudden lightness. I touched the back of my head, the stub of short hair.

I turned, but René had already secured my hair in a paper bag and whisked it to his desk drawer. Perhaps to avoid a scene? Little did he know how good it felt.

I stood. "My payment?"

René pulled a leather pouch from his smock pocket, slid out a few bills, shook out silver coins, and slid it all into my cupped hands.

"Half now and half on—"

"I want it all now or I will shout to the rooftop that you are a fake and a—"

He stepped back. "Keep your voice down, madame. This is a quality establishment. Fine then, four hundred francs."

"And more for the pins."

He slid the extra francs into my coat pocket. I counted it and then stepped to the door.

"In three years your hair will have grown long enough for another visit."

"*Au revoir, monsieur.* I won't be back."

I LEFT THE HAIR merchant's tent and, on my way back to Rue Daru, had the impression I was flying, so light after the surrender of my hair. Perhaps it was more the happy jangle of silver in my pocket, but I felt I could do anything. What to do first? Send word to Eliza? Hire a private detective to find Max? First I had a mission to accomplish.

I'd never handled so much money before, since no one in my family carried it and at boarding school we had no need for it. My first stop was to the sweetshop I'd been thrown out of, la Mère de Famille. This time they were more than happy to sell me my tin of candies and a box of their prettiest chocolates when I produced a palmful of silver francs. I then walked on to a merchant who dealt in knives and hatchets of every kind, then hurried to an open-air market. Though the selection was limited, I found a fat cabbage, good-looking carrots, and some lavender-colored beets to stuff into my net bag. I'd never shopped for food before and how satisfying it was, seeking out the best produce and bargaining for the lowest price.

I bought firewood and a few more things and hurried to the restaurant at Rue Daru, feeling invincible, bags bulging with food, a bundle of kindling under one arm. I called for Dr. Abushkin and handed him my bags.

I handed him a handful of francs. "This is to make soup for those working across the street."

"Where did you get such money?"

I turned my head.

"You sold your hair? How could you? A woman's *femininity*. Are you deranged or just hysterical?"

"After Karina—"

"You are suffering from a weak nervous system as a result of the terrible news, Sofya. Being on your own, without your husband, has affected your decision-making. Single women—"

"I will hear nothing more about my weaknesses, Doctor. I have many and I catalog them myself. Being a single woman suits me well and I'm suffering from nothing but a great deal of sadness. I know cooking that much soup is a great commitment but I will arrange help for you. I will come as well."

"*You* cook?"

"Yes. Twice daily. This should get us through the winter."

"Why spend all this money on soup for a bunch of women? Use it to get yourself a nice room in a good part of Paris."

"When you arrange to have weekly firewood sent here to the restaurant, can you add a bundle for the doll factory? And I would like to hire escorts for the women, can you recommend those you know and trust—to see them to and from their work? I have purchased a box of small knives I will distribute to each worker."

"Women with *knives*? Karina's murder was a fluke, Sofya."

"We are targets, you said so yourself, and I won't let it happen again."

"You're hysterical, completely understandable, Sofya. A woman of your gentle birth—"

"If you wish to help us, I welcome it. If not, please tell me so I can make other arrangements."

"You've become so like your mother."

I smiled at that, hoisted my kindling under my arm, my box of jackknives under the other and walked on to take on Mrs. Zaronova.

I FOUND MRS. ZARONOVA boxing up lace tablecloths, the women silent at their work.

"Kindling?" she asked. "I told you—"

I handed her the box of chocolates. "For all your hard work."

"What is this?"

"I came into some money and I wanted you to have them. I would also like to become a patron of this endeavor. I've arranged for a hearty soup to be brought here to the women twice daily. Come spring we'll plant vegetables in the lot next to the restaurant."

"How did you—"

"We're fighting back, madame. And in the interest of safety, Dr. Abushkin is arranging to have the women escorted to and from their homes after dark. I'll not have another murder in our community."

I stepped along the tables with my box of jackknives, slid one into my own pocket and began distributing them. "Carry this with you at all times. Even in daylight. Travel the city in groups of two or more. There's strength in numbers."

A woman with hair white as corn silk, plaited in one braid, stood from the bench. "I am Yana. Let me help with that."

I handed her the box and she passed through the tables offering knives to the women. How good it was to see them each sitting up a bit taller as they examined their new protection.

I turned to Mrs. Zaronova. "Take that dark paper from the windows."

"But—"

I pushed a stool to the wall, stepped up, and tore the black paper away in big pieces. Yana and others joined me and laughed as we ripped paper. Soon light shone through every window.

I turned to Mrs. Zaronova. "As your patron, I insist that these women also receive rest breaks and are allowed to speak to one another and that you allow the children playtime."

"Of course, madame."

I passed the bread down the tables, to the children first. Once everyone was fed I stood and admired my work and then headed home for a good night's rest.

Tomorrow I would find my son.

I WENT TO SLEEP quickly that night, knowing the workers at the cathedral were safe for the time being. Oxana was out for the night so I had the bed to myself. Who knew how good a lumpy mattress could feel? As I drifted off I imagined how lovely it would feel to hold Max's small hand in mine. I would visit every school in Paris if I had to.

Close to morning, from the very bottom depths of sleep, I heard a distant bell ring. I tried to retreat deeper into slumber but it grew louder.

I swatted at it.

A voice came, close to my ear. "Time to wake up, lazy girl."

Oxana. I batted at her with my arm. "Let me sleep."

"Well, that is terribly impolite."

I sat up with a shot. That was not Oxana. My heart pounded in my chest.

Could it be?

CHAPTER
46

Varinka

1919

I SAT AT THE KITCHEN TABLE THE FOLLOWING FRI-
day, dressed in my robe, and drank a quick morning tea, having just
pulled out the drawer of pots and pans for Max to play with. What a
good boy he was. As he played, I considered my Luna Park date and
Radimir's offer. It might be my last chance to free myself from Taras.
Why could Radimir not just accept my son? Would he be leaving
soon?

Taras entered the kitchen through the back door with a cold blast of
air and stepped toward me.

"Never at home anymore are you, Varinka?"

I pulled my robe tighter around me. "Do you ever knock?"

"I pay the rent here, last I checked." He slid one hand down the side
of my neck.

I lit a cigarette. "I have to get Max to school. He's already late. And
you smell like an opium den." I'd smelled that scent on villagers back
in Malinov, sweet and unmistakable, like a flower on fire.

I set my cigarette in the ashtray, a lazy trail of smoke rising to the
ceiling.

"You and your mamka can't just live here for free."

"I've been busy."

"With your new friend. Has you smoking now?" Taras came from behind, pulled a pair of dark gray manacles from somewhere and enclosed my wrist in one cuff.

I pulled at the metal, but he held it tight. How heavy it was. "This isn't funny, Taras. Let me go."

He closed the other end onto the table leg and walked away for a moment.

"Where are you going?" I asked.

"Just making sure the key is well hidden."

"You can't keep me here forever. Someday I'll just leave."

Taras shrugged. "I'll just find you."

"Not if I get enough of a head start. Where did these handcuffs come from?"

"I need them in my line of work. They're the strongest made, adjustable for any wrist size and pure steel."

He slid one hand under the lapel of my robe, across my breast. He kissed the scar of the burn on my cheek and ran his lips down the side of my face, his beard scratching the skin along my jaw.

"You're hurting me."

Taras murmured, lips close to my ear, "That Streshnayva daughter is here."

A chill ran down my arms. "In Paris?"

"Has been hanging around."

"Here?" A sick feeling clawed at my belly. Sofya? Come for Max?

"I put a message in the newspaper they all read but she didn't bite. If you could spy on her for me it might help us both."

"So you can hurt her?"

"I could use your help. She's all over the place."

"Do your own dirty work, Taras."

Taras trailed his lips down the side of my neck. "Come now, Inka. Afraid your new boyfriend will think less of you? And just so you know, Vladi's been in touch. Asking if the boy has been taken care of."

A shiver ran through me. "Tell Vladi whatever you have to. Max is staying right here."

Taras opened the front of my robe. "Then you need to make it worth my while. Admit it. You'd like to. Tonight."

Max watched us with a steady gaze and my cheeks burned.

"The boy—" I said, pushing Taras away with my free hand.

I turned in my seat to find Mamka standing near the icebox, a crochet needle in her hand.

"Get away from her, Taras," Mamka said.

I tried to stand, but the handcuff held me back.

She waved the needle at him. "Unlock her."

Taras stepped to the icebox and pulled out a glass bottle of milk. "Who said you could come home during the day, old woman?"

"I live here."

He waved her off. "Go sleep at that dress shop."

Mamka stepped closer to Taras. "Give me the key."

Taras walked away from her and I closed my robe best I could with one hand.

"How could you?" Mamka asked. "Animals know better."

"I'm sorry, Mam—"

"It is the very worst sin. Plus, that child sees everything you both do. You should pray for forgiveness."

Taras laughed.

Mamka came to me and tied my robe shut. "Someday you'll feel the consequences, Taras."

Taras stepped to the back door. "And you should pray you'll find the key or that kid will be late for school."

"I wish my husband never brought you into our house."

Taras bent to Mamka's face. "He *bought* me, old woman. Guess you need to feel the consequences."

Taras left and slammed the door shut behind him as Mamka tore the kitchen apart in search of the key.

Max stood from his play and stepped to Mamka. "The key is in the flour."

"Good boy," she said, then dug her hand into the flour bag and extracted it, her arm covered in white to the elbow. She unlocked me, pulled me up to standing, and I pocketed the heavy cuffs and key.

"Get dressed," she said. "I have something to show you."

WE ARRIVED IN THE Jardin du Luxembourg in record time, with Mamka pulling me along by the hand, Max trailing behind holding my coat hem. It was one of our favorite places.

"Where are we going, Mamka?" Would we walk all five hectares of the park?

She said nothing and continued to pull us past the long rows of queen statues, which stood on pedestals. Being winter, we had the park almost to ourselves, since only a few couples strolled the wide, tree-lined paths.

A woman turned to me as we walked. "What a handsome child, your son."

"Thank you," I said, standing a little straighter. How often that happened all over Paris. With our similar coloring, of course people assumed he was my blood.

Max lunged toward the pool near the front of the imposing, gray Luxembourg Palace. "Please, I want to sail a boat."

"The pond is closed."

"The carousel?"

"It's winter, Max. The horses are resting." I gave him one of my best funny faces and he turned away, face sullen. How grown up he was, his hair straight and darker now.

The heavy cuffs in my pocket bounced against my leg as Mamka pulled Max and me to a long, rectangular pool with a carved stone grotto at the head. In the arch a sculpture of a hulking, green giant crouched on a rock, leaning over two naked marble lovers embracing.

Max busied himself tossing pebbles into the pool.

"So, when were you going to tell me Taras was doing such things again?"

"I didn't want to bother—"

"He still watches you in the *bania*, doesn't he?"

I looked away.

"Since when?"

"Since he came back from prison."

"Does he . . ."

"No. We have an arrangement. But he says he wants more. Tonight."

I turned away. The shame of it.

Mamka stopped and covered her face with both hands, shoulders heaving in silent sobs. "This is a sick thing, Varinka. What do we do?"

I rubbed her back.

Max came to stand near her and touched the back of her coat. "Don't cry."

Mamka dried her eyes. "Why did I not see he was doing this? Obviously, I didn't protect you."

"I was ashamed to tell you. We had an arrangement. Rules that we could only go so far."

"I curse the day we took him in."

"I let him do things like watch me in the bath and he took care of us. He said it was my fault. I teased him."

She glanced up at me, her face blotched red. "By taking a *bath*? How can you think such a thing?"

"He says it was my fault what happened with Papa—"

"And you believe every lie?"

We both watched Max toss more pebbles in the water, sending watery circles to the pool's edge.

"And now he knows about Radimir," I said.

Mamka stood up straighter and fastened her top button. "You must leave immediately."

"My life may not be normal, Mamka, but it's the luck I was born with."

"Luck?" She held up one hand to the sculpture. "The Medici Fountain. Do you see who that is up there in bronze?"

Of course, I knew. The cyclops Polyphemus with his broad chest and nasty expression. But I said nothing.

"That is Polyphemus up there preparing to attack the young lovers below. You recall that much, at least?"

I remembered the legend well from Mamka's lessons. How often I'd asked her to tell me the story of handsome Acis and sea nymph Galatea, and how Polyphemus tried to crush his rival with a boulder.

"No need to be harsh, Mamka. Of course, I remember. Polyphemus wanted to kill Galatea's lover."

"Why?"

I stamped my feet to warm them. "He was jealous."

"Well, you are Galatea now, my dear, and luck has nothing to do with it. Until you are rid of Taras, you'll always be in danger. Radimir, too. I saw it. In the cards."

I gasped a little breath in.

"The coffin card for Radimir."

"But that is not always death—"

"I've *seen* it, Inka."

"He wants me to go away with him."

"Go."

"But won't take the child."

"Leave Max with me and go."

I gathered her close, kissed her cheek, and lay my head against her fur collar. How could I ever leave her? Or Max?

"You don't even know Radimir, Mamka."

"Your life will be hard, with two religions, but he's a good man." She held me at arm's length. "I heard Taras talking on the telephone last night. I think he's part of a kidnap team sending Whites back to Russia."

"For trial?"

"The ladies at work say most die before they make it back. By sudden accidents like a fall from a window. I think it's Taras who's been murdering women, all over Paris."

"How could—"

"Some no older than you. I found a shirt of his covered in blood." She released me, gathered her coat closer, and looked about. "He could be watching right now."

I took her hand, soft in mine. "How can I live without you?"

Mamka gave me her best reassuring smile, her eyes bright. "I'll miss you, Inka, but you will be *free*. Leave Max at school, hang a kitchen towel on your bedroom door, and I'll know you're gone and safe."

"I can't leave Max."

"Go, Varinka."

Would I ever see her again?

"What if Taras comes after you? A crochet needle will do little against him."

Mamka clasped my hand tighter. "I can take care of myself. I have Madame Lanvin and the others. But do it soon. If you want the good I've seen in the cards to come true."

"What, Mamka?"

"Something you've always wanted."

I barely breathed. "A *child?* Boy or girl?"

Mamka smiled. "You won't know unless you go soon."

CHAPTER
47

Sofya

1919

Hᴇʀ ᴛᴇᴇᴛʜ ɢʟᴏᴡᴇᴅ ᴡʜɪᴛᴇ ɪɴ ᴛʜᴇ ᴅᴀʀᴋɴᴇꜱꜱ ᴏꜰ the brothel dormitory. Was it possible?

"You look like you've seen the dead."

She sat next to me on the bed, the little red bell Agnessa had so often punished her with around her neck.

"Luba?" I whispered.

"You've come a long way from the Ritz hotel, sister. I'm assuming no room service."

I reached for her face, feeling it as a blind person does. My fingers traveled down her cheeks to her lips. "But I saw you, on the—"

She held my hand. A light from the street caught a reflection in her eyes, welled with tears. "The person you saw up there was the count I'm afraid, poor man. I escaped just before Vladi—" She paused, overcome.

"God be praised." I gathered her in a tight embrace. "The Heavenly Father saved you, Luba." How thin she was. I felt the bones of her back through her coat.

"It was Mrs. A., actually. I convinced Varinka to let me out and I tried to take Max but Vladi caught me. While he was getting his villagers roused up, Mrs. A. let me slip out of the quarters when she brought our food."

"Dear woman."

"And then I hid in the upper cabinets of the pantry."

"Smart girl."

"I came out when I heard Vladi and his mob in the courtyard, starting a great fire with Agnessa's dining room furniture. They shouted, 'Kill the pigs' and got Father. . . ." Luba paused. "I'll never forget Agnessa's screams—calling for God to save them." She wiped a tear with the back of her hand. "I saw it all from the woods. I wanted to run to them so badly, but there were villagers everywhere. I won't tell you what they did to Tum-Tum."

"We'll get through this, go back and punish them all."

"While I breathe, I hope," she said.

Dawn's first rays touched the room and showed Luba more clearly, her hair dyed white-blond.

She pulled at one lock. "I dyed it to be incognito. What do you think?"

"I think it suits you. I cut mine."

"Your pride, Sofya."

"It will grow."

"Any news of Afon?"

Still the master of changing the subject.

I smoothed the edge of my blanket. "I don't know if we'll see him again, Luba." How could I say, "Your beloved brother-in-law may have been captured by the Red Army and killed?" There would be time to tell the whole story later. "But I do know Varinka and Taras have little Max. I've been working as a collection agent for the owner here and saw Taras. At 24 Rue de Serene."

"Did he recognize you?"

"Not sure. But I think he's become even more dangerous."

"We'll get Max back."

"How did you make it here from Malinov?"

"Sailed to Constantinople where I sold women's silk stockings for a while, then spent a year in Rome and hitched a ride here with a circus."

I smiled. "Only you, Luba."

I took her hands in mine, a woman's hands now, so slender, rough and red, covered with black stains.

"Luba, your hands."

She shrugged. "Found a job at the Citroën factory in southern Paris."

"Of all people, Luba. You should be at university. Your hands will never recover."

"But I have. Flown out of the gilded cage."

"I miss it."

"I think about Cook's apple cake every day. My silk sheets. But too much time in the past hobbles a person." Luba paused for a moment. "It's so strange to be wandering the world, isn't it? Unable to just go home."

She nodded toward the plant on my nightstand, its two white buds just opening.

"Your rose." She stood, leaned down, and breathed in its scent. "Mr. Gardener's antique."

"When I went back to the house I found it in Agnessa's ruined hothouse. Kept it alive since I left Russia."

Luba stroked a petal. "Poor lost roses. Like us, I suppose."

As dawn broke in earnest, more light streamed in through the louvered blinds. I searched Luba's face. She was a teenager now; at fourteen more like Father than ever.

Luba placed her hand over mine and held it tight. "I have a plan."

"Of course, you do."

"And do *not* try and stop me, sister. I know what I'm doing. Meet me at that townhouse—where you saw Taras—at Rue de Serene, this afternoon at three. We're going to get Max back."

I reached for her. "Please stay. Where are you living?"

She bent to kiss my cheek. "The less you know the better, sister."

How blessed I was to have her back.

She looked down at me with such a serious face. Father's concerned look. "Three o'clock. Rue de Serene."

"Be careful," I said. I'd lost her once, I could barely think of losing her again.

Luba walked out with a hasty look back and it occurred to me that once I would have found her overly dramatic, but now I just thought she was the most courageous woman I'd ever known.

I reveled in the wondrous idea that my precious Luba was alive and well and more ferocious than ever.

I BOUGHT AN APPLE CAKE, sat on a bench in the Jardin du Luxembourg and savored every bite. It was a far cry from my usual meal,
half-eaten croissant and some melted ice cream from the trash basket at the puppet theater. I found a camel hair scarf abandoned on
a bench, frozen stiff, and warmed it with my breath. Once I draped
it around my neck I saw the quality of it, heavy and warm. Only in
Paris.

After wandering the park for some time, braving cold winds, I arrived at the Rue de Serene townhouse to meet Luba and approached
the café across the street, with its glossy black-painted front.

One table remained out there in the cold, two chairs around it. The
bar inside looked lively and I sat, dressed in my white dog fur coat and
hat.

That café table offered a perfect view of the townhouse, elegant in
gray stone, the windows on the three-story facade tall and wide. What
was Luba's plan? A bad feeling rumbled in my belly.

Soon Luba came along and sat in the chair next to me.

"So, what is this plan?" I asked.

"No hello? Some sisters would be grateful to have their son rescued."

"I'm worried about you, Luba."

"I did my homework." She sat a little straighter and nodded toward
the townhouse. "I'm going in there."

"You're out of your *mind*."

"Do you have another way to find Max? The thought of him with
them makes me sick, Sofya."

"You think I don't worry every waking minute? I've kept an eye on
the house, but never see Max. Or Varinka."

"I watched this place today since I left you. No one is home now."

"We'll go in together, Luba."

"No offense, but I work better on my own. Plus, Taras has seen you
when you came to collect. So stay over here in case he shows up. My
plan is foolproof. I'll go in the back door."

"How do you know there is one?"

"I checked." On the café table Luba spread out an imaginary map.

"The kitchen is on the ground floor, quite a big one. The bedrooms are bound to be on the third floor. I'll find the study on the second."

"What if Varinka comes home?"

"Her I can easily talk my way around."

"Taras is a killer, Luba."

"That's where this comes in." She pulled a white cotton cap from her pocket.

"A maid's cap."

She smiled. "Borrowed it from a friend. How will he know I'm not the maid? I can be subservient if I put my mind to it."

"I'm begging you not to do this."

"I won't even see him." She stood. "But one thing's for sure, you'll be too obvious out here in the dead of winter."

"I'm not leaving."

"Very well. We'll have a signal, as all good spies do. If you see someone return, stack your chair on the other. If I don't come back in ten minutes, contact the police."

"Wait . . ."

"I'm doing it, sister. For Max."

Luba hurried across the street, looking both ways for traffic, and stepped down the block on her way around to the back alley.

I stood and then sat again, gaze fixed on the townhouse facade. Where was she? I watched one crow fight another for a crust of bread and then searched the windows for movement. Had she even gotten in? How could I allow my little sister to take such a risk?

I saw movement at the second floor window and jumped to my feet. Luba came to the window and shook her head, hands palms up. I waved to her to come out, but she disappeared into the darkness of the room.

I sat again, the lining of my fur coat soaked with sweat.

Minutes passed and Luba came to the third floor window with a box in her hands. She opened it and shook it upside down with a scowl.

Again, Luba disappeared into the depths of the house. How much could I take before I just knocked on the front door?

Behind me the café door opened spilling golden light and warmth and laughter onto the cobblestones. A man emerged and walked by me. I turned and we met eyes.

Taras. I barely breathed. He wore a puzzled expression and a look I knew intimately from the brothel. The sleepy eyes of the opium smoker. Surely he recognized me? I turned away as he passed and he walked across the street to the townhouse, climbed the steps to the door, unlocked it, and stepped inside.

My heart hammered against the lining of my coat as Luba came again to the second floor window. I stood and gave the signal, sliding one café chair over the other. I jabbed my hand in the direction of the front door.

"He's in the house," I mouthed.

Luba turned from the window and I clutched one hand to my chest. Should I go around to the back door and enter as she had? Run for the police?

Instead, I hurried across the street, straight for the front door.

Sofya

I KNOCKED ON THE TOWNHOUSE DOOR, KNUCKLES BURN-
ing against the cold wood, more options buzzing in my head. Should I
go to the neighbors for help?

I knocked again and stood there listening to the children's voices on
the nearby playground, my heart battering my chest. What had I done
to my sister?

The door swung open and a slight, dark-haired woman wearing a
pink scarf tied about her head stood there. At her side stood Luba,
wearing her maid's cap, mop in hand, the cotton head wet and gray. I
knew the woman from somewhere.

"Be here next week," she said to Luba.

That voice. It was Varinka's mother. What a kind face she had.

"I will, madame," Luba said, bowing low. She stepped out the door
and walked by me onto the street.

Varinka's mother gazed into my eyes. "You take care, now. Mind
the steps."

We hurried away from the townhouse, Luba's mop head already
freezing stiff at her side.

"What happened?" I asked.

"I *told* you it would be fine."

"*Fine?* Taras came home. He was at the café all along. He may have recognized me. Did he see you?"

"I searched everywhere for school papers. Desks, cabinets. But then Varinka's mother came upon me—found me going through drawers in the kitchen. She asked what I wanted and then stepped to the library and brought them to me. She's on our side, Sofya. Wants you to have Max back."

"Any sign of Max? Varinka?"

"Just his old blanket on the floor of a bedroom."

"Did Taras see you?"

"I started to leave and he came into the kitchen. 'What are you doing here?' he said. He had been drinking, I think, or into the opium, for he swayed a bit standing there."

"Luba, I can't believe you did this."

"And then Varinka's mother said, 'She's the maid. Let her work.' She handed me this mop and said, 'She was just leaving to get us a new mop head.'"

"An angel."

"I did have a scare when Taras said, 'Wait. I've seen her before,' but Varinka's mother was quick and said, 'She's a French girl and cleans very well, now leave her be.' She handed me ten francs and said, 'Be on your way now and hurry. That floor won't clean itself.'"

From her coat pocket Luba pulled folded papers and we stepped into an alley to read them. It was an enrollment letter from L'Ecole Cygne Royal, the letterhead a crest with a swan.

"*Dear Varinka Pushkinsky, Your son Maxwell—*" I didn't stop to read the rest, but folded the letter, slipped it in my pocket as tears filled my eyes. I was going to see my son.

Luba put one arm about my shoulders. "There is no time for crying, sister. We have work to do." She smiled. "And ten extra francs to spend."

She reached into her pocket. "And look what I found." She pulled out Mother's emerald necklace and held it in the air by the clasp.

"Luba, you little genius. Where—"

"It was right in the jewelry box in the bedroom."

We left the frozen mop in the alley and headed back to Rue Chabanais. Halfway home, I touched the papers in my pocket to make sure they were real.

We had found my son.

THE NEXT MORNING LUBA and I went to L'Ecole Cygne Royal hoping to catch a glimpse of Max in the schoolyard. We arrived at ten o'clock to avoid seeing Varinka at morning drop-off.

Careful to keep to the opposite side of the street, we walked by the school entrance, *Ecole Maternelle* chiseled above the door. Above the blue door was a stone crest with three swans carved in it. Next door, surrounded by a black iron fence, stood a pea-graveled schoolyard. How neat it all was. Three metal, pastel bouncy horses, each atop a heavy, rust-colored coil, stood in a sandy area along the left wall. A pretty sandbox. Beyond the schoolyard, steps ascended to a pair of honey-colored oak doors with black hinges. Was Max's schoolroom beyond those doors? Would the children come out for play, even in the cold?

Just a glimpse of him was all I needed.

Luba and I jumped a bit when the oak doors burst open and children marched out in a wobbly procession, three teachers helping them down the stairs. The little ones, wrapped up in their heavy coats and scarves, headed for the sandbox. How quiet they were.

Soon another group arrived, older children. Luba and I strolled down the street and back searching for my son among the warmly dressed students.

The teachers stood near the sandbox in twos, chatting, hands in their pockets, stamping away the cold. Every now and then one would break up a spat or button a coat.

One teacher left the group and gathered the older children.

"Jacques dit touche tes genoux!" she called out. The children bent and touched their knees.

It was the famous copycat game, where a player was eliminated if he followed instructions without hearing the words *"Jacques dit."*

A young couple came along the sidewalk and stopped near us to watch the little game. Luba and I stepped to the fence and I searched the children's faces, best we could, since they were wrapped up in scarves and hats, until my gaze landed on one child.

Luba grabbed my arm. "It's him."

Could it be Max? He wore a navy blue coat and a nubby, gray woolen cap.

"Jacques dit tirez la langue!" the teacher called out.

The children stuck out their tongues, sending little white puffs of breath into the air.

"Lève un pied!" she said, catching all of them unawares. Each child lifted a foot and when they realized they'd been caught, one let a laugh ring out, a laugh that sent a chill through me.

Max. The boy in the navy blue coat.

I held on to the cold iron bars to steady myself. My boy.

He walked with another child to the sandbox.

The more I watched the more certain I was it was him. Afon's easy gait. My skin tone. If only he would come closer.

The young couple walked on and I considered my options. Could I call out to Max? The teacher was distracted with her *Jacques Dit* game, after all.

Max wandered in my direction, along the fence, running his mittened hand along the slats.

"Max, dear," I whispered.

He turned toward me.

"It's your mama, darling."

He stepped closer. Did he remember?

All at once a teacher from the sandbox stepped to the steps at the door and clapped her hands. "Lunchtime, children."

Max hurried to the door with one look back to me.

Luba pulled me close. "He knows you, Sofya. We must go talk to the headmistress. After we show her the papers we could leave with him today."

A lovely warmth spread over me as I pictured the three of us walking out the front gates, Max's hand in mine.

I snatched the dog fur hat from my head. "How do I look?"

"Terrible. That coat is frightening, but just remove it when you enter the building. And the hair . . ." She licked her palm and smoothed back my hair. "There. Like any French mother."

"At least I finally bathed."

"You could still use some perfume. Just keep your distance."

LUBA AND I WAITED in the outer room of the headmistress's office. Glorious scents of roast chicken and potatoes and cinnamon wafted into the room sending our stomachs growling. At least Max was being fed one good meal per day. I pulled my dog fur coat closer, having decided it best to keep it on, the dirty shirt and trousers underneath even worse.

A tall woman came to the inner office door and Luba and I scrambled to our feet. I ran my hands down my trousers.

She waved us into the room and stood behind the Louis Seize desk, posture straight, in a well-cut black wool dress, the white lace cuffs and collar delicate as a spider's web. It was a dark-paneled room, thickly carpeted, coals glowing in the fireplace, and it was all I could do not to warm my hands near it. Madame left the door open, clearly expecting a quick meeting.

"What is this about? You've come at an inopportune time. We consider lunch part of our curriculum."

Madame looked at me and seemed unable to look away, a slight furrow in her brow, as if watching a trained monkey in a calico skirt. Of course, she was mostly put off by the coat, for to a Frenchwoman, wearing a dog fur coat in public was worse than wearing a clown costume or paper bag. Add my chopped hair and maid's boots and there was plenty to take in.

I froze, unable to speak. How badly I needed Madame to understand.

Luba spoke up. "Good day, Madame Fournier, my name is Luba Streshnayva and this is my sister Sofya. We are here inquiring about a student."

"Name?"

"Maxwell Streshnayva Stepanov," I said.

"We have no student by that name."

With trembling fingers, I pulled the enrollment letter from my pocket and handed it to Madame. "The mother asked me to pick up the child and deliver him home, with this as proof of my legitimacy," I said in my best French.

She scanned the sheet and handed it back to me at once. "This says the child's name is Pushkinsky. We are authorized to discharge students to immediate family members only."

"There has been a death in the family," Luba said.

"Not surprised. Look, if I allowed every person off the street to come in here and take home a child—"

"May I be honest with you, madame?" I asked. "I may look terribly unkempt to you, for I have made it here from Russia by horse cart, but I am Max's mother. He is a noble child—my family is related to the tsar."

"I can't help you."

"I saw him today in the schoolyard. He looks unwell. He's not safe with those two. And once they know I'm in the area they'll take him and run."

Madame closed the door and stepped to the window, arms folded across her chest.

"All I know is the couple that enrolled this child threatened me and could be a danger to the students."

"But Max was stolen from me in Russia."

"What am I to do? A Cheka agent the size of an elm tree comes in here and suggests I will die if his child is not accepted."

"How do you know he's Cheka?" Apparently, the Red secret police was not so secret anymore, if Madame knew of them.

"I'm not stupid. Look, my mother is sick and needs me. I cannot risk it."

"If having Max here endangers your other students, why not let us take him?" Luba said.

"You don't understand. He threatened my *life*. Suggested he has the police in his pocket. Hinted he was responsible for the murders around Paris. I can only imagine what he'd do if this child went missing."

"Do you have a child yourself?"

"No." Madame stepped behind the desk. "I'm sorry, but you must take it up with the family."

"I have reason to believe Max is in grave danger," I said.

Madame looked at me for a long moment. "I'd like to help. The poor thing plays well but we think he is ignored at home. Eats like a starving farmer at snack time. Only cereal. And the mother is never on time for four o'clock pickup. But you must understand. This is a dangerous family."

"I promise you I will take him far from Paris. If questioned, you can honestly say you don't know where. Who could argue with that?"

She returned to the chair behind her desk and sat. "Go to the police."

"They do nothing," Luba said. "And they've started deporting some of us back to Russia—a death sentence. Who is to help us?"

"Who is to help *me*? We are all on our own these days. I must ask you to leave immediately."

I stepped toward the desk. "I was raised to be well-mannered above all else, but I am a desperate woman, madame. Please. Given time I can make you a very rich woman. I have emeralds—"

"Nothing is more important than our safety." Madame picked up the phone. "I would hate to see you sent back to Russia."

Luba and I started for the door.

"You're a cruel woman," I said, though the words somehow fell flat.

We left her there, one hand resting on the phone, and walked out of her office, further still from rescuing Max.

SNOW FELL AND WHIPPED our faces as Luba and I made our way to the Russian cathedral at Rue Daru to show Luba the new and improved doll factory.

"What if Varinka takes Max from Paris before we can figure out a way to get him back?" I asked.

"Something is going to help us," Luba said. "I feel it."

We walked along, the snow forming powdery drifts on the shuttered bookstalls. What a sight we were. Two dirty street women.

Luba kicked a stone through the snow. "This isn't such bad news, you know, about Madame Fournier. At least we understand her concerns about Max. That's the first step to a solution."

We came to the Russian cathedral and both of us stopped on the path. What a majestic sight, with its golden cupolas.

"I miss Mother," I said.

She brushed the snow off my shoulder and wrapped her arms around me. "Me, too."

We stood holding each other as the snow fell around us, warm as one, our silver thread stronger than ever.

Eliza

1919

THE DAY AFTER I FOUND MERRILL AND SENT HIM happily home with his fellow wounded fliers, I walked along Rue Saint-Honoré toward the Saint Alexandre Nevsky Cathedral. I was headed to the cathedral basement for a one o'clock appointment with Mrs. Nonna Zaronova and the Russian women who made so many beautiful things for the cause, a box of Whitman's chocolates brought from New York clutched to my chest.

I'd already spoken to the staff at St. Luke's Hospital in New York and they would meet Merrill upon his return and enter him into rehabilitative care to ready him to live in Bethlehem.

How good Paris looked even in winter, a layer of snow softening the hard edge war had brought. I walked a little taller knowing this enterprise helped so many Russian refugees. How exciting it had been to receive another shipment of goods from Paris, cracking the crate open in the kitchen at Gin Lane, to find the exquisite handmade dolls and lace-trimmed bedding.

You have improved the lives of over one hundred women, Mrs. Zaronova had written in her letter. The Woolsey women would have applauded.

I hurried through trim neighborhoods of townhouses, a certain satisfaction to the sameness of it all, their light facades of cut stone, mansard roofs, and black filigreed balconies.

All at once I came upon a cathedral soaring above, a lovely example of Neo-Byzantine architecture tucked away in Paris. How different it was from the surrounding architecture, as if dropped by air from Petrograd.

I stepped up and into the cathedral as a male choir dressed in white robes practiced "Gabriel Appeared," their voices echoing in the vast nave.

"Mrs. Henry McKeen Ferriday," I announced, my words echoing in the cathedral. "From New York. Mrs. Zaronova is expecting me."

The choirmaster waved me outside and down a set of concrete stairs. I entered a lovely painted crypt, flooded with light and filled with tables of women, happy at their work, chatting over the clack of wooden bobbins, sewing lace and handcrafting the dolls New York had come to love so. Many of the women finished bowls of soup, the air perfumed with the scent of carrots and onions.

A large, serious-looking woman hurried toward me. "I am Mrs. Zaronova."

She was different than I'd imagined her. Less refined and certainly more brusque. I handed her the chocolates and introduced myself.

"Your handicrafts are so welcome in America, Mrs. Zaronova. Anything Russian is so in vogue. You should see all the New York women in their beaded headdresses and their shorter skirts. New Yorkers snapped up every doll and piece of linen you sent."

"Would you address the workers?" Mrs. Zaronova asked.

I stepped up on the closest bench. "Hello, everyone. I am Eliza Mitchell Ferriday. You may call me Eliza. I am here from New York, as a representative of the American Central Committee for Russian Relief. I want you all to know how much I appreciate your efforts and the tireless work of Mrs. Zaronova. I hope our partnership lasts for a very long time to come."

As I stepped down from the bench, applause broke out and a white-haired woman approached me.

"I am Yara," she said. "My English is not good but I wanted to tell you there is someone else who you need to thank for all this. A very kind Russian lady who helped us make it so much better here." Yara leaned in. "They say she may be related to the tsar."

All at once I felt as though a bird were trapped in my chest, flapping her wings there.

"I would very much like to see her. What is her name?"

"I'm not sure, but I think I know where you might find her."

I FOLLOWED YARA, who turned out to be a very fast walker, across the street to a Russian restaurant. We entered, waving the cigarette smoke from our faces, and I took in the place, packed with people, very much like restaurants I'd seen in Petrograd. My favorite color, bright cherry red, was everywhere in that room. The tables and chairs were painted with it in a charming folk way with leaves and gay flowers. Red tablecloths, heavy red draperies on the windows. On the walls, painted black tole trays made very nice art pieces and shelves on the walls held every sort of knickknack. Russian nesting dolls. Lacquered papier-mâché bowls. Commemorative eggs with pictures of the tsar's daughters. I looked closer at the one of Olga, poor, lovely girl. Had it only been four years ago I'd met her in Petrograd?

We forged our way through the crowd to the hostess desk, raising our voices over the din of patrons at the tables talking loud Russian. A waitress squeezed by us carrying some sort of fried pies that smelled like lamb. A stooped woman holding an ear trumpet came to us and said something.

"She wants to know if we want anything to eat," Yara said to me.

"Some bread would be heavenly," I said. "Cheese?"

The woman held her trumpet to her ear as Yara translated. No wonder the poor woman had lost her hearing in that place.

Then, from the little Russian I understood, I think Yara asked the woman, "Is the lady who makes the soup here?"

The woman looked at me for a long moment and then disappeared through a red curtain into the back of the place.

I leaned on the hostess desk. "Where is she going?"

Yara shrugged.

We surveyed the tables, many filled with men and women arguing and laughing. Did any of them know Sofya? I considered making an announcement. In my bad Russian they would likely just talk right over me.

I felt a tap on my shoulder and a voice came from behind me, in English. "Excuse me, madame, but we have no bread and cheese today, only butterscotch crisps."

I turned and there stood a woman, so thin, dressed in cotton trousers and a man's shirt, a gray, canvas apron over it all.

She held out one hand to me. "Eliza."

It took me a moment to recognize her, but her voice did it. "Eliza."

I took both her hands in mine. Could it be? "Sofya?"

She nodded as tears welled in her eyes. "Careful, I may have every disease."

I cradled her dirty, beautiful, tear-streaked face in my hands. "I'd risk cholera to be with you again, darling. I've been so terribly worried, you don't know." I wrapped my arms around her and pulled her close. "At last."

I felt the bones of her rib cage as she convulsed against me with silent sobs.

"There, there. Everything will be better now." I smoothed one hand down the back of her head. "What happened to your hair, darling?"

She pulled away from me and dried her eyes with the back of her hand. "I sold it."

"Well, I like it very much. Every chic woman in New York has a bob." I pulled my handkerchief from under my cuff and handed it to her.

She dried her eyes. "You're always the one with the handkerchief, Eliza."

Luba came forward, now blond, which suited her well. How grown up she'd become.

I pulled them both to me, held them tight. "I'm not letting you out of my sight, darlings. We have so much to talk about. Yara tells me that you helped make the doll factory what it is today."

I turned, but Yara was gone.

"Just a little," Sofya said.

"Please, no modesty," Luba said. "Sofya transformed that place. It was a sweatshop."

I pulled them both to a corner. "You must come to the apartment immediately. Madame Solange can make you—"

"Soon, but we need to help Max," Sofya said. "He's been taken."

A bitter chill went through me, the loud talk fell away and I heard only her. "He isn't here with you?"

"A peasant girl I trusted took him when bandits broke into the estate and she has him here in Paris. Varinka. She won't give him up."

"Dear God. But you're his mother."

Sofya and Luba gathered me closer.

"We went to get Max at school," Sofya said. "But Madame Fournier, the headmistress, refuses to give him to us. Says the man Max is living with may be a Cheka agent—the Red secret police—and threatened her. She's terrified, poor woman."

"What school?"

"L'Ecole Cygne Royal." Sofya handed me a school letter.

Just seeing Max's first name in print brought tears to my eyes. "I know the school, of course." It was one of the most exclusive crèches in Paris.

"Can you help me get him from there? We must arrive before Varinka takes him home at four. These people, Taras and Varinka, are dangerous. Taras helped attack our family, he and Vladi, who stabbed you on the tram."

I reached out for Sofya's hand. "Oh no, my dear—"

"I think Taras is only here to kill nobility fleeing Russia. I must try again to get Max. Maybe you can persuade her?"

"Perhaps we can go to the police."

"The police will do nothing, Eliza. Did you get the bracelet?"

"Here." I held out my wrist.

"On folded paper inside are account numbers from banks all over Europe and their passcodes. Father left them with us for safekeeping."

I clasped one hand over the bracelet. "Heavenly day."

"The money from those accounts could be of tremendous help to the Whites."

"Perhaps it can buy us some help with the school," I said. "Maybe I could contact some official with influence." I'd left New York with a long list of Mother's acquaintances whom she'd asked me to check in with, including a former Russian officer.

Sofya leaned in. "My thought exactly."

I folded the paperwork and slipped it in my handbag. "Well then, I'll do my best. I know someone who might help. Will ask him to appeal to the school to release Max to us. He can offer Madame protection, certainly."

"I'm sorry to draw you into all this, Eliza."

"I do love doing the impossible. We've got a whole army of Russian émigrés staying out in Southampton."

"Of course you do."

She smiled and for the first time I saw the old Sofya.

"Luba can wait for us at my apartment and you and I will visit Mother's friend and then the school."

"We must hurry. Soon as Varinka knows I'm here she will leave town with Max and we'll never find him."

SOFYA AND I TAXIED to the Place Vendôme in eleven minutes flat and entered the grand lobby of the Ritz with just enough time to talk to General Yakofnavich and then make it to school to fetch Max. The lovely old place had survived Germany's bombs nicely and changed little since my parents took me to tea there weekly during our August stays in Paris.

The lobby stood as usual, the reception area, with its ten-foot-high ceilings and eighteenth-century furnishings, doing everything it could not to look like a reception area. Our footsteps echoed on the marble floor as we stepped to a lovely, leather-topped Louis Seize desk. Behind it sat the concierge—Charles, according to his name tag, who spoke at length to someone on the telephone while wearing the vigorously bored countenance Parisian hotels encourage in their concierges.

"Name?"

"Eliza Ferriday and Sofya Streshnayva Stepanov. Visiting from New York."

"Your business?"

I paused. How to phrase: *We need to deliver bank passcodes critical to saving the Russian White Army in exchange for help releasing my noble godson from a Cheka assassin?*

"I need to speak with General Yakofnavich. Important diplomatic information concerning the Streshnayva family. It's most urgent, Charles."

"On hold," he said. He covered the receiver with one hand. "The general has a food taster. Can you imagine? It's like a novel."

Was it my first-name familiarity that opened his spigot of gossip?

He leaned across the desk. "The general is a mean one. Someone's mad they lost the war. Even his two bodyguards fear him. Big ones, those two. They don't worry about having *their* food tasted. One ate a whole salmon, head and all."

I checked the wall clock. 3:30.

"Please, monsieur. We're terribly late."

Charles hung up the phone and waved in the general direction of the elevator.

"Fifth floor. Room fifty-two. Be prepared to do battle, ladies."

I held Sofya's hand as the elevator ascended and I practically vibrated with excitement. Perhaps I missed my calling and should have been a spy, or at least an ambassador.

A servant answered the hotel room door and ushered us into a fabulous suite, the type the Ritz was known for, with high ceilings, thick moldings, and a bed festooned with a tasteful print. Two onyx pillars tall and fat enough to hold up the Parthenon helped divide the bedroom from the sitting room, where a painted vanity and mirror sat. An elegant man stood near the window, flanked by bodyguards.

He stepped toward me dressed more like a Parisian gentleman than Russian soldier in what appeared to be a bespoke suit, his mustache fanned out like bird wings. Could Mother have known this man in another life? Would he help us?

I offered my hand to General Yakofnavich and introduced Sofya. He shook both our hands, then folded his arms across his chest and scowled at me.

"What brings you here, Mrs. Ferriday? I'm a busy man." He spoke good French with the trace of a Russian accent.

"I have a pressing matter to discuss regarding my friend Sofya here." My gaze went to the two bodyguards, both making my six-foot height feel small.

"My mother, Caroline Woolsey Mitchell, gave me your name and said—"

"Carry Woolsey?" His gaze drifted out the window and he smiled. "Such a fine woman. Handsome."

Mother may have claimed fuzzy memories of her connection to the general, but apparently, he remembered her well.

The General lit a cigarette. "And Mr. Mitchell?"

"My father? Gone for years now, sir."

He nodded at that. "Never remarried? Such a waste. She could row a boat, Carry Woolsey."

I shifted in my shoes. "General, I'm here to give you information. Coded passwords, actually."

He smiled. "That's a good one. Where did you get these passwords?"

"They were given to Sofya by her father, Ivan Streshnayva."

He hung his cigarette on the edge of a crystal ashtray, the size and shape of a small iceberg. "From the Ministry? Murdered on his estate, poor Ivan, like so many. Horrible."

Sofya stepped forward. "He gave them to me well before that."

"You have them now?"

"In a safe place," I said. "But we need something first."

The general glanced toward his bodyguards. "Money, of course."

"We need your help with a sensitive issue," Sofya said. "A Cheka agent kidnapped my son Max. Stole him in Russia and brought him here to Paris."

"You understand I can barely leave this hotel even with my security detail."

"Of course. Max attends L'Ecole Cygne Royal, where the headmistress refuses to give the child up since this agent has threatened her life. Can you help us, General?"

"Perhaps I can make some calls. Offer what help I can to Madame. Station a police guard at the school."

"The agent lives at 24 Rue de Serene," Sofya said.

"The police commissioner clearly needs to pay him a visit. One less Cheka agent is good for me, certainly. No promises, though, I'm afraid."

I slipped the bracelet off and handed it to him, my wrist already feeling empty. "The codes are inside, on a piece of paper."

The general gazed at it there on his open palm. "Thank you, Mrs.

Ferriday. This will help us take back what is ours. I'll do my best with Madame."

We stepped toward the door and Sofya turned back. "General, my husband is a White Army officer. Would you by chance know him?"

"Name?"

"Afon Stepanov."

I stepped to Sofya and wrapped one arm around her shoulders.

The general looked at Sofya for a long moment. "Of course, Ivan's son-in-law. I didn't make the connection. Good man. From the military academy."

"I've been hoping for news, as you can imagine. . . ."

"Military wives are strong women."

"Please, General," Sofya said. "We don't have much time."

"I believe he was with a regiment headed from Ukraine up to Siberia and he split off south of Petrograd to visit his family's estate. There'd been reports of criminal activity there."

Sofya faltered and I held her fast. "Coming to help us?"

The general nodded. "Nine of his best volunteered to accompany him, but they were attacked by a Red Army unit as they slept, just south of Tsarskoe Selo."

"He made it that far? And then what?"

"Well, I'd rather not—" The general walked to the window and stood, hands clasped behind his back, and gazed out onto the street below.

"I need to know, General."

I held her tighter.

The general kept his gaze on the street. "If you insist. All ten were hung, on telegraph poles just north of there."

Sofya folded her hands at her waist, her gaze steady on him. "There's no chance of a mistake?"

He turned his attention back to us. "My most trusted lieutenant and two others witnessed it themselves. They'd been out patrolling the area and came back to find the men murdered. They waited for the Reds to move on and then cut the men down and buried them in the forest just outside Malinov."

Sofya turned to me, eyes shining. "So he did make it home."

The general stood taller. "My deepest condolences, madame. This madness has made us all barbarians. But Afon was everything a soldier should be."

"Thank you, General."

Sofya took my hand and we started out toward the door.

"And brave to the end," the general called to us and we walked on to L'Ecole Cygne Royal.

CHAPTER
50

———

Varinka

1919

I WOKE, SHORT OF BREATH, MAMKA'S PLAN IN MY HEAD.
How good it would be to travel back to Russia with Radimir. But Taras
would track us. How could I leave Max? The worry gave me a headache and made me angry at every little thing.

To make it worse, Max fought me all morning about what to eat for
breakfast. We sat in the hot kitchen, the silver radiator near the door
hissing a little high-pitched scream, a reminder of Papa's lost samovar.

I set a bowl of boiled eggs before Max.

"Eggs are slimy," he said, scowling.

"Get your coat, then," I said. "We mustn't be late."

Max slid off his chair and took his navy blue coat from the peg near
the door.

I knelt to help him button his coat. How grown up he looked, his
hair straighter, no longer a mass of golden ringlets. In that coat, he
looked so much like his father, the soldier.

How warm it was crouching there by the radiator. I loosened the
scarf at my neck. "Your grandmother bought you those eggs. They
may be the only ones in Paris."

Max stared coolly at me. "She's not my grandmother."

Was aristocratic pride passed through the generations?

"What are you talking about?"

He shrugged. "She told me."

Hot prickles crawled up the back of my neck. "What did she say?"

Max grew silent.

I shook one finger at him. "You are lucky she loves you so."

He raised his chin. "Sometimes I remember things. About Russia."

"Don't think of it," I said and gathered his things for school. Certainly he would forget about Sofya someday.

AFTER I DROPPED MAX at school I made my way back to the townhouse, as one thought kept creeping up on me. Maybe Mamka and Radi were right. Maybe Max was better off with his mother. I stuffed that idea down. The rip of leaving him would be too great.

I was almost home when Radimir came toward me on the sidewalk. I stopped and stared, not expecting that. How good it was to see him.

He held his coat up around his neck with one hand. "Varinka. I have been looking for you."

"Come to say goodbye?" Surely, he had come to have the painful discussion of breaking things off.

Radimir held me by the shoulders. "I'm leaving. Come with me."

"Leaving this minute?" My heart beat faster.

"Tonight. I've already written for permission to bring my wife."

A hot gush ran into my arms. "Do you mean—"

I could not stop smiling. Married? I could tell everyone in Malinov. What a life it would be. Max. A husband. More children. Would we live in Petrograd? Once we were back in Russia I could work hard on being a better mother. Radimir said he did not welcome Max, but what if I brought him with me tonight? How could he deny me my boy?

"I am going to get the necessary papers now," he said. "I'll be at my place until six. Don't be late."

I HURRIED BACK TO the townhouse bedroom and stepped into my old *sarafan* and apron. How good it felt to be back in simple clothes. I slipped Sofya's mother's sable coat on over it all.

Into a pillowcase, I threw Max's things. A box of cereal. His blue blanket, threadbare now. His stuffed owl. I then placed a towel on my bedroom doorknob. Would Mamka be sad to see our signal there?

I crept into Taras's bedroom and stared down at him, asleep on his bed. My hands shook and I could barely open the handcuff, but I finally unlatched it, took a deep breath, and closed one end around the iron bedpost. What a loud sound it made.

I stood there, heart beating wildly. Would it wake him? I opened the other cuff and struggled it onto his thick wrist. I tried to click it closed but his wrist was so large.

Taras opened his eyes, still half asleep. "What's this?"

I pressed harder and the cuff clicked shut. I felt the key in my coat pocket.

Taras pulled on the cuff and the steel rattled against the bedpost. "This isn't funny, Varinka."

I stepped back. What if he broke the chain? I'd be dead for sure.

"I'm leaving, Taras."

He squinted at me. "Get over here."

I took a deep breath. "It's time for all this sickness to stop."

"The arrangement? It was you who started it—"

"I was *a child*, Taras. Even that young I knew it was wrong to do that with my brother."

"Half brother."

"Do you know how hard it was for Mamka to have her husband's love child living in the house?"

Taras tugged at his shackle. "Shut up, Inka. They *bought* me."

"Only to keep you safe. You think Mamka liked taking you in? They were kind to you and you paid him back by killing him and terrorizing me."

"Papa's death was an accident."

"Give up that lie, Taras. He scolded you for watching me in the bath. You didn't have to kill him."

"I did my time. And I *terrorized* you? I kept you and Zina alive. Sorry now I did."

"You should have protected me, like any good brother. This is sick, Taras. I want a real relationship. Love and children I could never have with you."

He tried to rise from the bed.

"Give me the key, Inka." He lunged toward me, pulling the bed by the cuff, moving it an inch.

I took another step back, heart pounding.

He yanked at the handcuff. "Where are you going? Off with your new boyfriend? I'll find you. I'll get Max and take care of him like I should have done long ago."

I stepped out of the bedroom, toward the kitchen door. How good it would feel to walk out, free.

Taras called after me. "I'll tell that new boyfriend of yours about us."

"I'll tell him myself. Goodbye, brother."

CHAPTER
51

Sofya

1919

ELIZA AND I LEFT GENERAL YAKOFNAVICH AND HUR-
ried across Place Vendôme toward the school, numb to everything but
the horrible words *Afon is dead*. But he'd come to save us, hadn't he?
Good Afon. As Eliza tried to wave down a taxi, the thought of Afon
hanging from a telegraph pole floated up in front of me. My brave husband had come so close to helping us. How happy he'd be we were
getting Max back.

Eliza checked her watch. "Almost four, Sofya. This may not work
today."

"We must try," I said.

I was all Max had now.

WE ARRIVED AT MADAME Fournier's office just before four o'clock.
Would Varinka be there? Would Madame relent?

A young teacher showed us into the headmistress's office where Madame stood behind her desk.

"You're back," she said, as if she'd tasted a bad clam.

"So sorry to burden you, madame," I said in my best French. "Since
I saw you last, we've secured help from powerful sources. This is Eliza
Ferriday from New York. She has found help from General—"

"I just received a call from the police, thank you. Said they are stationing an officer here. My own needs may be met, but I still must make sure this does not traumatize the child."

Eliza stepped toward her. "This is his mother."

"But will he remember you? Feel safe in your care?"

I shook my head. "I have no idea, madame."

Madame retreated to her desk. "Perhaps a temporary home would be better while he transitions."

"I'll not leave here without my son, madame. I am afraid Varinka will take him away once she knows I am in Paris."

Madame played with her pen and the sound of children's voices in the hallway rose as parents came to pick them up. "Well, here is what I can do. I'll have Max brought here and we'll see how he does."

"But they've been separated since he was two," Eliza said. "He may not recognize her."

"A mother and child always know each other, no matter the divide. Like chicks in the henhouse. If not, there are many families willing to take a child in."

"I assure you, he is her son," Eliza said.

Madame stood. "My final offer."

I nodded.

"Very well. I will bring the child and his teacher here. Do not overwhelm him with sudden movement. Stay calm. Let him come to you."

Madame left the room and Eliza and I exchanged glances as the mantel clock chimed four times, my palms moist. I paced the carpeted room. How long had I waited for this moment? But now it was here and I could barely breathe.

Soon the doorknob turned and the door swung open. *Please, God, let him remember me.*

Madame ushered Max into the room, followed by a sharp-faced young woman dressed in a flowered apron over her brown dress.

With shaking fingers, I brushed a lock of hair back off my face. Would he recognize me, so thin, with such short hair?

"This is Max's teacher Mademoiselle Slack, a saint I assure you, who has cared for this child through the most trying circumstances."

Max stood between the desk and his teacher. My pulse quickened seeing him there. He resembled Afon and looked so grown up, taller and thinner, his baby fat and golden curls gone. A handsome child, but with a certain hardness. Had he been mistreated? It was all I could do not to run to him and gather him up, to tell him how I missed him, how sorry I was I'd left him.

With a guarded look, Max gazed at each one of us in turn, with no change of expression.

I longed to reach out, but held back. "Hello, my little one."

His eyes met mine and I searched for a spark of recognition.

Max stepped to the desk and laid his cheek against the wood.

Tears flooded my eyes. Of course, he did not remember me. It had been years.

"He's just tired," Eliza said.

Madame ran her fingers through her hair. "This child is always tired."

Eliza turned to me. "Did you have a pet name for him as a baby? One he would remember?"

I shook my head. "Not really."

Madame rubbed Max's back. "He is not feeling good about this, I'm afraid."

From the outer office came the sound of the door opening and Eliza glanced toward it.

"They tell me my son is here?" Varinka called.

Varinka stepped into the inner office, an overstuffed valise in one hand and a full pillowcase in the other. She wore my mother's coat over her peasant clothes and looked ready to run out of there at any minute, her eyes wide.

"Going somewhere?" I asked.

Varinka stared at me. "I came to pick up my boy." She reached out her hand to Max, but he hid behind his teacher's skirt.

"He's just overwhelmed," Varinka said. "Would you all stop staring at him? This is too much for a young child."

I stepped toward her. "I will say what's too much for him. Being stolen from your family certainly is."

"What do you know?"

"I'm his mother, Varinka."

Varinka turned to Madame Fournier. "I don't know this person. I need to take my son and go."

I stepped closer to her. "Why, Varinka?"

"Come along, Max." She held out her hand for Max and the boy stepped farther behind his teacher.

"Why did you take him? I was so good to you."

"Good? That's not the way I remember it. The countess was a cruel woman."

"So you stole my child?"

"Shots were flying that night. I saved him. Though you were ready to leave for Paris without me."

"I—"

Varinka shook her finger at me, a red flush creeping up her neck. "Don't *deny* it. You all packed your things. Leaving me behind, never to see him again. Call that kind?"

"Please. Your feelings were hurt so you stole my *son* from me?"

"You barely cared about him—I could see. You only cared about your husband and your clothes and shoes. I *loved* him. Taught him things."

I held out my hand. "Give me my mother's coat."

Varinka took a step back. "Who says it's not mine?"

Eliza stepped forward. "I can attest to the fact."

"Take it off."

She paused, and then slid out of the coat and tossed it on a chair next to Eliza.

"He doesn't want to go with you," Madame said. "Can't you see?"

"I took the best care of him."

"So, it is true you took another woman's child?" Madame asked.

"You don't understand."

Madame turned to Mademoiselle Slack. "Please fetch the officer outside. Tell him we have a criminal here."

Varinka glanced at me, fear in her eyes.

Everything about me tightened. Why not let the girl suffer for what she'd done to us all? She and Taras tried to take everything from me. But life with Taras seemed punishment alone.

"No," I said. "Let her go. On the condition you leave Paris and don't return."

Varinka wiped her eyes with her apron. "I'm leaving today."

Madame Fournier stepped toward Varinka. "You and your husband must not enter the school grounds again."

Varinka stepped to the door, arms crossed over her chest. "He's not my husband, but don't worry, I won't be back." She crouched down to Max's level. "Goodbye, Max."

Max pressed himself tighter to Mademoiselle Slack.

Varinka stood and turned to me. "Please don't tell him I was a terrible person. His owl is in the pillowcase. . . ."

I kept my gaze on the floor. "Just go, Varinka."

"And he's not safe in Paris. Taras says he wants to——" She glanced at the boy. "Just take him away from here." Varinka opened the office door and turned back. "I love you, Max. I hope you remember that, too."

With one last look at the child, as if memorizing him, Varinka left the office and closed the door behind her.

Max emerged from behind his teacher's skirt and Eliza let out a deep breath. "Dear God, Sofya."

Every cell in my body relaxed and brought a new clarity of thought. "If you don't mind, madame, I do recall something Max might remember."

Almost at a whisper, I sang: "There was once a little boat. . . ."

I waited for a moment but Max remained behind Mademoiselle Slack, no expression on his face.

I sang on:

"That never on the sea had sailed.

Ahoy.

Ahoy."

Max stepped out from behind Mademoiselle.

I held out my hand to him. He hesitated.

"After five or six weeks rations began to wane. . . ."

He took a step toward me and then another and placed one hand on my knee. I barely breathed, as if willing a hummingbird to light.

"Ahoy. Ahoy," he sang.

I leaned closer to hear, his voice soft and sweet.

He looked up at me and I reached out and stroked the spot under his chin. The ridge was smoother and faded, but still there.

"Maxwell, do you remember me?"

He placed his hand on mine. How long had I hoped to feel that small hand again?

Madame produced a sheaf of papers for me to sign. "I suppose Maxwell can be safely discharged into your care."

Warmth spread through me. I stood, signed the papers, and shook Madame's hand. "Thank you."

I stepped to the chair and exchanged the dog fur coat for Mother's sable, Varinka's warmth still there in the silk.

Mother.

I held out my hand to Max. "Time to go."

He hesitated.

"Come along. We are going to Aunt Eliza's."

He looked up at me with his father's smile and took my hand. "I knew you would come."

Varinka

1919

IT WAS NEAR DARK AS I LEFT MAX'S SCHOOL AND RAN along the Champs-Élysées past the Grand Palais, happy to finally end it all. I just needed to get to the closest bridge at the Seine. The swift river would help me do what had to be done. I hurried the best I could, coatless in my long *sarafan*, the cold air stinging my lungs.

I replayed my goodbye to Max in my mind. How I would miss seeing his face every morning. Would he remember any of the good things? Our fun in Luxembourg Gardens? Mamka sewing him such handsome clothes?

Surely, Sofya would tell him I was a bad person. That I took him from her.

Tears froze on my eyelashes. I hugged my valise to my chest, which buffered the wind a bit.

What would Radimir think when he heard what I'd done? The truth about Taras and me?

I saw the river in the distance and picked up my pace. How would it happen? With an icy splash, years of hurt would finally end.

Stepping onto the bridge, the wind pierced the layers of linen, I felt the cold of the stone through my woven shoes. There was not a soul out in that cold. There would be no witness to what fell into the dark waters there.

Halfway across the bridge I stood, looking into the water, the stone railing waist high. I took a deep breath and pulled the handcuff key from my pocket. I stared at the silver glowing there in my palm. So much pain would go with it.

I flipped the key into the air and watched it fall into the dark water. Even Taras would never find it there.

I stood for a moment making sure the key sank and then left the bridge, valise to my chest, and walked on to meet my love.

CHAPTER
53

Sofya

1919

ELIZA STARTED WORKING ON THE VISAS FOR OUR trip to America right away, using every family contact and old favor she could. I mostly looked forward to the trip. After all, Varinka's mother had predicted Max would only be safe under the torch and I assumed she meant Lady Liberty's. But I missed Afon so terribly and couldn't shake the feeling I was abandoning his memory by going even farther away from Russia.

Eliza did all she could to help and served us breakfast in bed, had Madame Solange make us chocolate soufflés, and dropped everything to read Caroline's children's books to Max anytime he asked. Max and Luba picked up where they left off, often camping out together on his bedroom floor, her lap one of his favorite places. She helped me explain to Max what had happened, telling him his father was with his grandparents, up in the stars.

I loved the feeling of my son's hand in mine and held him close every chance I got, so grateful he was with me, safe.

His first night home, as I turned out the lights, I felt his soft kiss on my cheek.

"Good night, Maman," he said, there in the darkness.

It took me a moment to reply. "Good night, my darling boy."

AS SOON AS IT was safe I brought Max, under the cover of darkness, to the stables. I took no chances walking around in broad daylight. Washed and scrubbed and dressed in lovely borrowed clothes, I was even more at risk that Red agents in Paris would recognize me. Max as well.

When I requested sugar, Madame Solange had reluctantly put two cubes in Max's coat pocket, for to her mind they would be wasted on our mission. I still had money left over from the sale of my hair to pay the stable mistress. Was I too late? Had they taken good care of my dear Jarushka?

Max and I stepped into the stables and the mistress I'd left Jarushka with met us. She eyed me with suspicion. Did she not recognize me without the dirty face and terrible dog fur coat?

"I've come to talk to you about my horse Jarushka."

"You missed the deadline."

Tears filled my eyes. "But I was detained—"

"You have no one to blame but yourself."

I knelt next to Max and buried my face in his shoulder.

He stroked my hair.

A young girl hurried out from the direction of the stalls. "Please do not take her away from me. She is the horse of my dreams and I cannot go a day without her."

"My daughter," the stable mistress said. "Carmine."

I stood. "So, she's alive? May we see her?"

We followed the girl to Jarushka's stall, to find her there munching oats from a bucket, a crown of dried lavender and herbs circling her head. We walked in, our steps soft on wood shavings, and she nuzzled my neck and then tried to munch on her crown.

"Did you make her the pretty crown?"

The girl nodded and wiped away tears with the back of her hand. "I brush her three times a day and she kisses me while I do it."

"You love her very much, I can see."

"I ride her in the park."

"Well, Carmine, I have to take a long trip. To America. Would you take care of her for me?"

The girl brightened. "Oh, yes."

"I will write for her when the customs people say it is okay." I handed her mother the money. "This should take care of—"

The stable mistress waved the bills away. "No, merci."

I brought Max to stand near Jarushka. "Can you bring one hand, palm up, to her mouth? She'll kiss you."

Max lifted his palm, Jarushka kissed it and then she dug her nose into the space between his coat collar and neck.

"So soft." He laughed and wiped his palm on the front of his jacket. "She remembers me."

Jarushka nuzzled his pocket and took a sugar cube.

I ran one hand down her silky neck and she pawed the sawdust at her feet. Of course, she knew I was leaving. What a good friend she'd been.

Max and I stepped out of the stall.

"You be good for Carmine," I told her.

Carmine brushed Jarushka's back with long strokes. "I will guard her with my life," she called after us.

Max and I hurried off, and I looked back through tears as Jarushka watched us go.

CHAPTER

54

Sofya

1920

A FEW MONTHS AFTER I FOUND MAX IN PARIS, IN THE spring of 1919, Luba and I brought him to America to live with Eliza at Gin Lane. She said it breathed new life into the old place and our arrival also pleased Eliza's mother, who waited in the driveway with Caroline as we appeared, waving the Russian flag like a semaphore flagman on the deck of a destroyer.

How good it was to see that house again, where Max had been born. Had Afon and my parents not just stood on that terrace five years earlier? It was good to be safe in America, but dark thoughts of Afon's horrible death bubbled up at the most inopportune times and I missed my home. It was hard feeling connected to Russia so far away in the States. In France one could still feel close to home, but living in America the mail was so slow and made us feel farther still.

But I made do on my own. I started a garden business and that summer earned almost enough money to rent a little place for Max, Luba, and me.

Cook, living in upstate New York to get his chef's license, had not been back to see us in the year since we'd arrived. I had many loving people in my life and put the amorous part of me away in a box.

One fall afternoon before the benefit concert at Madison Square

Garden all that changed. Caroline and Luba had helped arrange the event—for 780 orphaned Russian children who'd been torn from their homes. Threatened by invading armies of Bolsheviks and pushed into Siberia, the Red Cross sent the children on a worldwide journey via ship, through the Panama Canal and up to New York City. We gathered in the dining room as the whole household packed musical instruments and gifts into boxes to distribute to the children. Nancy and Peg helped Thomas, just back from his service in France, struggle to get boxes into Eliza's mother's car.

I sat at the table checking their receipts as Caroline waved Eliza toward a cardboard box. "The guitars go there."

"Shouldn't we give the poor things balalaikas instead?" Eliza asked.

Caroline turned. What a lovely young woman she was becoming. Shy, but never timid, at seventeen so tall and slender, grown up in her dark gray suit. "They want guitars, Mother. To play American music."

"Twenty-seven guitars—" Luba said.

Caroline checked her list. "And one flute."

Eliza's mother smiled. "Ah, good. A nonconformist."

"We'll never make it in time," Eliza said. "The curtain's at six and Julia's meeting us there."

"Relax, Mother. Granny's driving. She'll have us there in record time."

Max, now a solid six-year-old, pedaled a little motorcar around the downstairs. As if he were a new child, he motored, the rubber tires quiet on the wood floors, out onto the veranda and around the backyard.

Luba tossed a doll into a box. "Better be careful or Max will drive that car into Manhattan."

At sixteen Luba was already as tall as Father had been and rivaled Caroline in height. Still dressed in her pink-striped junior nurse uniform from the hospital, she conferred with Caroline every now and then, taking her role as co-organizer seriously.

"No more riding, Max," I called after him. "Wash your hands for tea."

"Can't he ride a bit more?" Luba asked. "It's such a pretty day."

"He needs limits, Luba. He feels safer that way." How much more secure I felt about my parenting and my son thrived for it.

"Mrs. Montessori would be proud," Luba said and waved a letter from the post. "The change of name form came today."

I didn't have to say what we all knew. Across the Atlantic in New York we were safer than ever, but Bolshevism had taken deeper root in Russia and the safety of émigrés of noble birth was still not guaranteed. Plus, after the Bolsheviks triumphed in Russia a fear grew in America that they too would succumb to the rising tide of Communism. As the wave of anti-Russian sentiment in America grew, changing our names gave us the anonymity I craved.

Luba opened the envelope. "How strange you can just change your name in this country."

"We call it freedom," Eliza's mother said.

Luba pulled a pencil from her pocket and smoothed the form onto the sideboard. "I've always wanted to be named Lyra. It means Greek harp. Lyra's star Vega is the brightest in the night sky."

"Of course, you have to be the brightest," I said.

"Lyra it is," she said, writing. "Perhaps you could take the name Hydrus, Sofya. It means water snake."

"Thank you, sister."

She poised the pencil above the paper. "So, what will Max's new name be?"

"How about Cepheus?" Caroline asked. "It means king."

"I don't know," I said. "He already thinks he rules us all."

Eliza walked by carrying a saxophone in each hand. "How about John?"

I laughed. "We need something Russian but friendly, pronounceable for Americans."

We were silent for a moment, the wild cry of gulls and terns the only sound.

"Was his grandfather's name not Serge?" Eliza asked.

Luba fiddled with her pencil. "A bit boring, don't you think?"

"I like it," I said.

Luba wrote the name on the form. "Serge it is."

IT TOOK AN HOUR to load everyone up and by late afternoon Max and I waved them off to the concert. We enjoyed a lovely supper of cod straight from the Atlantic and Mr. Gardener's late summer peas. Once I read him a storybook in Russian, after his long day of motoring, Max fell asleep quickly and I walked about the house turning lights on here and there, as Mother had always loved doing. It was her favorite ritual, almost a holy one, lighting a candle here, a kerosene lamp there, as night fell.

I left the living room dark, sat on the smooth sofa, and listened to the waves crash upon the sand at regular intervals, a cool breeze from the open window playing about my bare arms. That time of night was always hardest, when thoughts of Afon crept out to haunt me. My rose sat on the sideboard perfuming the air, petals lifting gently in the light wind. Thanks to a new china pot it seemed happy to be back in its original home. What a trip that little plant had taken.

A flash of headlights panned across the living room wall and I felt the distant thud of a car door closing. I stood. Mr. Gardener? Had Eliza's group forgotten something?

I stepped toward the front of the house as the front door banged shut.

He entered the front hallway, the lamp on the table sending a pool of light on the floor.

"It's been a long time," I said. "Good to see you."

"And you, Sofya." Cook removed his hat, tossed it on the front table, and set down an enormous, framed certificate he carried.

"I'm now officially certified to cook in the state of New York."

I smiled. "Apparently if you survive carrying the diploma home you're free to prepare whatever you like."

"I received an A in chopping vegetables and now know ten ways to stretch a pot roast."

How nice it was to see him. What was that look on his face? Happiness? Ambivalence? Suddenly self-conscious, I looked anywhere but at him.

"I'm sorry about Afon," he said.

I folded my arms across my chest and nodded, afraid more words would bring tears.

"And about leaving you in Malinov. I couldn't get back—"

"Eliza told me."

"Your parents . . ."

"I still can't believe it's true."

Cook stepped toward me. "You cut your hair."

I nodded.

"It suits you."

I smoothed one hand down my short cut. "I won't be Sofya much longer. We're thinking about changing our names. Luba is now Lyra. I've decided on Vivian. What do you think?"

"Do what you want, but I think you're overreacting. No Reds will care about you here. I can't call you all by other names."

"You will if you care about us."

He stepped to me, took my hand, and kissed the palm.

"You're shaking," he said.

His left hand was bare, his famous ring gone. Lost? Sold or stolen along the way?

"Your ring—"

"We had to part ways. But now I have enough money to open my own place. I know how many restaurants fail, but I'm taking the chance."

"Where?"

"Here in town. I could use a partner."

"I've started a business myself. Just flowers but it—"

"I think you know what kind of partner I mean, Sofya. Maybe once you feel better. I know losing him cuts deep."

"I'm trying," I said, drying my eyes on my bare wrist.

He wrapped his arms around me. "Just try and love your life, Sofya. I think he would have wanted that."

I lay my cheek against his white shirt, and took in his scent, of men's talc and bay rum. How lucky I was to have someone so generous. But why could I not throw my arms about his neck and kiss him?

"Be patient with me," I said.

"Forever, Vivian."

CHAPTER
55
_____

Eliza

1920

HOW WONDERFUL IT WAS TO HAVE SOFYA AND HER family safely settled in at Gin Lane that autumn. After a few weeks Caroline asked if we could visit The Hay up in Bethlehem. I agreed, knowing she would be surprised by all the long-distance renovations I'd organized. Peg was in on the surprise and had kept the good bit of carpentry I'd arranged a secret. I sent her and Mr. Gardener ahead to prepare for our arrival.

Thomas drove us up to The Hay, Caroline in the front seat with him discussing politics. It was one of those first crisp autumn days that felt like fall, the leaves just starting to turn.

When we pulled into the crushed-stone driveway I almost didn't recognize the house, since local craftsmen had carried out all of my renovation directives. A cow brought in from Woodbury grazed on the front lawn and The Hay wore a fresh coat of white paint, the shutters glossy black, and a new cedar shingle roof that was still caramel brown, not yet weathered gray. The three barns to the right of the property had been painted as well and stood ready to host any number of animals.

Caroline ran to the front of the house across the long sweep of lawn that swept down to Bird Tavern. Now an upper-schooler, Caroline was especially proud to wear her Chapin School uniform, a more grown-up white blouse, dark green tie and skirt, and a belted jacket.

"We have a *cow*," Caroline called to me.

"And we shall have every sort of animal. Horses. A little Pekingese dog? Even a pig if you like."

It had been six years since we'd first seen The Hay. It had come a long way.

We stepped inside to the dining room, the table set with our best purple transferware and fresh flowers, and walked to the kitchen, following the scent of new maple wood. I'd had the hole in the subfloor repaired and a handsome black-and-white-checkered tile floor laid atop it and the cabinets painted deep robin's egg blue.

Peg met me in the kitchen and offered me a glass. "Wine, Miz Ferriday? Dinner will be done soon."

I smoothed one hand down Caroline's jacket sleeve. "How your father would have loved this."

"Especially the wine," Caroline said with a smile.

I realized with a jolt it was the first time in so long the thought of Henry was no dagger to the chest.

Mr. Gardener found us in the kitchen. "You won't believe this," he said with a worried look.

We followed him to the library. How beautifully Peg had outfitted that room, with the red-and-navy Tabriz rug I'd sent up from the city and a desk outfitted with all the best papers and pens. We stepped to the multi-paned bay window along the back of the room, which overlooked the sloping backyard.

Caroline hurried to the window and gasped.

Just outside the window, where our majestic maple tree once stood, sat a jagged, blackened stump.

"My goodness," I said.

Beyond the stump lay the fallen tree, parallel to the house.

"Last night, lightning sheared it clear off," Mr. Gardener said.

I turned to him, fists resting on my hips. "Well, that can mean only one thing."

"Take me two days to get this cleaned up."

"Means God wants us to have a garden, and we must start right away."

"Do you mean it, Mother?" Caroline hurried outside.

Mr. Gardener smiled. "I prayed for this."

"We'll have a boxwood knot garden here behind the house and terrace it down a flight of stone steps. And an herb garden there close to the house."

Mr. Gardener took a step back. "But we have no garden design."

"Here's your plan." I grabbed a notepad from the desk and sketched the same design found on the carpet at our feet, the rectilinear pattern so commonly found in rugs from the East, a strong border and a center medallion containing four triangles. "We'll have roses planted inside the boxwoods here and a small pool in the center of it all."

Caroline came running from outside. "There is a pony in the far barn, Mother. Just like the one Father promised."

"The only gelding with pinto markings in all of Connecticut. Just as he wanted you to have. And now for your second gift."

I linked arms with Caroline and we made our way up the front stairs, through my bedroom toward Caroline's, and along the way waved toward my silver-clad icon hanging on my wall, the one Nancy had gifted me.

"Oh, Mother, you've hung your icon."

How good my most treasured possession looked there.

We moved on to Caroline's bedroom and I stood aside so she could see what lay at the end of her room. It was a newly constructed extension to the back of the house, with several feet of new flooring and tall windows, which lengthened her room so it overlooked the backyard. The floor of the new area was lighter than the old, but the added space opened up the room considerably.

Caroline stood, looking out over the backyard, fingers to her lips. "It's perfect."

I stepped to her side and took in the lovely view, of the entire backyard, across the apple orchard all the way to Munger Lane. "You'll see the garden from here every morning."

"This room is big enough for three now. Perhaps we can invite some of the Russian women up here? I can ask Bird Tavern if they can offer them positions."

"That's a splendid idea, Caroline."

She slipped one arm around my waist. "They will like the garden, I think. May we plant eglantine?"

I laughed. "All the eglantine you'd like. And iris and Father's favorite peonies."

"And lilacs?"

"Of course."

I held her close. "I think Father would be happy for us, don't you?"

"So very happy," she said.

THE NEXT DAY A crew of men arrived with six draft horses to drag to the town green the donated boulder they'd crowbarred out of our meadow's earth. A bronze plaque was affixed to the boulder to remember the fallen of the Civil War and the Great War.

After the Episcopal pastor said a few words to recall the war dead, I walked across the street from the green to Merrill Brothers Store. I had readied the old place, a former home, and left it broom-clean with new shelves built in the front parlor, but left the rest to its new owner.

Merrill stepped out onto the porch. Given plenty of fresh Bethlehem air and a few Woolsey Civil War remedies like beef tea and spruce beer his hair had grown in nicely, almost all of his lesions healed and his vision improved every day. Though his doctor prescribed painful-looking physical therapy, the only lasting sign of his injuries was a slight limp, an imperfection that only made him more attractive in my eyes.

He came down the steps to meet me and we admired the handsome sign above the door that he'd commissioned, gold letters on black board. *Merrill Brothers.* Henry's sign at Poor Brothers had been similar.

"You hoisted it up there by yourself, Merrill? You really shouldn't—"

"Let me work, Eliza. It's the best way to recover."

"It's a lovely sign, Merrill, but Merrill Brothers? Why Brothers?"

"It sounds better than plain Merrill, don't you think?"

That was the type of good business decision Henry would have made.

"Would you like to sell apples at your store?" I asked. "Some are ready to pick in the orchard."

"I hate that you're tied to this place now, Eliza."

I brushed a smudge of dirt off his shoulder. How nice he looked, having exchanged his bespoke suits for a grocer's plain trousers, suspenders, and white shirt.

"I've got the baseball team lined up. First game next week and they've elected you as captain," I said.

Merrill smiled and stepped closer to me.

I held him at arm's length. "Just remember Caroline knows nothing of us. Mother, too. I will call you Mr. Merrill in public. How does that sound?"

We made our way up the wooden steps and stood in front of the door. "You must close your eyes, Eliza. I want this to be a surprise."

"Oh, really, Merrill." I squeezed my eyes closed and he led me in the door. I expected to see a crate of melons and a few bars of soap.

"It smells heavenly. Of bread and cinnamon and—"

"Good. You can look now."

I opened my eyes to a most charming array of dry goods. Glass jars filled with candies, Henry's favorite peppermints. On one side of the room shelves stood stocked with every tinned delicacy one needed for a party. Shelves on the other bulged with remedies and cures of all kinds. Witch hazel. Chamomile lotion. Epsom salts. Acorn squash in bushel baskets.

How different it was from Henry's store, with their whole floor of beaver hats and overcoats in the men's department, biscuit boxes stacked to the ceiling.

Why could I not stop comparing everything to Henry's store? He was gone. Why could I not move on?

Merrill watched me, eager for a sign.

"Oh, it is just what I dreamed it could be, Merrill, but if you will excuse me, there is something I have to do. Something I've put off for much too long."

AS DUSK CAME UPON The Hay I knew I had to confront the hay barn, where I'd spent some of my last happy moments with Henry, the place I avoided at all cost.

I made my way out to the barn, a glass of Dubonnet in each hand and stepped into that sweet-smelling place, hay boxes lined up against one wall. A family of barn swallows chattered up in the eaves as I stepped across the wide-planked wood floor. The scent of cedar brought Henry back in full color, standing there.

The trip he'd planned. The kiss.

Surely he could hear me, out there in our holy place?

I set one glass down on a hay box and looked to the rafters. How silly I felt out there, talking to the deceased. Where to begin?

I pulled my coat closer. "Thank you for finding this place, Henry." The birds quieted. Was he listening?

"You were right, of course. It will be a great comfort to Caroline. Ninety-six acres. Plenty of room to roam. I'm bringing a few of the horses up."

I sipped the liqueur and it burned my throat in a good way. "The pony was a big hit. And there are bluebirds here now. I'll put out some nesting boxes in the meadow."

It was as if I were making small talk at a cocktail party, just delaying the important issue.

I toed a knot in the wood floor. "So, I want to tell you I need to do something. I'm sure you'll understand. It may not seem too big of a thing to you, but it is to me."

Tears pooled in my eyes and I bit the inside of my cheek to keep them at bay.

I slipped my rings off my left finger. "Do you remember when you said you wanted to go with me everywhere? I said I wanted that, too, and still do."

I slid my rings onto my right ring finger.

"But I need to move forward, Henry. Just remember it doesn't mean I love you less. You are with me always, no matter where I go or with whom. No one can take that away from me."

I stood for a moment. Had he heard?

I turned and walked to the door as a barn swallow swooped down from the eaves and lighted on the edge of the glass I had set down. He dipped his beak into the golden liquid once, twice, and then flitted off back up to the loft.

Thank you, Henry.

I stepped out of the barn feeling lighter somehow.

On my way back toward the house I stopped to admire the sunset, growing pink and violet over Munger Lane.

From the driveway, Merrill walked toward me, carrying a stack of bushel baskets.

I stepped toward him across the grass, the air at my ankles chilly. "Hello, there, Mr. Merrill."

Merrill's smile glowed white in the growing darkness. "Hello Mrs. Ferriday. Just going to pick some apples for the store."

I reached for one of the baskets. "Let me help."

We picked apples as the sun went down beyond Caroline's playhouse, as the meadow turned to gold, and watched the bats fly above the orchard, silhouetted against the pink sky.

Mr. Merrill, Henry, and me.

Luba

1921

GIN LANE

PEOPLE ASK ME WHY I CAME TO AMERICA WITH MY SISTER, Sofya, and I tell them for the pistachio ice cream. They laugh at that and I don't have to think about my parents and everything we left behind.

Life goes on.

Scrumptious little Max, who now answers to Serge, is now Cook's apprentice and is becoming quite a good little chef, and is going to school here now, at seven he is the tallest in his class. He told his teacher they shouldn't get too attached to him since he was going back to Russia. Sofya tells that story with a smile on her face but she feels the same way, still has not fully unpacked, expecting "that affair with the Bolsheviks" to be over any day and the Whites to be back in power. But Great Britain just recognized the Reds as the official government of Russia and, if you ask me, the whole thing just gets worse.

As Eliza says, "Heavenly day."

It must be hard on Sofya that Max looks more like his father every day, his hair no longer blond, but a light cocoa brown. As I write this, she walks the beach looking at the ocean. Thinking of Afon?

She and Cook are doing well, like nervous fourteen-year-olds holding hands sometimes, and she wears the band he gave her. At Peg and Thomas's wedding he looked at Sofya the whole time and she pretended not to notice.

We're supposed to call Cook by his real name now, Yury. He's opening what they call a dinner theater in Quogue. I think Sofya has deep affection for him, but still she has a drawer in her bedroom where she keeps Afon's photo. She looks at it sometimes.

People say we're assimilating well, which I think must mean our English is getting better. I work at the hospital here and with my first paycheck bought a *True Story* magazine, the best textbook to teach myself phrases from toothpaste ads, like *What a lovely thing a swift little smile can be*, and I learned how important kiss-proof lipstick is. Many Russian girls are here now and I hear talk about building a church we can all go to in Sea Cliff.

Sofya had a row with Eliza after she sold Mother's emerald necklace. But my sister would not back down. She put the money in the Southampton Bank so I can go to New York University, which she says Mother would have wanted.

We planted Sofya's rose here in the garden at Gin Lane, and Eliza brought a minister to say a few words about Agnessa and Father and Count von Orloff. Cook and Mrs. Ferriday made Russian food to make us feel better, but it just reminded me of the things I'd never do again. Like see the Rembrandts at the Hermitage, the house cats at my ankles. Play game night at Alexander Palace with our Romanov cousins. Watch the stars from the steppe with Father.

What would they all say if they knew I was seeing the town policeman, a boy named William Maddox, with kind eyes and very white teeth, who asked me to Corine's for soda? He didn't know much about astronomy but he does now. He calls me Lyra, my new name, and sometimes I forget to answer to it, which he thinks is funny. "Who doesn't know their own name?" he says. Agnessa would've taken to her bed to learn I was seeing a policeman. How would my mother have felt?

Mother.

I think of them all often, on bad days with a stab of pain. When I see a pine grove and think of Afon at rest in Malinov under his favorite larch trees, back home without us. When I see a little brown dog with a wet expression. When I see Mr. Hildreth with his wire spectacles like Father's, or catch the scent of wild rose in the air that makes me ache for Mother.

But I'll keep my mind on my new American life, study hard my English, and not question a thing.

I swear by God's stars.

AUTHOR'S NOTE

WHILE WRITING AND RESEARCHING *LILAC GIRLS* I came to love Caroline Ferriday's mother, Eliza Woolsey Mitchell. The daughter of Caroline Carson Woolsey Mitchell, one of the famous Woolsey women of New York City, staunch abolitionists and philanthropists, Eliza saw what it meant to give back at an early age. She ended up devoting her time to the cause of the "White Russian" émigrés, former aristocrats in Russia who lost everything when the Bolsheviks finally seized power from the tsar in 1918. When the émigrés arrived in New York City, many of them destitute and traumatized, the men often found work but the women and children had a harder time. A fierce advocate for these women, Eliza helped organize the American Central Committee for Russian Relief, fought to find the émigrés work and homes, and opened her own New York City apartment and Southampton cottage to them.

At the end of World War I the West discovered the exotic Slavic countries of Eastern Europe and, as Russian émigrés poured into Paris, Russian art, handicrafts, and clothing were the height of fashion. Seizing on this trend, Eliza and the American Central Committee for Russian Relief commissioned Russian handicrafts from a workshop staffed by White Russians in Paris to sell at a series of bazaars to benefit the women.

Caroline Ferriday developed her own sense of service working at these bazaars, held at the Ferridays' Manhattan apartment at 31 East Fiftieth Street and at the Plaza Hotel, and she often tapped her fellow debutantes to work there. The young women, dressed in traditional Russian *sarafans* and *kokoshniks,* manned the sales of Russian hand goods made in Paris: rag dolls dressed in Russian folk dress, lace-trimmed bed linens, peasant blouses, and enameled boxes. These bazaars were wildly successful and the sales went on for years, a favorite subject of the group of society journalists known as Cholly Knickerbocker, and raised considerable aid for the White Russian émigrés.

Eliza contributed to many other charities as well, all while raising her daughter Caroline on her own, feeling the constant ache of losing her beloved husband, Henry. Henry was a successful dry goods merchant whose family hailed from Ferriday, Louisiana, on one side and England on the other. He spent a great deal of time in Paris as a child and young man, was a tremendous Francophile, and instilled his love of France in Caroline. Henry died from pneumonia shortly after they bought The Hay, never to spend a full season in the country home he loved.

Eliza met many Russian émigrés in the course of her work, including perfumer Prince Matchabelli and his wife Norina, and Princess Cantacuzène, President Grant's first granddaughter, married to Prince Mikhail Cantacuzène, a Russian general and diplomat. Princess Cantacuzène became Eliza's good friend and headed up the Russian relief committee, often helping with handicraft sales. Her book *My Life Here and There* provides a fascinating look into her twenty years living in Russia, from the American point of view of a woman who fiercely loved Russia.

Many of the autobiographies I read of former aristocrats from that period helped inspire and inform the character of Eliza's Russian friend Sofya Streshnayva. Mary Tolstoy, Marie, Grand Duchess of Russia, Countess Olga Hendrikoff, and many others helped me fill in the details of Sofya's life in Russia. But the one I drew upon most for Sofya's personality was Countess Edith Sollohub. Completely charming and unpretentious, Edith was the daughter of a high-ranking Russian diplomat, her privileged life derailed by the Bolshevik Revolution. Her books *The Russian Countess* and *Stories from Forest and Steppe* provide an intimate sense of what Russian rural life was like at the time and give insight into a grounded, intelligent woman who made the most of her terrible circumstances.

Varinka is a character of my imagination, though the book *Home Life in Russia* was a tremendous help in bringing her to life with its fascinating look into superstitions, customs, and village life. Being a peasant in Russia during that time was fraught with difficulty and this helped me show that.

Julia Marlowe was a great friend to Eliza Ferriday throughout her life. A famous actress of her day, *The New York Sun* wrote, "There is not a woman player in America or in England that is—attractively considered—fit to unlace her shoe." Julia and her second husband E. H. Sothern were enormously successful and served as Caroline Ferriday's acting mentors from her teens through years of acting on Broadway and touring. I was lucky to visit Julia's home, Wildacres, in the Catskills, and found her presence still there, the big rooms now in disrepair but still echoing Julia's wonderful life.

The character Cook was inspired by Serge Obolensky, a former Russian general from a wealthy family and a charismatic fixture in Southampton society. The book *One Man in His Time* is another fascinating glimpse into a Russian aristocrat who had to start over in a new land. Though he loved Russia, he moved on and adapted well to life in his new country, unlike many other displaced émigrés who "sat on their suitcases" waiting for the Bolshevik revolution to blow over. It never did, of course. In time, the Red Army was victorious over the Whites. On November 16, 1933, President Franklin Roosevelt ended almost sixteen years of American non-recognition of the Soviet Union, a final blow to those émigrés who still held out hope.

I traveled to Russia to research the writing of this book. It brought the country alive and, as always, visiting a setting made it much easier to write about. I found Russia to be a complex, fascinating country, and I'm glad to know its history better now in order to understand its place in our world today.

Though the Russian royal family makes only cameo appearances in these pages, the letters of Olga Romanov gave me tremendous insight into the family and their tragic end. Her father, the tsar, sealed his own fate with decades of corrupt mismanagement, concentration of wealth, failure to recognize basic human values as other European monarchies had, and constant oppression including inciting and turning a blind eye to deadly pogroms against Russian Jews. But it's hard not to pity his five children, who paid the ultimate price for their parents' misdeeds. I grew particularly fond of Olga Romanov, and the book *Journal of a Russian Grand Duchess* gives a poignant look into a bright young woman's life cut short.

Bringing the White Russian émigré experience in Paris to life was especially rewarding. Discovering Rue Daru, once the epicenter of Russian émigré culture, was incredible. The Saint Alexandre Nevsky Cathedral with its lovely, painted basement crypt, and the restaurant A la Ville de Petrograd, recently shuttered, are still there today. The brothel at Rue Chabanais still stands in Paris. Once one of the best-known and most luxurious houses of prostitution, it is now a private apartment building on a quiet side street, no sign of the thriving *maison close* it once was. It was closed in 1946, when brothels were outlawed in France. Paris's oldest candy store À la Mère de Famille at 35 Rue du Faubourg, Montmartre, was an especially delicious place to explore. Just stepping in the door takes a candy lover back to 1761. The Paris planetarium Eliza and Sofya take Luba to in the prologue existed. Though it has long since been demolished, the Globe Céleste was built for the 1900 Paris World's Fair, a massive, faux planet Earth, which delighted armchair space travelers. Patrons to the exhibit leaned back in easy chairs while "panoramas depicting the solar system rolled past."

My grandmother was a talented seamstress and I loved watching her sew. Perhaps that's why I enjoyed bringing Varinka's Mamka's sewing career to life. Lanvin and the other great couture houses of Paris employed hundreds of Russian émigrés in their workshops and the Russian skill with a needle supported the worldwide fashion trend toward Russian dress. The *kokoshnik,* the traditional Russian beaded headdress, became a fashion phenomenon and bridal fashion so popular Queen Mary wore a *kokoshnik*-like diadem on her wedding day.

I enjoyed my time in Southampton, New York, researching that lovely place and time. Hildreth's store, established in 1842, still stands on Main Street and remains a most charming, thriving home goods store, still owned by Hildreths after thirteen generations. I based my Pink and Green society women on the "Dreadnaughts" of Southampton, the supremely confident old guard elite who hosted the town's social teas. They set the dress code, strictly enforced social conduct, and seemed bent on making society life uncomfortable.

The Bellamy-Ferriday House & Garden, Caroline's home that was once called The Hay, was my own epicenter when it came to this story. From the archives there I have used Eliza's and Caroline's letters and other personal writing to bring this story to light; and the lovely old house has a character arc of its own. Following Henry Ferriday's death, Eliza added interior plumbing and a service wing containing a kitchen and servants' rooms; and the former schoolhouse was relocated to the orchard as a playhouse for Caroline. The Hay was a place Caroline, Eliza, and Henry Ferriday loved since the day they saw it, and Caroline and Eliza adored the gardens they created there. Even when in her beloved Paris, Caroline wrote "I realized that I had Bethlehem under my skin. In the midst of the delights of Paris, I would stop to wonder if the rose bugs were under control, or how the new regale lilies were doing."

Today you can tour The Hay, now the Bellamy-Ferriday House & Garden, all ninety-six acres bequeathed to Connecticut Landmarks by Caroline. The building where Merrill Brothers Store stood is now a restaurant on the village green and the boulder Eliza allowed moved from their property still stands on the green, an honor roll stone memorial to Civil War and World War I veterans.

For my next book I travel further back in time to the Civil War, to tell the story of Caroline's great-grandmother Jane Eliza Newton Woolsey and her family, their fight against slavery, and their struggle to establish the first nursing services in America. The Woolsey women.

More staunchly fierce women I've already come to love.

ACKNOWLEDGMENTS

Many thanks to those who made writing *Lost Roses* such a pleasure:

To my husband, Michael Kelly, who happily read every draft, shared my dream of continuing to tell Caroline Ferriday's family story, and supports everything I do with unflagging enthusiasm and love. Excited to share "yon crescent moon" forever with you, old Cary Grant.

To my daughter Katherine, for her supreme wisdom and encouragement, and to my daughter Mary Elizabeth, for her expert editorial suggestions and cheerful support. I couldn't have asked for a better model of the two loving sisters: Sofya and Luba.

To my son, Michael, for his manuscript advice, book trailer skills, and road-trip companionship.

To my son-in-law, Chase, for his sage advice and support.

To Kara Cesare at Ballantine Bantam Dell, the most caring, talented editor a person could wish for, generous in every way, who understood and embraced Eliza's story with such care and empathy.

To all of "Team Roses" at Ballantine Bantam Dell for their seamless collaboration and boundless enthusiasm: Debbie Aroff, Barbara Bachman, Susan Corcoran, Melanie DeNardo, Jennifer Hershey, Kim Hovey, Paolo Pepe, Kara Welsh, and Gina Centrello, to name a few.

To my amazing agent, Alexandra Machinist, who once upon a time plucked me from the slush pile, insisted these stories needed to be told, and made it happen.

To the lovely Betty Kelly Sargent for her early encouragement and expertise, and who said, "All I need is a chapter." Without her none of this would have come close to happening.

To my sister Polly Simpkins for her wisdom, generosity, unconditional love, and inspiration for the character of Eliza. And to my sister Sally Hatcher, who first taught me how loving sisters can be.

To Alexandra Shelley, independent editor extraordinaire, for her honesty and editorial help.

To Alexander Neave, Caroline Ferriday's cousin, and his wife Lynne, who so generously shared their memories of her.

To Rosie Furniss, who shared her great-aunt Mary Koutousov Tolstoy's story and wonderful book, *As the Old Order Was Changing*.

To Sheryl Hack, executive director, and the rest of the staff at Connecticut Landmarks, including Jamie-Lynn Fontaine Connell and Jana Colacino for taking such good care of Caroline's beloved home.

To the brilliant and tireless Bellamy-Ferriday House & Garden tour guides: Dorothy Ambruso, Sarah Baker, Gary P. Cicognani, Mary Dulude, Tyler Huntsley, Danielle Spino, Nikkii Todaro, and Marj Vitz. Thank you for your hours of service and for making the house come alive so beautifully for visitors. Caroline and Eliza would be proud.

To Bellamy-Ferriday House & Garden Site Administrator Peg Shimer for her hard work, unending support, and loving care of Caroline's house.

To Cathy and Doug Altenbern for rolling out the red carpet in Nashville, the definition of true Southern hospitality.

To the wonderful independent booksellers and librarians everywhere who worked so hard to get this family's story into the hands of readers.

To my French publisher Les Editions Leduc, Karine Bailly, and Danae Tourrand for showing me a fabulous French welcome and Paris over Russian vodka and caviar.

To Susan Van Winkle Pollack for pointing me in the direction of her father, Wm. Mitchell Van Winkle's, extensive rose book collection.

To Sophie Baker at Curtis Brown London for thirty incredible foreign editions of *Lilac Girls.*

To Josie Freedman at ICM Partners, Los Angeles, for helping make that incredible dream come true.

To Mollie Fitzgerald whose gorgeous red hair and incredible piano skill inspired the character of Karina.

To Yeda Zaitz Fish, for inspiring the character of Mrs. Zaitz.

To George McCleary, program planner and horticulturist, who knew "Miss Ferriday" and shared his stories. Together with his wife, Carol, he keeps Caroline's gardens just the way Caroline and Eliza would have wanted.

To filmmaker Stacey Fitzgerald, for her friendship, upcoming documentary about the Rabbits, and for showing me the importance of mutual aid and cooperation.

To Colleen Hildreth, who so graciously showed us around her family's store in Southampton and shared its fascinating history.

To the staff of Saint Alexandre Nevsky Cathedral on Rue Daru in Paris, who gave me access to and information about the crypt.

To Eleanor Southworth and Irina MacGuire of the Chapin School, who brought Caroline Ferriday's school days back for me in living color.

To our fabulous Russian tour guide Ilia Kruglov at Exeter International Travel, who went above and beyond to make sure I understood Russia and helped me gather the courage to eat a bear dumpling.

To the staff of the State Museum of Political History in St. Petersburg, who patiently answered my infinite list of questions about Russian political history.

To the Southampton Historical Museum archivist Mary Cummings for her help in making that charming town come alive.

To my mother-in-law, Marian, and five sisters-in-law for their unending support and continuing to show me how important a loving, encouraging family can be.

To Gary Parkes, who keeps my social media humming.

To Natalie Picot, the best research assistant ever.

To Barbara Bradbury-Pape, former site administrator of the Bellamy-Ferriday House & Garden, for sharing her vast knowledge of the lovely old house.

To Kathy Murray, who works hard to keep me in shape, body and soul.

To The Old Bethlehem Historical Society, keeper of Bethlehem's lovely past.

ABOUT THE AUTHOR

MARTHA HALL KELLY is the *New York Times* bestselling author of *Lilac Girls*. She lives in Connecticut, and spends her days traveling to visit Civil War battlefields and writing her next prequel to *Lilac Girls,* set during the Battle of Gettysburg. *Lost Roses* is her second novel.

marthahallkelly.com

Facebook.com/marthahallkelly

Twitter: @marthahallkelly

This book was set in Fournier, a typeface named for Pierre-Simon Fournier (1712–68), the youngest son of a French printing family. He started out engraving woodblocks and large capitals, then moved on to fonts of type. In 1736 he began his own foundry and made several important contributions in the field of type design; he is said to have cut 147 alphabets of his own creation. Fournier is probably best remembered as the designer of St. Augustine Ordinaire, a face that served as the model for the Monotype Corporation's Fournier, which was released in 1925.